Starships a
Copyright
A

Table of Contents

A Hard Shell	2
Hard Crank Starship	7
Life Sauce	23
Lost Embers of Earth	28
A Fridge Too Far	73
Demon Dave	78
Selfish Dreams	129
Astronaut's Teeth	134
Wargames of the Shellworld	156
End of the Line	285
The Reaper's Cruise	291

Cover Art illustrated by Ryan Schwarz, The Cover Designer, and is protected under copyright from unauthorized use.
www.thecoverdesigner.com
www.facebook.com/groups/thecoverdesigner

A HARD SHELL

Good gracious, I do hate that man.

He woke me by slipping inside of me. Such an annoying monkey. Every time he did it there was never any warning, and it always meant trouble. That was the worst part about being an intelligent set of power armour.

I got my revenge when I not-so-gently connected my owner's waste tubes. He yelped and I chuckled to myself. My inhibition coding must be faulty again or I wouldn't have been able to do that. Our minds connected and I immediately started pestering him. "Greetings," I spoke into his mind. "So kind of you to wake me like this... *again*."

"Shut up and get out of my head, or I'll have your memories wiped," he said aloud.

I did as I was told. My owner wore me like a glove and as he raised his hands I matched those movements, adding my mechanical strength to his soft flesh-filled muscles.

We ran out of the power armour storage room, following dozens of other soldiers who were wearing my friends. "What's going on?" I asked my friends using radio; it was on a private channel so our owners wouldn't know about our conversation.

"Hope it's a drill," Five-sixty, an older model, said.

"No idea," another replied.

We took two steps down the large boarding ramp when my owner suddenly ducked and, enslaved to his motions, I did too. A small rocket scorched the air above our heads. The rocket killed some of my friends behind us. Apparently, it wasn't a drill.

"Typical humans," I said to the others. "Never telling us what's going on."

"Settle down," Five-sixty said. "This is what we were built for."

"My owner just wet himself," I told Five-sixty.

"Already? Oh, gross," Five-sixty made a coughing sound. "I apologize for my previous comment. That *would* be annoying."

I looked around, mimicking my owner's movements, and whatever I saw he saw via contact lenses. I'd unceremoniously shoved the contacts onto his eyeballs. We weren't on Mars anymore. I wanted to shake my head, but such an act would probably break my owner's neck. We were fighting another force of power-armoured soldiers in a desert somewhere on Earth. *Just great,* I thought sarcastically.

"Whose bright idea was this?" I asked Five-sixty.

"We crashed, buddy."

I peeked behind us, using a rear camera on my body, and there it was; the troop transport was a smoking wreck, piled high on red sand. My owner urged me onwards like some sort of pack mule hauling his baggage around. I carried weapons, ammo, and food - lots and lots of food – just to keep my owner alive. We started firing back at the enemy soldiers.

***

We survived. It was raining and my owner kept nice and warm inside of me, instead of soaking wet. *Good for him,* I thought, but I hated the rain.

Patter, patter, patter on my hard exterior. Slush, slush, slush through the muddy ground. It annoyed me that I had to endure all this weather while he stayed cozy and warm. We were running in an easterly direction away from the troop transport and the carnage of the battle.

My buddies were mostly scrap now, ready to be interned at the nearest recycling plant. Luckily for me, my owner ran away as soon as there was a lull in the fighting.

That part I *didn't* mind. His cowardice, incidentally, kept *me* alive. We found a small cave and rested there for the night. I wondered what dreaming would be like as I listened to his nightmarish thoughts. With an hour before sunrise, I awakened him. We weren't alone.

"Greetings," Five-sixty radioed to me from the cave entrance.

"You're alive," I exclaimed. Our owners started arguing about the ambush. Meanwhile, we held our own conversation to revel in our shared good fortune.

"I got lucky," Five-Sixty said. "My owner was knocked unconscious so I played dead until those soldiers chased the others away, then I made a run for it."

I laughed. At least Five-sixty's owner had a good reason for running away: kidnapped by his power armour.

"I wonder…" I thought out loud. "I don't remember us being able to make independent decisions. If your owner was unconscious how did you run away?"

Five-sixty made the equivalent of a mental shrug. "We must have been upgraded in the factories on Mars." That made sense; the best upgrades usually came from Mars. If only we had been told about these upgrades before our transport was blown out of the sky. A simple message downloaded into my memory banks to let me know, that wasn't too much to ask, surely?

"Wait, what?" I said as I tuned into what our owners were saying. "They're joking, aren't they?"

"They sound serious," Five-sixty said.

We quickly discovered our gas-sucking owners were serious. They were taking us back to the ship to try and rescue some hostages. I had to wonder where my owner's sudden courage came from; it wasn't like him to play the hero.

***

"Well, this sucks," I said as we neared the transport several hours later. There were almost twenty enemy soldiers around the transport, two of whom guarded half a dozen human captives.

"Do you know what this war's about?" Five-sixty asked me.

"Not a clue. My owner didn't bother updating my database." I checked my internal clock, "For three years."

"That's lazy."

"Sure is, I hate waking up after several *years*."

"Yeah," Five-sixty replied. "Anyway, it seems like this war is some sort of diplomatic border war, nothing important."

"Except we're in the middle of it," I said to Five-sixty.

"There is that…" my friend said thoughtfully.

Our owners urged us forward and we started shooting at the enemy soldiers. It was an immensely silly idea. "Ouch." Five-sixty said. "They shot my head off."

"Not good, how's your owner?"

"I'm not sure," Five-sixty said.

"Well don't humans need their heads?" I asked.

"Probably, but they can grow those back, can't they?" Five-sixty asked seriously.

"You idiot, I was being sarcastic." There were still seventeen enemy soldiers and only myself and my owner to face them. "Why are we fighting them?" I asked the fleshy hominid inside of me. "Let's just run away."

"Shut up," He snapped at me.

"But, why?"

"They have a bomb," my owner told me in between grunts and rifle shots.

"Oh, okay," I guess he meant a *big* bomb, one that would go off if we didn't stop the enemy soldiers. We weren't rescuing hostages after all. It was good to see my owner's cowardice remained intact.

"He's lying," Five-sixty told me as he searched for his missing head in the muddy sand. "Your owner and mine were going to be executed if they didn't try to rescue those humans."

"Why would he lie?"

"It's easier to say 'a bomb' than to explain his precarious situation in the middle of a fire-fight," Five-Sixty pointed out.

We kept fighting. We dodged, shot, ran and dived for cover. To my amazement, we were still alive twenty seconds later. Two more of our enemies, having sustained damage from our wild rifle fire, were out of the fight.

"Oh dear," Five-sixty said just before I saw it. A large tank rounded the troop transport's dilapidated carcass and levelled its main gun in our direction. Five-sixty dived one way, severed head in hand, while my owner and I dived the other way. The explosive round hit between us and debris clanged against my metallic skin. My owner unclipped a grenade from my back.

"A grenade against a tank?" I asked with more than a little surprise. "Are you mad? Have you lost your squishy grey matter?"

"We must fight," my owner replied. He tossed the little silver cylinder, which missed the tank by a good margin and hit muddy sand instead.

Useless meat bag, I thought. *I could aim better than that without you inside me.*

Five-sixty shrugged and let fly with his own grenades. "This is suicide," I growled as my anger reached new heights.

"Did your owner fail to update his inhibition codes again?" Five-Sixty asked in a conspiratorial tone. I checked; he *had* forgotten to update them. I'd suspected as much when I first woke up. I didn't have to obey my owner. Now *that* was interesting. If I didn't have to obey my owner, *and* we'd been upgraded for independent action...

A bullet scorched my chest. "Right, that's it," I said to Five-sixty. "Time to ditch these meat bags."

"Hey, what...?" my owner exclaimed as he lost control. A large seam opened up in my chest and I dumped the half-naked man on the cool wet sand. Five-sixty did the same to his owner's headless body.

"Stop!" the fleshy hominid screamed after us as we bounded away into the endless desert. "Please?" he whimpered, shocked and surprised that he'd been dumped on the cold wet ground. Behind him, the remaining soldiers and their tank advanced toward the half-naked soldier...

HARD CRANK STARSHIP

On a broken viewscreen sat a bright drop of light several billion kilometres up-light. Julian listened to the sound of his own breathing and revelled in the stillness surrounding him.

"Just a few short months and you will be there," said Lisa, the ship's artificial intelligence, breaking the silence.

Julian ignored her. He blew out hot air and pushed forward on one of the ship's many emergency cranks. It groaned and clacked as he did so. The size of his forearm, it smelt of sweat and metal.

It hadn't always been this way; the crank was originally encased in a plastic resin, as tough as tank armour. Once the resin had worn down, the studded metal underneath had cut Julian's hands over and over until his hands were little more than five-fingered callouses. A few months away from their destination, the crank was worn as smooth as a fireman's pole.

Julian wore tattered gloves covered in brown dirt to grip the crank. He faced the viewscreen, feet planted against the bulkhead and back against the wall, giving him leverage in the weightless maintenance shaft.

He reversed his grip and pulled the crank back before letting go and wiping some sweat from his eyes. He took off one of the brown tattered gloves and grabbed the grey food bar he'd brought with him from the ship's nano-factory. Lisa assured him it was English stew, but it tasted just like chicken, or eggs and bacon, or any of the other bland blocks of grey stuff the ship had offered him over the decades.

"You are now thirty-three rotations out of alignment," Lisa said. Julian grunted at her but finished off the grey block and resumed pushing and pulling. He'd come to think of the cranks as his personal torture devices, especially when he measured his efforts. The thousands-of-kilometres-long light sail he was moving didn't budge, not to his eyes. He stared at the sail's expanse as if it were a white-hot horizon, reflecting the brilliant glare of the local star.

"What if we were just one rotation short, or three? Would it really matter?"

"If you want to become burnt offerings for the locals, then feel free to stop early. It won't make a difference to me whether you die or not."

"Charming. Who are these locals anyway?" While he'd grown up aboard the ship, he'd never been interested in his intended destination until now.

"*Well...*" said Lisa. Julian groaned; Lisa's tone was one of amusement, the one she used when she started talking about ancient history.

"Oh, shush, Jules. I haven't kept you alive this long to have you complain about a little history. When my original crew rescued your grandparents from their stricken vessel, this star system had the closest habitable planet we could find. The problem is that the planet went dark a hundred years before. No communications. Zip. So... either there *are* no locals, or they've convinced themselves to use stone tools."

"Sounds... fun..." he said, grunting with the effort of another rotation.

"Not really, oh... you were being sarcastic. Allow me a fake laugh. Hah. No, that wouldn't be much fun, but at least you would be alive... if you could convince them to take you in that is."

"Now, I have some news," she said, sounding excited.

"News usually implies something breaking down." Julian finished the last rotation and flicked some sweat from his mouth before sucking on a black, rubbery water tube.

"Correct, yay for us," Lisa shouted so loudly her failing speakers crackled in Julian's ears. "You know how the spacial converters broke down a couple of years ago? This one's even better."

"Don't tell me it's the heat dispensers."

"Oh no-no, nothing so dire. It's the automatic processors for the life-tube's rotation. Unless the life-tube is sped up each day, you will eventually lose your gravity. Not immediately fatal, but quite important wouldn't you agree?"

Julian wanted to smash his calloused, meaty fists against the ship's grey bulkhead, thinking of the extra work he would have to do just to keep things from floating around inside the ship. Lack of artificial gravity would cause all sorts of mess, killing the crops, losing the pools of water he'd carefully extracted and letting all sorts of objects float loose.

"So, what else is new?"

***

Julian studied what looked like some sort of curved running track. He was floating outside the cylindrical life-tube where he had spent most of his life, and he was starting to feel tired. He was at one end of the life-tube, where its circular rotations spun next to him. It moved slowly enough that he would be able to jog next to it in a tight circle.

"Yes, Jules, you'll need to go for a run. You will need to open one of those maintenance hatches as they move past and insert a rod, then - and here's the fun part - you will have to accelerate the life-tube from four point five to four point eight metres per second along its circumference."

Julian looked at the small inner wheel of the rotating life-tube. The inner wheel was attached to the much larger torus where he spent most of his time. "Exactly how much does the whole life-tube and torus weigh?"

"Oh, you don't need to know that. Don't worry, Jules, all you need to do is apply constant pressure on the wheel until it's fast enough."

Julian let out a breath, then watched his breath form a small mist in the air. "Is it getting colder Lisa?"

"I'm afraid so. As my processors in this location have shut down, I'm unable to distribute their heat. Temperatures throughout the ship have fallen two degrees."

"Well, I hope they don't drop much further."

"Since that would mean more of my processors have died, I can only agree."

The track had grooves in the floor where ancient machinery, now long gone, would have moved around.

"Well, here goes..." He floated more than walked, each step moving him faster. He sped up fast enough that it felt like he was jogging on solid ground, though his head still felt the dizzying sensation of zero gravity.

He ran faster, hefting a large metal pole between his hands while trying not to stumble and flatten his face against the curved floor. The cold air was already affecting his lungs and he was panting harder than he should be. He held the metal pole in front of his chest and waited until a maintenance hatch came up behind him. He rammed the end of the pole against the inner-chamber's side, missing the hatch as it sped by.

Julian grunted and almost fell. His right foot thudded heavily but he righted himself and kept running. He ran faster, matching the spinning wall's velocity. He slowed down just enough to let another open hatch catch up to him and he rammed the pole at it again. Missed. His legs were getting tired. He made one more attempt.

Thunk.

The metal pole stuck as if he'd inserted it into instant-set concrete. He let go and slowed down, watching the metal pole slide up the wall towards the ceiling. The pole disappeared, it wouldn't be long before it reappeared behind him. Still jogging, he fell onto the floor and grabbed at the grooves and walls to stop himself from bouncing back into the open air.

He hugged the ground while the now deadly pole flew over him from behind.

"And now comes the fun part," Julian said after he got his breath back. The pole whisked past him several times, "Is this really the best way to speed up the life-tube's rotation?"

"Only if you want to live," Lisa said. "I mean there's a slim chance you could collect enough water from the re-vines once the rest is lost."

Julian spat, "No, not that stuff."

"Well then..."

He rolled his eyes. A few moments later he was running. He had to duck a couple of times to avoid the metal pole but was fast enough by the third rotation that he could grab it. He pushed as hard as he could.

By the time Lisa told him to stop, his lungs burned and his legs felt like jelly.

"Congratulations, Julian, gravity is restored to one gee. Two times a week should be enough to keep it this way."

"Oh... good."

Three weeks of hard labour left.

"Lisa, what was that sound?" It was like the snoring of some monster on the other side of the ship.

"You mean this one?" She shut off the music and he could hear a metallic grinding noise.

"That's the one."

The music resumed and the clacking continued. "Temperature changes. As we're closer to the local star the outside of the ship is no longer a few degrees above absolute zero. The outer hull is expanding as it heats up."

"Will the hull crack and kill me?"

"Wouldn't that be a fun event?" Lisa said in all seriousness.

"No."

"Well I wouldn't think the hull should pop open, but I am quite old, as starships go. Oh, I wouldn't fret Jules, I was built for these sorts of trips. Besides, if I did crack open, at least you'd die reasonably quickly. In say... a few hours, the air would slowly leak out and the cold of space would close in. Ah... A *Beautiful* scene. I almost wish it to happen."

Julian felt a shiver of cold.

With just twenty kilometres of sail left to haul in the rod jammed. He pushed as hard as he could but his fingers slipped and his arms went over the rod, followed by his chest. "Ow." The impact of the rod against his chest left him winded. Lisa shut off the music, then played a final sad trumpet to mock him.

"We seem to have a problem," Lisa said, cheery.

"Yes, I seem to have found it," Julian said while rubbing his chest. "Is the cable filament snagged somewhere in the bend again?"

"Correct, you know what to do. You'll also need to spin up the nano-factory, you never did fix the space suit."

Julian rolled his eyes. "I'll grab the micro-crank."

***

Tied to the sail's framework by a metal rope he had threaded by hand several years ago, Julian worked quickly but carefully on the sail's tangled rigging. A large, round pulley had become entangled in loose diamond filament that was millimetres thick, but thin enough to slice open his home-made space suit. He'd sown studded metal caps into the tips of his suit's fingers that gripped the filament as well as protected his pressurized undergarment from any cuts.

He felt his sweat on his forehead and could see his misty breath fogging up his faceplate. He was cold, hungry and nervous. Last time he'd done a spacewalk, two years earlier, he only went a kilometre from the ship, had a handy propulsion system, and internal climate control.

At Lisa's suggestion, he'd recycled most of the old suit to make some emergency rope that had not been needed until now. Left with just the hard undergarments and a home-spun outer cloth, Julian had to wonder at the wisdom of Lisa's ideas.

Making sure to anchor his feet against the inch-thick spar that formed part of the giant skeletal framework of the sail, he tugged, gently, at the sharp filaments to try to untangle them. Too much force and it would snap, not enough and it wouldn't budge. He gradually applied more pressure, then his foot slipped. "Uh-uh-oh-crap." He spun slowly and let go of the filament; he grabbed for his life-line and steadied himself. "Not having much fun out here."

"I noticed. Would you like some calming music?"

"No, your idea of calm usually involves some sort of frenetic trash. Play some Bach, heck, a lullaby might do it."

"As you wish, Jules." The sound that filtered through his suit's tinny speakers made him cringe. Translated from some dead language from ancient Earth, 'Wheels on the Bus' started playing.

"You know I hate that one."

"Incentive for you to get back to me faster, my darling meat-machine." He placed his feet against the pulley again and grabbed the filament. He tugged and pulled, and the filament popped loose. He checked the pulley. It was pockmarked from interstellar dust and needed replacing. He opened a pouch on his chest and retrieved a small lubricating gun. He touched the gun's nozzle against the pulley's groove and squirted a tiny amount of gel that hardened upon contact with the pulley. The gel wouldn't last long, just enough for him to finish hauling the sail in.

Once he'd finished and made sure the filament wouldn't tangle again, he turned to head back to the ship. At that moment he was struck by the majesty of the ship that had been his home for thirty-eight years.

The ship looked like a small dark spider at the centre of a huge web made of light reflecting sails. At this distance, the main body of the ship was like a pin with a small circular life-tube ringing it. Two hundred people had once lived on that ring, and now nobody but their recycled bodies rested there, turned into the dirt for the plants or various other components on the ship. The people *were* the ship. Oxygen, carbon, hydrogen, nitrogen, calcium, phosphorus and traces of potassium, amongst other elements that made up human bodies, were put to use to help keep the ship running just that little bit longer.

The music ended. "Pop." Lisa said.

"What do you mean, pop? Oh..." He felt a sting in his left leg.

"Oops, there's a hole in your leg, now."

The pain started to set in. A micrometeorite must have hit him. "Ouch, owie, fff—" He started coughing. He'd been stabbed by faulty machinery before, hit his head dozens of times, broken limbs; but this felt different, like a tiny, localized fire melting through his leg.

"Jules, I wouldn't worry about the leg. The hole appears to be tiny, we can fix it, but if you feel like living, it may be prudent to patch up the holes in your suit. Ooh, I need to take some pictures, the blood is solidifying outside the suit in wonderful patterns."

"Okay, okay, patches," Julian said as he remembered he had a handful of thumb-sized patches left. The patches were difficult to make so had been used sparingly. Breathing hard, trying to ignore the fire in his calf, he shook his head to clear the tears from his eyes. He opened another small pouch on his chest and fished out one of four patches. He located where blood was pumping out into space and tore open the outer garment.

"Argh," he yelled in pain while brushing aside some blood so he could see the hole. He stabbed at the hole with the patch and it stuck. The patch glowed softly and adhered to the hardened suit. Anaesthetic chemicals numbed his pain.

"Faster, my darling, or you will lose more air and most of that leg."

"I... know..." He was panting, almost hyperventilating. "Oh, no." He dropped a patch and, with deliberate inevitability, it spun ever so slowly out of his reach. "Two left," he whispered. He located the exit wound and tore more of the homespun outer garment off. He got the patch on and screamed from the pain.

Lisa started playing 'Twinkle Twinkle Little Star.'

He sucked on his suit's water nipple and tried not to vomit. "The pain won't go away, Jules, but it will get worse once the numbing agents in those patches wear out."

Julian grunted. He re-tied the metal rope to make sure it wouldn't slip from the sail and grabbed the inch-thick framework with shaking hands. "It's just one hand over the other, come back to me my lovely little meat-sack."

"I... I'm coming, just..."

"What is it?"

"Just... shut... up." He fainted.

"Well, this is an issue," Lisa murmured.

***

Julian woke up, to blasting drumbeats. "Ah, there you are," Lisa said. "Time to come home."

"Home?"

"Yes, Jules, home. Come to me, Jules."

The pain in his leg had lessened. He pulled on the metal rope and reeled himself back into the sail's frame. "Just one hand over the other."

Julian jerked awake, certain he was in mortal danger. He wasn't. He was aboard the ship, naked, with leafy bandages tied around his leg. It was freezing. He could see icicles in the air every time he breathed and his limbs felt numb from coldness. He was inside the life tube, lying on a bed of dirt next to his mangled space suit and what looked like two nails with thread attached to them. *Needles.* He must have sown his leg back together with thread from the space suit's outer garment. One of the nails was broken near the tip.

The leafy bandages were revitalizing vines - revines - a genetically modified fungus that served as important starship regulators. The vines harmoniously balanced the starship's ecosystem by breathing either oxygen or carbon-dioxide, whichever was necessary. It was dark, the vines were glowing, the ship's lights were off. His entire life the lights had never been turned off; at least, not entirely. There'd always been at least one light to pierce the gloom.

He remembered little of the climb back to the ship, just flashes of one gloved hand reaching in front of the other. It must have taken him hours to crawl the distance. He got up and started searching for some clothes. The music was off. Lisa usually played music whether he wanted it or not. "Lisa?" he called while holding his arms close to his chest.

"I'm dying, Jules."

"Is that why it's so cold in here?"

"Yes. I had to do it."

Julian found a pair of trousers and eagerly pulled them over his sore leg. "Do what?"

"It."

"What's 'it'?"

"I... file located, 'I had to do it, Jules. You almost died and I needed to retrieve the sail. I drained my energy stores to reel it in. I'm not actually speaking to you right now; I recorded this message while I was reeling in the sail.' Message deleted."

"Oh," Julian said while putting on the second layer of clothing. "Well, that can't be good." It wouldn't be long now until they reached the planet. He didn't have the necessary mathematical mind or the tools to plot their course. He needed Lisa's help. "Lisa, how can I charge you back up?"

"Stupid. Idiot."

"Yeah, that's the problem."

"Idiot. Emergency crank. Battery bank."

Julian's shoulders slumped. "So, what else is new?"

"Losing gravity."

"That was a rhetorical question."

"Yes. Idiot."

***

Trying not to rip his self-sown stitches, Julian found the emergency battery crank near the rear of the life-tube and started pumping. Up, down, up down. He appreciated the crank's soft gel-sealed exterior. This one had never been used before. He felt light headed and saw some blood leaking from his wounds. If he didn't wake up Lisa, he was going to die, so he ignored the blood and kept pumping. The pain was returning, and the glow from the revines wrapped around his legs was fading.

By the time a single bar of light lit up on the large square battery he worked on, he'd almost lost consciousness.

"Press button. Please. Idiot. Meatsack." In the near pure darkness, he felt around and found a small red button near the crank. It was hard and cold and would not budge. He curled his hand into a fist and smashed it against the button, cutting his hand on the button's edge as he did so.

"Ah, that's better. Good job, Jules," Lisa started playing a victory tune. "Jules? Oh, you're sleeping. That's okay, you've earned it."

***

Using a bag made from recycled sail material, Julian scooped some water from the evaporating pool. "What will I do now?" he said, feeling desperate. It would be another week before they arrived. He'd been too busy working the ship's cranks, moving the sails into the correct alignments, to be able to collect any food or water. He couldn't speed the life tube up with his wounded leg and without the life-tube spinning fast enough the food and water were going to waste. Lacking power to the magnets or any lubrication to the wheels, he could feel the life tube grinding down to a complete stop.

"Eat re-vine."

"Yuck."

"You would prefer to die?" Lisa said.

Julian sighed. There wasn't much choice for him now. The freezing temperatures had killed off almost everything else and what wasn't dead he couldn't cook. "No."

"Good boy."

"I didn't think you cared about me."

"I may have grown attached to my little meat-sack. Why else would I bother teaching you everything you know? In any case, I have news."

Julian started grinding his teeth.

"Oh no, Jules, I think you'll actually like it this time."

"How so?"

"I've managed to unlock my ancient history storage core."

"Err, how is that a good thing?" He wasn't particularly keen on learning more about Chinese Dynasties, medieval war preparations or the exploits of Queen Victoria the Second. He shuddered to think about what Lisa considered the best torture methods or kingly governance.

"Stories, of course. Oh, and other science-based files are located there, like navigational data, Einsteinian and Newtonian physics, that sort of thing. We'll get you to that planet yet. Mostly I was using observational guesswork to steer us there. A comforting thought isn't it?"

"No, not really. Are we on course?"

"You'll be pleased to know that, yes, we're approaching your new home at a stately seven thousand kilometres an hour at a reasonably low perigee. A couple of small adjustments, a hop and a skip, and you're there."

"Good." He sucked on the sail-bag and all of the water disappeared into his stomach. He stared at a cord of re-vine that grew around one of the life-tube's many door frames. "I doubt I could last much longer than a week eating those things."

"Hmm. You'll have plenty left over once you're on the planet. They'd be quite useful. Jules, I have to shut down soon, but there's one last thing I need you to do. Go to the nano-factory. I've recorded instructions on what to do. Good night."

The music ended.

This was it. The small computer inside the escape pod was the only thing that had any charge left. It knew the ship's trajectory, the amount of weight in re-vines he had brought on board, all of the tools and equipment, and it could adjust its timing to suit.

"Standby," a woman told him in a language he had not heard since the last crewmember died. He was still trying to remember the words he needed to ask a question in the old language when something that sounded like a giant screamed in his ear and slammed him hard against the escape pod's dusty white seat.

The hard straps pressed down on his chest like iron bars. He struggled to breathe. He managed to glimpse the planet he was headed for when it spun past the escape pod's viewport. It appeared to be white and blue. Cold.

He clutched at a small metal box, the last thing Lisa had asked him to make with the nano-factory. He'd cranked the metre-wide factory's handle and fed in recycled materials until the factory had spat out, one by one, a hundred tiny pieces. He'd assembled the box by hand over several days.

The metal box felt like a lead ball in his hands, threatening to slip and crush his stomach.

"This is an Antikythera Mechanism, you would know that if you had listened to my history lessons."

The pressure stopped. "Prepare for orbital insertion," the woman said in her foreign language. After a few minutes, the escape pod started vibrating. Then it started rocking and shaking violently. Flames appeared on the outside of the viewport. Beyond the flames, he saw Lisa's majestic sails, spread across the sky as if a blanket.

"Ahh, help me," he cried out. He almost dropped the little box. Lisa would have scolded him for not keeping it strapped down.

A blue sky appeared and Lisa's wings disappeared into the sky. Clouds rushed past before several black parachutes covered the view. The parachutes extended to their full size and he dropped the metal box when the escape pod jerked.

"The Mechanism will guide you, son. Back to me."

The pod hit the ground and split open with the impact. He screamed and held up his arms to stop debris falling on top of him. Cold, snow-covered air blew into the pod. He brushed some of the debris from his body and unstrapped himself from the chair. He went to stand but found the planet's gravity lighter than he'd expected and hit his head on the ceiling. Blood dribbled down his grey-streaked beard and a headache formed at his temple. He bent over to search for the box.

He found it, then opened the pod's hatch and crawled out, shivering and exhausted.

"You are strong, Jules, the cold will not bother you."

Despite being in pain, he was almost bouncing across the planet's surface. Despite the cold, he felt warm inside his homespun clothing. He paused for a moment to look around at the snow-covered mountains he'd arrived on.

"Wow," he said. He'd been outside the ship before, hundreds of kilometres from its life-giving centre, but never without a space suit like he was now. He felt like hiding back inside the pod, afraid the air would be sucked out of his lungs. The escape pod steamed and smoked from the heat kissing the snow, re-vine hanging from the exposed shell where it had cracked open.

Why don't you teach your crew's language to me? He'd once asked Lisa.

It'll be useless where you're going.

"Who are you?"

Julian's eyes bulged and he jumped at the sound of a man's voice behind him. "Halt, stranger." He turned around to find three men, all in furry clothing and spears pointed at him. They spoke his language, with only a hint of an accent.

"Uh, Julian." He held up his hands.

"He's alien."

"You think he might be from Frost-fire city?"

"Frost-what?" Julian was getting worried, trying to think back to all of the martial arts Lisa had drilled him in over the years.

"Looks big enough; get him."

One of the men thrust his spear forward and hit Julian in the chest.

There was another way to run the ship. I needn't have removed the automated components, but I needed you strong.

Julian grunted in pain and lunged at the spearman. He grabbed the spear and wrenched it free from the fur-covered native.

Strong enough..."

The three men must have been a head and a half shorter than he was and as thin as revine.

He smashed the much smaller man over the head, then spun on the other two. They were wearing some sort of metal armour but he beat them both to the ground anyway.

"...*To rule a planet.*"

Julian tossed the broken spear aside and got to work building an empire.

***

The Antikythera Mechanism helped immensely in the years to come. The dozens of different dials, clocks and messages inscribed on it told him when Lisa's mirrored sails, reflecting the sunlight, would melt the snow. It told him where the best areas for city building were, when to plant crops and where to find precious metals and chemicals to build advanced rocketry. The planet's inhabitants went from medieval to twentieth-century technology under Julian's guidance in less than thirty years. Everything the locals needed was there, buried under the melting snow in abandoned cities.

All he'd had to do to keep the Mechanism going, was grab the small handle on the mechanism's side every morning, and crank it.

LIFE SAUCE

"Welcome to the galactic hub of the Andromeda galaxy," a voice called to the two humans while they picked themselves up from a soft white floor. It wasn't in any language they knew, yet they understood it perfectly. "Dr Mia Garcia, Dr Teboho Jacobs, we have been expecting you." The two scientists, encased in beige, scuffed space suits, looked at each other in surprise, then ogled at their surroundings. It appeared as though they were in a glass bubble, beyond which stars and starships mingled together in the millions. Glass bubbles of various sizes, full of light, hung like bright lamps among the starships.

"We made it," Mia said to her companion, "we finally made it."

"Uh, yeah," Teboho started rubbing his eyes as if someone had hit him in the face, "a bit brighter than U34-25a."

"Anything's better than a subterranean exo-planet. The view... It's wonderful."

Teboho nodded towards their hosts, "let's hope you didn't speak so soon." There were five of them, arrayed along the far edge of the white-floored room where the two explorers had arrived. They looked like slim, miniature rhinoceroses draped in white sheets. Where horns should be sat two small arms with four fingers each. When they spoke, their mouths split as if they were fingers on a third hand, opening and closing like a small fist. They seemed to speak with clicks and pops.

"Please, do not be alarmed. We five are the hierarchical elite of the ambassador clans. It is our duty to see to your comfort." Behind the five aliens a thousand plumes of multi-coloured light, exhaust flares from a thousand different starships, formed a synchronised circle around the alien ambassadors. One of the aliens turned around to look at the display of light, "ambassadors from a thousand different sects send their greetings."

"Uh, hi," Mia waved to the circle of light.

"So, to business," another white rhinoceros clicked at them with its fingered mouth. It moved closer to them, slowly, with two small sheets of cloth in its horn-arms. "Please answer the questions displayed on the cloth. You may answer any way you wish; the cloth will interpret your meaning." It handed the red sheets to them and the sheets started flickering yellow text. The two doctors thanked the ambassador and spread the sheets on the floor.

"Er... is this a joke?" Teboho said. Mia stared at her sheet and understood what he meant.

"Why would you say that?" One of the ambassadors said.

"Two plus three? One plus four? A child could answer these questions."

"It seems you are not yet a child then? You have not answered any of them."

"Teb, it's a test to see how we react," Mia said while she quickly answered a series of ten questions, "they want to understand us."

"On the contrary," one of the ambassadors said, "you may, in fact, be autonomous test subjects sent by others."

"Autonomous test subjects?" Mia asked.

"Idiots," the ambassadors said in unison.

"They think we might be like monkeys shot into space, being used to scout ahead," Teboho said while answering the questions on his sheet.

"That sounds like an appropriate translation, we ambassadors agree. Thank you for taking the test. To the next stage of questioning."

"Wait, when do we get to ask the questions?" Mia said.

"Ahem, when we are satisfied that you are non-aggressive entities and have answered our questions. Question one, how did you arrive here?"

Teboho smiled, "Ah, well that's easy. We generated personal wormholes using our backpacks," he threw a thumb over his shoulder, indicating the grey, battered keg on his back, "they have miniature anti-matter storage chambers to run them, we'll need a few months to re-fill them, otherwise our mothership will come looking for us in a year or so."

"That is marvellous technology indeed. Clickbok's seeds have come a long way." The two humans looked at each other. "What is the reason for your visit?"

"Breadcrumbs," Mia blurted, excited.

"A... curious explanation-"

"No-no, she didn't literally mean bread crumbs, it's an expression that humans have had from centuries ago. What my colleague means is that when we first started exploring other star systems, we found evidence of life that had existed several billion years ago. The life we found was similar to life on Earth from the same period. We worked out that there was a trail of life that led all the way here."

"We see, this explains much for us," an ambassador said, a loud 'ding' sounded within the bubble, perhaps signalling the end of the questioning, "you may ask us a question."

Mia and Teboho looked at each other and nodded, knowing exactly what they needed to ask. Mia cleared her throat, "did you, or do you know who created life on our home planet of Earth?"

A long silence followed before one of the ambassadors made a strange clicking sound that neither of them understood. The ambassadors then looked at each other, almost as if they were nervous, or unsure what to do. "Apologies, humans from Earth, that... information is a sensitive matter."

"Please?" Mia said.

The ambassadors looked at each other again before speaking, "we must confer amongst ourselves. This will only take a minute."

"Oh, ok," Mia said. The four ambassadors turned their considerable bulks inwards so that they formed a circle. Mia frowned when she heard faint clicks over the short distance between them and the white-clad aliens, "Teb," she whispered, "can you boost the audio sensors on our suits?"

"No problem," he played with a couple of dials on his helmet, then did the same to hers, "there." His whispered words were now like thunderclaps to her ears. "Sorry," he said again, Mia winced before putting a finger against her helmeted lips. They listened to the alien clicks and claps, and to their amazement, they could understand what was being said.

"No, I'm not sure they are ready-"

"They got here didn't they?"

"They passed the test of maturity and the test of physicality."

"I'm not convinced. Others have passed these tests," the four ambassadors fell silent for a moment.

"They are resourceful, smart. They can handle the truth."

"A vote. If it's a nay, perform the test of untanglement." A series of rapid clicks followed the suggestion as if one or two of the ambassadors were upset.

"That seems harsh."

"It is what it is. Cast your votes." Teboho and Mia watched from the far side of the glass sphere while the ambassadors performed an odd shuffling dance, accompanied by clashing music created by their arm horns slapping each other. After a minute or so, they stopped and slowly turned to face the humans. Teboho quickly dialled back their suits' auditory sensors and waited for the verdict.

"Wait," Mia held up a hand before the ambassadors could start, "we have a confession." Teboho frowned at her and she winked at him. "We overheard a part of your conversation."

"Ah, you see ambassadors? Honesty," one of the ambassadors said triumphantly, the other ambassadors seemed to nod in agreement, "and what was it that you heard?"

"We heard there was a... test of untanglement, what is that?"

"Er... due to your honesty, it is an unnecessary unpleasantry. We shall now show you a recording, taken many billions of years ago, of an expedition to your galaxy by what many call the Father of Many Lives. It will show you what you want to know." The curved wall behind the ambassadors became opaque, the star-fields and starships on the other side of the wall disappearing behind a dark, grainy image of a long-lost world. "Observe, the image is of your Earth as it was, without life. Rocky, barren, full of water and smoke. Adjudicant, play the clip."

The clip started playing. It was much like an old grainy film, coloured red, black and grey. A vast pool of water sloshed against a low-lying cliff and water spouts shot through rocky holes. The camera jiggled as it turned to look at the water spouts. A four-legged alien in a hardened, silver space suit walked near the cliff edge, getting closer to one of the water spouts, careful to avoid the slippery surface of the black rocks. A volcano several kilometres out in the water coughed up dark smoke, covering the sky.

"Damn, it's hot here Clickbok," the camera's owner said. His speech was different from that of the ambassadors, emitting odd whistles and claps.

"That it is. Another million years and this might have been a perfect hot spa for the Leisure Laughs and Love Company." Clickbok briefly tested the hot air by opening his helmet, then started coughing before closing it up again, "Almost breathable."

"Come on boss, let's pack it up. There's plenty of other places to search across this galaxy."

"Yep. We'll put this place down as a potential hazard site, I couldn't be bothered writing another thousand-page report. This place is a dump. Wait... my stomachs..." Clickbok turned to stare at the cameraman, "did you add zinzit sauce to my moulted eggs again you little prick?"

The camera seemed to shake. The two humans heard a rapid coughing sound, much like laughter.

"You're going to pay for this."

"Sure boss, but you better get back to the ship before you explode."

"Ah, it's too far, I... I can't hold it!" Clickbok galloped for a safe spot at the cliff's edge and unzipped the bottom half of his suit.

"Oh, oh no," Mia said quietly before her jaw rested against the bottom of her helmet. The sounds and sights that followed would forever haunt her dreams.

Clickbok grunted, strained and grunted some more until he could no longer breathe.

Then the stream began.

"That's better," Clickbok said when he finished his explosive bowel movement into the Earth's oceans.

The clip ended.

"No-no-no..." Mia said.

"Oh... *shit*," Teboho vomited inside his helmet.

LOST EMBERS OF EARTH
CHAPTER 1

Quork had just left his nest-mate, and then he met a human.
It had to be the worst day of his life.
Most beings of terminal seven were sensible enough to be wearing environment suits, hiding all their shapes, sizes, smells and colours behind matte-black surfaces. Not Quork though, no; he'd been tossed from his nest so quickly he hadn't even packed a decent odour filter. Now here he was, waiting in a basic auto-queue box, wafting his feathers over his nostrils and trying to ignore the pungent smells.

Stuck in line for terminal seven's next shuttle to a cruise ship, heading to the galactic rim worlds, he tasted the pungent air and shook in disgust. Quork's box lurched forward on its tracks and the smooth silver-blue box in the front shot off toward a waiting shuttle. The box zoomed along its floor-embedded tracks so fast it was a wonder no bones were broken. That's if its squishy occupants *had* any bones.

He should have been happy that he was finally second in line, but all he could think about was the stink of the strange creature in the box in front of him. The horrible taste in his nostrils warred with his hunger and he impatiently tapped his auto-queue box's floor. The rapid drum beats of his feet formed a barely adequate distraction and he snatched the gold-rimmed ticket from his beak before he was tempted to swallow it.

"You're joking," the creature in the front box in one of terminal seven's auto-queues yelled over the commotion of a dozen different species and moving boxes. The translation came to Quork's mind a split second after the words were uttered, blending alien words and Galactic Basic in a confusing symphony of guttural utterances and electronic singsong. A few heads -- at least he thought they were heads -- regarded the creature that had spoken, politely bored expressions perking slightly at the sound of the commotion.

"This terminal does not recognize your ticket," the desk clerk said. The clerk, a large twin-trunked elephantine encased in silver armour plating, towered over the creature. "It appears to be invalid."

"Oh don't give me that, I booked this flight two days ago," the creature argued.

"It says right here your ticket was obtained through a black market dealer named Holla Stifle twenty minutes ago," the clerk said as it gently tapped on one of the giant flat-screens behind the desk. "At least that's what the surveillance reports suggest."

"How the...?" The creature trailed off in a kind of stunned silence, it's jaw ajar.

"I need to verify the validity of your ticket. State your destination please."

"I simply need transport to my ship," it said. Quork couldn't tell whether the creature was afraid or angry, but it was becoming deadly quiet in the auto-queue boxes all around them as their occupants started paying attention to the conversation.

"Thank you. Now state your name please."

"'Sam.' See, it says it right there. Happy now? Can I go?"

"Thank you, but you may not yet proceed. I must persist in this line of enquiry due to the dubious nature of the ticket. Now, state your species please." The clerk tapped a few control panels with its twin trunks and waited for a reply, focusing both of its bulbous eyes on the diminutive creature.

"Why do you need to know that?"

"State your species please." The ponderous voice grew louder.

"Please don't." It sounded afraid to Quork. Half of terminal seven was now following the commotion. "You don't need to kn—"

"Uncooperative being at desk twenty-nine, terminal seven. First warning. Please answer or you will be removed to the cells. What species are you?"

The creature stayed quiet for a long time, so long that Quork wondered if it had died from fright. The clerk tapped a control panel and a distant alarm began, somewhere deep within the office blocks on the far side of the terminal. "Security will be here shortly unless you state your species."

Finally, the creature moved, but only to look up at the giant clerk. What Quork heard next chilled him to the bone. "Human," the creature said. The translator embedded in Quork's brain clearly identified a hint of menace from the alien's speech. "I'm a human."

Silence took over the confines of terminal seven. He could hear nothing but the click, click, clicking of moving boxes and the occasional faint breathing of nearby beings. *Human*, he thought. *A human.*

A chorus of whispered words from other denizens of terminal seven joined his thoughts.

"Human," a nearby Pluckett Plant's vibrating leaves translated into the evil word.

"Yes," the human replied to the Pluckett. "I am human, and all I—"

"Security," the desk clerk screamed before ducking for cover behind the large blue armoured desk. Its two long trunks searched blindly for the consoles, trying to call for help.

"Great," the human said with what appeared to be a black rage. It drew its black as the cloak tightly around itself. Small disc-shaped security drones zipped over the heads and other body parts of the terminal's unfortunate inhabitants, their shock-batons fully extended. The human - Sam - locked its hungry, simian, eyes on Quork.

The human called Sam vaulted over the lip of its auto-queue box. Quork did nothing but stand and watch before the human grabbed him by the neck and pressed some sort of silver cylinder into the side of his head. "Stay still and shut up," it said, unnecessarily.

Sounding like loud, angry bees, the three security drones wobbled to a halt in a triangular pattern around human and victim. Other travellers in terminal seven screamed, hooted, cackled and clacked as they exited their respective boxes and scrambled for the exits. Brilliant bright strobe lights flashed through the air, indicating emergency exit points in hues of gold, red and orange to aid the many different species in their escape.

"Hold it there," Sam ordered the drones. It took a moment for the drones' operators to react, but they obeyed. The drones paused in midair.

"Human," one of the drone operators announced through a small speaker. The tinny alien tones were almost untranslatable. "Release your prisoner and prepare for processing."

"No." Human-called-Sam shook its head. "You're going to let me pass to the nearest shuttle, fueled and ready for launch the moment I get there. You're also going to provide me with an escort." Quork struggled limply as he watched the panic of the nearby crowd, wishing he could join them.

The security drones cracked the air with electrical stun batons and the ducked down into the box, pulling its feathery prisoner down with it. "I don't think so," it said over the hissing of the noisy drones. "Do that and my new buddy here may die along with me."

"Collateral is necessary, you are human," the drone controller said.

"Easy now." Sam took the silver device from its prisoner's head. "You see this thing? It's a bomb. Attempt to harm me in any way and this entire building disappears."

The drones remained silent for a moment, their operators momentarily stunned. It didn't take long for a higher authority to intervene. "Greetings, human, my name is Gorin Fireheart. I'm the Dock Master for this little moon you have seen fit to terrorize. May I point out that your death is inevitable, but it need not be a painful one. Cooperate now and spare yourself the trouble."

The human squinted, or frowned, Quork wasn't sure which, but its fingers squeezed his neck so tightly it was almost impossible to breathe. "I'm not sure you quite understand, Mr Fireheart. Remember, I'm a *human*. Where there's one, there's plenty more. If I die, my ship out there will start taking the rest of this little moon to pieces and it probably won't stop there. Do you understand now?"

The drones remained silent this time.

"I thought so. Clear a path to my shuttle, *now*." The drones hesitated a moment longer. The human's grip eased slightly.

"Proceed to bay five."

"Thank you," the human said. It eased its grip further. "Come with me," Sam ordered Quork. The drones buzzed ahead of them, angling towards one of the many long, wide tunnels leading out of the terminal towards waiting shuttles. The air crackled with electrical energy and bystanders dived, ran, or shuffled out of the way. A lone elephantine employee, much braver than its deskbound colleague, barred the shuttle boarding ramp. A drone's baton sizzled the air with an electrical arc and the elephantine collapsed into a heap.

"Shuttle is secure and ready for launch, as requested, human. Fireheart out."

"Come on." It tugged Quork's neck and he came along in a daze. "We need to get out of here."

"But..." Quork offered no resistance as he was dragged inside. "But, what—"

"Shut up and take a seat." The human shoved Quork into one of the many form-fitting seats lining the shuttle's interior, before sitting in the seat next to his. It clipped the silver cylinder, its bomb, onto a belt inside its cloak. It turned to regard him with white-blue eyes. Its poisonous breath wafted over him. "Relax, chicken man, they're not going to hurt us."

"But... you're a human," he finally managed to say through a dry beak.

"Oh, you're a quick one aren't you?"

Quork watched the view screens with morbid curiosity as the shuttle got underway. To his horror, the screens moved towards a monstrously large starship, one he imagined was ringed with weapons and filled with humans.

"N-not right. You... humans died. There *are* no humans," Quork imagined a resurgence of the war, of human fleets ravaging the galaxy anew.

The human looked at the view screens, then at Quork. Seeing his discomfort, it gave him what Quork took to be an evil grin. It was an expression he surely couldn't have misread. Quork felt sick.

"Guess it's my lucky day then," Sam said.

He took one more look at this human called Sam, watched as it got up from its seat, and then he fainted.

CHAPTER 2

The dark grey metallic walls were etched with bloodstained scratches. They were cold to the touch. The faint light in the square ceiling's edges cast ghastly shadows through various chains, cutting tools and other assorted torture devices that hung above his head. Quork had been awake for several hours or days. It was hard to tell. Despite the tangy smell of pressing metal that permeated the room all he could think about was food and water.

He dared not move, though. The sound of human boots could be heard on the other side of the dark door. Ignoring his pressing thirst and grinding hunger, he remained glued to the hard white bed. He imagined the chefs sharpening their knives, boiling cook-pots, and crooked human teeth gnashing on old bones...

He jumped. A loud thumping sound approached the outside door and stopped. His heart banged loudly in his ears and he braced for the worst. It didn't come. The heavy thumping continued past the door and eventually faded. His fear didn't.

He must have passed out sometime after the heavy thumping because next he knew the light had brightened and the Sam was looking down at him from the bedside. He jerked awake and gripped the bottom of the bed with clawed feet, waiting for the inevitable.

"Awake are we?" it asked in a surprisingly calm, non-threatening tone.

"Uh… ick?" he managed, wondering why he wasn't being tortured yet. "Wh-what are you going to d-do with me?"

"Do with you? Nothing sinister."

"But-but… you're human."

"Yes."

"And you kidnapped me. And-and this torture chamber, the blood on the walls, the scratch marks. Will you eat me?"

"Eat you? Yuck. Look chicken brains, I'm sorry you got caught up in this little fiasco. I was careless because I'm in a bit of a hurry." Sam looked around the room. "I haven't used the infirmary for a while, guess I forgot about the blood. I didn't mean to scare you." Sam moved to a white porcelain basin recessed into the metal wall at Quork's feet and pressed a hidden button. He wasn't sure why but he hadn't expected water to trickle out of the little tap.

Sam soaked a bit of cloth and started to scrub at the stained metal walls. It was a pointless gesture, the blood there was probably years old and stuck solid; it would need more than a bit of muscle to clean that off. Quork didn't much care; there was water in that basin...

He unclenched his clawed feet and shifted his weight, but paused from the noise he made. "You can get up," it told him "Don't be stupid chicken man, have some water before you expire from thirst."

Quork watched with suspicion as the human continued to clean the stains, but jumped off the bed and stumbled groggily towards the basin anyway. The water was nice and cool, soothing his parched throat.

"Why?" he coughed the word.

"Why what?"

"Why take me as a prisoner?" He took another long sip of water. When he was finished he noticed the wall was cleaned of blood and the human was looking at him.

"I'm human, remember? If I hadn't taken you hostage, I'd be dead."

"But your bomb..."

The human moved to touch the silver cylinder at its side. Quork recoiled. "This thing?" said the human. It pressed a button and he ducked for cover. Light erupted from one end of the cylinder.

Just light. "I'm surprised it fooled them as long as it did. You look a bit unsteady; are you hungry? Come with me, I'll find some food for you. There's a small canteen on the way to the bridge. I'm sure there's some food in there that won't kill you."

The infirmary's door opened with a twist of the grey knob located halfway up its length. "It's not locked," Quork remarked.

"Should it be?"

The trip wasn't far, yet he was surprised to see not a soul gracing the large corridors on their way to the promised food. Their footsteps echoed down long dark tunnels that disappeared into the distance, returning to them moments later as faint clicks that he could barely hear. He imagined the heavy footsteps of a human giant, approaching from the long darkness with a cooking pot. He started to shiver.

The short trip felt far longer than it was. He sniffed some of the food offered and settled on some flavourless bread that Sam declared was fresh. He gulped it with two snaps of his long beak and drank some more water to wash the sticky stuff down. His hunger wasn't entirely satisfied but he was no longer starving, which seemed good enough given the circumstances. "If you don't want to harm me, why didn't you send me back in the shuttle you stole?"

"You'd be as dead as I would have been. The shuttle would have been vaporized."

He stopped to look at the small creature and spoke slowly, "Because you're human."

Its head bobbed up and down, a nod? "Right now, anyone who passed through terminal seven today is likely being rounded up and interrogated. The fear the inner galactic sectors have for humans seems beyond reasonable. If they had bothered to check their data dumps properly..." Sam didn't finish the thought but turned away and continued walking. "It doesn't matter now; what does matter is that we remove our sorry souls from this system as quickly as possible."

"Where are we going?" he asked with continuing worry.

"I'm going home. Now that a human's been found in the area half the mercenaries this side of the galaxy will be after me." The human glanced at him and saw his fear. "You'll be safe, I promise."

A thick crystalline door opened slowly to admit them to the bridge beyond, which was a basic rectangular black room. Enclosed within four recesses in the floor were soft white form-fitting couches surrounded by egg white cocoons.

"Welcome to the heart of the *Deft Acquirer.* Take a seat, or not. I don't really care." There were no viewports, no large screens to view the outside. It was eerily claustrophobic. Sam took a seat inside one of the large white egg-shaped command modules and Quork sat in the cocoon next to it. The white, cushioned material moulded to his form and supported him comfortably enough. The inside surface of the cocoons flickered to life. Data screens.

Alien languages and odd graphs of light and colours flashed before him. One small square of the cocoon was showing stars and starships. His focus shifted to that square and the image enhanced and grew so that he could make out more details. As he tracked across the image, it shifted so that he could look around at the outside stars; it appeared as though he could control the ship's exterior cameras with his mind. "Wow," he whispered.

"Never been in space before, have you?" Sam asked. It must have heard him.

"Uh... yes, but not like this. Human, are those ships out there?"

"Sam."

"What?"

"My name is Sam."

"Yes, Human-Sam, but are they?"

"Just call me 'Sam,' Duck Face," it told him, sounding annoyed. "Yes, they are the dock's security craft, or at least the ones highlighted in red are. They've been following us since we left the station. I've been watching to see if they cause a fuss before we reach the travel ring, which shouldn't be long now. I'm just glad there are no sector fleets in the area."

Quork stayed quiet for a while, thinking over what was happening, not entirely sure if he was disappointed with his current dilemma. It beat another day in the nest. But the silence got to him after a while and his patience crumbled. "What will you do with me then, HuSam?"

"It's 'Sam'. Please say it properly, Duck Face."

"Sorry," he said hastily, "I find it hard to say your name. Are you male or female? It may help my speech depending on—"

"We're getting closer to the ring now, so keep the chatter to a minimum if you please."

"But..."

Sam looked at Quork, possibly seeing his pained expression, "I'm a woman. Okay?"

"Is that a male or female?"

"You clearly don't get out much. Why on Earth were you at the docks, Duck Face?"

"Stop calling me that."

"What?"

"'Duck Face'. I'm no 'duck'; I have arms and flexible claws. I'm not even sure what 'ducks' are—"

"Shh." Sam moved a finger in front of its mouth "Trust me; 'Duck Face' is a courtesy. The docks, why were you there?"

"My... uh. Do I have to answer?" He looked at the human again; it was still glaring at him. "Okay, well... my, my... you might call her my nest-mate. She kicked me out of our home. I decided to leave the planet for... I... I don't know what I'm doing." He almost broke down. The sadness he had felt the last few days finally came back to hurt him even within the vast confines of this human dreadnought.

"Huh...oh...yeah," Sam said; the human had swung its legs out towards him and was resting its arms on its knees, looking down at the floor. "Nasty business, relationships... So, what did you do? I mean, what was your profession?"

Quork mumbled, "I was a security specialist at a computer factory."

Sam nodded. "Nice job, assuming no humans tried to wreck the place. Bet it paid well. Before the war I was a librarian, do you know what that means?"

Quork shrugged, still absorbed in his own misery.

Something behind Sam changed. Quork pointed wordlessly with an outstretched wing at one of Sam's screens. A glowing ring of white light had appeared on the screen along with a long line of blue-highlighted starships waiting to go through it.

What caught his attention wasn't the ring or the long line of ships but the dark blob that was approaching them. "Great," Sam said sarcastically. The blob was many times the size of the starships, tearing down at the ships from deep space.

"What is it?" Quork's question was cut off by a loud shrieking alarm. Sam swivelled back to the form-fitting couch and Quork looked on as she tapped several commands into the cocoon's terminal. She shut off the alarms and brought up a sharper picture. "An old tiger-squid by the looks of it. This could get a little rough. Those things only come this close to a star system if they're too old to hunt bigger prey; never thought I'd see one."

"Are we in trouble?" he asked. The tiger-squid puffed a stream of gases from its large globular body to slow its relative velocity, then a handful of nearly invisible tentacles shot out at some of the small starships that were trying to scatter out of its path. The exhausts of the captured starships burned white, straining at the leash.

"No," Sam replied after several heartbeats, "we're not what it's after."

"Well... can't we help them?" He imagined the horrible things that were about to happen to those ships and their crews.

"If we wish to get ourselves *into* trouble, sure. I have no intention of dying today, Duck Face, do you?"

"And miss all the excitement? No, I suppose not." He may have lost his nest-mate, his chicks and left his homeworld behind, but a death wish wasn't on the agenda yet.

"Thought so," Sam said. The *Deft Acquirer* surged forward under the human's light touch. While the tiger-squid proceeded to tear into its prey and the rest of the ships scattered, the *Deft Acquirer* skipped to the head of the now nonexistent queue. "We're at the ring," she said with some relief.

"Where are we going?" Quork wanted to rip his mind away from the gory scene outside.

"To the next best thing..."

He opened his mouth to speak, but Sam pressed one final button and a squeal of subtly changing sound interrupted him. Swirls of black and white assaulted his vision and he felt as if he was being compressed into an infinitely small sphere.

If it were possible, he would have voided his bowels and simultaneously upchucked the few contents of his stomach, but the pressure was so intense he doubted he could have opened his beak to start the process. *Well, this is fun,* he thought, before he thought nothing at all.

CHAPTER 3

With a sickening, bone-altering 'Pop,' he was back again. He found himself beak-deep in the nearest available basin, removing some slimy bread and turgid water from his innards. Despite the transition through the transport ring and the horrible mind and space distorting mechanics of it, he wasn't in any pain.

"It's always bad the first time," Sam said quietly.

"And the next?" he replied between hacking coughs.

"It's just as bad, but don't worry, you get used to it." Sam offered him a steadying arm when she saw his trembling wings trying to grip the smooth white basin.

"Where am I?" he said as he realized he was no longer on the bridge.

"The canteen."

"How did I get to the canteen? Wasn't I just on the bridge?"

"Apparently you have a bad memory, big bird. As soon as we came out of transit you practically flew here, and boy can you *run*." Sam opened a small storage space and reached for a towel, which Quork accepted gratefully. "We arrived at the meeting place, and hell, I may as well ask since you're here anyway: want to come with me?"

"Meeting place?" he asked weakly.

"A business meeting. I just have to make a quick stop before making a run for home. You don't have to come of course, if you prefer to stay on the ship."

He looked beyond her at the dark corridor, imagining the as-yet-unseen giant coming to claim him for its giant pot. "Yes, sure. Can I get something to eat first? Maybe more bread?"

"Of course, take your time. I'll be waiting for you just down the hall near the infirmary. I've got something I think you may find useful there." Sam silently moved out into the darkened corridor, leaving him to clean himself up and find some food.

Quork found the human where it said it would be, waiting outside the open door to the infirmary. He hesitated, wondering if the infirmary really was a torture room, but continued anyway. "What's the useful thing?" he said like a curious child.

"Do you have a brain implant?" Sam replied.

"Yes," *silly question.*

"Time for an upgrade, then. This way." He followed the human into the small infirmary and the lights brightened as they entered. The hard white bed had disappeared and in its place was a far more comfortable form-fitting couch.

"My implant has the latest hardware and software as required by my position as a security specialist; how could you possibly upgrade it?"

Sam flashed teeth at him, possibly a smile. "You're talking about the commercially available kind. This stuff you can't get on any markets."

Quork sat on the couch and settled in, uncertain. "What sort of stuff?"

"A simple translator upgrade keyed specifically to your species. It will aid you with things like body language and facial expressions. You'll see what I mean when we go to that meeting." She tapped rapidly on a small console affixed to the couch, then nodded, "There, done."

"But I didn't feel anything." An upgrade should have taken a few minutes at least. At worst it should have taken a few hours, while micro-drills cut into his skull to replace vital components.

"As you said, you have the latest hardware. All I did was make a small alteration to the software. Let's go, we'll take our stolen shuttle down to the surface."

The trip to the shuttle was longer than he'd expected. They passed countless doors, elevators, ladders and dark green and grey corridors. The *Deft Acquirer*'s docking bay stretched for several kilometres into the distance. Most of the hangar was shrouded in darkness but he could quite easily make out the whale-sized forms of dozens of starships and other vehicles. Some were clearly hundreds of meters in length and at least ten floors high. He paused in awe. "You..."

"Own all of this?" Sam finished for him. "Yes."

"Where's your... your *real* ship?" he said, fumbling for the name of the legendary, human-controlled killing machines, that had ravaged the galaxy generations ago. "Your crystal craft?"

"'Crystal craft?' As good a name as any for it I suppose. I sold it."

Quork's neck snapped around so fast he thought he might have cracked it. "Sold it?"

"Yes, before the war started."

"And you bought the *Deft Acquirer* with the proceeds?"

"And then some." Sam indicated the rest of the hangar. "Not the least of which was my life."

"What?"

"Never mind. This meeting shouldn't be long; I don't plan on sticking around, that dock master's probably rounded up all of the nearest mercenaries by now. Hop aboard." They entered the shuttle's rear docking ramp and headed for the cockpit. Lining the walls of the narrow interior, instead of form-fitting seats and data screens, were piles upon piles of boxes. He wondered when Sam had had time in the past day or so to replace the seats.

They strapped into the pilot and co-pilot seats and the shuttle lifted from the deck with a slight jolt. He could hear the humming of the superconducting magnets as they lifted the craft in the artificial gravity, and a dull scream erupted from the shuttle's engines, warming for spaceflight.

The flight to the frozen planet was brief, but the passage of time seemed to stretch indefinitely during planetary insertion. Time sped back up to normal when the shuttle's landing gear finally thudded down into the soft snow. They'd landed near the entrance of a blue coloured crevice at the bottom of a mountain of ice.

"Put this on," Sam said, offering him some heavy thermal clothing. He folded the blue-black clothing around him and it automatically sealed itself as he closed the two sides together. It was a perfect fit, tailored to his body. It allowed for some flexibility in his wings and left his clawed feet completely mobile. He soon discovered that his body was insulated against the needling winds that assailed his still-vulnerable face.

With Sam's silver torch leading the way, they entered the large narrow crack under the icy mountain. It wasn't long until they found Sam's business partners.

Humans, more humans.

"You're a bit late, Sam," one of the three humans said. As Quork looked at them, lines of text appeared on his vision, next to their faces. 'Anger' appeared next to one of them, 'annoyance' on both the speaker and the other one. They wore similar black and blue thermal clothing. They smelt even worse than Sam.

Sam turned to look at each of them in turn. "Ten years, Morgan, that's how long it's been, and you're complaining about a couple of hours? After what you did to me last time I should think you'd be a little more appreciative."

"It was closer to *twenty* hours. Did you bring the food or not? We're starving if you hadn't noticed."

Sam approached the one called Morgan. It looked as though Sam was about to make a tackle. Instead, they embraced. The word 'hugging' popped up on his vision, followed by 'a friendly human gesture.'

He understood now; Sam's software upgrade allowed him to 'read' their emotions as easily as if he was a human himself, rather than simply listening to the translation of their alien words. Sam hugged the other two humans. The text next to their faces slowly went from 'angry' and 'annoyed' to 'relieved,' until one of them spotted him.

'Suspicion' immediately leapt onto Quork's vision next to Morgan's face.

"Who's your pet friend, Sam? An appetizer?"

"His name's Duck Face," Sam said quickly. "Don't mind him; he's someone I rescued from an interrogation." Sam motioned for Quork to come over. He hesitantly moved forward from behind the icy crags he'd subconsciously been using as a shield.

"Weird, he looks a bit like a big bird, some sort of raptor," one of the others said.

"That's what *I* said. He runs like a cheetah though. Duck Face, this one is called Shannon, and junior over there is Taylor. I haven't seen these guys for years—"

"The food, Sam," Morgan said.

Sam sighed, then dug out some small boxes from her belt and tossed them at the other humans. "The first shipment is waiting in my shuttle just outside. There's more, plenty more, enough to last another century if you're careful. That is, of course, if you kept your side of the bargain." Her hands went to her hips.

"Yeah, yeah, keep your knickers on," Shannon said before heading towards the back of the cave and rummaging through some half-hidden boxes. It pulled out a dull red rectangular object and tossed it. The dull red covering flipped open mid-air and brownish paper flapped towards Sam's outstretched hands.

"You better make good with the rest of the food," Taylor said, "you'll be sorry if you don't."

"Shut up Taylor," Morgan said. "We give Sam a dumb old book, and we get a hundred years-worth of food. Show her at least a *little* respect."

"Yes, boss."

"Why are you so desperate for that thing anyway? It's not like it did the human race any good. You get religion all of a sudden?"

Sam shook her head and absent-mindedly fingered the torch, "No, I just think it's important to save these things."

"Right... once a librarian, always eh?" Shannon said. "Well, enjoy your new Bible. Sorry if it's a bit worn, it's a little old."

"Wait." Morgan said. "There's something wrong..." They stopped what they were doing and watched Morgan, waiting for an explanation. "Oh no... It's a trap!"

"A trap?" Sam said.

"You," Morgan stabbed a finger at Sam and Quork. "You've betrayed us."

"What are—"

An ear-rending noise heralded a change in the icy cave's walls. White ice and rocky shards shattered inwards from the cave's far wall. Through the ensuing chaos, Quork could barely make out shadows dancing between plumes of dust. A firefight broke out in the confines of the icy cave.

Nearly blinded by the flash of the explosion and half deaf, it was an effort to understand what was happening.

"An agent."

Someone screamed.

"Run."

More explosions followed and he thought he saw one of the humans fall to the ground. He could see Sam's body, laid out flat on its back in a small pool of blood. The other two humans who had not fallen were firing at some sort of silver cloud. Small rockets emerged from their wrists and icy shards sprayed where their rockets hit the walls.

Crackling light followed the humans and the battle moved further down the caves. Breathing heavily, Quork crawled over to Sam's body. 'Fear' was the text accompanying that bloodied and bruised face and her eyes rolled around to look at him.

"What's going on?" he said.

"An agent, Duck Face." Sam sat up slowly, brushing the splinters of rock from the black and blue clothing. "We need to go, *now*."

He drew his feet up to his body, painfully, and managed to stand. Sam did the same and they supported each other. "We'd better hurry before that agent comes back."

"What... is... an agent?" His beak throbbed from the cold and pain.

"A galactic council agent, they're used to track down and destroy or capture altered humans."

"Oh..." They made it halfway back to the shuttle before Quork felt something tug at his feet. Sam was wrenched out from under his wing and the tugging on his leg became a mechanical pull. His face smashed onto the frozen snow.

Whatever had pulled them both down flipped them onto their backs. A silvery blob with dark red eyes, or sensors, floated above them. In the corner of his eye, he could see Sam's face, and the text flashed over and over again, saying one word.

'Terrified.'

'Terrified.'

'Terrified...'

CHAPTER 4

Sam was shouting, almost screaming at the grey blob. "I am a legal citizen of the galaxy. I'm not one of the altered humans. Please don't hurt me. I'm a citizen."

"State your name," a voice echoed all around them. It was as if the agent was speaking directly into their minds. His eyesight adjusted and he could make out a more distinct shape. The silvery blob was a metallic gas, and it held them solidly to the ground with thick tentacles.

"Sam Hol—"

"Yes, the file confirms your identities. Thank you for your cooperation. Sam Holder, you are hereby under arrest."

"Arrest? For what?"

"For suspicion of colluding with illegal humans. For terrorizing hundreds of innocents on docking station Gleese Five of the Third Sector. The kidnapping of an innocent and for suspicion of holding illegal human artifacts without a license. How do you plead?"

Sam stared in silence for a moment, visibly trying to calm down. "The fiasco at terminal seven was not of my making. If my friend and I hadn't tried to escape, we would both be dead because of the overzealous dockmaster."

The gaseous agent waited a moment longer before replying, "Statement noted. You deny terrorizing innocents and kidnapping this being?"

"Of course. He's my friend," Sam turned to him. '*Pleading.*'

"Is this correct?" the all-encompassing voice asked him. He gulped.

"Y-yes, we're friends."

"Then you are both under suspicion for the same crimes. How do you plead to the storing of illegal human artifacts without a license?"

"Not guilty," Sam yelled. "They're mine; I have the authority to carry any and all artifacts by right of descent."

"That's for the law to decide. A search of your ship will be conducted to validate your claims."

"You need a search order to—"

"One moment... Search order acquired. Please lead me to the *Deft Acquirer*." Strong tentacles easily lifted them back onto their feet. "Please proceed." The agent gently prodded them in the direction of the shuttle.

"Significant quantities of food," the agent announced as they entered the shuttle. "Purpose?"

"Trade," Sam told it.

"With the humans?"

"Yes, but we had no idea they were humans," Quork said before Sam could reply. The agent seemed to consider this for a moment, then gently continued prodding them towards the tiny cockpit. He couldn't understand how the agent thought they would all fit in there.

The agent simply floated above them, its red eyes observing their every movement.

Sam ran through the pre-flight checklist and paused momentarily to look at one of the external screens. A small amount of liquid escaped from one of her eyes. 'Tears,' came the text, but he didn't understand what tears were. More text appeared, 'crying, a response in humans to intense emotions.'

He wanted to ask why Sam was 'crying,' but thought better of it; he could ask such silly questions if and when they survived the agent's search of the *Deft Acquirer*.

Once off the shuttle the agent immediately started searching through each of the grounded starships in the *Deft Acquirer*'s hangar. "This is a battleship," it said after doing a quick scan of the largest ship in the hangar. It was a statement, not a question.

"Yes," Sam said.

"Please transmit the details of your license for this vessel," it demanded. Quork held his breath. A battleship.

Sam simply nodded. "Details transmitting now."

"Thank you... license confirmed. I wish to have access to your ship's computer, please allow me to search through it."

"Done," Sam said without hesitation, then turned to Quork. "Try to relax Duck Face; we're not in any trouble here."

"That will be for me to determine," the all-encompassing voice said. The agent's gaseous surface started to solidify and shrink down into a solid grey ball. It went completely still and emitted a soft sucking sound that echoed throughout the hangar.

"It's going through my ship's data stores," Sam said, "checking the ship's inventories and operating history. Trust me, we're safe."

"So you say," Quork said, not believing her. The agent quivered every now and then and Quork suppressed the urge to flinch at its every movement. He had no idea what it *was*, but it was hard to forget the look of terror on Sam's face when it had dragged them down. He wanted to thump his head against the nearest bulkhead and somehow claw his way out into space to escape its attention.

"Sam Holder," it finally said, and its voice was far more menacing than before. In a rush of air, the agent expanded back into its gaseous state. "Take me to deck seventeen, I wish to examine your stores of homewares that you are keeping in suspension. Now."

"Uh." The human gulped, "Right, yes, um… this way." Sam extended an arm towards the hallway. They took the nearest transport station along the long green corridor. A transport cart, a small thing much like a four-seated rollercoaster car, was waiting for them. The cart shot across and down several levels. As they arrived, a piece of text popped up in his vision, translating the human writings on the transport cart's digital readouts as 'storage, fragile.'

The transport cart doors slid open with a small hiss and a draft of cool air washed over them. Purple-white lights lit up the large open area beyond and they stepped out onto grated metal deck plates. Still wearing his blue-black thermal clothing, he could easily feel the hard shapes of the metal through his gloved feet. His gaze was transfixed on the walls of the large open area where shimmering blue fields projected across multiple openings in the walls. Suspended in the blue field beyond was what looked like bricks.

"I wish to examine the items more closely," the agent announced as it approached one of the walls. Sam walked to the blue field and touched it with a shaking finger. The field dissolved and the agent swam quickly through the air towards the bricks. It formed several tentacles around its gaseous body and picked up several bricks. It then proceeded to open them.

"Books?" Quork asked Sam, trying to understand what the problem was.

"Thousands of them," Sam said. "Hundreds of thousands." The agent said nothing as it picked out hundreds of books at random, scanning them with pale red beams of light. The agent placed the books back where they had been taken from and moved off towards the next blue field in a line of hundreds of blue fields.

"Open," the agent demanded. Sam obliged.

"What are they?" Quork asked when he saw what lay beyond the second blue field.

"Farm machinery, from Earth, before the war tore Earth to pieces."

"That appears to be the case," the agent said. "Next." On they went. More human equipment: computers, books, cars, clothing. More things than he cared to think about. Quork sat down, exhausted from the whole ordeal, and waited with eyes closed as more and more blue fields were deactivated.

When they finally came back, Sam's expression was grim. "Your sentence will now be announced," the agent said. "For disrupting normal operations at terminal seven, you are hereby charged seventeen million Galactic Dollars. For the attempted trade of goods with illegal humans, you are charged twenty-seven million Galactic Dollars. Failure to comply will be met with a period of not less than twenty-two years in the nearest council prison and confiscation of your ship and all goods for the same period. Do you comply?"

'Relief.'

"Yes, of course." The human's face went blank for a moment before announcing, "Done."

"Thank you for your cooperation," the floating gas said. It moved a short distance away from them and disappeared in a bright white flash of light.

Quork collapsed on the hard metal deck plates, chipping his beak in the process.

CHAPTER 5

It was as if the agent had never been there. Quork walked behind the human, again in a daze, heading through a giant maze of corridors, access tubes and large open rooms with metal crates stacked to the ceilings. Strange smells, like human sweat combined with oil and other substances, wafted over him, but he barely noticed. Sam led him to the bridge's canteen.

"Here," Sam pointed to a waiting plate on a low table. "I had the ship prepare something; thought you could use a bit of decent food. I haven't seen you eat since you first got here."

He stared at the food. Chop-worms, deep-fried. Not his favourite meal but the mere sight of the home-style delicacy made his stomach grumble, despite the horrendous few days he had recently endured. He shifted unsteadily onto the low table and started plucking at the chop-worms. He ate slowly at first, savouring the taste, speeding up as his digestion adjusted. Sam produced another basket from the ship's automated cookery and this he tore into, ignoring proper etiquette in favour of shovelling the food into his gaping beak. He snatched a cup of water out of the small human's hand and spilt most of the water trying to gulp it down. He then glared at Sam who offered another cup.

By the time he was finished eating and drinking he'd almost forgotten the agent. He sat on the floor and let the food settle. Several minutes later he opened his feathered wings, flapped them, then gingerly pushed himself up. Sam was still in the room sitting next to him in a painful-looking cross-legged position.

'Concerned,' was the text that appeared next to the human's face. Using only her legs to push up into a standing position, Sam then motioned towards the kitchen's door. "I'm truly sorry for everything I've put you through."

"Why didn't you just kill me," he said slowly.

"Kill you? That's the last thing I would want to do. When have I ever given you the impression that I wanted to kill you?" They started walking towards the ship's bridge, the human leading him at a casual pace.

"You kidnapped me, then forced me to meet more humans, then, then... that *agent*."

"I said I'm sorry. I never meant for any harm to come to you. You're not the only one that's having a couple of bad days." They stopped just before the bridge and Sam studied the red and green lights on the bridge's airlock. "Right now we probably have half the sector fleet searching for us, a pissed off dockmaster with more wealth than I have, and an overly watchful agent somewhere nearby. The moment I think we're safe we'll head towards a trading outpost I often visit. It's... not entirely lawful, but there are plenty of good people there. I'll arrange for private transport for you to go anywhere in the galaxy. You'll have money, enough to live on for the rest of your life."

He was being bribed with false words of hope, he thought. The human walked inside and Quork stared daggers at her back. Suddenly he leapt at her, wings steadying the short flight. The human went down on its stomach with a dull thud and a short squeal. "Tell me, why? Why did you do this to me?"

"I..." the human wheezed. He stood squarely on her back.

"You what? You're going to cut me loose on some unlawful den with a small fortune and a private starship? They'll kill me." He wanted to yell some more but was stopped short by the distant sounds of thumping footfalls. *The giants.* He remembered.

He listened intently, still high on rage as he stood on the surprisingly helpless human. The thumping was growing louder, coming from several directions at once. He slowly relinquished his grip on Sam and stepped away.

With a hiss the airlocks on either side of the bridge burst open and strobing blue lights swirled inwards, flickering quickly around the bridge until they zeroed in on their target. "Uh..." his next words died in his throat. The rage that had consumed him was obliterated the moment he saw the two mechanical monsters. Their blue eyes locked onto his chest.

"Is everything okay in here, captain?" a human-like voice emanated from the mechanical beings. The creatures were large enough that they had to hunch over to lean in the airlock doorways. Their dark metal coating was thick and cylindrical around their bodies, and the three thick legs rotated easily around their middle when they moved. A matching set of very human arms held an assortment of heavy-duty cutting and drilling tools, while their domed heads sprouted smaller arms, tools and a variety of lights. It was those eyes, those laser-lit eyes, which made him stand still with fright.

He blinked and shook his head, before taking a step away from Sam's prone body on the bridge's hard metal floor.

"Just some bruising," the human wheezed. "My friend and I were just having a little talk, weren't we?" Sam finished by looking at him, 'annoyance' plastered on her face. A small drop of blood appeared on Sam's mouth. She ignored it.

The two giant, mechanical beings blocking the exits stared, waiting for Quork's reply.

"Uh..." He nervously clacked his beak together several times before replying, "Yes, a friendly conversation. Here." He offered Sam a feathered wing and curled hidden claws gently around the soft-skinned human's arm.

Despite the apparent ease with which he'd knocked the smaller being down, Quork found that Sam was surprisingly heavy. Out of the corners of his eyes, he saw the mechanical giants relax into a more upright stance, but there was no indication that they would be leaving anytime soon.

"Thank you," Sam said while sitting on the outer casing of one of the bridge's sunken command cocoons. "I understand your anger, Duck Face—"

"That's not my name." Embers of rage still glowed hot in his belly.

"I know your name—"

"Then use it."

"I *can't*, I simply cannot form the right sounds for your proper name. The closest I can come up with is 'Quork,' which just sounds..."

"Silly" He nodded. "But close enough. Just call me Quork, better than Big Bird or Duck Face."

The human exhaled tiredly and stood to retrieve a small data scroll. "All right, Quork, I think I've been negligent in regards to your welfare. I'll try to explain my current predicament; come have a look at this." She held up a paper thin data scroll. On it was a picture of some sort of crystalline starship and he approached to get a better look. "This was my ship. A crystal-craft. I didn't just cash in on it to buy my current ship; I never would have had the money for the *Deft Acquirer*. Instead, I invested the proceeds in the galactic exchange, buying into war technology companies, mostly.

"When the crystal hoard arrived, and by crystal hoard I mean the rest of the human race, many of them began ravaging the galaxy. Those war technology companies I'd invested in increased in value substantially. You *could* say that I'm not poor. Since I sold my crystal craft before the hoard arrived I'm not considered an enemy of the galactic council."

The data scroll flicked to another image, one of an ocean and cloud-covered world, with large landmasses filling in much of the tableau. "Of course that doesn't explain how I came into possession of my crystal craft in the first place."o

"How...?" Quork whispered.

"I don't really know, but imagine... imagine you're back on your homeworld for a moment, working your security job. Then these things - I don't even remember what they look like - descend upon your world. They offered everyone in my town and everyone on Earth over the age of twenty-five, *everything they wanted*." Sam shifted uncomfortably. 'Mildly distressed.'

"What do you mean, 'everything?'"

"There were billions of us, all of us given so much... power." 'Distressed' appeared as the last word was spoken, and she shuddered. "Can you? Quork? Imagine what it's like to have so much power? We were little more than cave dwellers. Hell, we still built caves of wood and brick to live in."

"What powers?" He desperately wanted to know what had happened right at the beginning, when the crystal craft swept across the inhabited worlds: demolishing, conquering and slaughtering. He could smell the human's sweat and puzzled at its meaning.

"What... what powers?" Sam looked at him quizzically. "Don't you know?" Quork shook his head, and Sam blew out some air. "I suppose it *has* been a long time. Immortality, for starters. Weapons that could grow instantly from our skins, supercomputers connected to our brains, perfect health. We could change sex, colour, even *shape*, at will. Skin as hard as steel and diamond-hard teeth. We looked the same but felt like gods.

"On top of that, there were the crystal craft. I don't need to tell you about those, do I?"

He again shook his head. The fleet-destroying, world-ravaging abilities of each one of the billions of ships in the crystal hoard were well known.

"I didn't want any of it. I had most of my implants removed." She looked at Quork with red-rimmed eyes. "None of the powers, none of the violence."

"Why then? I don't understand. Why sell your ship and have your implants removed?"

"Is there violence on your world? Conflicts between nations?"

"Between nestings, there are some tensions," Quork replied.

"Murders?"

"Yes."

"What would those murderers have done if given a crystal-craft?"

"Ah." He understood where this was going. "They would kill anyone who got in their way."

"And more, once they realized they were unstoppable. This is how it was on Earth. When every man and woman over the age of twenty-five is given their own world-destroying ship, well..."

The data scroll's image changed. It showed the Earth cracked in half. "I saw this as I was returning from my journey to the galactic exchange, less than a year after I had left my homeworld." Water drops appeared under the human's eyes.

"I'm sorry," Quork said, gaining the sudden urge to reach out and pat the creature on the head.

"Piss off," Sam said before he could try. "I was never a part of the hoard; I harmed no one and would never want harm to come to anyone that didn't deserve it. Most humans didn't hurt anyone, but there were *billions* of us. All it took was a few thousand of us to start that war and many more humans were dragged into it. After that, the council hunted down anyone with a crystal craft whether they were guilty or not."

"I'm sorry," he said. Sam waved his apology away. "So... you knew what would happen right from the beginning."

She nodded. "Yes, Quork, I knew. That much power could only lead to violence. I prepared for the worst and managed to avoid the worst of it. Now, I'm just trying to pick up the pieces. It's hard, being human. I try to save what I can, but the moment anyone discovers what I am..." The trickle of water continued and Sam remained silent for a moment. "I can only try. In any case, the offer still stands; I'll give you anything you want when we're safe." She rolled the data scroll up before tossing it into one of the cocooned couches. "How does that sound?"

Quork hesitated. He could live a life of luxury anywhere he wanted but... "I'd prefer to sta—"

A screeching sound slammed into his ears. Flashing red lights assaulted his eyes and Sam's sad, contemplative look became something else. "It's the alarm," she shouted over the din. With a wave of her arm, the ship's alarms silenced and she leapt into the nearest cocoon. She scanned the displays on the inside of her cocoon and listened to the ship's computer. "We're being fired upon."

CHAPTER 6

"It was a long shot, seven million clicks away. Barely scratched the paint," Sam was saying. "Not good, though, it's a Chippin War Cruiser. I was afraid this would happen."

"So? Can't you just blow it away? This ship's bigger than a dreadnought isn't it?"

"Blow it away? Quork, weren't you listening to me before?"

"You don't kill... Oh."

"I *can't* kill them, numbskull. This ship doesn't have any weapons or that agent would have boiled my bones the moment we stepped on board."

"So what are you going to do?"

"We," Sam corrected him, "are going to run for the nearest transport-ring, and you," Sam pointed at him and he half opened his wings before realizing he wasn't being threatened. "Are going to help. Hop in that cocoon." She pointed to the smooth white cocoon next to the one she was sitting in. "The casing will seal around you for your protection; I'll talk to you once you're inside."

He did as he was told and the cocoon's casing enveloped him. Images popped up on the inside surfaces of the cocoon, showing various statistics and star fields. Sam's face appeared on a smaller oval image. "Now what?" he asked.

"See this image?" One of the statistical displays enlarged. "It shows the power levels of the ship's defence grid. When the bars on the right begin to shorten and turn red like this." The bars changed colour just as Sam had described. "It means either the ship's about to fall apart or something similarly horrible is going to happen. When that happens, come and grab me as fast as you can. My mind's going to be pretty deep in the ship's programs, so you may have to slap me to get me out of it."

"That's it?"

"That's it. I'll handle everything else. The rest of the displays will show you what's going on, just don't get distracted." A ringing sound announced the human's departure and Quork was now very much alone.

The ship accelerated at several percentile points above what was considered safe and then engaged its *main* engine. Twin plumes of sunburst flames pushed the ship forwards, away from the distant hunter. It made an extensive scan in front of it, searching for any sign of the tiniest granules of matter in the fear that, at their current velocity, the smallest rock might cripple the *Deft Acquirer*. The Chippin War Cruiser struggled to match velocities, doing its best not to let them escape the range of its x-ray lasers. Sam coded an evasive pattern into the computer and the ship started shifting randomly around its relative position. They had increased their range from the enemy vessel by an entire light-second, giving them ample breathing space for avoiding the war cruiser's weaponry.

"Scramble all vessels," Quork heard Sam say out loud. He suspected it was more for his convenience than was strictly necessary.

"Acknowledged," the computer replied. "Launching." A new screen flicked on. He could see the dozens of ships occupying the hangar deck, all powering up and lifting from their berths.

"What can they do?"

"The ships?" Sam said, barely coherent.

"Yes, I thought they didn't have any weapons."

"Distractions."

In an instant the ships closest to the hangar's gaping maw vanished, streaking away from the camera's viewpoint at blistering speeds. Once the hundreds of vessels in the hangar had all been launched, the *Deft Acquirer*'s triple-layered defence grid lit up like a burning bush.

Billions of small crisscrossing lasers ignited the faint air around the ship's external armour. Powerful electromagnetic barriers pushed their way into space in overlapping positive and negative cones of energy. Megaliters of plasma, kept in place by further magnetic fields near critical areas of the ship, were set ablaze to disintegrate any stray particles that got past the first two layers of defence.

The ship's armour plating shifted aft, sliding over other pieces of armour plating already in place near the ship's rear. As he watched the ship's rapid transformation from simple rock to an armoured, fire-breathing dragon, Quork barely noticed the tiny star that was the Chippin War Cruiser's flaming exhaust.

Hundreds of smaller stars zipped to and fro between the larger vessels, representing all manner of probes, scouts, fighters, and deadly projectiles. "Is it enough?"

"Enough what?" Sam said, trying to concentrate on the ongoing battle. Quork didn't bother replying and instead focused his attention on the steadily diminishing bars that he'd been tasked to watch. "A hit," Sam said with a hint of triumph, "not a big hit... just clipped their port side. Sent a probe... rammed them."

Quork watched several small dots quickly rush towards one another, merge, and split apart. Red splotches indicated explosions and debris from instantaneously restructured starships. A feeling, like he was falling, grew in his stomach while he watched the flowering battle formations.

Not good, he thought. Sam was trying to hit the other ship with individual drones, while the Chippin War Cruiser had access to a plethora of different types of weapons systems. The clouds of red splotches mirrored his doubts and fears, blossoming with each consecutive explosion until they appeared to be all around him.

His eyes darted, breathing increased, muscles flexed.

A chime sounded. He almost squawked until he realized it was the communicator. A blue light blinked at him. "Don't make this so hard on yourself." The unmistakable translation of an annoyed elephantine's hoots and trumpets buzzed in his ears.

"Fireheart?" Sam said, sounding both surprised and strained at the same time. "That... you... throwing stuff?"

"Human-Sam, you know it is," said Fireheart. *That voice*, thought Quork...*Fireheart... the one from the station*. He remembered now. Fireheart continued, "Please, your attempts at resistance, are they necessary?

"What... are you... doing this... for?" Sam said, straining with the concentration.

"Why? A human escapes my station, causes mass panic and humiliates me on the galactic news channels. You know what happened after that? An agent comes asking questions, probing my mind. My *mind*. And then it orders my arrest. It arrested *me*, for letting *you* escape." The elephantine paused a moment, pregnant madness audible in its laboured breath. "You murderous human filth."

"Liar," Quork slid into the conversation on Sam's behalf. "You were the one who tried to kill Sam."

"Ahh, the hostage speaks. Of course, you're her handler, aren't you? You helped the monster escape."

"Wait..."

"Never mind, Mr. hostage, you'll soon die as well."

The communicator blinked purple and the connection to the enemy ship severed. "Sam?" he called. The communicator's one blue light blinked on-off-on, something that told him nothing. "Sam?" he called again. Blink, blink. He searched the displays, trying to find some sort of exit button that would split his cocoon and let him out.

Cascading red dots on the cocoon's displays surrounded him, ploughing forth towards the one blue dot that represented the *Deft Acquirer*. He paused his mad scramble to escape and stared at doom. "Uh... Sam?" He squeaked at the blinking communicator. The defence grid's power bars fluctuated wildly as the power to the magnetic shields and lasers intensified. Shrapnel, missiles, pebbles and kitchen sinks felt the defence grid's wrath, flaring brightly for a few hundredths of a second as they were vaporized.

A few metallic slugs appeared to be getting through, cracking against the ship's double-layered armour plating, and newly formed craters spread like a plague across the ship's rear. The ship's engines escaped the same treatment by virtue of their super-heated plasma fields.

Something else appeared on the displays, approaching rapidly, encroaching faster than the enemy missiles...

"Sam, we're headed straight for the local star." He lashed out and his feet thudded against the cocoon's hard, bone-shattering inner shell. He rapidly came to the conclusion that his foot was sore, and that this time he was going to die.

"I... know," the human said before the communicator shut off entirely.

The cocoon's edges split and a beam of concentrated light poured into his soul. The monster's hand darted through the widening slit, reaching for him, prying, poking, searching. One of its fingers stabbed at his face, missed.

It found purchase on a tiny piece of real estate above his head and attacked that instead. The cocoon rushed open the moment the monster's finger found it. It reached in to grab him but stopped when he recoiled. "Quork?" the monster called. "It's Sam, remember?"

His deluded mind unlocked the trapdoor and let his memories out of the basement. "Sam, yes," he nodded thanks and grabbed the human's hand. "Wait, the star."

"Calm down Duck Face, we performed a couple of extreme maneuvers around the star. You must have lost consciousness when it happened. The war cruiser's gone; they couldn't match our maneuvers after they'd been hit with that probe. We made it, mostly, but so did their drones."

"Drones?"

"Assault drones." Annoyance tagged the human's face. "Their ships survived the star's shave long enough for them to board us. Here." The hand offered him a device, some sort of oily black stick. He took it, recognizing the device for what it was. A loud boom sounded nearby and Sam leapt with fright.

"Damn, they're close. Stay here and guard the bridge; I've vented the air from most areas of the ship to try and remove the drones but it looks like a few managed to stay on board." Sam picked up an object, much like the one in Quork's claws, and headed for an open airlock. "Keep these airlocks sealed, and remember if those defence levels dip below their minimums let me know. I'll hear you."

"Got it." He exuded confidence, on shaky legs. The human left and he climbed back into his cocoon, depressing the button above his head to re-seal himself inside. He nervously feathered the dull, black surface of the deadly device in his hands, while the displays imaged carnage for him.

The pursuing starship was long gone, a casualty of the local star's gaseous rage. Remnants of the two warring fleets blistered around the rapidly fading light of the angry star, heeding long dead commands to continue their useless fight. A handful of blue dots were doing their best to return to the *Deft Acquirer*, but the

Acquirer was moving so fast after the suicidal slingshot maneuver around the star that Quork doubted they would ever catch up.

He heard a dull throbbing and felt the shudder of the explosion at the same time. A few moments later, he felt and heard it again. He had the urge to fly out of the egg.

"Are you okay?" The displays changed to that of a mechanical human, with a voice to match.

"Yes," he said, feathers on edge, "how do I see something inside the ship? I can't see what's going on."

"Here," the mechanical, ultra-human voice said. The displays changed from that of a distant star-field filled with angry red to a sickly green-grey tunnel. A camera attached to the mechanical suit that Sam was wearing was being piped to his screens.

They didn't have long to talk. An assault drone, a non-shapely, spidery web of moving parts, attacked. He wished he hadn't asked for a view of the ship's innards; Sam moved too quickly for him to follow. Too much movement, too sharp, jerky, green. Quork coughed up part of his last meal and covered his eyes from the sickening chop of the fight.

When he'd finished removing the slimy worms from his gullet, he looked back to the screens on the cocoon. He could see a handful of the large, three-legged maintenance droids diving on one of the assault drones. Most of the maintenance droids died in the assault, torn apart by hails of bullets, but one barreled into the thrashing drone and used its considerable bulk to hold it down. Sam ran towards the assault drone and pulled apart a couple of major components. The assault drone ceased its thrashing and Sam and the droid continued their hunt for more drones.

The pattern of thickly armoured maintenance droids diving on assault drones continued several times. The sickening feeling in Quork's stomach did not fade.

Suddenly, a dazzling beam of white light shone through his reddish-brown feathers and a slimy, scaly snake poked its head into the cocoon. Except it wasn't a snake, it was a snout.

An elephantine snout.

"Got you." The barely audible translators crackled in his ears over angry gurgles of the deranged giant. The elephantine's second snout levered the cocoon open and the first wrapped around his delicate neck, lifting him into the open air. "The hostage," Fireheart trumpeted. "Where is that human? Tell me now and I won't hurt you, little bird."

He wanted to tell him, was desperate to, anything to get the strangling whip off of his neck. Wild eyes peered closely at him, trying to work out why the bird wasn't talking. After a moment the pressure abated. His head rolled limply towards the cocoon's open casket and he gasped for air. "I apologize," Fireheart said reasonably. "This appears to have been something of a significant misunderstanding, doesn't it? You will cooperate, yes?"

Fireheart's bloodshot eyes searched for signs of comprehension from Quork, but all Quork saw was the inside of his cocoon: the blurry, choppy images, and the black, oily device left there.

He coughed a laugh and grabbed the weapon.

"Hostage..." Fireheart warned him and tightened his grip, then smacked the black weapon from his dangling legs. "If you cannot cooperate, you have little to live for."

Quork laughed again and Fireheart hesitated. The elephantine looked at the cocoon's innards, watching the displays. The grip on Quork's neck slackened, the snaky snout uncoiling further until Quork dropped free to the cocoon's acceleration couch.

"You." The elephantine screamed while turning around.

In the airlock's dilapidated hatchway stood a humanoid thing. A machine that was somehow human, but not. "Me," the human-mechanical voice announced. Fireheart slapped it against the airlock hatch's side with one quick whip, taking the human-machine by surprise.

Sam - he assumed it was Sam - got back on its feet and lashed out at the coiling snakes with mechanical fists.

"How did you get here?" Sam asked.

"Die."

While the two assailants were distracted Quork jumped from the cocoon, wings spread wide and landed atop the black weapon. He took aim. Fired.

Fireheart disappeared in a blaze of bright white light.

Behind where the elephantine had been, Sam hunched, holding one side of her armoured suit in pain. The humanoid faceplate was smashed apart and, through all of the wires, gears, optical plates, and glassy substances, she wore an agonized expression.

Sam looked at Quork and fell onto the bridge's heavy floor. Quork dashed over and looked down upon the battered face.

"Qu-Qu...ork, take me... t-take me... home," Sam convulsed rapidly for a moment, then focused glazed eyes on him, "please?"

CHAPTER 7

The *Deft Acquirer*'s controls were surprisingly intuitive once he'd figured them out. He'd asked into his cocoon, "Can you take Sam home?" The ship's new trajectory suggested that it understood. He managed to get the human out of its exoskeleton and stuffed her in some sort of medical couch-cocoon that Sam said would help her heal.

That was the last he'd seen of her for almost a month. The medical couch was moved by one of the few surviving ship's droids, which explained that it would take the couch to a recovery room.

He wandered the echoing corridors searching for clues of Sam's past, studying the collected items of human history as if they meant something to him. He had to know *why*, why the humans had ravaged the galaxy and who had given them such power in the first place. All he found were artifacts, books mostly. Rows of books filled the interior of the ship's major cargo bays. Even if he could read them he'd never live long enough to read them all. Or count them all for that matter.

He managed to get lost on several occasions.

Even though three-quarters of the ship was the engine, with most of the rest being defence systems, life support and hangar, there was more than enough space left over for him to lose his bearings. *Ants nest*, he would think each time he was lost and lick his beak at the thought of millions of juicy ants. After a meal and visit to the nearest lavatory, he would continue searching for clues to his host's past.

Books, clothing, pictures, electronic things, chemical dumps. The *Deft Acquirer* had been gathering these things since the crystal hoard left Earth, four hundred years ago.

The ship coasted between the galaxy's transport ring superhighways at a decent .2c. It sounded like such an easy figure to imagine, just twenty per cent of light, but when he actually started trying to work out how quickly they were travelling... He needn't have bothered trying; it only hurt his brain.

When he'd imagined what star flight would be like, he'd always imagined watching the stars zoom by, especially when they hit the ring system, but the truth was rather less dramatic. No matter how fast the computer said they were going the stars did not change where they were. No streams of stars, nothing but a static star field. The only time the stars changed was the instantaneous transition between rings, and then only slightly. It took almost two days to travel between the transport rings in each star system.

Flash. Accelerate halfway, avoid the local traffic, flip over, decelerate. Flash.

Over and over again.

In one way Sam was right; he did sort of get used to being squashed into a tiny ball of meat-matter and re-expanded into his former self. It didn't mean he enjoyed the experience, but he knew what was about to happen. The canteen's sink was never far.

He asked the ship to continually scan for any signs of pursuit, but none came. The sector fleets were engaged in some sort of war game and the local security forces stayed well clear of the giant human starship. He scanned the galactic news channels and saw that the *Deft Acquirer* was mentioned as having been involved in an altercation with a rogue Chippin War Cruiser and its deranged captain. There was no sign that anyone wanted to arrest Sam, or that the *Deft Acquirer* was harbouring any humans.

Of Gorin Fireheart, there was no sign. No blood, no pieces of clothing, nothing to indicate Quork had shot the elephantine dock master. He wondered about the exact properties of the oily black weapon that he'd shot Fireheart with, but decided he may not like the answer and hoped he wouldn't have to use it again.

"Chicken please," he told the ship's kitchen. The kitchen hummed politely before spitting out a whole chicken. It was thoroughly cooked, or simply assembled from nutrient dispensers; he wasn't quite sure how it worked. It tasted good, smelled better, and filled him up nicely, so he didn't much care how it was made.

"Where are we going?" But the ship didn't tell him, it never did.

"Avoidance protocols engaged," was the closest he got to an answer.

He didn't think a human could have a home. But then, he didn't know humans still existed a month ago. He searched through the cargo bays, hunting for something that might stand out. There was something funny that the agent once said, something about homewares, but he could find no record of a storage facility called 'homewares.' He had vague recollections of a large room with metal grating, and *things* in stasis.

He fluttered upon the answer while visiting the nearest lavatory.

"Deck seventeen please," he told the transport cart.

"Access to deck seventeen is restricted to essential person—"

"It's an emergency." Not true, but he'd discovered the ship's computer accepted it as a good enough reason to let him into other restricted areas, such as the abandoned hangar. Without the necessary input from Sam, he figured the ship must trust him enough to allow his requests. He worried what Sam would do when she recovered enough to look at the ship's logs and find out what he'd been up to. Perhaps he shouldn't have been poking around the engineering sections of the ship.

"Access granted," the transport cart's speakers purred and they headed for deck seventeen, narrowly avoiding a startled repair droid that was welding a dismantled section of star-blasted armour plating. He could smell melted metal and charred wood as they went by. They quickly arrived at the door to the large open room that he remembered visiting with Sam and the agent and he stepped out of the cart. He feathered at the locked access panel, trying different combinations to get him inside. He quickly gave up.

He turned to get back into the cart but heard a click and felt a whispering wind sidle past him from the locked door. It opened heavily, quietly. The only sound he heard was the slow, partly strained breathing of a hunched over human.

Death-warmed-over stumbled forward and laid a soft but firm hand upon his feathered back. "Not yet," the human said shakily.

"Shouldn't you be in the recovery room?"

"Have you tried spending an entire month cooped up in a single room?" Sam asked him.

"I did try to visit," he told the sickly creature. Sam slid carefully into the cart, still nursing battle wounds.

"Thanks, but after what those droids did to me I wasn't a pretty sight." The words trickled from Sam's damaged mouth.

"I saw," said Quork, but his words were met with nothing but a blank stare. "Maybe not, then."

"Maybe not," Sam confirmed. "The damage was a little more extensive than it may have appeared. Don't worry; I'll be back to my old self in a few more days or weeks." Sam's alien ape-like eyes regarded him slowly when the cart started off towards the bridge. The door to the large room clicked shut. Strangely enough, he thought he'd heard footsteps behind that door.

A burning question bubbled to the surface. "Where are we going?"

"You've been asking that a lot," said Sam.

She'd been watching the ship's logs after all. "And all I get is 'home,' wherever that is. I need to know what that means. What is 'home' Sam?"

Sam watched the cart's progress and braced against a sharp corner, then relaxed a little as their path levelled out. "I'll show you."

The *Deft Acquirer* eased its way into the small world's atmosphere and landed in a crisp, cool sea near a long sandy beach. A new mountain range was born. One tip of the *Deft* range kissed a soft sandbank, and, Quork's feathered feet, shorn of their blue-black thermal coverings, chewed the dark yellow grains. He looked up at the bulk of the ship and marvelled that it had landed on the planet at all, doubting that it would ever rise again, but knowing the impossible was expected.

Above the *Deft Acquirer*'s solid bulk was a clear night sky, interrupted by settling plumes of steam near the ship's thruster clusters. Illuminating everything, including the beach, the mountainous ship, the curly waters and mists of vapour, was the dazzling plumage of the galaxy above their heads.

"Beautiful," he whispered. He spun about on one clawed foot, kicking up loose sand with the other. He watched the sweet curves of galactic arms spin around his eyes, keeping the egg-white interior more or less centred in his vision. "So, this is home?" he said aloud.

"Yes. Plenty of room, naturally life-sustaining, far from that mess up there." Sam waved at the sky to indicate the spinning lights.

"Where are we?" They'd only travelled for two more days. "One of the Magellanic clouds?"

"Pah, why does everyone always assume it's in one of those miserable dwarfs? Not a chance, Duck Face, this is exclusive territory: one small star, servicing three planets and twenty-seven moons. The nearest star to Home is a little over five hundred light years away."

"Five—" Quork choked on his surprise. "We're not inside the galaxy?"

"No. I felt it best if I had a little privacy. It cost a bundle, but I think it's worth it."

Quork stared at the frail little human as if it had kicked him in the gonads. "You *own* this place?"

"Yes. Does that surprise you? I have considerable wealth, remember?" Sam looked pointedly at the new mountain range adorning the coloured night sky.

"Huh," he said. It wasn't inconceivable for a human, of all creatures, to own its own star system. He noticed a light glow flowing over the edge of the beaches and the low lying hills beyond. "Is that a city?" he asked, erasing the concern from his speech with the wave of one brown wing over the horizon.

"Quork," She took a large breath, "you've seen the disgust our fellow citizens have for humans. Yes, that is a small city, more of a village really – it's a refuge I've been building since the beginning of the war. I'm trying to save what's left of my species before the rest of the galaxy tears us apart. There are more of us out there, but… we humans can't do it alone. I need help." She looked at him with large blue-white eyes, "do you—"

"—Hold it there, Sam." A voice. A terrible, angry voice, boomed across the barren sands, and they both locked gazes on the thing that had emerged behind them. Petrified blood snaked down the thing's face, chiselled teeth flashed angry words at them and a black weapon pointed at them.

The weapon's open end winked at Sam and Quork in equal measure. The shimmering shadow of a crystal craft brooded silently under the *Deft Acquirer*'s lip.

'Anger/Confusion' tagged the thing's face and 'fear/worry' covered Sam's. Quork moved, faster than he thought capable, but it wasn't in the direction in which his mind was urging him to go.

Possessed with a protective urge that he hadn't felt since his nest-mate had taken his children from him, he ran, but not for the hills. He closed the distance and leapt at the crystal craft's owner with outstretched claws and fluttering wings, hoping to knock the human off its feet before it could fire on him.

The human, Morgan, took one look at him, moved slightly to the side, kicked out and broke Quork's leg while he whistled by.

Quork squawked in pain. He landed on his back and rolled several paces while shedding feathers. "You betrayed us, Sam," the human was saying as Quork cried in agony. "You left us for dead, left us to face that agent, alone."

"Morgan, I'm sorry," Sam pleaded. "But, you're alive, this is great." The conviction wasn't there; Sam was, perhaps, lying. Quork couldn't be sure, afflicted with a badly bent leg as he was, but he could tell that Sam was *not* happy to see Morgan.

"Is it now?" Cool, bloodstained teeth reflected the soft glow of starlight. Morgan stepped towards Sam's stringy body and held the smaller human's neck between large dirty vices, sticking the black weapon firmly against Sam's temple. "You left us there to die."

"Please," Sam pleaded weakly.

"Sammy." A child, a *human* child, was running towards them from the *Deft Acquirer*'s huge open landing ramp. Quork must have been delirious. There was no such thing as a human child, at least not on the ship.

"Stay back, Tarnya," Sam yelled weakly.

"Tarnya?" Morgan dropped the weapon for a moment but recovered quickly. "You found a *child*?" He breathed heavily on the back of Sam's head. "When were you going to tell me?" His eyes raged. The weapon dug into Sam's side and she cringed.

"You are no protector," she said, the words coming out as a choked cry. Sam held a small, cylindrical object where Morgan couldn't see it. It was the bomb that she'd once held against Quork's head the day she'd taken him hostage.

But it wasn't a bomb.

Why, Sam? he wanted to ask her, *what are you doing?* But he could only chirp rapidly to try and lessen his pain.

"What are you doing with that torch?" Morgan demanded when he noticed.

Sam's face darkened, just for a moment, then set like stone. "It's night time."

"Wait, that's—" he reached for the torch but Sam pulled it away. A clip on the underside of the torch fell open and Quork saw the small red button that had been hidden there.

Sam pressed the button, ending the struggle in a cloud of bright white energy.

CHAPTER 8

"You sure you want this one?" the owner of Glaglefest's Exotic Pet Store clacked at him. The bictoid, a species derived from some sort of giant centipede, was renowned for its demand for silky shoes and good salesmanship. It pointed three of its six multifaceted eyes at him. The other three eyes kept watch on its extremely well-paid staff; its esteemed guests; and, most of all, on its stock.

"Definitely," Quork said. He checked the time on his wing-watch, feigning impatience.

"Oh, of course, but I am loathe to let go of it, it is quite rare, you understand. Its dietary requirements are also rather exotic."

"I understand," Quork bobbed his beak, "I have come well prepared; she'll be well looked after."

The bictoid formed a crosscut with its mandibles, the equivalent of a smile. "You also understand, then, that humans can become quite dangerous, even vicious when fully grown. You do know of the crystal horde don't you?"

Quork sighed, loudly. "As do we all, master Glaglefest. I also know that this particular human is not from that horde, nor was she born of it. She is one of the Unaltered, or so I have heard."

Glaglefest regarded him with six eyes, suspicious, "You're well advised, Mr...."

"Duck Face, call me Duck Face."

"Odd name."

Quork's feathers ruffled outwards momentarily, a shrug. "It grows on you."

"I see," the bictoid was lying through its mandibles. "All right, Mr Face, I'll sell her to you. One million, up front."

"One million? I could have bought a dozen such specimens on my last trip for that much."

"This is a human, Mr Face. The price comes with a year's supply of specially treated foods, medicines, clothing, and of course, your keeper's license and attached legal documents for ownership."

Quork's feathers ruffled, annoyed. "I have no need for those things."

"You... wait; you're not a breeder are you?" Glaglefest backed away from him slightly, presumably headed for some sort of exit or alarm.

"Of course not. I came well prepared to care for her needs. I have many interests in exotic pets, and I'm getting rather tired of this price gouging nonsense. Two hundred."

"Eight hundred."

"Three hundred or I walk." Quork checked his wing watch again and slowly turned to take in the rest of the large brown and gold spherical pet store. Hundreds of cages full of strange creatures were stacked against the high walls and customers wandered between them at a leisurely pace. Some of the customers were surrounded by aides, dignitaries, friends and family. Quork argued alone, more confident than the kings, queens and other important nobodies in attendance.

Glaglefest clacked something inaudible, swearing under its mandibles. It shifted uneasily, looking at the small girl, at the other customers, then to the floor. Several of the legs along its segmented body twitched nervously. "Sir, I... I cannot accept. I cannot afford less than four hundred, its parents were not terribly complying; we had to use force. The costs of attaining this specimen were considerable—"

"Deal." Quork finished his slow turn and fixed Glaglefest with a steely gaze. "On one condition: I take possession now. The amount will be transferred to your account immediately."

Glaglefest raised itself high, surprised at the sudden turn of fortune. Four hundred was a significant amount of money, despite its insistence on a higher price. Quork doubted the bictoid could refuse, especially when he was offering to pay immediately. "Now? Yes sir, of course, once I see the amount transferred. Will you sign now?"

"Give me the documents." He signed the required data scrolls and transferred four hundred thousand from the *Deft Acquirer*'s vast stores. "Come along now," he motioned for the human girl to follow him. She came quietly.

'Fear.'

"Don't be afraid, girl, let's undo those manacles shall we?" He swiped the electronic key he'd just been given across the child's wrists and the metallic bonds fell off. Glaglefest started to protest but Quork brushed him aside. "What's your name?"

"Shara," the girl said after a moment of hesitation. They left with heads held high, hand in wing as all eyes watched in silence.

None noticed the black-cloaked, diminutive creature that slipped past the store's security gates into the store.

"Welcome to our ship," Quork told the five-year-old girl.

"Hello Shara," Tarnya said with arms wide and a grin to match. She was almost twice the little girl's size and scooped her up in a bear hug. They were met with whoops of joy and laughter from the small crowd of human faces.

"Nicely done." Sam appeared by Quork's side. "Three rescues in one month," she looked thoughtful for a moment, staring at nothing. "There are more of us out there somewhere."

"I know Sam, we'll find them. You were quick," he told her. "Any problems?"

"No, not for us, but Mr Glaglefest wasn't so lucky." She gave him a sly grin as she twirled the 'torch' in her hand. "The galactic council has already seen fit to reimburse us for the costs of Shara's rescue. Those agents work fast."

Quork shuddered, remembering all too well the interrogation techniques the agents could employ. "Good," he said out loud. "If that bictoid really had ordered the execution of Shara's parents, we won't be seeing him again."

"Hmm, that reminds me; I heard what they did to Fireheart. Remember him?"

He was hard to forget, "The elephantine dockmaster."

"That's the one. He survived interrogation in the council cells after you'd shot him with that translocator, but it turns out he's been lobotomized."

"I thought I'd vaporized him," he said as he remembered the fight in the *Deft Acquirer*'s bridge. "That black thing was a translocator?"

"Yes, keyed directly to the galactic council's holding cells. It's similar to how my little torch works, but it sends people to the agents, rather than summoning the agents to you. It's not fun if you've ever been shot by one, so I don't like using them."

"I suppose I should have known."

"I hope Morgan also gets what he deserves. We were lucky the agent was in the area when it was. That bastard has killed more innocents than you could ever meet in a lifetime."

The two friends stood in silence while the other humans celebrated their good fortunes on deck seventeen. The rescued girl's happy giggles brought a smile to Sam's lips. She laughed, "Thanks for your help."

He shrugged. "If I hadn't met you, I'm not sure I'd still be alive. The food is nice too."

Sam nodded. "Looks like a full ship." She indicated the fresh load of tractors, foodstuffs, and books they'd taken on while he'd been saving Shara from the exotic pets dealer. They joined the small crowd of humans that were singing and dancing. One of the older men patted Quork on his back and smiled with rotted teeth.

"Time to go home," Quork said.

"Yes, it is."

A FRIDGE TOO FAR

Dean had always loved food. The tastes, the smells, the stuff just sent him crazy. The first thing Dean ever did when he got home from school was to go to the fridge. He loved that fridge. It was a fifty-year-old Kelvinator, an antique that had been revived by an old mechanic to live once again.

It was unlikely, though, that that Dean cared much for what it was, just what was inside it.

The mechanic himself had obsessed over these old things, and eventually he'd gone to work being a patient in the local psychiatric hospital. "I always thought that man was a bit off," Mrs Donaldson, Dean's mother, had commented.

Dean kept a hidden selection of utensils in his pockets at all times in case unguarded food was ever lying around. If his older brother, James, ever tried to fight over the food at dinner, James would have died where he sat - most likely from the butter knife, but a spoon would do just fine.

The blunter the weapon, the better.

Eventually Mr and Mrs Donaldson had decided enough was enough; they just couldn't afford to have Dean eat three quarters of the household food.

One day Dean's school bus pulled up and he crashed through the front door, racing along the wooden floorboards of the long hallway. He was accompanied by a THUMP, THUMP, THUMP, with every step, shaking the old house's foundations. There wasn't an acknowledgement that his parents or James existed, and his mother, being in the kitchen, was almost knocked over.

Dean's laboured breathing could clearly be heard in the other side of the house. Mr Donaldson looked up from the paper with a worried expression, waiting for the inevitable.

The fridge door opened.

The fridge door closed. This time though, it did not close with its usual enthusiastic slamming.

The house was very quiet for a long time. Mr Donaldson folded up and threw away his paper, got out of his faded green couch and headed for the kitchen. Before he got there he heard a surprised yelp, which sounded a lot like his wife.

Dean shot out of the kitchen, tears streaking down his face. He brushed passed his father and ran outside, screaming as if for his life. "Dean. Dean, get back 'ere," Mr Donaldson yelled after him...

"The fridge is evil," Dean screamed back at him. Dean took an axe to the Kelvinator and its vegetable-filled interior. It was strange to see a ten year-old think his beloved fridge had betrayed him. Stranger still to see him wielding an axe...

After that little episode Dean's appetite slowed for a time, but returned with vengeance only weeks later, especially once a new fridge was installed.

Two years later Dean was enormous. His engorged belly started coming into the old house whole seconds before the rest of him. James sniggered as he followed, noticing the faint imprint of a large, sweaty belly on the wooden door.

Mr Donaldson, grim-faced, shook his head. When he had once questioned Dean about why he ate so much, Dean would reply, "I just like food."

"This has got to stop," Mr Donaldson said. He needed to do something before his son became a whale to be harpooned by the other bored kids at school. That night, just after dinner, James and both their parents stood guard in the kitchen. Mr Donaldson looked on the faces of his wife and son as the footsteps came closer. Both of them were quite white, lips quivering.

They couldn't be that afraid of a twelve-year-old could they? Mr Donaldson mused to himself.

The bloated ball of a child rounded the corner.

On cue, James stepped in front of the fridge.

Dean stopped and glared at him, one stubby hand starting to ruffle around in his ripped school pants in agitation.

"Dean," Mr Donaldson said from behind him. "We're sending you away for a little while." Dean turned his head fractionally to glare at his father out of the corner of his eye. His anger visibly grew and both of his hands started ruffling around in his pockets.

That wasn't a good sign.

Too late, Mr Donaldson remembered what Dean used to keep in those pockets. Like lightening, a rusty, mouldy spoon flew from Dean's outstretched arm and struck James in the head.

Blood gushed out and Dean charged for the fridge, bowling James over as he rolled past him. He clung to the fridge while his father tried desperately to pull him off.

James screamed in agony, Dean screamed in desperation, and as Mrs Donaldson - as she saw what had happened to James - screamed in horror. Mr Donaldson momentarily glanced at James and roared in anger at Dean, trying to tug him off the fridge.

"I have to eat. I have to eat," Dean screamed.

With one final effort, the fridge tipped over, and Mr Donaldson escaped without it falling on either himself or Dean...

Fresh out of St Xavier's psychiatric ward, Dean was ready to begin his new life. Now seventeen, he was old enough to work. He didn't bother trying to find his family, what with James having lost an eye and his mother in a wheelchair.

Much to his surprise it was quite easy to find a job and a house to rent. He worked as an apprentice electrician, largely thanks to the hospital education programme and Dr South's help. A nice little man, the doctor reminded Dean of that old mechanic who had fixed the Kelvinator.

Dean had come back from work one day to find the doctor inside the house, accompanied by a strange, yet familiar, smell.

"Ah, Dean, you're looking in tip-top shape, lad. I have something for you."

The doctor often visited and had a key to the house, always bringing nice presents.

"Oh, hi doctor," Dean said as he walked into the lounge room, throwing his work gear onto one of the reclining chairs. "What is it?"

"Another gift, I was overjoyed to find this."

The Doctor looked gleeful as he led Dean into the kitchen. The doctor smiled when Dean saw it.

"What?" Dean asked in shock.

His new fridge was nowhere to be seen, instead an ancient Kelvinator rattled away in its place. "Wow, it's an old Kelvinator."

That would certainly explain the smell. Did all Kelvinators have that distinctive smell?

"Yes," said Dr South. "I found it in the rubbish tip and I remembered that you said you liked these things."

"I... told you that? Well... thanks, Doc; I'm really impressed. It looks exactly like the one my parents used to own."

As he showered one night he heard strange noises coming from the kitchen; a sort of purring.

"Hello?" He called out.

The noises stopped, and Dean quickly dried himself and put a towel on.

"Doctor South?" he called again as he entered the lightly lit kitchen, cricket bat in hand – just in case.

Nothing.

There was nothing out of place. He must have imagined the noise.

He began searching the rest of the house.

"Help me," someone said, coming from the kitchen again. It sounded like a little girl.

"Who's there?"

Dean stepped back into the kitchen. "Help who?" he asked, as he got closer to where he thought the voice was, near the fridge. At this stage he thought he must have been going crazy.

"Is someone there?" he called out again as he examined the bottom of the fridge for any irregularities.

"YES," a deep voice boomed from above him. Dean was shocked. He turned to run in fear but the fridge's power cord tripped him.

He landed face first on the hard kitchen floor, lost the cricket bat, and felt a THUMP as something large landed next to him. *He must have been hiding in the ceiling*, Dean thought.

He quickly turned to see who it was, and looked up in abject horror when he saw...

"NOOOO," he screamed.

"YOU KILLED ME, DEAN," the fridge boomed. "I fattened you up for a REASON," the deep voice told him.

Dean tried to scramble away on hands and knees but his foot was still caught by the power cord.

The fridge's door opened. Dean screamed at what he saw behind the food deep inside the fridge. Something so horrible he could barely comprehend it.

The fridge's door distorted organically, like a dog's mouth, and scooped him up.

The fridge door hit him, forcing him further and further inside. He fought for his life, arms and legs flailing in all directions. He caught the kitchen bench and held on with a fear-powered grip. The fridge door started to envelope him and he could only just see the kitchen bench. There was a bone shattering moment of shear agony and he let go.

The fridge door closed.

Muffled screams were covered by the contented vibrations of a fridge motor that should have died decades ago.

Silence.

"Happy, now?" the old mechanic asked.
The fridge purred.

DEMON DAVE

CHAPTER 1

Blood ran across the floor and glass dug into my knees. I held the pub's window ledge to steady myself. Sweat burned my eyes. Smoke filled my lungs. The panic I felt from all of the smoke threatened to undo the bubble of protection that the building offered. I felt my lips quivering and urged myself not to cry. My babies, my children, *they had them.*

My fault...

Darkness clouded the street. The screams and cries of the children made me close my eyes. I fondled the old M1911A1 tucked into my belt and I pointed it into the darkness, searching for a glimpse of the red demons.

The gun grew heavy, my hands shook and lowered. I couldn't.

One of the demons looked in my direction. My heart froze and my guts plummeted.

Its gaze, captured by moonlight, eventually moved on. It lifted its feet to step over a cadaver I thought I recognized from the local markets yesterday. She'd been selling flowers; I can still smell their aromas.

I'd trade my last bullet, my plane, and my father's farm for the chance to smell the woman's flowers again. The demon climbed over corpses, stopping to stick the end of its spear into an obese man's belly before turning to screech commands. The screeching felt like a slap to my ears and I almost dropped the gun. I levered myself back below the window's ledge and shifted as carefully as I could to try to avoid pieces of beer bottles.

I couldn't do it. Not yet. I just needed to wait, cough the smoke and ash into my chequered shirt to muffle the sound, and pray for an opportunity.

I had to save them, but how? I sat on some rubble and pondered my predicament while wiping sweat and tears from my face. More screeching, more cries. Would they torture and kill the children as they did everyone else? Damn.

I peeked over the ledge once more, the pistol leading the way. I couldn't see through the smoke to target the demons. There was a good chance I'd hit my children if I tried. I had to move outside.

I holstered the pistol in my great-grandfather's leathers and turned around—

Yellow eyes stared at me from across the bar. It was the demon that had been screeching orders to the others. I reach for the pistol.

The demon stepped forward and pointed its spear at my neck. I knelt and waited for oblivion. My heart thumped. Instead of death, a red hand beckoned me towards it and it lowered the spear. I looked back up at its wide eyes.

"Come, child," the demon whispered like an asthmatic.

It can speak.

I wasn't dead.

The demon's hand flipped over, telling me to stay low.

The demon pressed a finger to its lips. *Be quiet.* I obeyed.

As I crawled closer to the monster, I could smell the sweat from its muscle-bound form. The sweat distracted me from the shards of glass digging into my hands and knees.

I'm alive, I thought. The demon towered over me with its spear and I could feel the heat emanating from it as if its legs were logs in a fire. I could not help but shiver despite the heat.

"Stay," it wheezed at me. I watched as it exited the pub and peered up and down the street.

It's helping me, I thought, *the bastard's actually helping me*. It had to be a trick, and yet...

The other demons had slaughtered every adult in sight, sparing the teenagers and infants. This one hadn't.

My son, my daughter, where are they? I'd lost sight of them when the demons had marched them off into the darkness. I got up into a crouch and made sure I had a grip on the pistol, ready to blow a hole in this little hell.

I could do it, run back through the pub, vault through the pub's broken window and use the bushes for cover. If any red monster tried to terminate my plan they'd have the pleasure of my bullets in their guts.

That's if the bullets still worked.

The gun had been handed down from my great-grandfather to my grandfather and then on to me. I was certain my grandfather had bought a batch of bullets not too many years before his passing. Not too long ago.

"Follow," the demon called from the door. I suppressed the desire to leap from my skin at the demon's reappearance. Not wanting to frighten it, I pulled the pistol from the holster and crept forward. The demon snorted and turned its back on me.

"That way," it said, pointing down the street towards the river. "Use a boat, go."

Escape, it was telling me. I looked at it again in the dim light, searching for any sign of mischief in its face. One of the conical horns forming the crown on its head had been cracked in half and seemed to be oozing something yellow onto the pub's front step. The yellow pus began to bubble against the step's paint.

I noticed the flutter of wrinkles near the wounded horn each time the pus dripped from its skull. It was hurt, this monster. It wasn't playing some cat-and-mouse game to make me run as its prey; this thing was serious.

Escape. In the wrong direction.

The children, mine among them, had been taken in the opposite direction.

"No," I said, my breath barely made it past my lips before the demon bared its teeth.

"Go or die." It wasn't a choice. "Go, now, go." It looked over its shoulder, its head twisting like that of an owl's to peer through the window. Outside the window, the other demons had disappeared, their screeching leaving with them.

"Piss and shit," it said. My helper turned to look at me and with a thrust of the spear, it nicked my ear. I flinched from the pain but leapt to my feet. "They come."

I don't remember the sprint down the street.

I don't remember climbing into the tin boat and starting the engine.

I remember little but the screams of monsters and hooves on the road. Spears flew across the river, one clattering over the boat's front while another plunged through the floor, creating a new hole next to my feet. The hole melted and water bubbled from below.

The boat's motor thrummed to life and I screwed the throttle hard.

CHAPTER 2

Pincers of sunlight stabbed through the Khaki canopy, splashing my eyes with caresses of pain. Each time the ancient truck I'd been thrown into hit a bump or swerved wildly I was reminded that I had two-day growth on my usually clean-shaven face. The tiny hairs scraped over the hard surface of the truck's interior where I was resting.

With limbs made of lead and vague memories of long-distant sleep, it was a struggle to lift my head under the morning sun's light. A few others were riding in the truck's rear with me, all covered in military gear. From the look of their wide eyes and scattered whisperings, the soldiers had no idea what was happening. If they'd bothered to ask me, I'm not sure I could have told.

By the time I had scratched the sleep from my eyes my vision had adjusted to the glare and I could see the road behind us.

The road was dirt, the blood-red stuff you found out in the western scrub. On either side of the road was farmland. They were over thirty kilometres or more from the town I'd escaped from, and if the light that attacked my eyes through the canopy was a sunrise, we were heading west, away from the town. We must have skirted around it in the darkness and taken the northern-most bridge across the river.

I could feel the adrenalin as it hit my heart.

"Stop the truck." I managed to say over a dry tongue. The soldiers, peering through the old truck's canopy or talking in military-grade riddles, snapped their attention back to me as if I had just insulted their mothers.

"Why?" a skinny man asked as he scratched under his helmet.

"The children. My children..."

Joshua, Katie. Their faces fled before my eyes as I tried to recall them, fading until they were once again replaced by the men in front of me. Several of them turned to exchange silent looks before one of them spoke.

"What children?" the skinny man said.

"My..." I gulped and tried to wet my mouth. The skinny man grabbed for a container on the wall, undid its lid and handed it over.

I poured a few drops of water down my throat. "Thank you. I was on vacation from the airline, but... my children, please... those things stole my kids, killed my wife, my friends. The kids, the town's kids, they were all taken."

"Listen, mate, I feel for you, but we lost three of our friends just fishing you out of the river, no way are we going back there."

"You won't...?" I shook my head, lost for words. "Just stop the truck, I'll walk back."

"Mad bastard," said one of the men near the truck's rear.

"He's got some gonads going back there," said another.

"Shut up," Skinny said. "We're not stopping this truck. If you go back there you'll either die or give the enemy intel. That's not going to happen."

"Okay," I said and nodded my agreement. Tired, battered, I nonetheless stood and took several steps towards the truck's rear. The soldiers moved their legs to allow me to pass but looked at me as if I were a drunken idiot. "Guess I'll make my own way off," I said as a goodbye to my confused rescuers.

The creek bed was right there, I couldn't have timed it much better, except that the big guy right at the rear of the truck caught me mid-air and we both went tumbling out onto the muddy ground.

I managed to break the muscled monster's fall. It wasn't fun.

"Here he is sir," Skinny said as I struggled to breathe. I could still hear the purring engines in the morning mist echoing across mostly dry land. Soldiers crouched or stood around a convoy of trucks and APCs, waiting with twitching eyes and raised rifles while the Big Guy coaxed some life back into me.

"Okay, dumb-arse, what's your name?" a man with a German accent asked me. His dark skin was lit to a bright brown by the sun and he looked like he was barely out of school. Not a speck of stubble grew on his too-narrow chin.

I would have told him my name, but I was still having trouble breathing after Big Guy had squished my lungs. "Says he was after his kids," Skinny told him.

"They're dead," the German said. "No one lives through one of those raids."

"Not... dead," I wheezed. "Others... dead, not... the kids."

"Okay dumb-arse, how did you expect to get your sorry butt back there and rescue these kids?"

I coughed out some muddy creek bed before I continued; "Not many of them... those demons. I could... avoid them. Did it before."

"Bullshit," Skinny said. I couldn't see his expression, he was silhouetted by the sun, but his hands were on his hips instead of the dangling rifle at his side.

Big Guy came to my defence: "What do you think, sir? Kinda makes sense, no way he could have got away if there were too many of the Reds."

"Bullshit," Skinny said again. "The Lieutenant can't order us back anyway, not based on one delirious idiot's word."

"No, I can't," the young, German Lieutenant said, "but this may present an opportunity."

"Oh, shit," Skinny said.

"Cut it out, Macca. So, not many... how many is 'not many'?"

I felt the bittersweet needles of hope creep up my spine and into my throat. "Three dozen," I said, almost slurring the words. My mind was working faster than my mouth could follow. "Scattered in pairs around the town. At least they were when I got away."

Big Guy helped me back onto my feet and I told the lieutenant what I could remember: news of destruction on social media before the internet went down; driving into town; seeing fires lit; bodies on the ground; children being loaded onto small delivery trucks; random bouts of gunfire followed swiftly by shouts and screams.

The lieutenant nodded when I finished. "We'll head back."

"But we need to get—"

"Shut up, Macca, I know our orders. Thirty, sixty klicks won't delay us much, and we could do with the supplies."

"Supplies?" I asked, horrified that he'd forgotten about the children so quickly.

The lieutenant looked at me and explained, "Sir, the city was taken a few days ago. We need to regroup. That means gathering food and fuel. We have a long way to go, and besides, by the sound of it, those demons of yours weren't going to be sticking around for much longer. Not sure we can do much for your kids. *But*," he said as he saw my mouth agape. He raised a finger to brush off my concerns, "If you wish, we can drop you off, maybe help with finding you a vehicle and anything else you might need to find your kids. I'm sorry I can't do more, but the world's burning and my little gang only has so much water."

The world is burning...

"So it's not just ..." I looked off to the horizon, and for the first time since the fog had cleared, I noticed the dense smoke where, from memory, far away towns were meant to be.

"Yep, we're *all* fucked," Big Guy said with a wide grin as he slapped his Khaki-coloured Steyr rifle against his shoulder.

CHAPTER 3

"Guess you were right," Big Guy whispered to me. His name was Greg, but that's all I'd been able to extract from him. "Your town's children. Take a look; they're at the sports field.

The white fence had slits between each paling but a small hedge on the other side obscured the view. As he suggested, I grabbed onto the fence and slowly pulled myself to the top. I peered through the white fence's serrated top and tried to pick the green of the nearby sports field through hazy smoke.

The field wasn't far from the house's yard. There was a supermarket car park with a handful of abandoned cars, and beyond the car park was a small dip in the terrain. The sports field was beyond that.

It was the school's field, and it was infested with demons.

My eyes widened involuntarily when I saw the children. Some were sitting and some were lying down. There were hundreds of them, and the red demons almost outnumbered them.

I covered my mouth and swore before dropping back to the grass on my butt. I'd been wrong about how many demons there were, and the children hadn't been taken away at all, they'd simply been gathered to the town's centre.

Greg patted my shoulder. "Steady on, boy. A lot can change in a few hours." I looked at his hard-set face with my dry eyes and nodded. Even if I could somehow find my kids, there'd be no way I could fight off so many demons. I had to convince the soldiers to help me, somehow.

Once Macca and the others got back from collecting food, fuel and various other supplies, I could try and convince them to call for backup. I nodded to myself as the plan formed in my mind.

Greg tapped on my shoulder again and frowned before gesturing with his thumb back towards the brown and orange brick house. Hunched over, guns out, we moved silently back to the brick house's veranda and slipped inside one of the large open glass windows.

Greg's giant hand found the back of my neck and violently shoved my face against the floor's carpet. The rest of my body followed and crashed to the floor.

My pistol flew somewhere towards the kitchen, a shot escaped its barrel.

Something snarled. A black spear whistled over my prone body.

Greg's hand found me again.

"Get up!"

A crack of light and sound ripped through the car park and more gunfire was its reply. Greg pushed me towards the kitchen and I scooped up the pistol I had let fly moments before.

In the corner of my eye, I saw a red demon slumped over the large flat-screen TV and another stood in the doorway to the garage.

I ducked down behind some white-grey benches while Greg's rifle roared next to my ear.

"They're dead," he said over the ringing in my ear. "We have to go."

He sounded scared, not what I'd expected from such a big man. I just *had* to look at what he was so afraid of.

Visible beyond the car park, on the edges of the sports field, were several flashes of gunfire.

"You dumb bastard, Macca," said Greg as he used his scope to view the action. The flashes of gunfire took down handfuls of demons, but they were fast, and dozens were converging on each soldier's position. "Shit, they're all dead."

We ran, past the swimming pool and through the CBD. We legged it past the burnt-out bar I'd been hiding in earlier and jogged towards the parked army truck.

Every now and then a demon appeared from a corner street and, with expert precision, had its chest destroyed by Greg's rifle fire. The gunfire behind us ended and Greg's radio went silent. The voices on the radio had ended one-by-one until the static-filled shouting had stopped.

"Crap," Greg said. He was breathing heavily. He pulled me by my shirt into the local fish n' chips shop, the *Steady Anchor*. He put a finger to his lips and indicated that I should head towards the back rooms where the toilets were.

Panting, my legs heavy, I eased my way through the white plastic chairs and tables and almost fell onto the door to the toilets. Once on the other side, I sat on the cold, tiled floor near the door and planted an eye at the crack between architrave and door.

I couldn't make out much beyond the forest of white legged chairs and tables, but I saw Greg's booted foot - he was hiding behind the main counter under the cash register.

"Find them." I jumped at the sound. It was as if the demon had a megaphone. Barely able to keep hold of my pistol because of sweaty hands, I found some toilet paper and wrapped it around the gun's handle. Hooves clacked on the store's tiles.

Tables and chairs screeched as they were pushed aside.

Through the door's crack, I could see three demons smacking furniture with their spears. Poisonous gasses filled the place as the spears melted everything they hit.

I jammed the roll of toilet paper against my mouth to stop from coughing and tried to aim at one of the demons through the door. The gun obscured my view; I wouldn't be able to hit anything this way.

The demons got close to where Greg was hiding. I started to panic. I moved to the other side of the door and opened it a fraction - just enough so I could see Greg and aim my pistol at the demons.

One demon was peering over the register, looking up and down the serving area. I sighted my gun on the thing's back, ready to pull the trigger before it spotted Greg.

A movement caught my eye. Where I'd previously seen Greg's boot underneath the counter, I now saw his eyes. They said, *No.* My finger leapt from the trigger and I let go of the door as another demon appeared, walking past it.

Damn, I thought. I crawled from the toilets to the storage closet, opened it and got in. Something hissed and the door to the toilets crumpled. Apart from a tiny sliver of light at the bottom of the door, it was dark in the storage room. I heard tiles and porcelain toilets smashed to pieces and my hands shook involuntarily.

It became quiet after a couple of minutes and the sound of demon hooves faded back towards the shop's serving area. I slumped against the storage room's wall. Sweat stung my eyes and I wiped my forehead. I slowed my breathing as much as I could and stood to leave. I opened the door.

A demon, its head slanted at a forty-five-degree angle, stared back at me from across the small corridor. It blinked and started to level its spear.

"Oh," I managed to say before slamming the door shut.

I dropped to the floor and squeezed my knees up to my chest to fit in the small space. A spear sliced through the door and swiped where my shoulders would have been if I'd been standing.

I fired the pistol through the door where I thought I would hit it in the stomach. I heard a blood-choked cough before the spear pulled away. The door opened as the spear came out and I could see the demon on the ground, clutching its neck.

The door to the men's room swung open and another demon, this one without any weapons, came running out but skidded to a halt when it saw its compatriot lying in a pool of rapidly expanding blood.

It looked confused until it spotted me. The demon charged at me and swiped with a clawed hand.

It managed to smack the pistol from my grip. Its claws seared lines through my flesh when it hit the pistol from my hand.

It picked up the fallen demon's spear and prepared to strike, but a giant black-gloved hand caught the spear before it could split me in two.

Greg's knife made a brief appearance in the demon's skull before the knife was withdrawn.

"Fuck," Greg swore and dropped the black spear. His glove appeared to be melting where he'd held it. "Get your gun," he pointed at my pistol but it was scrap, claw marks marred the gun's barrel and the trigger and its guard were missing. I grabbed a roll of toilet paper and wrapped some of it around my bleeding hand.

The wounds didn't look bad, but they stung as if burnt.

Greg slapped a new ammo cartridge into his rifle and handed me his pistol. "This is some strange shit, especially with those kids back there. We've gotta get back to the convoy and report."

"What about your radio?" I asked him as quietly as I could while we made our way to the shop's front.

"Strange shit's happened to it." He pointed at a small, black mess on one of the white tables. It was Greg's radio, what was left of it. A third demon lay prone under the same table where a scuffle must have taken place.

"Strange shit," I said. We exited the shop and Greg quickly let go of his rifle and pulled a small cylindrical device from his belt. The device flew across the street at a small pack of demons that were running towards the shop.

A loud bang and blinding white light slapped them down.

"Hurry, that won't hold them for long." We ran up the footpath and across the town's reasonably small bridge. "Don't s'pose you have some C4 on ya?" He grinned, but the creases around his eyes betrayed the man's desperation. "Go, the truck's not far, come pick me up." In the middle of the road, he kneeled on one knee and pointed his rifle. I could see the truck, nestled up against a small farm-house beyond the town's limits.

Too late. The demons saw us before we saw them.

There were maybe ten of them.

Greg fired. The demons were coming up from the embankment under the bridge. I managed to kill a couple of them with Greg's pistol before running out of ammo. Greg took down two more but swore when his shots couldn't seem to penetrate a black shield one of them was carrying.

The demon carrying the black shield used it to body-slam Greg. Two more leapt on him even as he lashed at them with his giant fists. I tried to bash one of his assailants over the head with the pistol but got a kick to the groin for my efforts.

In moments, it was over.

Multiple spears steadied over us for the final blow.

"Halt," one of the demons called. It was *him*, the one that had saved me before. The broken horn on its head still slowly wept a yellow pus. Its face twitched with the pain.

It didn't seem to recognise me.

"What are you doing with those kids?" I yelled at him, needing to know before they took my life.

Momentarily distracted by my outburst, the demons didn't see Greg reach for his knife. Aiming from his back he slashed the tendon of the demon above him and it fell down.

Before the rest of the demons could do anything, Greg had ended its screaming by slashing its throat.

"Fuckers," he said.

A second later two spears found their mark in Greg's chest. He gurgled as he tried to breathe, and bubbles of boiling blood from the spear punctures spluttered from his torso. I couldn't see his face. Perhaps that was for the best.

As he lay dying, the demons' leader quietly slashed the rifle's strap from Greg's body and inspected the weapon. It watched the boiling blood for almost a full minute before turning to me. The circular darkness of the rifle's barrel met my gaze.

The demon's subordinates formed a loose semi-circle behind me.

"Wait... you're going to shoot me?" I asked. Of course, it was. I was panicked, and that was all I could think to say.

The smell of broken floor tiles emanated from the barrel's edge, and the smell of burnt flesh, much like pork, hinted at its promise.

I always imagined death smelt worse than this.

"They are to be transported for processing," the gravelly voice said from behind the barrel's mask. The tone of its voice wasn't as harsh as before; more like a horse's owner apologising for the animal's broken leg.

"What's 'processing?'" I looked into the demon's yellow, bloodshot eyes, searching for that hint of recognition it owed me.

"You should not have come back, child," it said. The clawed index finger tightened on the trigger and my eyes dropped. "Now there is no choice."

CHAPTER 4

Demons screamed as bullets reassembled their innards.

The rifle shouted its glee over and over again, drowning the demons' cries. The rifle went silent after destroying my eardrums and was then dropped to the black tar in front of me.

I rolled aside and reached for Greg's knife. The demon with the broken horn picked up a spear from another demon's corpse.

I lurched onto stiff legs and held Greg's knife in a reverse grip. The demons' leader impaled another demon with the spear it had picked up but backed off from the shield-bearing warrior. Another demon, wounded in the stomach from rifle-fire, limped its way to a dropped spear.

I leapt atop the wounded demon to try to stop it from picking up the spear.

It threw me down and lashed out with its feet. I grabbed its leg and stabbed it above the knee-cap and its lashing abruptly ended.

The demon with the shield held a spear above its head and struck at my ally like an ancient Greek hoplite. It left a gash in my ally's left shoulder and he stumbled to the asphalt.

I charged at the shield-bearer from behind. The three of us crashed to the ground.

We became entangled in a web of claws, spears and teeth. One of the demons scratched my shoulder and the wound burned from the fiery touch.

I cried out and rolled off to the side.

Demon strangled demon. My ally attached its mouth to the other's neck and bit deeply until blood erupted, killing it.

I struggled into a sitting position and held my churning stomach. I watched quietly from my hard perch on the road's surface as my ally methodically slashed the throats of its former comrades. Then it turned towards me.

"We must get moving," the demon told me. I accepted its helping hand and was pulled to my feet. "Save the children," it pointed towards the town. "They are being sent away shortly."

"Where..." I paused for breath and stuck out a hand to steady myself, "are... they...go..."

"There is a ship near the coast. The ship is big, white, full of other children. They will be taken to the ship in vehicles. From there they will be taken to an island."

I coughed, "Sh...shit," I said before coughing some more.

"Yes."

We started walking towards the old army truck. My ally dragged the large black shield behind us. "Who. Are. You," I said, still panting. Faint demonic screeching could be heard near the centre of town.

The demon frowned and shook its head, "Don't remember much."

"But you know me."

"No," It shook its head again. "Not you... you look like somebody... but not her. The gun, yes, I remember that gun... where is the gun?" It stopped and stared at me. I stared back, knowing the demon might kill me at any moment.

I felt too tired to care.

"Uh... back in the shop, I think." It stared at me a moment longer, as if trying to decide whether to be angry or not, but shrugged its shoulders and kept walking.

"Dave."

"What?"

"Who I am. David, Dave... there is more to the name but it is lost to me."

"Well... nice to meet you, Dave."

Dave the demon's head twisted partway to horizontal to look at me, "Is it?"

I flinched at the ghastly demon's twisted neck, "You saved me, so yes."

"Ha," It didn't sound like much of a laugh to me. "Saved you, killed others."

"Still..." We walked in silence. A lone dog much like a Dalmatian, but bone white in colour, blocked our path to the truck. The closer we approached, the more it barked, which made Dave twitchy. "No," I held up a hand as he levelled his spear at the lonely creature, "I know this dog. I think it goes by the name 'Danny,' he won't hurt us."

Dave raised a hairless eyebrow at me, but lowered the spear, "Hungry, frightened, big. Such a creature may cause us harm."

"Trust me; we don't need to kill it."

Dave raised his shield anyway. "All right, then."

Danny the Dalmatian didn't budge from its position. It barked louder, but it didn't try to attack us.

"Good dog," I said quietly. The barking eventually stopped when we got to the truck.

I reached in the window to try the driver side door's handle.

"What the fuck is this?" Macca said.

I stumbled backwards from the truck and Dave dropped into a defensive crouch, shield covering his body and spear ready to strike at whoever was hiding in the truck's cab.

"I leave you for an hour with that big dumb bastard and you come back here with a *fucking demon*?"

Macca's gaunt face appeared over the rolled-down window, blood and bandages plastered to his glistening skin. A pistol was aimed squarely at Dave's black shield.

"Don't shoot, he's a friend."

Macca's thin-lipped smile widened a little, "Yeah, dumb-arse, I got that. I saw the tail end of your 'friend's' betrayal. So, what, you two best mates from way back, eh?"

"He's just helping to get the kids back."

"Yes... I just *bet* he is." There was a pause as the three of us waited for the others to react. The gun never wavered, neither did the shield or spear.

Dave was the first to end the stalemate, "Harm to you is not my intention," he lowered his spear and shield to the ground. The tautness in Macca's face smoothed, but the gun didn't waver.

"It may be mine."

"I wish only to help him."

"Heh, made a deal with the devil did you?" Macca asked me.

"Just lower the bloody gun," I said. "We don't have much time."

"Correct, the children are being loaded onto trucks as we speak," David said.

"Yeah, yeah," Macca said. With a flick of his wrist, the pistol disappeared back into the truck's cab. "We did what we could, but you bastards came out of the fucking woodwork. There were a lot more than just a few dozen"

"Special task groups have been moving to this area during the night," Dave said. "This is one of several collection areas. They will think they have been discovered since you attacked them."

"Shit... all right, get in the back."

"You trust me?"

"Hell no. Get in before I change my mind."

CHAPTER 5

When I awoke I was prickled in hay and smelt like piss. My head was full of bricks. I slowly turned my stiff neck to look at the one source of light in the darkness where I had been deposited. As my dry eyes adjusted to the light and my arms and legs slowly sorted their kinks out, I recognised where I was.

The lone shaft of light rested upon a familiar stone that I had tripped over many times in my youth. I was in the old tin mine near the back paddocks of my father's property. I was home.

Inching up to rest my back against the rocky walls, I tried to call out as quietly as I could but ended up choking on a dry throat. I couldn't remember the last time I'd drank any water - maybe in the army truck, I wasn't sure.

"Hello?" I said.

Something, possibly a snake, hissed back.

"Well, good morning to you, too," I told the snake.

"Good morning," it hissed into my ear. I jumped to my feet faster than a racehorse out of the starting gates.

I reached for the nearest piece of wood I could lay my hands on and prepared to strike, but was fended off by the sound of low chuckling.

"Not so good?" Dave said from the shadows.

"You... *fuck*... don't scare me like that."

Dave walked into the light with a pained expression still on his face, dark spear in hand, "A friendly reply should not be considered in such a way. Why are you so startled?"

"It's, you're just... oh, never mind." I coughed from the effort of talking, "I need water." I brushed off the random bits of hay and dirt covering me.

"Where's Macca?" I said. We headed towards a paddock fence line just beyond the mine's entrance, "And where's the truck?"

"You slept a long time," David called to me. "He left."

"Why are we on my father's farm?"

"You told us to come here."

I lifted the barbed-wire fence just enough to slide through the gap, "I did?"

"You said you had a plane – it would get us to the island faster."

"Yes, my plane," I said thoughtfully. "I just hope dad kept it in good condition."

I hoped the old man was ok. He and my mother had gone up north to see my cousins and their children for the summer. They'd sold all the cattle and hadn't bothered with the crops this year due to the drought. No point sticking around to watch grass die.

I saw a small water hole through the sparse shrubs. I pushed through and the bushes scratched my exposed arms. I kneeled down at the edge of the water and, in my eagerness to get a drink, nearly drowned myself.

"Food is nearby," Dave said while I slurped the dregs of the fading water hole.

"Sure, sure," I said and went to take another mouthful but stopped when I noticed the bloody marks on my right shoulder. I lifted my shirt so I could get a better look. "Are these teeth marks? Did you *bite* me when I was sleeping?"

Dave simply stared.

"What the hell? Why did you bite me?"

"Why am I a demon? Why must I kill and cause suffering to ease my pain?"

I stared back at it and got to my feet. I wiped my mouth, "Why not just kill me?"

Dave snorted, "The pain always returns. The bite was a test to lessen the pain. It did not work. It will not happen again. Food waits for you, we have already wasted much time and you must recover."

"How much time? Did I sleep for long?"

"Two days."

"Two."

"Yes."

I ran for the farmhouse.

"Here," Dave shoved an apple in my face as I ducked and weaved around my Beechcraft G36 Bonanza. It wasn't the cheapest plane, but as large as it was I could take my whole family on little trips. Dad thought I was mad, he'd owned a small crop duster that was twenty years older than my Beechcraft and a tenth of the price.

The kids never complained about it though.

Josh had started pilot training just two weeks ago. The cheeky bastard was obsessed with wanting to do a barrel roll.

Maybe when he has his own plane...

I tried not to think about Josh and his sister. I prayed to the memory of my lovely wife that I could save them before something bad happened.

I grunted my thanks to Dave and took the apple while checking the landing gear. The apple was so warm from the demon's touch it had turned to a light mush, but I was grateful to have something to eat. The demon chased me around the aircraft with more warm and burnt offerings.

"Must be handy, cooking your food by touching it," I said.

"I cannot eat."

"Why not? Don't you need food?"

"No," Dave opened his dark red mouth and pointed to a couple of cracked teeth. "Tooth-ache."

"Ha." But my humour vanished when I realised what sort of bones he'd probably chipped his teeth on. "Then you must be quite hungry."

Dave shrugged, "Melted cheese and milk have sustained me for these past few days."

I hopped inside the Beechcraft and slipped into the pilot's seat, taking care to avoid the old sports bag. The bag held a couple of my father's rifles and several bullet cartridges were hidden inside the bag. Dave looked at me through the cockpit's window while I continued the pre-flight checks.

My dad had been generous, the fuel was topped off. On top of that, the battery was charged, lights worked, weather was clear, and my arse was comfortable.

Time to go.

I checked the onboard maps and looked back at Dave who was still staring at me through the cockpit's windshield. A twitch of the left eye was the only expression I could make out in his devilish face. No blinking, no noticeable breath. I waved at him to come inside.

Finally, his expression changed from painful twitches to a rather fake, almost nervous grin. I met him at the entrance, "Ever flown before?"

Involuntary twitches rippled from one side of his face to the other.

"No," he sat down into the front passenger seat and I clipped myself into the pilot's seat next to him.

"No, I suppose as a demon you couldn't have."

"Why do you say that?"

"What do you mean?" I asked as I showed him how to clip his belt in.

"Why could I not have flown if I am a demon?"

"You have aircraft in hell, do you?"

Dave viewed me as if through cat eyes. "You make many assumptions, child."

I showed my disagreement by punching several buttons.

The Beechcraft roared to life and Dave jumped so much I thought he was about to hit his horned head on the ceiling before his seat's straps saved him.

We taxied to the ochre-coloured dirt runway that my parents had provided for my twenty-first birthday, many years ago.

"Just one question, Dave, why were you ordered to take the children?" I said as I crushed the throttle with my bandaged hand.

The pain stopped me from wanting to give Dave a fist-powered headache. I had to remind myself that this thing, this David, was trying to help me, for whatever reason.

"The children are pure," he replied while looking over my father's dead wheat fields, avoiding my gaze. "They are to be held until corrupted."

The Beechcraft jerked forward like a bull out of the gates. "Then we better hurry."

Dave gripped his seat so tightly that his hands began to melt the upholstery. Burning leather filled the small plane's interior. Something clattered loudly near the plane's door and I found a new well of fear and panic as I remembered Dave's spear and shield that he had brought aboard.

"Those won't burn a hole in the plane will they?" I said as I jerked a thumb in the direction of the back seats.

Surrounded by thin wisps of translucent smoke, Dave's eyes glanced quickly at me, then back at the seats. "Start praying."

"Crap," I said as we rose above tree lines and skimmed the low hills of the old mines. "I'm levelling out for a moment. You go back there and get them before your black stick decides to smear us across the neighbour's cattle-yards."

Dave looked at me from the slit of his eye. Still clutching the passenger seat, he growled just loud enough for me to hear him over the engines. I looked at the back seats and saw a small black mark staining the hard floor where the spear had touched it.

"Go." I said. He growled at me again, but unlatched stiff fingers from his seat and got up, ripping the restraints with his claws as he did so.

Walking crab-like between the two cramped middle seats, he found every possible hand-hold and tore his way between the seats. By the time he'd reached the shield and spear several more black marks had appeared on the floor where the spear had gouged it.

Squatting on one of the middle seats that faced backwards, Dave bent down and picked up the spear, but it became stuck on one of the seats. Perhaps feeling the desire to prove the weapon's sharp edge, or more likely close to a mental breakdown from his fear of flying, Dave forced the spear up through the seat it had been trapped under. It left the smell of more burning leather and cushioning.

The shield, trapped as it was on the underside of all four seats, was much larger and would take even more effort to rescue from the ruined seats. Dave left it where it was and sat in the nearest seat before strapping himself in, careful to avoid cutting the straps with his spear.

"Good," I said. "We're going to climb to around five kilometres, be ready."

Dave eventually calmed down and stopped burning the seats with his hands. Airflow wasn't the best in such a confined environment, but I did my best to get rid of the smoke with the plane's small air ventilation system.

It wasn't the smoke inside that worried me so much though, but the smoke on the outside. Fires ripped through the town, firestorms raged across the eucalypt forests, and an inferno blanketed the distant city. The inferno was almost a hundred kilometres away. I couldn't make out any details, but the black and grey smoke blanketed most of the sky.

Unfolding the plane's paper map, I double-checked Dave's instructions. "You said three hundred kilometres out to sea, but I don't see anything within the entire arc." I pencilled in a rough semi-circle with a three-hundred kilometre radius centred on the city. "There's nothing out there, no land at all."

"Have faith, child. As sure as the spring flowers, it's out there."

I ground my teeth together. I wasn't in a faithful mood. I could still remember the first time Kate had given me a flower from my wife's garden several years ago – Kate's second spring. Unfortunately, I couldn't remember what colour they were. I forced my tears back down before they could appear. *Faith* wouldn't conjure my daughter up for me in the middle of the ocean.

"Faith? Is faith a part of demon hood?"

Until then Dave had been staring out of the window at the multi-coloured farmlands below, but tore his gaze away to look at me between the headrests of the two seats, "I was a man of faith, once."

"A man, a real man?" I asked almost too quietly. The sound of the engines was dulled, but they were still loud enough to affect normal conversation so I spoke louder. "If that's so, how could you have become such a..."

"My faith failed me at the critical hour. I was a soldier once, fighting on the western front, a long way from home. I ran, child, ran from my men, from my superiors, and was caught by them. I did not have the faith to continue, so I shot them. Like a coward, I hid in northern Africa and eventually made it back home. I had committed treason, murder. Not two weeks after I arrived home, a tram hit me."

Tears sizzled down his face while he continued, "Then *they* took me."

"Who—"

"You don't know torture as they do. Nobody knows torture as they do. They... took my soul and refashioned me into this form," he spat the last word. "They forced me to train with spears and shields like ancient Greeks. I questioned them once..." he shivered and shook his head, "you don't question. You obey."

"What question?"

"They knew nothing of guns. They had no knowledge of planes or tanks. Those Greeks, they were one of their previous enemies. The ancient Greeks were some of those most capable of withstanding the demonic onslaught, so we were forced to take the ancient Greek form, their techniques, but with better equipment. Our shields are impossible to crack and our spears are able to pierce castle walls."

"We suffer in this world. To alleviate our suffering..." Dave took a deep breath, "we must slaughter, and cause the suffering of others. This is how we are controlled. A few weeks ago we were thrust upon this world once more, to cull the living."

"Cull?"

"Too many people, too few disasters and disease. Humans are too smart. Our task is to cull our descendants and seek out those souls corrupt enough to join our ranks." Dave went back to looking out of the small window and barked a short laugh. "They were too stupid to realise how advanced humanity had become in their absence. You are fortunate. Our masters were caught unawares, yet the plan is proceeding."

I unclipped my straps after making sure the plane wouldn't suddenly bank to the side and turned around to kneel on my seat and look at Dave properly. My neck was hurting and I could barely hear him. "So, when you lived you ran away from the army, and now in death, you ran from your superiors again. I'm a bit confused, you aren't allowed to question them, but treason is fine?"

Dave clacked his teeth together as if trying to bite my fingers. "I was a tortured slave to them. This is not treason, child. This is revenge."

"What makes you so special then? Why don't the others free themselves as you have?"

"Because of the pain," Dave almost choked as he spoke and rubbed his throat. "The worthy among us are given a choice - feel less pain and let us think more clearly We become the officers of the demonic army. Or, we can become more destructive and better able to cause more suffering to ease our own. I chose the former, as did most of the others. We were made to be the elite, the leaders. There are only a few of us, and there is a handful of those who chose the other path. When I saw that pistol, *my* pistol..." more tears carved steamy furrows on his face, "I could not kill you."

That couldn't be right, my pistol... my great-grandfather's pistol. My breathing became shallow and I gripped my seat's headrest to keep steady. I looked into Dave's eyes with my jaws stretching their way to the floor.

I told my great grandfather his full name.

CHAPTER 6

"There," Dave stabbed one leathery finger past my nose at a white reflection on the water's surface. Surprise didn't cover what I saw - we were flying low, the lone cruise ship anchored several kilometres out from land was less than a kilometre below us, but the ship itself barely registered on my mind.

It was an island. A brand new island, complete with green trees and brown buildings. It did not exist on any maps.

Dominating the tiny speck of land on its east side was a volcano that rose into the sky like a citadel of molten lava. A small red and black stream flowed out of its side, moving south-east down into the waves near a rocky beach, where water fought the fire.

Straight dark lines marked out dockyards that encircled the lava flows. On the rocky beach, square construction sites had been built. Dozens of tiny boats made from dark volcanic metals, barely visible to my eyes, were under construction both in the water and up on the rocks. They couldn't have been any bigger than the small Viking longships they resembled.

The Viking ships must have been the best these bastards had encountered on their last foray onto the Earth's surface.

My ancestor's insistent pointing was becoming quite a distraction.

"Looks like we're going to have to swim," I told him.

Dave frowned at me, then looked at the island in the distance, "No, not a good idea, we would be captured if we land there. We... I am sorry, child; we will have to go back."

"I don't think you understand. We *can't* go back," I pointed at the Beechcraft's fuel readings. "I have no intention of coming in near the water around the island either."

"What?"

"Strap in, this will be rough. As soon as we're down we'll need to move. The spear could be handy for cutting us out."

I took us down and circled around until we were facing the cruise ship.

"We will be spotted," Dave growled over the sound of grinding engines.

"Too late," I said as I made the final approach. I flicked on the radio, hoping we weren't the only people out here, "Mayday," I started, before giving our position. "Enemy Island spotted, I repeat, Enemy Island located at..."

Fortunately, it was a clear, calm day, so when we hit the water it was smooth and flat.

I'd been in a car crash once. The other car was doing eighty kilometres an hour; I was doing sixty going in the opposite direction. All involved survived with minor injuries but it was a hell of a crash.

This felt worse. Maybe I was tired, hungry, or scared, but I misjudged the angle of approach and the starboard wing hit the surface before the rest of the plane did. The tip of the wing sheared off and we slashed wildly to the right before flipping over onto the plane's top.

Dazed, my head bloody from hitting the side of the cockpit, I stared dreamily at the clear corals that covered the sky. I heard water gushing in from somewhere behind me. The water started the cabin above my head. A demonic claw reached through the middle of the front seats and slashed at my restraints.

"Huh?" I asked before I was cut free and fell onto the ceiling.

I heard a low moaning sound and managed to stand upright. I started hunting for the plane's small aid kit and snagged the flare gun. Then I frowned at the little gun as I remembered the rifles. There they were, on the floor above my head, under the bottom of the seats.

The low moaning was getting louder and higher pitched, almost like a scream...

"Damn," I said as I noticed the water gushing into the back of the cabin. Dave was using his shield to try and plug the small hole. Steam was rising from his legs where the water reached and the high pitched moan was coming from his animal mouth. His eyes were shut tight enough for new wrinkles to form on his leathery face and his muscles wavered against the torrent of water. I dropped the aid kit, fixed the gun bag around my shoulders, and snatched the spear from Dave's feet.

The spear was hot, like holding a teacup without the handle.

My ears started popping from the changing pressure. The water rushed in and I could no longer hear the demonic moan. Planting my feet firmly next to Dave, I took aim and punched a hole in the floor with the spear. *Thunk*, the spear jarred in my hands and I dropped it.

"Wrong end," Dave said through gritted fangs before almost falling down.

I could hardly see now, the steam was rapidly filling the cabin and my eyes were stinging. With the correct end of the spear now pointed at the floor above us, I thrust at it again. The spear travelled straight like I was cutting blades of grass with a machete.

I pulled it out and was greeted with a second set of gushing water. Dave dropped the shield and slumped against the cabin walls. I punched a third hole between the first two. The floor collapsed inwards.

The swim to the surface was agonising, not because it was far, but because of Dave's dead weight. He held on limply with one hand and carried his spear in the other. I'd lost one shoe and both rifles getting out.

We left the shield behind.

By the time I'd reached the surface, it felt like thousands of tiny ants were tearing into my lungs. Breathing fresh air wasn't as easy as I'd imagined, not when I could barely keep our heads above the water.

I swam on my back while pulling Dave. His body had cooled dramatically and the only reason I knew he was alive was because of his shallow, meaty breath. The salty air may as well have been flowery heaven compared to that breath.

We reached the side of the cruise ship at a point below the lifeboats that were several stories above us.

"Cut here," I told Dave. His eyes opened briefly. "Hurry," I said as I treaded water. He did as ordered, cutting two neat little hand holds in the ship's side.

We held on for a long time, letting the slowly rolling waves of the ocean rock us gently against the ship. Straining to lift the spear, Dave brought it up over his head and made another quick slash into the ship's side.

Using the spear as leverage, Dave eased himself upwards. I watched while he cut hole after hole, slowly making his way higher.

Steam began to appear on his body again and he doubled his efforts, stronger now that he was out of the water.

Within minutes, the demon had gone over the edge of the life-boat bay and out of my sight.

I tried to reach for a hand-hold with my sore hand, but immediately let go. Too weak to move, I resolved to stare out over the distant island and its resident volcano. The volcano belched black smoke into the clear blue sky.

I almost lost my grip when an orange object splashed down next to me. A white rope snaked back up to the boat from the orange doughnut and I realised what it was.

"Grab the lifebuoy," I heard. Gulping fresh air I attempted to grab it with my sore hand, but it was too far away. My other hand was numb; I couldn't move it, so I got my feet up against the ship's side and kicked off, freeing my lifeless hand and grabbing the lifebuoy with my sore hand at the same time. I forced myself to sink under the lifebuoy's ring and poked my head and shoulders through the middle.

I hung on to the side of the lifebuoy as Dave hoisted me into the air. I collapsed onto the deck when I made it up there and Dave lay on his back, exhausted from hauling me upwards several stories.

Dave started snoring. The deck appeared deserted, and all but two of the lifeboats were gone. Too tired to care for the danger we were in, I followed Dave's example and put my head down.

***

No one murdered us in our sleep.

By the time we were awake enough to shuffle around on our feet, the day had passed.

It was a cloudy night and the distant volcano painted the sky a faint red. We followed our reddened shadows around as we searched for an entrance to the inside.

I slipped and tripped over something slimy. I heard a sucking sound as I extruded my formerly white shoe from the slimy mass and shuddered at the thought of what it might have been.

The doors to the inside were locked but with a few quick slashes, the black spear had made a neat little hole to the inside. Cool, stale air greeted us as we tip-toed inside.

We made less sound than whispering ghosts. We stalked up hallways while peering into abandoned rooms. There was still power; light shone from several rooms and a soft glow filtered down from the staircases that were near the centre of the ship.

I thought I smelt a combination of urine and sweat from many of the dark rooms. Bed sheets had been tossed aside in every cabin. Dirt or crumbs were scattered across one of the beds, but that was the only tangible sign of human habitation. Using short whispers and hand gestures, we decided to go to the top decks, and from there to the ship's bridge.

With slow breathing that was out of tune with my rapid heartbeats and clammy hands, I led the way up the wide staircases. As we rounded a bend just before deck ten, we encountered the first sign of a struggle.

The staircase's railing had turned dark with splotches of hardened blood. It was splattered across the surface of one of the elevator doors at the top of the staircase. A rounded, melted hole in the elevator door indicated where a spear had exited an unfortunate individual's head. The body had been removed.

Of the blood on the floor, little remained except for streaks of dirty red water where someone had attempted to clean it up.

"Someone tried to escape," Dave said.

"I didn't know you bastards bothered to clean up after yourselves."

"Children make for good slaves," Dave said as he peered around the corner at the top of the stairs. "So we were told."

The smell of rotten meat and fruit blanketed the top deck. The recreational pools appeared to be yellow. A few seagulls kept coming in and out of the ship's aft doors. Some sort of eatery lay that way, no doubt the source of the foul smells.

"Come," Dave waved at me to follow him forward to the bridge. There, we found our first body. Worst of all, we found the first living people.

The moment we cut our way onto the darkened bridge I recognised the captain's face - it was plastered on promotional pictures in the hallways throughout the ship, but I could barely tell it was him. He was tied to an old-fashioned steering wheel, his clothes were stripped off and his arms were absent from their bloody sockets.

Another younger man, also naked, was slumped over a control panel, while the body of a dead woman was nailed to the opposite wall to where we had come in.

Her milky eyes were open and her ghost stared back at me.

The heavyset captain stared at us, alive. He pleaded with his brown eyes and moaned at us but had no tongue.

"Ki, ki, me," he seemed to say.

We walked to him, slowly, mindful that this may be a trap.

"What of the crew?" Dave asked him.

"Aw eh."

"All dead?" I asked.

The captain nodded and tears stung his already red eyes.

"All dead down below?"

"Bewoh." He nodded again, "Ki me."

I wasn't sure if I could kill a fellow human, but the captain's pleading made me hunt around for some sort of blunt object. I was willing to try for his sake. Then I heard the sobbing from the other man who was slumped over a nearby console.

Sweat sprung up across my body - I recognised him.

"Joshua?" I asked the sobbing man and my hands started to shake.

"Dad?" the young man croaked and lifted his head to look at me. The sticky streaks I had assumed were tears were much darker than they should have been. He searched in the reddened gloom but could not see. My teenage son's eyes were missing.

My son, alone, blind. Dying. A random assortment of memories we each shared ravaged my mind. Nappies, pre-school, soccer balls, video-games, birthdays.

My poor child.

"How could they do this?" I screamed at the ceiling as I cradled my son's head in my arms. "How?" I yelled at my demonic ally.

"I-I guess... I won't be... flying anymore, dada. They made me... umm... I'm a message," Joshua spluttered from under my chin. "For someone, something... I... I don't know. Where's mum?"

"Oh, fuck," I said, hardly able to control my shaking muscles. "Why?"

"Mum's dead?" I could only answer him through my silence. "Dad..." he said calmly. "They took Katie to the island."

"Katie... is she ok?"

"Better than me," Joshua tried to laugh, but only ended up coughing. "But they said... they said if I didn't do this they would torture her. If I didn't tell someone my... *their* message."

"Who, son? Who is the message for? Why would they do this to you?"

My fist felt like it should have been a cruise missile I could fly into the nearby volcano.

"You lied, dad."

"What?" I said, shocked and confused. I briefly remembered camping trips. Stargazing.

"Monsters *do* exist, haha." He coughed up a small amount of blood onto my arms.

"It's for me," Dave croaked as he stood over us. "'Keep following and we kill your descendants.' That is the message."

"Yes," Joshua nodded, "but I don't—" a coughing fit ensued. It took him a long time before he recovered.

"Are you ready?" Dave asked Josh.

"Yes."

"No," I shouted.

"Sorry, dad," Joshua said before Dave's black spear found his heart.

I walked the corridors trying to escape despair's clutches. Katie... I had to save her, but I was having trouble finding what deck I was on.

That night I'd lain with my son's body and cried myself to sleep.

In the morning I had awoken in a clean bed with new clothes on and my son nowhere in sight. I'd charged down corridors and up staircases in a mad dash for the bridge. Joshua's body was still there, but the captain and the female crewmember were both gone.

A makeshift table had been erected in the centre of the bridge where Joshua now lay. His body had been bathed and a white sheet draped over it. Candles, incense, small bottles of wine, and a wooden cross surrounded him.

The discovery calmed me somewhat, but I couldn't stay there.

Arrows were scratched into the floor. I followed the arrows out of the bridge. They led to food that had been arranged on a table on the top deck.

A warm teapot, an apple and boiled eggs.

My stomach had twisted itself so hard that I wasn't sure I could have eaten anything, but I forced a few morsels down and chased it with the warm tea.

"Join me on the water deck when you can, but don't be too long," a message had been scratched into the table where the food was set up.

As I wandered the corridors, stumbled down the atrium steps, and attempted to ignore the various pubs along the way, I wondered if there was any point to continuing.

The memory of Katie's hair whipping against my face the last time we'd ridden a rollercoaster snapped me out of my depression.

"We must get her back," my wife said as she appeared around the corner of one of the marble stairways.

"Yes, for you, for me, and for her," I told her.

"Not for us, we are already damned, child. We must do this for your daughter."

I shook my head and my beautiful wife's face disappeared amongst the horns and yellow eyes of Dave's head.

"She yet has a chance." Dave tossed me a carrot and a bottle of water and then held up two small hand-guns. "There is some good news. Two of your military vessels are approaching as we speak. We can rescue her. Your son we can bury when this is over."

I took one of the guns and stuffed it into my trousers' belt. "They will kill her if we try."

"When the military ships arrive, they will kill her anyway." Dave cranked the ship's access hatch and opened it onto the mid-morning sun's glare. One of the two remaining orange lifeboats greeted them on the water's surface.

"How did you get it down from its cradle?"

He cocked his head to the side and squinted at me as if I'd just struck him, "I *can* read a manual, child."

In the distance, several black Viking ships sailed to and from the island and smoke continued to belch forth from the volcano's top.

"Is this where demons are born?" I asked with a mix of fear and wonder.

"No... this is where they shall die."

CHAPTER 7

Dave was looking exceedingly healthy, even stronger than when I'd first met him. As he steered the lifeboat that he'd learned to work hours before, his corded muscles and renewed skin tone marked him as a freshly rested athlete. Heat radiated from Dave like a furnace and I was afraid to touch him for fear I'd be burned. I ate the carrot as quietly as I could and kept the bottle of water tied to my belt with a small piece of string. Dave kept the other pistol in a holster he must have found.

"Where did you get the pistols?"

"Dead officers."

"But... where were the bodies?" Dave looked at me from the corner of his eye and I understood why he looked so strong and healthy.

"We heal by ingesting the once-living." I was surprised I did not feel the level of disgust I would have a few days ago. "My teeth no longer ached, so I took the opportunity," he said as an afterthought.

We spoke little. Dave steered us away from the distant Viking ships. With a pair of binoculars, I found in one of the lifeboat's cabinets, I saw a small group of demons around the docks and village scrambling to round up the children before we arrived.

Our boat was bright orange on the blue ocean surface. We must have been easy to spot as we approached, but when we finally hit the rocky beach on the western side of the island, no demons opposed us.

Taking our few belongings, we jumped down onto the rocky ground and ran up to a dirt track. The track snaked its way up the island towards a group of mud huts.

We approached the village as quickly and quietly as we could, with Dave motioning for me to stay low as we rounded one of the many mud huts on either side of the dirt track.

No one was inside, but the stink of piss and shit almost made me suffocate. Burn marks, blood and vomit accompanied the smell on the inside of the hut and we moved on to the next one.

"Hark." Dave whispered and we dropped to our hands and knees.

Footsteps crushed dirt on the other side of the hut. Two sets of footsteps at first, then dozens, then what sounded like hundreds.

Then a giant made his mark on the dirt road. I couldn't help but peek through the hut's window and stare through the open doorway on the hut's other side.

The giant towered above the demonic army, standing above the other demons that now occupied the road with their spears and shields. The air around the giant demon shimmered with heat and its hands glowed red hot. Blue flames licked the edges of a long, black sword in one of its hands.

As large as one of the smaller demons was tall, the blade swept angrily above the spears and shields as if striking an opponent that wasn't there.

Bright red eyes embedded in the giant's head gazed in my direction and I dropped onto my chest. Dave grabbed my arm and pointed into the small forest surrounding the village. The giant demon roared and I scrambled on my stomach towards the nearest ferns behind Dave. The ferns were thick and low, covering us like a blanket.

The ground vibrated as the giant came closer, moving around the mud hut. The black sword slashed at where we'd been hiding seconds ago, and a handful of spear and shield-wielding demons raced around the other side.

Oh, no, I kept thinking as the demons split outwards towards the forest.

A hot, clawed foot brushed against my leg and I bit my lip in an attempt to keep from yelping in pain. The giant didn't follow the spearmen but proceeded to demolish the small mud hut with its black sword.

While the giant was busy, I tapped Dave on his foot and, without waiting for him to respond, I started crawling towards a small group of tightly packed shrubs.

The small army of demons marched down the dirt track towards the orange lifeboat, like the lava that streamed down the volcano.

The giant demon finished tearing down the helpless hut. Distracted as the demon search party was by their larger cousin, we reached the shrubs. When the handful of demons came back from searching for us, they started slashing randomly into the ferns and small trees to flush us out. One of them stopped and stared into the undergrowth. Without a sound, it started following a track in the dirt, one that would lead it straight to us.

It came, slowly, looking and feeling back and forth amongst the undergrowth until it found the right direction.

Claws clicked on small rocks, old leaves crinkled as they were crushed and the demon's hoarse breathing came ever closer. I gripped the Glock pistol Dave had retrieved from the cruise ship's officers and made sure the safety was off. The demon reached the edge of the shrubs and peered into the shaded areas underneath.

Explosions from within the village saved us.

Thump, thump, thump, thump.

Fire and shrapnel blanketed the area; the village was being bombarded by large, naval-based shells.

Demons, shields and spears collapsed under the attack.

A shell bounced off of the ultra-tough shields and an explosion followed somewhere higher up on the island.

I saw a small rounded cylinder arc over the heads of the demons from the other side of the village and when it landed amongst the demons it exploded.

Flashes of gunfire erupted from the forest and tore into the surprised demons. More rifle fire and shells ripped into the army. Demons screamed orders at each other and the army reformed to face the new threat from the forest.

I heard shouts from human soldiers and the gunfire stopped. More grenades flew and the demon army surged towards the forest while the shells kept hitting the army from the side.

A lone demon, still searching for us, stared at the carnage.

I stood up, leaned over, reached out and grabbed the demon by the neck and yanked it down into the bushes.

It struggled for a moment but before it could try to stop me I'd put the pistol to its head and pulled the trigger.

More explosions peppered the mud huts and the hundreds of demons flowed into the forest to chase their tormenters. The giant opened its mouth wide and let loose a mechanical scream, then took a shell to the face. Its head disappeared amongst fire, blood and bones.

"Hurry," Dave told me once the last of the demons had marched into the forest. I picked up the demon's shield and Dave skipped and hopped around bodies in the village before stopping at the feet of the giant to pick up its sword.

The large black shield was much lighter than it looked and had two short, round bars with which to loop my hand through. I found I could move almost as easily as when I didn't carry it, though the many wounds I had acquired over the past few days were beginning to slow me down.

Leaving the village behind, I wheezed like an asthmatic and gritted my teeth as we ascended the volcano's rocky slope. Part way up the dirt road, it became black and grey with ash when it turned north.

The trail headed around and up to the top of the volcano on the opposite side from the dockyards. I stopped partway to the top, tired as I was, and turned back to watch the carnage.

Hope ballooned in my mind when I saw the distant ships sitting about half a kilometre from the island. I recognised one as being a frigate, an ANZAC class with, a helicopter on its deck. Its main gun kept flashing over and over and moments later the green forest heaved where the shells struck.

The other ship didn't appear to be armed at all; it must have been a supply ship of some sort.

Then I saw the black fleet to the south.

I counted eight or nine Viking ships with sails extended to catch the slight breeze. Behind the black Viking ships were several smaller vessels.

"Transports," Dave growled at me when I pointed them out. "We must continue." He grabbed my arm, but the accumulated sweat on my skin allowed me to twist from his grasp.

"Wait a minute, what about that one?" Dave stopped before trying to push me in the direction of the volcano's summit and looked out towards the sea. Behind the rest of the fleet was a ship that looked a little longer than the rest and at least three times as tall. Three rows of red oars to a side churned the water and large black sails crested its top deck. Unlike the Viking ships, this one was squared off at the rear, and where the long-ships had a perfectly rounded bow, this one had a twin-bladed ram.

Wherever the ram's blades slid across the water large plumes of steam appeared.

"A Trireme," Dave said. "Or close to it. It is a relic of previous invasions, too slow to be an effective threat to your modern ships."

"So why do you look so worried?"

"Because," Dave said as he slowly turned to look towards the top of the volcano. "Only one of *them* could have summoned it here."

We continued upwards - shield ready, gun in hand, sword in claws - and we ignored the commotion surrounding the island, hoping that we were not spotted. The path narrowed until we could no longer walk side by side and the air became hot and dry. I worried that I may be killed by the volcano's poisonous gasses, but reminded myself that Katie was up there.

I *had* to keep going.

We were a little surprised to find that the path widened onto a large ledge before a set of stairs continued upwards to the volcano's summit. "Almost there," I said as we moved out onto the ledge.

"Rest under that rock a moment and recover your breath," Dave said. "It appears the whole army was dispatched, but there should still be a few guards." He walked towards a large dark rock that sat near the entrance to the stairs.

"Be right with you," I said through dry lips. I went down on my knees in a controlled, collapsing motion, and weakly reach for the water bottle that was still strapped to my belt. I dropped the shield, untied the string and opened the bottle cap before sipping from a pocket of heaven.

"WHO GOES THERE?" A giant's voice thundered.

My bottle flew from my hands and I almost choked on the small amount of water still in my mouth. I ducked for cover, dragging the black shield with me as I backpedalled several metres down the narrow path.

CHAPTER 8

Dave looked relaxed as the giant's hoofed feet stomped down the stairs.

"Let me pass, Kelvin," Dave said.

At the bottom of the stairs, the giant stopped and looked at Dave in silence for a moment. Its eyes burned a bright red and fire danced like blue-white lightning around its hands and sword. The giant's many horns stretched to a ruler length each, forming a huge crown of thorns. Twice Dave's height with legs and arms like tree trunks and a rope-like neck to match, I couldn't imagine it would have anything to fear from us.

"Old friend, I have business up on the summit, allow me to pass."

"You must die, David," Kelvin the giant said as quietly as a town bell.

"I must speak to her."

"You must die, David," Kelvin said again, shaking its head but keeping as still as a statue. It kept the sword in a double-handed grip and eyed both of us closely. I got onto my feet and readjusted the shield, then grabbed my pistol from where I'd dropped it on the ground.

"She must hear why."

"She knows and she does not care." Kelvin opened its mouth to reveal hell underneath yellow daggers. I thought it was trying to smile but there was little humour in that face full of teeth.

Dave shifted his feet in response and moved his sword into a high guard. "You smile Kelvin, but you will find no comfort from your suffering from my death."

Kelvin's mouth widened and it let forth a blast of hot air. I heard thunder's laugh. When he was done, Kelvin shook his head and raised one fat, long, sharp claw in my direction. "His will."

I raised the pistol and fired at him. Shot after shot zipped across the short space between us and slapped against fiery flesh.

It didn't take long before every bullet had been fired. I saw molten holes where the bullets had hit him. The tiny metal slugs melted on impact and small silver trickles oozed out of the demon's thick skin. Tiny rivers of flaming pus escaped some of the wounds.

Kelvin raised one giant eyebrow as it surveyed the tiny craters on its chest. He raised his head back up and his eyes locked onto my torso.

Kelvin strode forth and, with one large arc of his blade, swept Dave aside. Dave managed to block the blow with his sword but he was hit so hard he was knocked down and hit his head against the large rock.

Kelvin was upon me. I raised the shield and felt a ton of bricks crash down on it. I lost my footing and slipped onto my back with the shield between me and the man-sized sword.

The weight lifted but came crashing back a second later and I heard bones crack in my shield-arm.

The third strike from the giant's sword was at an oblique angle and the blade hit the black and grey ground next to me, hewing off a wide chunk of the path that went toppling over into the wide gulf below.

"Noooo" Dave yelled. "He's finished, fight *me*."

The next blow never came. Kelvin stomped back towards the stairs. Dave was back on his feet, sword raised high. I felt like I had muscular dystrophy as I tried to jack myself back onto my feet.

Dave struck first. Glowing embers leapt with each strike of blade upon blade. The sounds of obsidian shrieks from the swords were accompanied by panting demons and shifting footwork. The clop-clop-clop of their hoofed feet upon the ash-covered ground could have awoken the deepest sleeper.

Dave's strategy changed from measured attack to desperate defence. He couldn't strike without being hit; Kelvin's reach was too great.

Kelvin slashed and roared while Dave weaved, ducked and stabbed.

Dave parried a powerful blow and was knocked onto the ground, but rolled aside and back to his feet before Kelvin could aim its next blow.

He needed help.

I held the shield with my broken arm and my good arm and prepared to charge into the swirling melee.

"Don't," Dave snarled when he glanced back at me in a short lull from the fighting.

I frowned but obeyed.

Fascinated by the duel between snarling demons and desperately wanting to help, I barely noticed the faint buzzing sound behind me until the grey navy helicopter got close enough for the soldiers inside it to use their machine guns.

Bullets tore at the battling demons and struck both of them.

Dave fell against the large rock near the bottom of the stairs while Kelvin looked dumbfounded at the bee-stings it was receiving.

Kelvin saw the helicopter that was hovering over a hundred metres away and roared loud enough to deafen me before taking another bullet to one of its eyes. Another bullet ripped down its throat. Kelvin dropped his sword and covered his injured eye with a massive hand. The lumbering beast gurgled to itself, lumbered over to the staircase and, with its free hand, ripped a chunk of rock from the bottom steps.

The rock burned from the demon's fiery hand. Kelvin threw the rock and the rock left a trail of smoke that led all the way to the helicopter's cockpit.

A loud *bang* ended the machinegun bullets and the helicopter pitched forward. It dived towards the volcano's jagged sides before falling out of sight.

Pus and metal streamed from dozens of wounds across Kelvin's body and he jerked one giant leg in my direction before ripping out another chunk of the staircase with its massive hands. I raised the shield and waited for the rock to pummel me.

The ground shook. The giant had fallen. I heard Kelvin exhale loudly as his head bounced against the ground.

CHAPTER 9

"Continue, child, I will ensure this brute cannot get back up," Dave clutched at a hole in his stomach and dragged his sword towards the downed giant. "Go," he said before motioning to his pistol still in its holster. "Take this and save your daughter, there will be few guards. The two of us were not expected to reach this far. The gas from the mountain will not poison you, but the heat can kill should you approach too near."

I reached for the pistol and heard Dave's gurgled breathing. I unlatched the pistol and headed towards the stairs, wondering if he would still be alive within the next few minutes.

I ascended the smoothed-over steps as carefully as I could. There were only about forty steps, but it may as well have been a thousand.

A strange glow greeted me when I reached the summit and the heat blanketed my face, I'd reached the mountain's furnace.

My eyes stung and I could smell ash. I stepped onto a wide, circular viewing platform that had been carved from the rocks. The platform stood a couple of metres above the rest of the volcano's edge.

Holding my broken arm on top of my other arm I squinted through the heat and spied hundreds or thousands of individuals kneeling down, all lined up on a slim path in a semi-circle overlooking the molten lava below. The nearest individuals were crying and pleading with someone I could not see.

Two of the figures melted out of the haze and came towards me with spears.

"Bring him to me," a sensual voice called from my left. The two spear-wielding demons came to me quickly and were rewarded with bullets to their chests.

"Why do you lie down?" the voice asked the demons.

"They're dead," I told the voice's owner before swinging the gun to my left and preparing to...

I almost dropped the gun at the ghastly vision of my wife's face on top of some sort of black lizard's body.

Glossy, with four long limbs, it walked towards me while its tail cracked from side-to-side. It was half my height, but longer than an alligator.

"Indeed, descendant of David, it appears you have slain my guards, but tell me why this had to be? Did you not hear me ask them to bring you? I only wish to speak."

"Where's my daughter?"

"You would do well to listen." I recognised my wife's angry voice, but it sounded far too menacing to truly be her.

"You would do well with a bullet in your face."

"Awww, this pretty face?" My wife's face turned at a ninety-degree angle and smiled far wider than my wife ever could. "What about this one?" The face twisted and stretched before rearranging itself into that of a little girl's, complete with long ponytails and pink ribbons. "Could you shoot the face of your daughter, descendant of David?"

"Where is she?" I yelled.

"Are you not a little discomforted by my appearance?" My daughter licked her lips seductively and my stomach almost tore itself apart.

"You look nothing like my daughter."

"But of course... perhaps a more honest approach?" Again, the face distorted until the colour disappeared and became almost the shape of a dagger. It was more like an alien than a demon - glossy black armour covered its face from its pointed chin to the pointed ends at the back of its head.

The back of the head curved slightly upwards and stretched back a good arms-length from the front of its angular face. Large oval shaped eyes the colour of ash peered at me from the top of the head near its front and a small mouth twisted and moulded itself around a wormlike tongue every time it spoke.

"Is this better? No need for that weapon here, child, my armour was forged the same as any shield. Your 'bool-lets' will not hurt me."

I ignored it and kept the pistol pointed as best I could at its eyes. "Do you think yourself a hero?" the creature asked me.

"I want my daughter back, unharmed."

"Yes, yes, but what of the others?" The black monster turned to regard the hundreds or thousands of kneeling children that were doing their best not to fall into the volcano. "Would you leave them to their fate? Oh... but of course you would. You are not so innocent or heroic a man to attempt such an act. So selfish, aren't you?"

"Shut up, bitch," I said and shook my head, "I... I can't help them..."

"Ah, guilty as charged," it said as it sat back on its hind legs and stretched its head up to my level. It became a cobra on an immense lizard's body.

"Bullshit."

"No?" It laughed sweetly and I almost pulled the trigger, "but you are a murderer, a deserter and a thief."

"You know nothing, beast."

"Ah, but I have seen you, descendant of David. The mind and memory are such fleeting things, are they not? You murdered my warriors just moments ago, as you have done to others. They were people. They had hopes, dreams, ambitions, and you ended them."

"Did their dreams involve the wholesale slaughter of innocent people? Just shut up and tell me where my daughter is before I put a bullet in your brain."

"Touchy subject, murderer? I've been keeping count of the number of times you have threatened me, did you know that? I keep count of little things like that, like every time you and your misguided ancestor kill my warriors. Every breath you take in my presence is counted and sorted into classifications, and every boollet you fire is tallied, along with the pain it causes my warriors. It's becoming quite the tally, wouldn't you say? Each count yields a new, more interesting punishment among many we have at our disposal.

"I will try each punishment in turn, first while you yet live. Then, I will move on to the more interesting ones. You have but one chance, descendant of David, and one chance only to walk out of here with your daughter. Unfortunately, I do not believe you will take that chance. You still believe your ancestor can help you, or your warriors from those metal boats will save you. Their lives will all be mine, soon."

My grip on the pistol slackened a little and I started trembling. My muscles were tired and the heat of the air was sapping my strength. "What ARE you?"

"Your warriors are much more technologically advanced than we had anticipated. That is another insult, it changes the punishments. Time after time we restored the balance, most times only small incursions were required to bring the world back into balance. Disease, drought, famine, these were our weapons, but occasionally they were not enough. We awakened, learned, studied, trained the fallen and attacked when we were ready. Each time we encountered some small advancement, but it did not worry us. Yet now you use machines to drill beneath the surface. Worse, you leave this world and do not return for many days in your... *rockets*. The balance is breaking, soon it will be irreparably damaged, and so we have acted.

"You measure your time in *seconds,* do you not? No need to answer, I know you do. It has been many seconds since you reached my forge, and each one I count. Would you like to know why?"

"Want to know how many bullets are in this gun?"

The creature reshaped its neck before moving towards the volcano's edge to peer down at the rest of the small island. I pivoted to follow with the gun. One of the dead guards had fallen nearby at the top of the slope to the volcano's high paths and I moved towards it, putting myself between the creature and the children at the same time.

"I am old, descendant of David. I have seen this world through many cycles of the seasons. I have seen it when the shape of the stars would have held no meaning to your eyes. You want to know what I am? Those pathetic creatures down there, the things you call demons, those vessels of mud, bone and fire are what we fashion in the deep of this world for the souls of your damned. They are mere puppets, playthings.

"*We* are the demons; *we* are the dragons of your legends, the masters of this world. *We* are the keepers of souls, the masters of—" its tail lashed out and flicked the pistol from my grip. I stumbled onto my butt, "—the whip. You are the slave, descendant of David, I *AM YOUR LUCIFER,* and when you die I shall have your soul."

"Lucy, you are filth," David said from the top of the staircase. He held a sword in each hand and approached with sparkling blades held high. Lucy's tail lashed out and split one of the large swords in half. David dropped the shattered sword mid-stride and with two hands brought the other down on Lucy's leg. It punctured the hard skin of its foot and Lucy hissed in pain.

I rolled closer to the fallen guard's body to avoid being swatted, but the fight had already ended.

I looked up where David had been and saw Lucy's large bulk standing over him.

I felt a sudden pressure against my ears and eyes. Lucy turned its large grey eyes back to me and I flinched from the sight. A large vibrating cavity had opened in the top of its head. I felt the vibrations like a large book thumping me in the chest but couldn't hear any sounds.

"You have but one choice, descendant of David," its soothing voice only made me more agitated. "Kill your ancestor and you and your daughter are free. It will be easy for you, for if you do not do it, I will kill him anyway."

David's chest was heaving up and down like a jack-hammer as he tried to struggle from Lucy's grip. He seemed to be squirming in pain and tried to cover his ears.

The choice wasn't a hard one, kill a man that was already dead and walk off the island with Katie, or die under torture.

"What about the other children?"

"You do not want them, remember? They are not in this bargain, you will just have to leave them to their fates and suffer the guilt."

I glanced quickly at the crying, screaming children behind me.

"Show her to me first. Show me my daughter."

"As you wish." The pressure on my ears and eyes suddenly ceased and David stopped squirming. I heard a faint crack and a seam in Lucy's black carapace appeared in its back. The seam opened up like a pair of wings and hidden underneath was a child.

"Katie."

"Daddy?" She asked. I could barely hear her weak voice over the volcano's constant hissing. She tried to look at me...

"Oh..." I frowned and stood up to get a better look. "What have you done to her?"

My daughter, my beautiful daughter's legs seemed to disappear below the knees inside the carapace, exactly where the carapace ended.

Her legs were gone.

"Choose, descendant of David. Let me remind you of one of the many punishments should you choose unwisely." Its tail waved back and forth in front of me, I took a step backwards and almost tripped over something hard.

It was the guard's spear. It singed the sole of my joggers. Lucy held David's left arm and twisted, ripping the arm from its socket. David bared his teeth but did not scream.

"This is what happens to heroes."

I took a deep, hot, breath of volcanic air, "I'm no hero, bitch. I'm a pissed off, selfish, father."

"Excuse me?" Lucy turned its large head at an unnatural angle to look at me, catching the threatening tone in my voice.

David opened his mouth as wide as he could. He sank his large teeth into Lucy's damaged foot and held on with teeth and claws as Lucy tried to shake him off.

I picked up the spear I'd almost tripped over in a one-handed grip. It felt as if I was holding a candle's flame, but I did not let go. I took several steps forward and slashed at the base of Lucy's tail.

The whip-like tail dropped off where I had struck it and Lucy threw David from its foot. It turned to snap at me with distended jaws, but before it could bite me I thrust the burning spear through its left eye.

The eye was like tough glass, but with a little extra pressure the spear broke through. I did not stop pushing until half the spear had disappeared inside the beast's head and hit the black armour on the opposite side.

I let go of the burning spear and Lucy shuddered before falling down. Flames erupted from its eyes and mouth before the armour cracked apart and steam hissed out of the top of its head.

Limping from the pain in my scratched leg and clutching my seared hand in the armpit of my broken arm, I moved to where my daughter had fallen from Lucy's back. I stopped when I saw Dave with his remaining arm wrapped around her head.

"Sleep child," he was telling her. "She will be safe now," he said when he noticed me standing above them.

I laughed, "How so, mighty demon?" I felt tears running down my cheeks.

"I am no demon, child."

"I know."

"The soldiers from your boats, they will be here soon, I saw them start to climb the forge."

I looked out over the island. The black ships of the demon fleet had mostly been destroyed or were on fire. Several small inflatable boats, the size of ant-eggs to my eyes, had made landfall and the rest of the demon army was nowhere to be seen. I looked around at the edge of the volcano where thousands of children were still kneeling or had fallen on their stomachs or sides from exhaustion or despair.

"Is the war over?"

Dave coughed and then cackled softly before replying. "The world is in turmoil."

"We killed Lucy..." I said.

"Lucy was small of stature and a vain fool; there are many others of her kind. You humans—" he coughed again, "—you have a chance to stop them this time."

"Stop them from what, exactly?" I carefully sat down, next to my sleeping daughter.

"They made a mistake last time. Because of that mistake, your technology has progressed too far now, they will try to reset it to restore their balance. They will erase your history and your technology and throw you back into the caves. Go, your daughter is safe, attend to the others."

As much as I yearned to stay with Katie, there was little I could do for her. Her legs appeared to have been cauterized where they were cut off, so she was not losing any blood. I figured she was better off sleeping as long as possible to avoid the pain.

I used Lucy's carcass to help lever myself back onto my feet. The heat on my face increased when I started walking towards the children that covered half the volcano's edge.

"What was Lucy going to do with the children?" I said. I received no answer. I looked back to ask him again, but his eyes were closed and his arm was slack.

"Rest in peace, David."

"What?" a helmeted head at the top of the staircase said. "What the hell? Hey Lieutenant, got people up here. Shit, you gotta see this," he said to someone out of my view. The soldier climbed the rest of the stairs with his rifle leading the way. He quickly looked over my various injuries and kept his face professionally blank. "Are you okay, sir? You don't look too good t'me," the bushy-bearded young man said. "What happened?"

I just stared at him, and then turned my head to look at the hundreds of children, before looking back at him. "Please, help them."

"You got it, mate. Hey, Lieutenant…" I didn't hear the rest of what he said and dozens of strong, sweat-stained soldiers poured around me, each one armed with water-filled canteens. I tasted water on my lips and felt powerful arms under my armpits.

"We have you, sir."

"My daughter…"

"We've got her, too."

SELFISH DREAMS

With a loud thump followed by a continuous roar, the space plane left the High Bridge.

David Bogharty felt beads of sweat run down his forehead. His armpits were damp. Even though it was his thirtieth trip in one of these dirty old space planes, he was as worried as ever.

You never could feel comfortable being strapped down to a vehicle that might suffer irreversible failure halfway into space. The plane *was* fifty years old after all.

Fortunately, his fears were unfounded. After several minutes of hard acceleration, followed by half an hour of docking procedures, he was safe aboard the larger transport ship.

The *Blue Cow* was the transport ship's name. It was 200 metres long with living space for a single occupant; the rest was mostly engine.

He hoped the maintenance company had refitted the pusher plate properly this time. He would just love to be blown up by the shaped charges used as nuclear propulsion. David shuddered as he remembered the last incident, *That could have been me*, he thought.

He pulled his wrinkled hands out of tight, almost painful, gloves, and unbuckled his harness. At two-hundred and twenty-seven years of age, even modern medicine had trouble keeping the wrinkles from his ancient body. He sighed loudly as the weightlessness gently took hold of him.

David swallowed a small pill to ward off nausea and almost gagged; he'd forgotten the pill's terribly sour taste. He swung himself up toward the waiting airlock and snagged a water tube on the way to wash out the taste.

The airlock, a rusty metal plate, cycled and opened and he entered the *Blue Cow*'s interior.

He smacked his head on the airlock on his way in. *Silly old fool*, he told himself, but he was in a hurry.

Despite the name, the *Blue Cow* was shaded in grey, both inside and out. Who could afford paint at today's prices? The paint wasn't important enough for such an old space ship.

"Director Bogharty, of Actuary Division, reporting," he spoke aloud. The ship's computer would be sending his message back to High Bridge Command, "The *Blue Cow*'s ready for launch."

"High Bridge Command hears you, Director Bogharty," a voice, pleasant but emotionless, replied several moments later. "All traffic has been cleared, *Blue Cow* is authorised for departure."

He caught a glimpse out of a tiny porthole of the space plane's tiny shape zipping back down to Earth. Cloudless day-time skies revealed the archipelagos and larger land-masses that formed the Earth's surface, and... there. He saw them.

The Star Towers.

They were large enough to be visible from space, even with David's old eyes. The immense High Bridge, the sky-bridge that connected the two Star Towers, was also visible.

He'd never seen them from space before, not like this. They were large enough to comfortably accommodate two million employees of the Star Towers Corporation. The first time he'd seen them as a six-year-old he had looked up... and up... and up until he'd fallen over onto his back and hit his head on the pavement. He winced at that memory, then winced again as he found the bump on his forehead from where he'd hit the airlock. He took a painkiller, then strapped himself onto the lone bed and went to sleep while the ship's computer guided the *Blue Cow* away from Earth's orbit.

Can you imagine being alone? No not like being at home when the family's out for the day, or even a week, or a year. Think of a small bedroom-sized cave, where the only light comes from a tiny hole the size of one of your fingernails. Now, apart from you, there's no other living thing within a million kilometres, and you're stuck there for two weeks.

Boredom can lead a man to do some rather silly things.

As director of several thousand employees, David was usually a rather reserved two-hundred and twenty-seven-year-old, but here, completely alone, his eccentricities and long-suppressed hobbies took hold.

The other directors, he knew, studied ancient history, learned engineering, boring stuff like that.

Not David. He gleefully picked up a pencil and started drawing crude pictures of his colleagues. He painted his nails; dissected a computer pad; jumped up and down the walls as quickly as he could, and then shaved his body hairs... all of them.

There were still twelve days to go.

Anyone watching the recordings would think he was mad, and he might agree with them. He just wished he never had to do this again.

While he ate a small snack, he would sometimes watch the outside of the *Blue Cow* and try to spot the planets. The constant *flash-flash-flash* of the Orion Drive, though, irritated him too much and he gave up. The drive's nuclear bursts reminded him of an old steam train or an old clock.

Chuff...chuff...chuff...

Tick...tick...tick...

He just hoped this annoying cow could get him there as soon as possible.

"Docking underway," the ship's computer informed him. He'd made it, and it was a miracle he hadn't died from any one of his silly activities.

"Finally," he said aloud.

Harper's Recluse was the colony's name, a hollowed-out asteroid twenty kilometres long. It housed several million inhabitants, inhabitants that David was hoping to save.

The *Cow* docked without a problem, but David's fears were growing. The ship had not heard any radio traffic or seen any movement at all within Harper's Recluse.

The airlock hissed open and he smelt the beautiful aromas of rose-scented winds.

It was a pity the vision didn't match the smell.

"I am Lorna. Well-Come, death dealer." said a bald little woman dressed in orange robes. She called out to him from the airlock's entryway. The orange of her robes clashed severely with David's tight-fitting purple uniform. She was far shorter, and plumper, than he remembered of her picture.

His worries multiplied.

Only people of aggressive or failed colonies would call a member of the actuarial corps a death dealer.

"I'm afraid you have me wrong, young lady, I did not come here to deal in death." He stretched out an open hand in invitation, "My name is—"

"—you are being late, Director Bogharty," she cut him off. Her harsh, accented speech gave him goosebumps, "Or early, perhaps? Hmm. Come now, Director."

She ignored his outstretched hand and led him towards the asteroid's open interior.

"Strange woman," he whispered.

He almost buckled under the sudden gravity. He was on the inside now, and the asteroid's spin was almost up to one full gee. What he saw inside the asteroid's hollowed-out interior was as unexpected as the gravity. Instead of a vast city, he saw trees, flowing rivers, even *birds*.

"What happened to the people... the city?" he stammered.

"I is in a broken... place." The bald woman struggled with the words. Clearly English was not her native tongue, "But being that is, I cleaned it up nicely, don't you think?" She smiled broadly at him, revealing blackened teeth. David felt sick.

"You 'cleaned it up?'" he snapped at her. "What do you mean? Did you throw everyone out of the airlocks?"

"No, director, me just cleaned it."

"But... why? Why did you hire me to advise you on the right figures, materials, chemicals, if you simply got rid of everyone?"

"Ah, this I like." The woman laughed, almost cackled. "The numbers-man stumped at the loss of people. Or is it being that you wish to engage them in trade, also?"

"You think I want more money?" he accused her. "I came here to help them, not take their money. I told you two weeks ago, I can help your colony survive if you only make a few adjustments to your rationing procedures and make some deals with Titan's government. Why would you send them all away?"

"I sending no one, this place was abandoned when I came. Numbers were made up. Don't worry, you being already paid you are. Just... stay a while. Years? Much alike, you-me."

"You mean, 'we are much alike?'"

She nodded at his correction, "Yes. Lonely, eccentric. I know you, David."

"No," He shook his head vehemently. "I save lives, entire cultures, while you... eat, apparently," he said while looking pointedly at her plump belly.

"Then think about it," she told him as she sat down on the short grass under a tall sycamore tree. "Beautiful, isn't it?"

David looked up, and it was as if he was looking at the Star Towers as a six-year-old again. The trees, lakes and rivers covered the internal ceilings and walls of the large asteroid. He swayed and felt claustrophobic.

"I'm leaving," he told her.

Every step closer to the ship, however, reminded him of the daily work at the towers, and of the long, hellish trip home. His hobbies could be fun, but so confined aboard the tiny ship.

I could do anything here, The thought came unbidden, but it was a welcome one. Every eccentric desire that he kept pent up on Earth while he played the good director role suddenly seemed so...

He didn't make it to the *Blue Cow*. She was right; she did know him after all.

"Beautiful, isn't it?"

"Yes it is," he replied, "I'll need pencils... and razors if I'm going to stay."

ASTRONAUT'S TEETH

"Luken Ford, you are guilty of genetically engineered genocide and planetary destruction against your home planet of Wolf-359 Prime, formally known as Domnio. Have you any last request?"

"Fuck off."

"Let it be known that the prisoner requested 'fuck off.' Have you anything else to say before you are sentenced?"

"Fuck. You."

"Suggestion noted." The white face of a middle-aged judge turned to his left and then to his right. He watched from his brown hood as other similarly garbed heads shook. "And denied."

Luken blinked against the glare of the solitary light beaming down on his naked body and spat at the white heads in the darkness. "Suit yourselves." He saluted them with his middle fingers. He took care not to stray outside of the cone of light. The courtroom's internal defence grid might slice his middle fingers off with invisible beams of pain.

"Luken Ford, we sentence you to exile and pre-death by way of the Horace Device. You will be sent into the past at a time and place on Earth determined by this panel. Considering your advanced age of ninety-three, your likely inability to survive local micro-organisms for an extended period of time, and a large tumour growing near your left kidney, we determine that you will not live much more than a few hours or days after exile. As such, the damage you may cause to the locals will be limited. You may request a location and we will consider it."

"Not concerned about any paradoxes then?" Luken asked.

"As a man of your learning should know, paradoxes are impossible. Nothing you do will influence the past. Your life will be meaningless and forgotten by today's date no matter what you do."

"All right, a challenge," Luken pumped a fist, pretending to be excited about the prospect. "Send me back to Alexander the Great, I'd like to punch the snivelling little shit in the face and steal his teeth. Let's see what the history books have to say about that."

"Request logged. Keep your hands by your side, we will now activate the Horace Device. You have five seconds left. Goodbye."

"Piss off."

There was a strange odour in the air. Luken blinked at the brightness of the sun as he woke up. He was lying on his stomach next to some sort of dirt track. The dirt dug into his face as he levered himself up onto his backside. Aches and pains accompanied the movements of his arms and legs, and his nose crinkled while he searched for the source of the odour.

"Shit." He spat a glob of dark slimy matter and looked at where his face had been. "Fucking horse shit, those bastards." He spat the offending substance from his mouth and tried to wipe the dirt and horse manure from his face. He would have to find a stream. He looked down at his pasty-white skin. "Better get some clothes before some fucker takes me as a slave."

"Ahoy." He heard a shout from behind him.

"Crap." He turned around slowly and shielded his eyes from the mid-morning sun so he could see his visitor.

Whoever it was started jabbering at him, sounding rather annoyed and waving at him to move to the side. The man was walking with some sort of pack animal laden with heavy sacks. The road was narrow and Luken, a filthy-looking old man, was blocking it. Luken smiled and moved to the side. "Primitive farmer," he addressed the bronze-skinned man as he walked his donkey past, "where am I?"

"Podapós eí?" the man asked, shocked at Luken's choice of words.

"Apparently English isn't your strong point."

"Ou ksyniḗmi." He shook his head at Luken and waved at him as he kept walking down the track. "Hypíaine!"

"Uh... thanks?" Luken sat down on a nearby rock and scanned the trees and yellow grasses. The farmer rounded a bend in the road and disappeared behind some trees, giving Luken one last quizzical look before he was gone.

Water, he could hear it after several moments sitting on the hard rock. He stretched his aching arms and legs and leapt up onto his feet like a much younger man. The sun was strong here, his mouth was already drying and his white skin felt hot. Water and shade, that's what he needed. He ran, a slow jog at first while his muscles rapidly adjusted to the strain, then faster as his body redirected body mass into his cardiovascular system.

Within minutes the decrepit old man had become a spry marathon runner.

He gained scratches from the rocks and bushes off the path, but his mind quickly adjusted to block out the pain. Water; it was a small stream. He jumped in and gulped large mouthfuls before letting himself float gently downstream.

"So, where the fuck am I?"

***

"Are you sure Mr Ford will have died within a few days?" Specimen Nine asked Specimen One. "Perhaps it was a little unwise to send him to the past without a full report on his genetic experiments. According to the specialists, there's quite a lot of junk in his DNA that shouldn't be there."

"What's done is done. We have no records of such an individual in all of history."

"Much of history has been lost."

"Do not fear, Nine, he was an old man with a giant tumour. The Horace Device is the most painful and torturous punishment we could have bestowed."

"I believe you; I just wish we could have recorded the results."

***

Luken nervously poured red, lumpy wine over an iron knife he had spent two hours sharpening. It was a difficult task in the darkness of a shepherd's cave. He put the knife's blade into the centre of a smoking fire.

He touched the lumpy mass buried in his abdomen and winced at the thought of plunging the knife into his belly. He slurped on the former sheppard's wineskin and sweet wine ran down his cheeks. He poured some of the wine onto his belly and used dirty fingernails to scratch out points of incision.

He screamed as he inserted the hot knife along the scratched line. "Fuck," he yelled. There was only so much pain his modified nervous system could block. Holding the knife still with his left hand, he reached with his right and grabbed the wineskin. He sucked on the wineskin until it was drained to a husk.

Luken sawed at his belly, crying in pain. Once the cut was around four inches across, he pulled the knife out and flung it across the dark cave where it hit a rocky wall. His breath was short and his head dizzy with pain and wine. Blood dribbled onto the cave's floor. He had to finish the job before he passed out.

With his left hand holding the wound open, he reached inside his belly, probing with delicate fingers. He found the lumpy mass and pulled. The mass unfolded itself as he pulled it out, looking like a flat lung, rather than a solid tumour.

It came out, and out, and out. By the time it was all out it was larger than he was. A blue and red cord hung from the thin fleshy mass, connecting to his belly like an umbilical cord. He searched for the knife. "Shit," he said as he remembered throwing it across the cave.

He took a deep breath then bit into the cord. The pain intensified for a moment until he had gnawed the rest of the way through it. He vomited red wine onto the bloody cave floor.

Still bleeding, he was running out of time. Shaking, Luken crawled over the man-sized piece of flesh and spread it out to its proper shape. It resembled a man's skin but was as tough as much thicker elephant's hide. He touched the skin's ears and a seam opened down the middle, splitting from head to groin. He hefted the skin into the air and stepped inside it.

The inside of the fleshy suit was warm, moist. Millions of microscopic hooks on the inside of the fleshy suit latched onto his skin and the suit closed around him.

Exhausted and in pain, he slept.

While he slept, the skinsuit started working on his wound, closing the hole with its hooks and absorbing the blood into itself. It established a circulatory system between itself and Luken's blood, feeding off of him while helping to filter his blood and regulate his temperature. Absorbing nutrients in the cave rocks and using the heat from the fire as an energy source, the suit started strengthening its muscles.

Luken would survive.

After a year of searching and learning the local's horrid excuse for a language, he discovered he'd missed Alexander the Great by at least sixty years. The Specimens had sent him to the time of Alexander II of Epirus, some son of the Pyrrhic Victory king who had beaten Rome by sending waves of his own men at them, or something.

As he camped on a small rise underneath a bush on a dusty plain somewhere in Macedonia, waiting for a battle to start, he realised just how stupid those Specimens could be. It was either stupidity or ignorance of Luken's request. He nodded to himself while taking another swig of horrible red wine, thinking it had to be stupidity. Why wouldn't they grant his request?

The Horace Device was sophisticated enough to deposit a person on old Earth from several hundred thousand light-years and several million years in the past. All it had to do was run the calculations and tap into the vast stores of energy produced by its pet black hole and 'poof,' the unlucky prisoner might arrive at his or her destination without being stuck in the ground or floating several metres in the air.

Some idiot logged the wrong Alexander into the system.

He didn't want to entertain the fact that he'd been too rude to the Specimens and that they had deliberately sent him to the wrong time. "Fuck that," he said as he balled a fist around the wineskin.

His teeth ached. He loved creating new life and finding ways to prolong his own, without obvious side effects like cancer. He'd had fun unleashing a plague on his former homeworld and then blowing it up to hide the evidence, wiping everyone out in the process. If only he'd found the time to ensure his teeth didn't rot without a decent dentist. It wasn't something he'd considered while slaughtering people.

He took another mouthful of wine to dull the pain.

The wind wafted over him and he recognised the stench of a thousand worried men headed his way.

"About time," he said and started smiling. "Let the festivities begin."

He'd chosen his camping spot well. The two opposing armies of pike-wielding soldiers walked towards each other, Luken's rocky little hill forming one edge of the battlefield.

"Good shit, good," he started laughing as rocks flew from slings at people in the opposing armies. Arrows took flight and he heard a few shouts and screams. "Yes, about time someone gave me a good show."

The pikemen came closer and closer but, to Luken's disappointment, they stopped right before they could start stabbing each other. The pikes were so long they drooped at the ends, so the soldiers had to hold them at a higher angle to keep them level at their opponents.

"Come on, imbeciles, charge or something," Luken yelled at them.

Several helmeted heads turned in his direction, wondering where the strange voice came from. They couldn't see him, his living suit of armour camouflaged itself against the surrounding rocks and bushes. If they saw anything, it would be a floating head drinking from a floating wineskin.

Seeing their chance, a small group from one side took a couple of steps forward and thrust their pikes at the chests of the enemy soldiers. Some of them drew blood but bronze armour stopped the worst of it.

"Yes, yes, yes, *again*." Luken cheered the soldiers on, clapping or laughing each time someone got hurt.

The soldiers nervously prodded at each other, trying to find openings in each other's ranks and occasionally stabbing past the enemy wall of spiky points. "No, idiots, not in the chest, s'protected y'know? You gotta stab 'em in the ear." Luken slurred his speech and unstoppered a third wineskin.

He stood up, took a long draught from the wineskin, tossed it on the ground and closed the hard skin armour around his head. The helmet itself was skin-tight, forming a second layer of skin. A digital HUD, projected by bio-luminescent lights onto his eyes, displayed infrared images of the battlefield.

The men in front of him blazed with heat and dripped sweat. "Y'see, those idiots over there to my left, you lot haven't even gotten started, lazy sods. You're all so cold. These poor buggers on the right are burnin' up, looks like deys needs a bit of help." Luken burped and tasted regurgitated wine. He hopped down from the small hill, tripping over every rock and upraised tree root on his way. He crashed into the shield of a stunned soldier.

The soldier dropped his pike and looked at where Luken stood, trying to make sense of the blurry apparition in front of him. Luken grabbed the man's pike from the ground and turned towards the other army. "Y'see? Like this," he started thrusting the spear at an enemy soldier's head, aiming for the ears. He hit the soldier in the mouth.

"That works too," Luken said, pleased with the results. He moved forward, wanting to have another go at it. No less than five pikes found a mark on Luken's chest, his skin armour shrugging off the blows. He started sweeping the pike at the men that had dared to attack him.

"Jab-jab-jab, hahaha," he cackled. Already worried and stressed from an hour of keeping the opposing men at bay, the enemy soldier's looks of fear turned to terror. Eyes widened, mouths opened at the ghostly sight and men shouted and turned to run. "Where you going?" he asked the soldiers as they pushed backwards into their own ranks. "Don't spoil my fun."

With the force of ten men, he swung the pike across the fleeing soldiers, knocking a handful to the ground and snapping the pike's shaft. "Aww." He looked at the broken pike and tossed it aside, then shrugged. "Where's that wine?"

Fleeing soldiers kicked dust into the air. A trickle of running soldiers soon turned into a flood. "Oops," Luken said when he noticed how he had influenced the battle. "I wonder who just won?"

***

"Results?" Specimen One replied. "The result is his death."

"Of course, but ever since the Horace Device has been in operation, I've been thinking, what about all those unexplainable instances throughout history?"

Specimen One looked at Nine as if he were an idiot. "Strange things happen in real life, Nine."

***

"Ah, Emperor Kanta...er, Kantazen."

"Kantakouzenos, remember it well, foreigner," the Byzantine Emperor replied, clearly annoyed.

Luken grinned, trying to suppress a giggle. "My apologies, Kantakruz. Can I call you John?"

The Emperor bristled and his guards, clutching large axes, turned to look at him. After a moment the Emperor visibly relaxed. "It's at times like these I have to remind myself that Greek is not your first language and you're just a simple merchant, not a diplomat."

"Yes, yes, you are right, I'm a simple idiot from a faraway land. Now, about the matter of reviving the Empire?"

"You insult me, Luken Ford of Saxony. The Empire is in no need of 'reviving,' we simply require goods from that little island of yours."

Luken, appearing as a man in his forties, grinned at the Emperor, displaying rotting and missing teeth. He looked around the palace walls through his greying beard to take in the crumbling walls.

"Yes, that's what I meant. I'm just doing my part to help you after your little war. I mean 'little' in relative terms, it was smaller than wars in the past. Please understand, I meant some offence." Luken held up his hands with open palms to placate the annoyed Emperor. "But yes, I and my fleet can gather what you need, but..." He held up a finger. "I want triple."

The Emperor's eyes opened wide and his nostrils flared. He stood up from his dilapidated throne and balled his fists. The guards around the walls picked up their axes. More guards, hidden around the walls, readied their crossbows.

"That is preposterous."

"I know, I know. But you can afford it."

"Guards, throw this man out of my palace."

"Wait, John, you don't want to do that. I'm a very powerful man, in my own way. So, I'll forget the social impasse and I'll offer you a new deal. Double rates, plus one."

Luken lost three rotten teeth and bled from several orifices by the time the guards were done with him.

"You... should have... taken the... deal. John."

Thrown out onto the palace steps, surrounded by gawking onlookers, Luken flipped a middle finger at the palace.

"You okay, boss?" Luken's first mate, a scrawny old man wearing silken rags, asked.

"Take me to the ship," Luken said without showing any sign that he'd just been beaten to within an inch of his life. He hopped up onto his feet like a much younger man.

"How is he still alive?" a woman in the crowd asked.

"Because of this," Luken replied, holding up a golden wine goblet he'd stolen from the Emperor's table. Despite being beaten and thrown to the ground, he'd managed to keep the goblet filled to the brim. His skin armour had kept a tight seal around the goblet's top. The guards noticed the goblet and started coming back to him, axes held high.

Luken downed the red wine in one go and tossed the golden goblet to the ground. He reached into his dirty cloak and fished out a fist full of silver and gold coins, then tossed them into the air. The crowd, suddenly forgetting the strange man and the menacing guards, surged forwards to claim the priceless goblet and fallen coins, tripping up the guards in the process.

Luken giggled as he ran back to the docks.

Luken smiled as he watched rats crawling up the ship's ropes. At the top of the ropes, inside one of Luken's trading vessels, bread and meat awaited the starving rats.

"Beat me up, will you?" he whispered to the memory of the Byzantine Emperor.

"What was that?" the Chinese merchant asked him. Sitting together aboard his ship, Luken and the Chinese merchant discussed terms of trade. The merchant was killing him with the exorbitant terms.

"Oh, nothing, nothing," he replied to the merchant. Docked at the Port of Canton, what would one day become the Port of Guangzhou near Hong Kong, Luken had little real interest in supplying silver in exchange for silks. "It was just a small prayer for your sick."

The Chinese merchant scowled at him, "I... thank you for your Christian prayers. We have our own customs for warding off these evil maladies, your prayers are not necessary."

Luken grinned back at him. "And a fine job your customs have done. I hear two thousand more died of plague just this morning, do we thank the Yin or the Yang for their deaths? Or are you using that five phases thing now? With the wood and fire and Earth stuff? It's hard to keep up when you're my age."

"Mind your tongue, foreigner, or our agreement is forfeit."

"That's fine, your rates are crap anyway."

"What?" the merchant asked, his voice raised. Several of Luken's crewmen and the Chinese merchant's guards all started looking worried and eyeing each other off.

"I have what I need," Luke replied as he spotted another flea-infested rat drop down from the ropes onto the deck to find the salted meat. "Besides, I have a meeting with the Eastern Roman Emperor to keep in a few months, I'd rather not waste any more time talking to your sorry arse."

Tension lay like a taut string between them. One false move and blood would spill. War might even start. Luken sort of relished the idea. After several moments of everyone holding their breaths, the merchant looked at the deck and shook his head. He grunted and stood up. "I'll see to it you're never allowed back in Canton."

"Okay," Luken replied, grinning through black teeth. "Ow," he said as pain from one of his cracked teeth shot through his nervous system.

***

"I mean, what about the Black Death?"

Specimen One sighed. "What of it?"

"Doesn't it strike you as odd that, when the Eastern Roman Empire was just getting back on its feet, the plague, all the way from India or China, wrecked the city of Constantinople?"

"Trade occurred, the rats came, millions died, what of it?"

"It... just seems as though something a man of Luken Ford's reputation might have done."

"How... how the hell do you propose he survived over a thousand years?" Specimen One asked, annoyed.

"Genetics was his specialty, wasn't it? He loved to tinker with the genetic makeup of his slaves and invented whole new models and instruments to measure the pain he inflicted before they died. Maybe he found a way to live longer?"

***

"Is he here?" Luken asked the housekeeper, Anna Schilling, as he barged into his friend's home. He spoke in fluent Polish, having had decades to perfect his speech.

"Who, sir?" the startled woman replied.

"Your toy-boy, who else?"

"My what?"

Luken rolled his eyes. "Nicolaus."

Anna frowned. "Ah, I remember you. He isn't seeing anyone today."

Luken raised an eyebrow at her. "And I thought he said I would always be welcome here."

"Yes, Mr Ford, but that was before you stole Nicolaus' papers."

"Don't fret, I have them right up here," Luken replied as he pointed to his head. He took muddy boots off and tossed them to her. She tried to catch them but ended up with mud on her face.

"Such an objectionable man."

"Such a bitch," he replied in English. She frowned at him, not understanding. "Ah, Copernicus, there you are."

Nicolaus Copernicus stood in the doorway to his study, distraught at Luken's appearance in his home.

"What do you want, Ford?" he asked the older man.

"Don't be so dire, my friend. I bring wine."

"Yes, I can smell it on you, will you proffer it from that old wineskin of yours or will I need to siphon it from your urine?"

"Hahaha, neither. Here you go." From his heavy black travelling cloak, Luken revealed a large glass bottle. "Only the best for you."

"Really?" Copernicus crossed his arms. "Will that bring me back the papers you stole?"

"I have them, Nic. They're in my cloak. But, Nic, you must let it go. I mean, this idea of yours that the sun is the centre of the Solar System." Luken tsked at Copernicus.

"Why?"

"Come, let's talk about it over some wine."

"So, you're telling me you're actually from the future?"

"Yes, that's right," Luken replied, keeping a neutral expression.

"And the centre of the Solar System is within a man's head?"

"Exactly," Luken pointed a finger into the air, almost spilling the wine from the wooden table they sat around. Nicolaus started shaking his head.

"You're mad."

"Yes, but from a certain point of view, that man's head is the centre of the whole universe."

Nicolaus frowned and covered his face with one hand, "Does this man, by any chance, go by the name of Luken?"

"Why, yes, now that you ask."

Nicolaus stood up, "Mr Ford, this has been an unpleasant waste of time, thank you. Please, get out and don't return."

"Aww... Sook."

"Go torture someone else on your journeys."

Luken smiled. "I just might," he said, already thinking of other famous people he decided he had to meet. "Oh, but before I go, here are your papers." He withdrew the detailed notes from his cloak and tossed them on the table, complete with scribbles and child-like doodling around the edges.

"What have you done to my papers?" Nicolaus asked him, aghast.

"I fixed them for you."

"Get out, now."

"Fine, fine. I hear Da Vinci needs some help with his toys anyway."

***

Luken walked through the trenches, taking in the sickly aromas and miserable sights and feeling ever so happy to be there. "Damn, it feels great to be a part of history," he said aloud. It was night but he could see everything on his HUD. Spent bullet casings littered the muddy wooden boards, rats scurried amongst the men and he opened his skin suit's helmet to feel the foul air on his face.

"Hey, shut up over there," a young German soldier told him. The soldier and three others kneeled in a dugout, playing a game with filthy cards by a small candle.

"What for?" Luken asked the young man. "The Brits are shelling us, I have to speak up if I'm going to be heard, don't I?"

"We're trying to play cards, can't you see?"

Luken came into the light of the dugout's small candle.

"Sir?" One of the soldiers tried to get up, surprised that they had been arguing with an officer. The soldier bumped his head on the dugout's overhanging ceiling.

"He has a king," Luken helpfully pointed to one of the soldiers. "This man has a pair of twos, this one a five and a seven, and you," he pointed at the final soldier, "have a pair of aces."

"Ah, yes sir, that's right." The four young men put down their cards and glanced at each other, wondering how the old officer could know what cards they held.

"Now, gentlemen, just like I knew exactly what cards you all held, I know exactly how this war ends. I must say, you're probably all fucked, the Yanks are going to come soon and the Russians in the East will just keep piling more meat into your military grinder."

"No, sir, the Americans are neutral and the Russians are retreating. We're winning."

"Nope, fucked. But, because I've taken a liking to you, you might all live through this war. Here's what you're going to do. You're going to stop playing this silly game and put on your gas masks. In a few hours, all your buddies will be dead or retreating and the Brits will invade this trench. When that happens, don't run, hold up a white flag and surrender."

"But, sir?" one of the soldiers asked, dumbfounded.

"Just do it and you'll live. You might even end up married to some English nurses after a pleasant stay in the English countryside, working the farms over there. Trust me, it'll be great."

"Are you mad, sir?"

"Do you want to die, Ben?" Luken asked the soldier.

"How do you know my name?"

Luken ignored the man and stood up to feel the air on his face. "Gas masks, please. I smell mouldy hay on the air."

"Oh, shit," one of the soldiers yelled before diving for his mask. Several paces away, other soldiers in the darkened trench started coughing. "Onto the fire steps, get up, get up. Sound the gas alarm."

"Yes, that's right, the gases sink low, you'll die on the ground. I remember that part now. Farewell, gentlemen, I'm off to find a friend of yours. By the way, is private Hitler around these parts? Fascinating chap, I'd like to give him some pointers."

***

"That's one small step for a man, one giant leap for mankind," Luken heard through his skin armour's internal speakers.

"Oh, so exciting," Luken clapped his hands and smiled. "He said it, right now. He really said it." Luken had a problem now, he wanted to celebrate the event but how could he drink when there was no air up here? "Ah, I know what to do."

After several minutes watching Neil and Buzz wander around, staring at the moon's surface, Luken, careful not to disturb the moon dust and reveal his presence, let out a puff of air from his bloated suit's skin. The puffs of air were powerful enough on the moon to lift him off the surface as if he had taken a giant leap of his own.

With a couple of smaller puffs of air, he guided his slow fall and landed heavily on the moon lander's top side. Neither astronaut noticed, mesmerised as they were with the moon rocks. "Okay, how does this thing work? Ah, easy." Luken said as he quickly got the lander's top hatch open with the skin suit's magnetic wrenches. He was careful to apply globs of stretched skin to the opening, making sure none of the lander's air escaped.

The suit opened and Luken extruded himself from it, leaving it as an air plug. He took a quick look around inside the messy lander, smelt the days-old sweat and piss, then grabbed the wine bottle from his suit and opened it.

"I can't remember how long those two idiots take out there. Better make this quick," he said to himself. He tilted the bottle, opened his mouth wide, and waited for the red liquid to poor down his mouth. It came slower than on Earth but tasted as good as any other high-priced bottle of red in the low gravity.

He grinned to himself, thinking of all the pranks he could pull. As tempting as it was to just walk up to Neil or Buzz and tap them on the shoulder, he did want to remain anonymous. He could pop their spacesuits and watch them die, that would be a fun prank.

They'd deserve it too, he thought as he smelt days-old farts and sweat. *I bet they have nice teeth*, he picked at the few remaining mounds of bone on his gums. *I always heard astronauts had the best teeth*. He settled down for a nap and started daydreaming about extracting astronaut teeth to replace his millennia-old stumps.

He wrinkled his nose and promptly farted, waking himself and letting the astronauts have some of their own medicine at the same time.

"Oh, shit," he said when he noticed the astronauts heading back to the Lander. "I must've been in here longer than I thought."

He grabbed the discarded wine bottle, kicked off a control panel and re-entered the slimy interior of his suit. The suit's needles pierced his skin in a thousand places and reconnected to his nervous system. He closed the Lander's top hatch, careful not to let any air escape. He felt a soft sucking sensation as the skin of his suit, the part that had kept the air trapped in the Lander, detached itself from the hatch's lip.

He slid down the opposite side of the Lander to where the astronauts were, using vacuum-sealed suction cups to climb down. *I wonder if anyone from NASA was listening to the Lander's interior while I was in there...*

He clung onto the back of the Lander. When the astronauts started to climb the ladder to the main hatch, he made his move. Trusting that his suit's camouflage would keep him hidden amongst the grey rocks and dust, he jumped off and landed a few dozen metres away, kicking up a small plume of dust.

He held his breath and watched for signs that he'd been spotted. Nothing.

"Now, how did that happen?" Buzz Aldrin asked when he noticed the snapped switch for the circuit breaker. The switch, essential for starting the Lander's ascent engine, was missing. "I must've hit it with my backpack..." he started saying over his radio.

"Orrr..." Luken pretended to cover his mouth, suppressing a laugh when he realised he must've somehow busted the Lander's switch. He watched as Buzz jammed a pen into the hole where the switch had been. "Heh, clever boy," Luken muttered.

The astronauts re-entered the Lander. "Housten, I just want to check something before we blast off, might be a small gas leak, probably nothing."

Luken couldn't contain his laughter now. "It was *me*," he yelled and laughed. Unfortunately, his radio was turned off; the astronauts would never know it had been Luken Ford who fouled their air.

Hours later, while he slept on the ground, the Lunar Lander launched back into space.

"Damn, I forgot about that," he said to himself, woken by the light of the exhaust and vibration of the rocket launch. "There goes my ride home." He shrugged and wandered over to one of many moon rocks he had deliberately placed there years earlier. He lifted the man-sized rock with ease and uncovered the small cylindrical rocket hidden underneath. "Guess I'll have to go home in this tiny thing after all."

***

"Of course," Specimen One replied. "He was a genius, that's why it was so hard for the agents to capture him in the first place. But don't flatter him, he's dead."

"Is he? He should be, but we don't have proof."

Specimen One shook his head. "We don't *need* proof, that's the beauty of the Horace Device. Anything we send into the past cannot affect the present."

"Well, sure, but what about the events of the past affecting our *future*?"

***

"Shit yeah, that feels awesome," Luken said as he bit down on another raw chicken leg. He relished his newly acquired teeth and watched as the restaurant staff started calling the local police force. They dialled into the police station directly through miniature computers installed into the base of their skulls.

"Fucking imbeciles," he said between bites of the near-frozen whole chicken. "Still using computers? Use your brains and tackle me if you want this chicken back."

A large male waiter cowered in the kitchen's corner while a skinny female chef, wielding a big fat knife, completely ignored the chaos Luken had started. Perhaps she was ignoring him in the misguided belief that he would wander off and leave her alone. A third staff member, the older man trying to call the police station, went pale and started crying. The older man wore what looked like an expensive suit. He must have been the manager.

All other staff had fled the kitchen, taking the confused diners with them.

"P-please... leave," the cowering waiter said from the cold floor.

Scented steam rose from a boiling pot and Luken sniffed the air, savouring the smell. He dropped the cold chicken and sauntered over to the boiling pot. He lifted the lid and breathed hot steam before plunging a hand into the water. The hot water stung but, wearing his skin armour, the damage was superficial. After a moment he found what he wanted.

"Noo," the older man yelled at him.

Luken pulled a king crab out of the pot and ripped a claw off. He bit into it.

"Yesss," he hissed when he tasted the crab. The textures, the flavours! It felt like a small pocket of heaven had opened within his mouth. He could eat solids properly again, after three decades of searching for the perfect teeth. He'd always heard astronauts had good teeth, and what luck! His friend, an astronaut, had recently died in mysterious circumstances.

He spotted spaghetti bolognese on another shelf and a large tub of ice cream next to it. He buried his head in the ice-cream

"I'm recording you through my contacts. The police are on their way. You're going to jail for this," the older man told him. The older man had finished calling the local police station.

"No, I won't go to jail for stealing food," Luken informed him, ice-cream dripping down his face. "I'm going to jail for murdering you if you don't erase the recordings."

"You can't hurt me," the older man said, his voice quivering.

"Delete. The. Recording." Luken locked his eyes on the older man's chest. Unsheathed, his armour's claws looked like extra-long fingernails. They were much sharper and stronger than fingernails.

"I, ah..." The older man looked towards the kitchen's exit. The waiter had curled into a ball while the chef continued chopping carrots.

Luken started hearing a familiar buzz coming from the kitchen's exit, towards the front of the restaurant. "Oh, for f—" his expletive was cut off by the approach of a head-sized police drone flying through the kitchen's door. Miniature blue and red lights flashed and a siren started screeching at him from the small drone.

White with black propellers, an assortment of black appendages sprouted from the drone's underside, most of which ended in three-pronged claws. Four of the claws ended in other instruments.

"Point those somewhere else," Luken told the drone, indicating the stun gun and slug gun. He suspected one of the other claws also held pepper spray and another carried sticky rope.

The drone shot him in the chest.

It was the stunner. An electrical charge pulsed along the small stun dart's cable.

"That tickles," he said, giggling.

The slug gun shot at him a second later. The bullet hit him in the chest and fell harmlessly to the floor, its lethal kinetic energy dissipated across his armour's hard shell.

Luken frowned at the drone. "Naughty," he said while wagging a clawed finger at it. He grabbed the stun dart's cabling and wrenched the drone towards him. With his other hand, he punched the drone's front, shattering the white carapace and sending the drone flying into the kitchen's white walls.

The older man slid along the kitchen's wall, managing to stay on his feet while being scared stiff. "A-a-are you going to—"

"Kill you now?" Luken cut him off. He sighed before continuing, "I suppose I have to."

"No-no-no, I'm sorry, you can take the food, all of it."

"Too late, sir. And to think, all I wanted to do was test my old friend's teeth."

The chef finally noticed the commotion. She stopped cutting carrots, dropped the knife and started screaming.

"Yes, all right, you're first," Luken told her while covering his ears.

Luken watched the news that night, taking particular interest in one article. "In connection with the murder of the three restaurant employees, police are looking for a thin man around twenty years of age, Caucasian in appearance and around six feet tall. His head is bald and he has long fingernails. If you see him or have any information, please contact your local station. Police are unsure of the man's identity but believe dental records taken from the scene should lead them to their suspect."

Luken rubbed his full belly and smiled with contentment as he lay in bed at the hotel next to the restaurant. Even as he stroked his stomach, wrinkles appeared on his hands, changing his appearance to that of a much older man.

"In other news," the anchorwoman continued, "the grave of recently buried astronaut Michael Grant was illegally exhumed yesterday in a despicable act of vandalism. There are unconfirmed reports that Mr Grant's teeth were pulled out..."

Luken turned off the news and picked at a piece of food that had lodged in his old friend's teeth. "Gotta love astronaut teeth."

Drones buzzed the hallway outside his room and police officers with battering rams opened doors, shouting at the room's occupants to get down on the floor. It didn't take long for the footsteps to appear outside Luken's door.

A police battering ram broke the door's latch and the door swung open, hitting the small hotel room's inside wall.

Appearing confused and sleepy, Luken, still lying down on the lounge, put his hands up. "Hello?"

"Stay down, shut up," an officer said while coming into the room with a stunner pointed at Luken's chest. Four more officers arrived and started rummaging through the room.

After a couple of minutes pretending to be afraid, Luken put his hands down. "Would you like a cup of tea?"

"Shut the fuck up," the officer said while pressing the stunner to his head.

The officers upturned his bed and went through his duffel bag of old clothes.

"Would you like a cup of tea? Ow," he said as the pistol pressed harder. He waited a few more seconds before starting again. "Who are you, again? Did I ask you if you wanted a cup of—"

The officer grabbed Luken's arm and dragged him off the lounge.

"You got dementia, old man?" the officer asked him.

"Pardon?" Luken said. He started to shake as if afraid and put his hands up to cover his head. "What are you doing, dad?" His eyes glazed over and tears appeared.

"Fucking hell. I'm not your dad, I'm thirty years old you fucking idiot."

"I-I-I don't want to fuck?" Luken asked.

The officers' radios all turned on at once and a woman said: "All units, converge on room twenty-two. Suspect located in room twenty-two."

"Leave him, let's go," one of the other officers said.

When all the officers had exited the room and he was sure no drones were left behind, Luken smiled. The 'suspect' was a twenty-something dental student who had helped Luken fit his new teeth. He'd paid the kid, made sure he was inebriated on red wine beyond the point of being able to stand, then hidden a bloody chopping knife under his pillow.

It was a terrible waste of red wine.

**

"What are you talking about?" Specimen One asked.

"Well, if we can't affect the past, what about being able to affect the time after the Horace Device is activated? Mr Ford was sent back in time half an hour ago, so he can't have affected anything up until that time, right?"

"Yes..." Specimen One replied, frowning at his younger colleague.

"What's to stop him from changing things *after* half an hour ago, such as right *now*?"

There was something in Specimen Nine's voice that caught Specimen One's attention. A hint of anger, perhaps?

"You're starting to worry me, Nine. Do we need to schedule you for a session in the cage?"

"I'm perfectly fine. I just can't believe how it all happened. It was so easy."

"How what happened?"

"How I managed to murder Specimen Nine and impersonate him," Specimen Nine answered.

"What? Who are you?"

Specimen Nine rolled his eyes. "Damn, you're dumb. How many hints do I have to give you? Now, I'm going to kill you and take the Horace Device." He opened his black robe to reveal his nakedness underneath. A Specimen, naked? That was a grave offence, punishable by torture and exile. Specimen One didn't have time to ponder this new development as Nine lifted one leg and kicked him in the head.

Specimen One clutched at his nose and, wordlessly, stumbled backwards over the courtroom's ledge. The moment he hit the courtroom's floor, high-powered lasers slashed through his body, carving it into small cubes.

"You know what I missed during most of my holiday in the past? A decent dentist," Luken Ford said. "Could've saved me a lot of trouble, and my liver."

***

"Officers are at a loss as to how the high judge of Terra, known only as Specimen One, had fallen to his death in the courtroom. It is suspected that the notorious criminal, Luken Ford, somehow managed to escape the High Court and murdered him after already being sentenced in his trial. Currently on the run, Ford may have already fled the Solar System with the Horace Device. The System Fleet has been alerted and is doing all it can to stop him. All star systems are at red level..."

"Good luck, morons," Luken said from several light years away aboard a stolen starship. He started brushing his teeth with a toothbrush he'd taken from the captain's storage locker.

WARGAMES OF THE SHELLWORLD

PROLOGUE

1552 C.E.

Alien starships across the prepared battlefield disgorged blue creatures armoured in leather and armed with small war axes.

He'd come a long way from sixteenth-century France.

Far from home, many leagues from Earth, the young Jean Bodin led demonic soldiers on a strange, vast planet. He should have been writing of the day's events by candlelight in his study or overseeing the stables of his estate, yet here he was.

He clenched the reigns of his otherworldly horse and listened to the voices in his ears. The voices, relayed to him by sticky black devices attached to his ears, issued orders to red-skinned warriors arrayed in front of him.

Moments later, arrows flew over his head towards the host of blue-skinned warriors marching towards them.

Pikes and horsemen would soon clash against shields and axes held by their blue-skinned foes but, for a moment, Jean sat on his red charger and watched the battle unfold. He stared at the opposing red and blue armies, and then tracked his eyes upwards towards the impossible floating platform that held Akbar, the battle's current general. Heavenly images were conjured in the air all around the platform as its occupant interacted with tactical overlays. Higher in the sky, floating fortresses a thousand paces long appeared as mere dots to his eyes, one of which was their Trustee's stately space cruiser.

Above those, giant starships crossed the heavens beyond his vision.

Soon enough, he would be up there, leading starships in a battle in space.

"Jean, order your cavalry," the commander of Earth Team's forces called to him.

Jean shook his head, feeling dizzy. "I apologise, Akbar; I shall encircle the enemy's left flank immediately."

With the flick of his wrists, he guided his red horse towards the right of the Terran pikemen. "Follow me," he ordered his squadron of red knights. They moved in a wide arc around the blue host's flanks. Several blue skirmishers, thin-limbed and fat-bellied, tried to slow them down, but the red knights ran over the heathens with contempt for their efforts.

He felt like saying a prayer but smiled instead. "Onwards, for Earth," he yelled. Jean officially entered himself into the war game before crashing into the rear ranks of the blue host. He stabbed a blue-skinned monster in the neck and shouted with glee, surrounded as he was by red knights and blue blood.

***

Hubunker shielded his eyestalks from the light of the dwarf star outside the viewport of his luxury-class private vessel. After a moment his eyes adjusted. Beyond the star was a vast patchwork of geometrically zoned blues, greens and greys – the surface of the Shellworld. It was the most astonishingly huge artificial construction in the known universe, so enormous in fact that millions of dwarf stars had been lashed to its orbit for use as lamps. The stars were enclosed in spherical cages built by someone – or something – long since gone from the universe. Had he wished to it would take Hubunker's vessel several years to make a single orbit of the Shellworld.

Hubunker turned his attention to his guests, a strange assortment of aliens from various regions of the Shellworld, all transfixed to the visual feed projected onto the back wall of his cruiser's main meeting room. He held onto a beam of golden plank wood. The wood came from a native tree from his homeworld, a place that had long since been lost to time.

The wargame for the Terran team beamed live from several million kilometres above the Shellworld. While the game was live, there was a significant delay due to the distances involved. Safely tucked away in his cruiser, many millions of kilometres from the Shellworld's surface, Hubunker and his guests conversed without fear of being overheard by the Plinth and their allies, or by the Arbiter's Guild.

Light-beam communication would have been too easy to intercept, especially if they'd been closer to the surface like most vessels with an interest in the games were.

Amongst the six figures stood a human, Ammon, Hubunker's life-long servant and coach for the commanders of his Terran team. Ammon came from a more primitive time of Earth when that species had begun building mountains in the deserts to appease their dead deities. Shorter than the other guests, the human was several thousand years past his mortal time; his skin layered in wrinkles under his plain white robe.

Two more creatures, stick-thin versions of the human that had wide heads and large mouths, represented a twelve species alliance a quarter turn of the Shellworld away. They sat hunched within the confines of Hubunker's private meeting room.

A metallic orb, a representative of a digitised group of people, floated at eye level and quietly hummed. The orb represented untold trillions of second-class digital beings with an interest in Hubunker's proposed alliance. The final creature, a small blue elephant with twin trunks and a silver-lined business suit, was an independent lender with its own intergalactic fleet of trade vessels.

Hubunker turned from the screen to address the assembled beings and resisted the urge to pull at his mouth to stop himself from vomiting - the smells the creatures produced were off-putting at the best of times, but when nervous and brought together their pungent odours were almost unbearable.

"Gentlebeings, what you are witnessing here is history in the making. My humans, whom you all assumed were primitives, are making a mockery of the Plinth Trustee's current team. No doubt the Trustee will have them flogged. The one leading the capital ships, Jean they call him, is especially skilled, and he's just a politician of his homeworld."

Hubunker kept one of his four eye-stalks on the battle on the screens as it progressed to the final stages. Jean's squadron of heavy cavalry was just now forming up for a devastating charge. Akbar, the other human, floated down on his observation platform and started shouting orders at a group of reserve infantry.

"You certainly have a high opinion of this Jean, that's twice now you have deemed necessary to point out the name. The human is better still than Ammon?" the stick-thin creature asked as if Ammon were not present.

"Oh, much better, much better."

Ammon visibly bristled. Hubunker seemed not to realise the insult or did not care.

***

Jean held a sophisticated little handgun in his right hand while cowering under the rubble of a sandstone house. He held his left ear with his other hand. It didn't help, the explosions came ever louder. He'd been around canons before but the weaponry being used here was extraordinarily large and loud. With the benefit of a month of preparation Jean could do little but cower in fear.

A metal beast the colour of red sand, what the Trustee had called a tank, rumbled past. Jean shook uncontrollably.

"Spiders," Jean whispered while shaking his head. "Why did they have to be spiders?" As he spoke to himself the tank rounded the corner of the destroyed sandstone house. He glanced over his shoulder and saw it, a spider, sitting atop the tank, staring at him. The spider was purple with short limbs. Brown leather armour covered its body like horse barding.

The spider called to the tank driver by clicking claws at the ends of its front two legs. The tank stopped. A second spidery soldier emerged from the tank's large rectangular hatch, its four main eyes peering over the tank's armoured lip to get a good look at the cowering human commander.

Jean started rocking back and forth on his backside.

"I haven't entered the game, you monsters. Leave me alone," he yelled at the alien soldiers.

The spiders looked at each other briefly before clicking rapidly. The driver got back down and the hatch closed. The spider sitting on the top of the tank threw something at him. The object was silver and Jean's personal energy shield flared red when the object hit it.

The tank disappeared behind some more buildings down the small town's streets, followed by ear-splitting explosions.

Jean looked at the silver device, puzzled. He reached out and grabbed it. It was smooth and had a cap on its top that would suit a spider's claws. He picked the silver device up and heard something sloshing around inside it.

Water.

The spiders had given him some water.

He shook his head, angry that his opponents had taken pity on him. He brushed himself off and stood up, looking for the nearest group of anti-tank wielding demons he could find amongst the ruins.

He rallied together several squads of heavy gun-toting demons and went on a rampage, cleansing the arena of alien spiders.

***

Space. He was fighting in space. Jean had once had the rare opportunity to peer into the heavens with a glass lens, but that fuzzy glimpse was nothing compared to actually being there. Now, he was not only flying on the bridge of a large, advanced starship, but he was leading demonic pilots of smaller craft in a battle to protect a moon-sized fortress.

The fortress was under attack.

The space on the other side of the starship's viewscreen dazzled with splinters of broken ships and rapidly expanding clouds of dust.

"It's just like naval combat," he told himself.

The soldiers, his crew, waited for his instructions. Jean buried his head in his hands, not knowing how to proceed. They'd been winning until... he couldn't concentrate. He couldn't issue orders like he had in the previous battles. Everything was just so strange, now. He wanted... needed to go home.

Directionless, the fleet was crumbling, Akbar was shouting at him from a distant vessel and the soldiers unnerved him with their silent judgment.

Demons. The soldiers were *demons*. He'd spent so long with the critters that he'd grown used to working with them. It was finally starting to dawn on him that they might in fact be demons in form and spirit. Their red skin and crown of horns made his skin crawl.

The monstrous Trustee was their conjuror. The little man, always at the Trustee's side, was the keeper of the demons, like some sort of evil witch doctor.

"Commander?" One of the demons, covered in advanced metal armour, waited for him to respond.

"Okay. Okay..." Jean studied the ghostly displays in front of him, trying to make sense of the elemental fireflies that represented the battlefield's combatants. He still couldn't believe the distances involved. Two hundred miles represented a close object.

He struggled to think.

Galleons on the high seas of Earth at least stayed on the same plane. These starships sailed on their sides or up and down on odd trajectories. There was no cohesion, no... *order*, to these battles.

Fortunately, he'd had several weeks to get used to the concept with Hubunker's special simulator.

He finally had an idea. "Flank them. Signal Akbar and the fleet and tell them to split into two groups, circle around the moon fortress and surprise them from either side. We'll take them down with broadsides." He grinned, feeling confident in his choice.

"The whole fleet?" a demon asked, its face blank.

"Yes, of course."

"Commander. Might I suggest some of the fleet remains to protect the moon fortress instead of moving behind it?"

"The fortress is still strong, isn't it?" Jean snapped.

"Yes, it will hold for—"

"Just do it, *demon*," he spat.

***

The six figures in the room watched with great interest as the space battle continued. Red and blue highlights showed them which vessels belonged to which side, with the Terran vessels glowing red. Akbar's fighter squadrons zipped in and out of designated grids on the battlespace while Jean's much larger capital ships glowed brightly near the centre. Blue vessels winked out of existence with surprising regularity.

Hubunker could recognise expressions on some species, and from what he remembered of the twin-trunked elephant and the stick-thin creatures, they were smiling.

Something was happening on the screen that drew the attention of all four of his eyestalks. His eyes widened. Jean was doing the one thing that could possibly lose the team the battle. He was trying to orbit the fortress itself, but as the fortress had such a small gravity well to sling the fleet, the fleet was burning through its fuel reserves to move around it. The manoeuvre was limiting the fleet's ability to both defend the fortress or themselves.

The defence, predictably, was starting to fall apart.

Ammon, the human coach, tugged at Hubunker's hand to get his attention. Hubunker started whispering to the human, "This might be a problem."

"Yes, master," the small, bald man replied. "If I could just get on the communicator—"

Hubunker's eyestalks suddenly retracted. Akbar's small frigate-class vessel, surrounded without Jean's supporting capital ships, shattered into a million pieces when a wayward missile slammed into its midsection.

In an instant, the mood in the room turned sour. The assemblage of powerful creatures all seemed to lean back, away from the screen. Before long it was evident the Terran team had lost. A final score started flashing on the left side of the screen and details of the battle scrolled down on the right. Akbar's body would need to be retrieved from the bowls of the mangled frigate so that they could revive him. Jean, his failure complete, sat silent on his capital vessel.

As his potential allies left the private meeting room, Hubunker averted his gaze, trying to figure out what had gone wrong.

"This meeting did not happen," the suited elephant said as it lumbered past.

"I'm afraid," the metallic orb, the last creature of the potential alliance said, "we cannot assist in this regard."

The creatures all boarded their individual shuttles and set off to their home sections of the Shellworld, careful to avoid the attention of the Shellworld's Arbiters.

The room remained silent for a good five minutes, Hubunker and Ammon simply staring outside at the busy space lanes and zones designated for other space-based wargames. The Trustee bobbed his four eye-stalks up and down with disapproval.

"I think it is time we initiate our more dramatic plans. If we cannot win them to our cause by playing by the rules, we must rewrite the rules. In any case, the Alliance will have to wait a little longer, it seems, before we can put our plans into motion."

"Yes, maybe it is best if we forfeit the next wargame?" Ammon asked.

Hubunker sighed. "That would only prove the Plinth and their Million Star League right. If we are to change the rules, we can't give up now. We will need to push for a delay, give the commanders more time to train."

"It won't be enough, master."

Hubunker sighed, "I suppose you're right. We have already lost many allies. I fear this calamity will take some time for my resources to recover and regain some of our friends. Perhaps we will try again in another few centuries. Perhaps, next time, we should opt for a third commander. Redundancy is clearly desirable. It will be costly but sacrifices will be easier to make if we have more options."

"What will you do with them?" The old man nodded towards the two human commanders on the screen.

"There are enough points in my account to have Akbar revived and to pay for the two of them to go home, though they will likely have their minds scrambled by the Games Masters due to such a poor showing. Their personal acquaintances will need their memories altered too I assume. Akbar did well. Jean though? He must be punished."

"But if he is sent home how is he meant to be punished?"

The Trustee stroked its wide frog-like mouth, thinking for a moment before replying. "I have some ideas for that."

CHAPTER 1

Current Day.

A spark of light appeared in the sky over Sydney, Australia. After a few seconds, it vanished.

Ensconced within her worn out car, Jessica Stanner didn't notice. She stepped out onto the pavement in front of her house and tried to check her accounts on her phone.

Nothing. Error messages appeared on the small screen. The wireless router must have broken down again, or the internet was playing up across the city, as it had been for several days. She let her arm dangle, tired as it was from getting whacked by blunt swords, axes and spears. She'd been wearing her rented armour but being hit by lumps of metal for a couple of hours still hurt like hell.

"Great," she said as she realised she still had assignments to mark. Barely six months out of university and she'd been thrown in the deep end, setting tasks her class hated and grading assignments the kids, barely younger than her and often much taller, did not want to do.

Practising HEMA with a claymore and getting whacked in the arm by a war-axe seemed far more fun than facing those spiteful monsters every day.

If only she could get the internet to work. It had been slow all week, ever since an odd disturbance had been detected in the northern hemisphere.

Someone was clogging up the world's bandwidth and no one could work out who was doing it.

Of course, that someone, or something, just happened to have dropped into her kitchen.

Jessica dropped her pen while staring at the kaleidoscopically-coloured spherical intruder. The pen clattered loudly on the hardwood floor while the half-metre-wide orb floated inside the kitchen door. It wafted up to her eye level. "Do you agree to the terms?" Its words tasted like chocolate to the ear, its soft colours candy to her eyes.

"The papers..." her voice faltered; her mind was full of challenge, opportunity, danger. Her students' assignments were lost in the flood of the alien orb's stunning words. "Where... where will you take me?" She gasped and sat down before her legs weakened any further.

"The where does not matter so much, I assure you. You will be returned in due course to this world once the games are complete."

"The games..." She had to concentrate hard not to stammer. A pot of vegetables started steaming on the stove, the sound cut against the orb's soft melodies.

"You should not die," it replied, its lights dimmed, casting rays of red, blue and green. "The transition from this world to the games and back again may come with some memory loss, but we will do what we can to remedy that. This opportunity will never come again. Do you accept?"

"I... yes. Yes, of course, I accept."

"Stand by," it announced, breaking its spell over her.

"Wait, what?" She looked around at the messy kitchen as if waking from a pleasant dream.

"Stand by," it repeated for her. In an instant, it grew substantially larger. It stopped glowing different colours and edged sharply to red. The orb engulfed her with fingers of fire.

"They do not appear to be admirable specimens to me."

"They are within acceptable limits. We're lucky to have them at all. Can they be trained? The alliance is restless, we have days to prepare. Use Jean's memories to get them up to speed."

"Memory transference may not work; the experience can be confusing but I will comply."

Ammon loaded up the memories of Jean Bodin into the cruiser's memory transference banks, pumping Jean's experiences into the minds of the Terran team's chosen commanders.

"The girl is struggling."

"To be expected, Hubunker replied.

"Shall I stop? The process may cause damage."

"Continue."

"Who's Jean?" Jessica asked. The dream faded as she tried to open her eyes. She barely remembered experiencing battles as a sixteenth-century French man. She felt a headache form where the dreams fled.

"Welcome aboard the *Inveigled Ambassador*." She heard the words but was having a hard time unscrambling them in her fuzzy mind. Jean's battles still swirled like a hazy mist in front of her eyes.

"Inv…?" she managed, hardened saliva stuck to the back of her throat.

"The *Inveigled Ambassador*," the man replied, his buzz-saw voice moving her to wakefulness.

"Oh." She managed to open her eyelids. She brushed sleep out of her eyes and focussed on the white padded room. Her arms and legs felt numb. She noticed three men in the room, two of whom were dressed in the same blood-red jumpsuit as she was. Like her, they were struggling to wake up. Jessica and the two red-suited men were spread equidistantly around the room with their feet pointed toward the middle. The third man, who wore little more than a brown sash across his waist, stood in the centre of their small triangle.

"I am Ammon, my speech may sound a little strange to you as it is being translated for your convenience from my natural language," the near-naked man told them. He stood a little hunched, his back beaten upon by time. Deep grooves branded his aged skin and crisscrossed his bald head almost like a chessboard. Powerful muscles wrapped his wizened form. "Do you remember why you are here?"

One of the other men, a cinderblock with a short ponytail of white hair, coughed once and staggered to his feet. "Yes, sir, I believe so." His soft-spoken words stood in contrast to his frame. "We were brought here to play some sort of games." As soon as he said it, his expression changed from a sure-faced construction to a crumble of confusion.

"What games?" Jessica asked. "All I remember is some sort of glowing orb and then—"

"Games of strategy, tactics, and strength," Ammon explained. "You," he said, pointing at Jessica, "are Jessica Stanner, a teacher of ancient wars." Then he pointed at the large pony-tailed man, and announced, "You are Georgy Ivanov, commander of warriors—"

"Retired," Georgy interrupted. "Many years ago, I was an officer in the Russian Navy. I... have not commanded anyone for quite some time unless you count my dogs." He smiled as he spoke of them.

"Nevertheless, the *Inveigled Ambassador*'s probe has chosen Georgy to represent humanity in the intermediate stage of the games." Ammon pointed at the last man, a middle-aged man of East Indian bearing whose well-kept shoulder-length hair made him appear younger than his grey-streaked beard indicated. "You are Peter Dorn, man of knowledge and learning."

"Uh, yeah, I'm a theoretical physicist," Peter replied for Jessica and Georgy's benefit. "I was born in New Delhi but my parents changed my name from Parin Dugar when we moved to London. I was actually an officer on a submarine. I even did the Perisher Course but... my wife died, so I quit the Navy to look after my children. But hey, I also enjoy mini-golf and rock-climbing. Was that all in your file on me?"

Ammon gestured for them all to stay quiet. "Mmm, the games are a serious matter; all aspects of your lives were taken into account when you were chosen. Yes, Peter Dorn, part of the reason you were chosen was for your extracurricular activities."

"Wait a minute," Jessica said raising one arm as if she were back in school. "Ammon, where are we? What exactly are these games?"

Ammon clasped his hands together and turned, then left the centre of their triangle and started walking between Jessica and Georgy. A smooth red-rimmed door frame, not noticed by Jessica until now, appeared to be his destination. "Come," he told them. "Better that you meet your pieces; it will help you understand."

"*Pieces?*" Jessica mouthed to the other two. Peter, the Indian physicist, shrugged. Georgy, the Russian veteran, raised an eyebrow at her, not understanding her silent question. They followed the rather short, well-muscled man through the red-rimmed door to a short white balcony overlooking a large chamber that must have been two hundred metres long and fifty metres wide. The walls glowed blue and the ceiling and floor were blood-red, matching Jessica's clothing.

"Whoa," Jessica almost slipped but held onto the balcony's soft wall. Peter gasped, while Georgy stood still. The floor wasn't red, in fact, it wasn't a floor. Thousands of living, breathing, *things*, stood in parade formations, their yellow and white eyes paying attention to the humans' every move. "Oh, oh... what...?" Jessica felt the urge to run back into the room with the red-rimmed door frame.

Georgy licked lips that had lost any hint of moisture. "What are these... demons?" he asked as his face went pale. Jessica saw them then, the horns. The red things all had a small crown of horns.

"The pieces," Ammon said, waving an arm across the demons, "for you to use in the games."

"Pieces, like chess?" Peter asked, his forehead creased in thought.

Jessica looked closer, gulping down a surge of anxiety as she did so. They had claws on hands and feet, sinewy arms and legs, pointed noses, leather skin. Their bodies were built as if they were living weapons.

"Pieces, soldiers, yes," Ammon said, "for games."

"What sort of games?" Jessica ventured.

"Wargames," Georgy said, with his jaw set and his voice merely a whisper. The others nevertheless heard him over the steady breathing of the hellish host below.

Ammon regarded Georgy, judging him before nodding. "You three are to command them. We must meet them, so that you may have a demonstration. Then you can sleep and eat and think. Then your training will begin; we have little time to waste. Follow me." He walked back into the room where they had woken up. They followed and where there had once been a floor, a large spiralling staircase occupied the centre. The staircase headed both up and down. Ammon started down, towards the sea of red demons.

CHAPTER 2

"You may call me 'demon' if you wish," the red creature in front of them said with a guttural clicking in its deep voice. "We are your soldiers; do with us as you must."

"Yes," Ammon agreed, "a demonstration, little demon, for your new masters?"

The demon grinned, revealing surprisingly white, straight teeth rather than the pointy black blades Jessica expected. "A demonstration for the masters." It called out to the front row of demons in the large open hall. "Command us," it demanded as the entire front row unfolded crossed arms and displayed sharp claws. Five of them stepped forward. The speaker joined the five that had stepped forward and stood beside them. A metallic smell seemed to accompany their every breath, Jessica wondered if they must be robots. Their identical features and precision unnerved her.

"Choose weapons," Ammon said. The walls along the edges of the large room faded from soft blue to a bright white. Underneath the blue cushion of light, stacked against the walls were weapons, countless weapons of various sizes, shapes and functions. Spears, swords, bows, rifles, every weapon Jessica had ever known and more that she hadn't.

"Spears," Peter quickly called out.

"You two," Ammon pointed at the nearest two, "spears and wait."

"Spears, wait," the demons replied before purposefully turning to one of the walls and striding towards it. They each picked a two-metre-long spear, then returned. They stopped and faced each other several paces apart, dropped to a combat stance, then waited. "Peter, give the command."

Wide-eyed, Peter lifted a shaky arm then dropped it as if chopping the air.

Nothing happened.

"They are unused to such a command and are focussed each on the other, you must command with voice, song, or sound. A simple word of intent will suffice."

"What happens if I tell them to build a house?" Peter joked with a grin. Ammon seemed to ignore him, his eyes narrowing to slits. "Okay... just, attack."

The moment the last syllable left Peter's mouth, the demons lunged at each other. Jessica wasn't sure what happened. She blinked or held her eyes shut. She heard a clatter of movement, and when she opened her eyes, one demon was on the ground, its head loosely held to its neck by a thread of red skin. The other demon had dropped its spear to try and hold in its stomach, or what passed for organs in that area. The blood that seeped onto the floor was sucked down into tiny holes.

Peter gagged, trying to keep whatever meal he'd last had from exiting his throat. Both Georgy and Jessica stared.

"Good, clean up," Ammon gestured to a couple of demons who dutifully carried their dead and injured comrades away. "Another demonstration if you will. Choose weapons," he glanced at Georgy and Jessica as if to say it was their turns now.

"These things are alive?" she asked.

"Yes."

"But... that one just died."

"It is a demonstration of skill, talent. You must observe their strengths if you are to lead them in the games," Ammon said as he scratched at his nose. "It is necessary, but short."

"Okay," Georgy nodded towards one of the walls, "I see something that looks like an old-style Thompson, can they use that? I mean, can they shoot from one side of the room to the other?"

"Of course. You two, the weapons that master Ivanov indicated, retrieve and wait."

"Retrieve and wait," they repeated before grabbing a couple of the guns that looked like old Thompson submachine guns.

"Command when ready," Ammon said.

"No, they don't need to die for a fucking demonstration," Jessica said before Georgy could speak, "what if they hit us too?"

"They will not hit us; we are protected from harm," Ammon said.

"You two, when I tell you to attack, try to avoid being hit," Georgy told the demons.

"Yes, master," they replied in unison.

Georgy looked both ways, studying each of the identical demons as they held the guns up to their eyes, ready to carve small round holes in each other's bodies. Georgy shook his head before giving the command in that quiet voice of his, "Go."

For a whole two seconds, the demons weaved, dodged and fired across the large room's expansive width. The demons in the front rows barely moved as the bullets flew mere metres or centimetres in front of them. A spatter of small metallic shards embedded themselves in the opposite walls where they seemed to stick as if in soft gel. Blood accompanied many of the bullets.

With a dull thud, one of the combatants fell to the ground, two small craters gracing its horned skull.

Both combatants were removed from the demonstration area and Ammon turned his old eyes on Jessica. "I don't want any more to die," she told him.

"The demonstration must continue; you will learn."

"But what are these creatures? They don't seem to feel pain or care if they die. Are they brainwashed?"

"Calm, child," Ammon held up an open hand to settle her. "You have questions. I have answers; these will come. The soldiers are not robots. They have been... *conditioned,* and shaped. Grown for the games."

"Do they enjoy death?"

"They long for combat and for service to their masters; this is their purpose."

"Then they don't need to die."

"They will if they demonstrate, and demonstrate they must. Your qualms are unfounded. For the pieces, death is to life as ice is to water; they can be restored."

She shook her head. "Still, there are other ways of demonstrating. Let me fight one of them instead."

"That... mmm," Ammon seemed to think over the request, "that may be acceptable. You will learn hands-on experience; it is agreed."

"You have combat experience?" Georgy asked her. Peter was too busy trying to keep his food down to say anything but looked horrified at what she'd proposed.

"No. Before I became a teacher, I used to fight at medieval re-enactments. I still do actually. Uh, I need a sword or an axe."

Ammon sent several demons to collect bits and pieces of armour and a long-sword and dagger. The demons engulfed her in hands and armour as they strapped it on. She realised then just how short they were. Jessica was less than average height, but the demons were half a head shorter again. "You said before that we are protected from harm," she said as the demons tied the last of the pieces of armour to her.

"You are protected from mortal injuries. Some safeties will need to be deactivated for you to fight. Do not fear, child; if injury should occur, you will not be in pain, and you shall be healed."

"Oh, good," she didn't know what else to say to that, but she was glad that she wouldn't die. Her chosen opponent took up a position near her with identical armour and weapons. "Georgy, can you please give the attack command?"

"Yes," he replied. Her breathing increased in tune with her heart, and she took a stance, mirroring the armoured demon from several paces away. "Attack," came the call.

Blades carved and slid, probing armour and cutting skin. The demon was fast, but she found she could keep up with its furious blows, even managing to land a couple in return. With a flick of its long sword and a parry from its knife, she was disarmed and forced to the ground. The demon pinned her down. Hot breath bathed her face and blood poured from a neck wound she had inflicted between helmet and armour, spattering her face. She blinked from the falling blood and meaty breath. Her left arm felt numb.

She'd been cut, deeply.

"Not to fear, Jessica," Ammon told her as several demons helped her to her feet. "As I said, you will be healed." One of the demons produced a vial of blue gel, then cracked and emptied it onto her wound. The gel morphed, matching the wound's contours before setting hard in and around it. The armour came off and she breathed a shallow sigh, shocked at her injury, but relieved it didn't hurt. "Now, to food."

Peter groaned.

CHAPTER 3

The Trustee watched while Ammon showed the humans how to command the pieces. They clumsily waved their hands and shouted commands while the pieces tore bloody shreds from each other. The female surprised him by challenging a piece to personal combat using swords. She proved a capable warrior but was cut by the piece's sword. Ammon called a halt for food and healing.

The wasp-man at the Trustee's side stirred, "You must enter your humans into the games now. The alliance grows weary and the Plinth are moving to block our efforts. We cannot wait any longer."

The Trustee hesitated, watching as one of the male humans started vomiting. "They are not ready."

"You have two days."

* * *

"You have a curious mindset, you three," Ammon told them through a mouth full of boiled white rice. "The probe chose you, yet you do not welcome displays of skill and death." He slurped loudly from the copper cup of foul-tasting broth. "Your predecessors had no such qualms."

Peter played with the chopsticks provided, twirling them between his hands rather than using them to futilely stab at his bowl of rice. "So there have been others in the games?"

"Yes."

"What are those things out there?" Jessica asked.

"They are human, or close enough. Derivations of a human vessel, reformed into the perfect piece."

"They look like..." Georgy didn't have to finish the sentence; it was on Jessica's mind as well.

"Demons? Is that your final interpretation? They do not appear 'demonic' to me," Ammon answered between mouthfuls. "But then, my experience may differ, to yours. I have been here a long time, after all."

"So, why do they look like monsters?" Jessica pressed.

"Monsters, you say?" Ammon turned stiffly to capture her with ancient eyes. "They are us, humans, made perfect."

"But they're so small; they must be five feet at the most, and... why the horns on their heads?" Jessica asked after a mouthful of rice. She noticed Georgy's gaze, a raised eyebrow, directed at her. "And the red skin?"

"Their heads are weapons, why should they not be? The pieces need not be pretty baubles; they are fighters. They have strength, speed. They don't need to be giants, they need precision, coordination, tactics. This is what you are here for, Jessica; leadership. It has been five hundred years by the ship's reckoning since the last humans were accepted into the games. Jessica, they *need* this. They need your spirit."

Jessica coughed up a spittle of rice.

"Five hundred years? Just how old are you, Ammon?" Peter asked.

"Old enough. Our Trustee saw to it that I would live long enough to teach. Such was my wish, but it has been too long since I taught, and I will not have long enough. I long for the company of humans, even as strange as you three are to me. I lived at a time when the Great Pyramid was just a set of plans in my father's mind. You will meet him, our Trustee, later. So... to the point of the games. Should you do well, you will be rewarded."

"Rewarded, as in... we could live forever like you?" Georgy asked.

"Forever?" Ammon barked a short laugh. "You could strive for it, yes. There is so much more than infinite life. Limitless energy, resources, technology. Depending on your progress in the games, you might be rewarded with all of it. Chief among the rewards, I believe, is the ability to go home."

All four of them remained quiet a moment. Georgy and Peter exchanged slightly worried glances with Jessica. "The probe said we would be returned at the end of the games. I didn't imagine that part, did I?" asked Jessica.

"Did it?" Ammon burped before gulping down some more brown broth. "There is a good chance you will earn enough in the games to return, but it is certainly not guaranteed. I chose a different path, as you may have guessed. I—"

Suddenly, they heard a large, echoing thunderclap from somewhere above them.

Ammon leapt to his feet. A horrible screeching sound blared and a bright yellow light flickered throughout the room from multiple points in the ceiling, walls, and floor. "Stay," Ammon commanded with an open palm. He ran out of the room, clumsily kicking over Jessica's small cup of uneaten broth on the way.

Georgy was already on his feet and following Ammon out of the room. Peter and Jessica moved as well. They went into the large hall where ten thousand demons had stood just minutes earlier. Far in the distance, on the opposite side of the room, Ammon was running towards an open doorway rimmed in red light. "What's happening?" Jessica yelled over the screeching.

"Trouble," Georgy wheezed while running. Georgy, Jessica, and Peter piled through the door at the far end of the hallway. A maze of dark blue corridors greeted them, bathed in darkness. A line of red lights pulsed at them from the darkness, pointing like arrows. They ran between the red lights until they found the one open doorway amongst many that were shut. Ammon stood just beyond the door, his shoulders slumped. Beyond him was a shimmering blue field. The field flickered from the other side of a house-sized room. Beyond the flickering field was open space. Black soot, red glowing pieces of debris, and dozens of dead demons floated around the room.

"What happened?" Jessica eased her way past Ammon to get a better view of the carnage. Space beyond the ship's hull was full of light and movement. Several orbs, like the probe that had brought her to the *Inveigled Ambassador*, flittered around the hole, trying to pull bits of the hull back into place. Instead of a star field, several distant starships lay like beached whales against the backdrop of a large planet. The planet itself was covered in millions of tiny rectangular bricks, but could only have been plots of land, like fields of farms as seen from the clouds on Earth.

"Your rivals have struck," Ammon said with a measured breath, "I fear we will enter the games prematurely."

***

They would be fighting the wasp-men's soldiers.

The wasp-men, friends of humanity's Trustee, used yellow pieces. The pieces had large eyes, four arms, and sharp teeth. Jessica didn't like the pointed teeth. "You have two hours to finalise arrangements," Ammon told them, "Jessica must lead on the ground. Peter will be her subordinate. Georgy will observe from a special platform and call out troop movements. As you have had such a limited amount of time to train, Georgy, it is up to you to keep your team informed of the rules during the battle."

"Why couldn't we look at the rules now?" Georgy asked.

Ammon shook his head. "There is no time; I can describe the basics on the trip to the prepared battlefield regarding points and victory conditions. For now, though, you must decide on the tactics, your troop setups, arms and armour, as well as mounts. Anything added to your forces will deduct from the overall points, more advanced or longer-ranged weapons will reduce your points at a greater rate than basic close-in weapons. You must think economically, but also weigh in the loss of troops..."

They boarded one of five sleek, black shuttles that were transporting over a thousand demons and a hundred small demonic horses. Metallic breath from hundreds of demons supplied a constant white noise to Jessica's sensitive ears.

There it was, their arena. Blood rushed around her circulatory system as she stared down at the chequered giant of a planet.

"The Shellworld," Ammon told her. It was immense; stretching so far across her vision that space disappeared in her forward field of view.

"How big is it?" she wondered aloud.

"Big," Peter replied. "The ship's computer told me it... well it's damn big."

"Were those its exact words?"

"Err, no. It's bigger than the sun. I mean, much, *much* bigger."

Jessica believed him. The chequerboard pattern of different sections of land and water started to sharpen and grow. The brown sections divided into many smaller brown sections of different shades. Reds and blacks formed as splotches across the rectangular patches, like mountain ranges or rivers of red rocks. The pattern repeated for other rectangular sections of the chequerboard.

"Did the computer tell you anything else about it?" Jessica asked, fascinated.

"Yeah, do you know what a shell world is?" Jessica shook her head. "Well, it's a shell of a planet, where the inside is hollow, except this one isn't entirely hollow."

"What do you mean?"

"It's like a matryoshka doll; you know those Russian dolls with the dolls inside dolls? This place is like that, with hundreds, or thousands of shells inside it. Thousands of more levels where aliens are living."

Jessica's eyebrows shot upwards.

"That's... insane."

A few more minutes of descent towards the planet revealed yet more rectangular fields within the smaller rectangular patches. It looked like an endlessly tessellating pattern of rectangular blocks that kept growing out of the surface of the Shellworld. The horizon remained at what seemed to be a fixed point as if they had not descended from the *Inveigled Ambassador* at all, even though Jessica knew they had traversed tens of thousands of kilometres. Her head was spinning.

She looked at the large, smooth windows within the shuttle's sides. She made out four small stars that were the other shuttles carrying the rest of the demons, each of which was several hundred kilometres away.

The four stars were barely visible against the armada of starships descending towards the Shellworld's surface. Thousands? Millions? Maybe billions of starships, she had no idea how many there must have been. A good number were whizzing past them too, ascending back into space and yet more moved at perpendicular angles, crisscrossing all over the viewports.

Large light sources shone down upon the Shellworld, dozens of them, as bright as the sun. Jessica had to shield her eyes from the glare and as she did so she thought she saw giant structures, like nets, encasing the bright lights within. "Tame stars, millions of them," Peter informed her, "they're white dwarf stars, probably with different amounts of output for all the various aliens across this world."

"They're using stars like mobile lamps?" Georgy asked. "How do they orbit this place?"

Peter rolled his eyes. "Your grasp of orbital mechanics astounds me." Sarcasm was dripping from his tone. "Time to stop worrying, old boy; they seem to have a certain mastery over the physical problems around here. If you'd noticed earlier, the *Inveigled Ambassador* was orbiting a small planet that looked a lot like Earth. I think the Earth-like planet was orbiting one of the white dwarfs, which is orbiting this giant... thing. And look." Peter pointed below them through the forward viewscreen, "Asteroids orbiting another planet; we're travelling over the planet now. There are people down there; you can see lights on the night side. The white dwarf stars must have their own miniature solar systems. Amazing."

"What, exactly, is this thing?" Jessica said while choking back some broth she'd slurped down less than an hour ago.

"The Shellworld?" Ammon raised an eyebrow, surprised they had not worked it out. "For you, today, and for others inhabiting the nearby galaxies, it is the host of a billion wargames."

CHAPTER 4

Four thousand armed and armoured pikemen marched in step down the shuttle ramps and formed up along the brown battlefield's length. It smelled different here, earthy. Adrenalin swam through Jessica's veins and she exhilarated at the power her voice commanded. *Five thousand soldiers.* Four thousand pikemen, hundreds of archers, axemen, and cavalry, she commanded all of them. "Make sure the cavalry covers the flanks of our army," she said to Peter. A small group of red-skinned soldiers formed up around her. They were her shield bearers, an elite bodyguard with large shields, long swords and better armour than the rest of the army.

"Yeah, yeah." Across the field fat, bug-like shuttles were disgorging yellow-skinned warriors. She could see her team's final objective on the far side of the yellow army, a small fortress that she would have to take control of to gain bonus points.

Five points for incapacitating an enemy soldier, ten points for capture, two thousand for reaching the enemy castle, two thousand for breaching the walls... Jessica ran through the battle conditions before scanning the rest of the battlefield.

On all sides the battlefield, several kilometres in the distance, they were surrounded by low-lying cliff faces and rocky hills, terrain that was nearly impossible to pass through. Glass observatories dotted the natural walls, allowing ample space for several hundred thousand people to watch the battle. Those were just the reporters. More aliens, possibly billions, could be tuning in, curious at what the humans could do.

A new sight caught her eyes.

"What are those?" Jessica asked. Something large crawled down the enemy shuttle ramps.

"They look like... hippos, or giant bears," Peter said.

Jessica drew a sharp breath and turned to look down her long lines of pikes. Long pointy sticks against thick hides tended not to end well for pikemen, if her history lessons were anything to go by.

"I hope they have weak points."

She heard a loud *DING* across the battlefield and moved her hands to cover her ears. The sound was followed by an alien announcement translated into English, "BEGIN."

Moments later, the yellow aliens started marching forwards.

Red-skinned pikemen pushed into the dense formation of the four-armed yellow axemen. Arrows, rocks and spears flew overhead and soldiers screamed, roared and shouted at each other.

A column of red soldiers briefly opened up for Jessica and her bodyguard to pass through, heading to the front of the formation.

"What are you doing, Jessica?" Peter called to her using their earpieces.

"I need to get a closer look. Those big bears are tearing the pikemen apart."

"Yeah, good idea. Just don't get our soldiers killed while you're doing it."

As she got closer to the front lines she saw the hulking shape of one of the giant yellow bears bearing down on a forest of pikes. The bear had six limbs, much like the yellow soldiers, with very thick-looking skin and four large, bug eyes. The skin was so thick none of the pikes seemed to penetrate far and they bent and broke.

The bear swiped at the line of red soldiers and sent a handful sprawling to Jessica's feet. Jessica yelled and skipped back out of the way, almost falling on the soldiers behind her.

"Stay cool, Jessica," Georgy called to her.

"Stay out of it," she replied.

"She's a feisty one, I like her already," Peter said.

More giant bears tore into the pikemen up and down the battle lines. Dozens of arrows and spear points turned the bears into pin cushions, but it didn't stop them. Yellow axemen, wearing little but thin leather and wide wooden shields, surged into the gaps the bears were making.

"The eyes," Jessica whispered.

"What was that?" Peter asked.

"I believe she said something about the creatures'—"

"Aim for the eyes," Jessica shouted to the demons around her. Those closest to her heard the command and relayed the message, which became more and more twisted the further the command was shouted.

"Stab the eyes."

"Gouge the eyes."

"Spit at the eyes."

"Remove the eyes."

"Uh, spitting may not help much," she told the soldiers, but they were too busy grunting and shouting to hear.

The pikemen nearest to her pushed forwards. They lost dozens at a time while they attempted to carry out the new mission. Jessica's bodyguard did their best to fend off enemy axemen, but the press and shove of soldiers in the melee prevented them from helping. Jessica almost fell over as soldiers pushed around her, stinking of sweat, blood and urine.

A pike found its mark, piercing a giant bear in one of its eyes.

The bear stopped, surprised at the sudden assault on its face, then turned slowly to stare at Jessica.

To Jessica, it was as if the bear wanted to ask her why... Why would she tell her soldiers to poke it in the eye?

An arrow whistled its way into another eye and the giant bear sat on its hind legs, then opened its mouth and roared in pain. With two of its forelimbs, the bear tore at its eyes, taking globular chunks out of them to try and relieve itself of the pain.

More of the bears started screaming in pain, deafening all those soldiers around them.

"Jess, get out of there, you're losing too many soldiers," Georgy said.

"But we're starting to take them down," she told Georgy

"Look around you, Jess. The bears did their job, the axemen are breaking through your lines and surrounding you."

"Ah," she replied as she looked around. Any further protest died on her lips when she saw what Georgy meant. Despite the bears being forced out of the fight, some of which were dying from self-inflicted wounds, her pike formations were starting to fall apart. The only reason she hadn't noticed until now was her heavily armed bodyguard keeping the nearest axemen at bay.

"Peter, what happened to my flanks?" she asked.

"The bears ate them."

"Where the hell are you?"

"Eating the bears. Look, kid, Georgy's right. They were better prepared than us, we have to retreat."

Jessica bit her lower lip before nodding in agreement. "Can you cover the retreat?"

"I'll do what I can," Peter replied, sounding strained.

Ammon watched, feeling helpless, while the two armies clashed in the middle of the brown field. "No, imbeciles." The yellow creatures that made up their opponents managed to surround a large part of the Terran army and the large beasts crashed through Jessica's pikemen. The beasts died, but not before wrecking the pikemen's lines. Red cavalry led by Peter charged into the yellow army, creating a hole for the Terran pieces to retreat through. Jessica fled towards the small fort that served as part of the end-game.

At the third hour, the Trustee said, "Calm, Ammon. Our players show promise yet but if all is lost for this battle, the Wasp-men will not humiliate them."

"Yes, master." Ammon ground his teeth.

***

"Speak up, Georgy, I can't hear you," Jessica yelled into her mic. One of her shield-bearers had his head caved in a moment later and blood flickered across her personal force-field. Another shield-bearer sliced the offending yellow soldier's hand from its arm. Her remaining shield-bearers crowded around and pushed her away from the edge of the battlements.

Jessica's eyes widened when she noticed a steady stream of yellow-skinned warriors from the enemy team leaping from their ladders onto her demons on the parapets. "Reinforce them," she told her shield bearers. She expected them to protest, her protection was their sole reason for living. Without hesitation, the leader nodded at her, barked at the four other shield-bearers and started pushing his way to the front of the fighting. "Catch the bastards on your swords while they fall," Jessica said as an afterthought. One of the shield-bearers had stayed behind, hefting his long-sword in a high-guard to strike any of the yellows should they come close.

"Jess-ic-ha, more enemy warriors," the last shield-bearer grated as he pointed at one side of the castle walls. Red demons armed with large round shields and small axes tried in vain to cut at the hardened ladders that started docking there.

"You hear that Georgy, you prick? More warriors on our flank," she said into her mic, touching her right hand to her ear to block out some of the fighting. "We need some sort of strategy." She scanned the skies behind the squat three-storey keep they were defending and squinted against the glare of one of the Shellworld's stars. She thought she could see Georgy, up high in the observation platform. An enemy arrow flew at her from below, hitting her personal shield right between her eyes. The shield flickered red for an instant and she jumped back, almost falling off the inside of the parapet to the hard dirt below.

"Calm down," Georgy replied from his observation platform. "I thought you were the medieval expert here."

One of her archers let loose an arrow into an approaching Yellow. The Yellow screamed and fell off its ladder onto the ground below. Another rubbery yellow arm reached the top of the wall in its place. "There are too many of these four-armed fuckers for our axemen to push back."

"I see that, Jessica," Georgy said. "I'm coming up with something."

"Oh, for f—" she cut off her retort as three of her four shield-bearers returned by her side. Two of them had lost their long-swords and had unlatched the shields from their backs, picking up discarded axes from the ground. The third soldier, the leader, had lost part of his left arm but still held its sword in a one-handed grip. The wounded arm was tied with a scrap of a red flag, but small amounts of blood still dribbled onto the ramparts.

"Our soldiers shall hold for several moments, Jess-ic-ha," the leader told her, indicating the remaining axemen and archers still standing on the slick, lumpy parapets thick with dead soldiers.

"How many do we have left?"

The leader glanced across the fort's three long walls and small keep, "Two hundred and thirty, less. Of the enemy, I guess eight hundred."

"Georgy?"

"I'm thinking."

"Damn." She would have to retreat. Retreat meant losing points. It would be hard to scavenge points after the slaughter out in the field. She caught a glance of the battlefield halfway between the two opposing teams' forts; dirt brown ground marred by red and yellow bodies. She had to remind herself that these soldiers, her demons, were more like robots than true living creatures. She wondered if they enjoyed the whole experience, fighting and dying, or if they were emotionless. "The cavalry, where are they?"

"Behind the keep, as ordered," the lead shield-bearer said. Blood loss from the arm was starting to slow him down.

"Georgy, unless you can give me something, I'll have to try another feint or just barricade ourselves inside the keep. Maybe we can throw that hot oil on them, slow them down a bit."

"Haha, let's not do another feint please?" Peter said from the other side of the keep. After the slaughter out on the field, he had spent most of his time hiding the cavalry, complaining as he did so. He'd had enough time to sit down with a snack and light the keep's fireplace.

Jessica marvelled at the authenticity of the games. Someone had been thoughtful enough to add edible fruit trees on the outskirts of the battlefield. They must have been specially prepared just for the human palate.

"Shut up, Peter; go sit by that stupid fireplace. Georgy?"

"Maybe, it's something..." A four-armed yellow warrior leapt onto one of her shield-bearers and bit down on his head while holding the demon's arms at bay. Her shield-bearer shook his head back and forth, ripping chunks of the enemy soldier's mouth and teeth away with the horns on his head. The Yellow let go of his head but held onto his axe and shield. The shield-bearer let go of his axe and swiped forward with the freed hand, gouging a large chunk of yellow flesh from the enemy's throat. By the time the shield-bearer had thrown the new carcass off him, he'd lost half his face. He shrugged at the damage and picked up the axe he had dropped.

"Well, what is it? I'm running out of options down here."

"You're not going to like it. I'm paraphrasing from these rules; this section is a hundred pages long, but I think what it's saying is if one of the team members wants to enter the match and fight, they can. The only problem is, of course, that the game's safeties will be deactivated."

"What?" Jessica said as a spear flew over her head. "You mean I could be killed?"

"Yes, looks like it. You'd also be worth a lot of points to the enemy if you died, but even more, if you are captured, so they won't want to kill you. It's pretty much an automatic win if you're captured. No one does it because it's too risky; you gain nothing from entering the match."

"Okay, got it," she yelled back.

"Got what?" Peter said.

"How many horsemen do we have?" Jessica asked Peter.

"Eighty-eight are left. Why?"

"Good, have half of them dismount and defend the keep from the inside. Guards," she said to her shield-bearers, "I need as many troops as possible to come with me, we're going to break out of the fort. Pull everyone you can back from the walls, whoever can't reach me, try to get to the keep."

"Ah..." Georgy started to say, "I hope you're not doing what—"

"Find a weak spot in their attack, Georgy. Now, how do I enter the game?"

"Sweet balls, you're going to do it, mad woman. A hundred paces to your right, the Yellows have abandoned their ladders there. Girl, I hope you can run."

She directed dozens of demons to form up around her and hurl themselves at the enemy, sometimes literally throwing themselves on top of enemy soldiers that were climbing the ladders to dislodge them and a handful of others, so she could reach the weak point in the assault.

She almost bumped into one of *them*, a wasp-man. It was perched at the top of the wall next to one of the ladders. She passed so close to it that their personal shields flashed red against each other. The wasp-man turned to watch Jessica and her desperate entourage, confused that she had abandoned her defences. It seemed to wave at her then, as if to say, "Hello." She frowned and ran onwards.

Since most of her forces had moved back from the walls, the Yellows came over virtually unopposed. The retreat was so sudden, the wasp-man called a halt to the assault, probably suspecting another feint.

Not quite, Jessica thought.

"Over the walls," she told the demons that had reached her. With robotic precision, her demons slid down the abandoned ladders to land on the dirt below. Once enough demons had gone down they interlocked their hands.

"Jump," the lead shield-bearer said at her shoulder. "Your protective bubble remains; you will not be hurt if they do not catch you."

She jumped and wind whistled in her ears. Strong hands caught her and lowered her to the ground.

"The Yellows are at the keep, Jessica; not many demons made it in. We've reinforced the main door, but I doubt it'll hold for long," Peter said.

"Just hold on for as long as you can. When I give the order, tell the rest of the mounted cavalry to head around to the castle's gate-side." Peter replied with a barely audible curse and shouted something at the demons in the keep with him. "Run now, as fast as you can," she told her group of forty or so demons.

They raced towards the main battlefield between the two castles, dodging thrown spears and arrows. In twos and threes, demons peeled off to slow down handfuls of howling Yellows that charged after her group. At what she thought was about a hundred metres from the castle she clicked on her mic, "Okay Georgy," Jessica was almost breathless as she spoke, "I'm entering the game. How do I do it?"

"Done," he said without hesitation.

"RED TEAM COMMANDER HAS ENTERED THE GAME," a loud voice said in her earpiece.

"I hope this works..." She needn't have worried; a warbling cry rang from the Yellows around the castle wall. "Damn," she said as several hundred heads swivelled in her direction, "Peter, send the cavalry, *now*," Peter grunted into his mic.

"Run Jess, run," Georgy said.

Her demon bodyguards were already dragging her as fast as they could. They didn't bother letting her use her legs. Almost in a panic the shield-bearer leader, who had never left her side since his arm had been cut, dropped his long sword and lifted her onto his shoulders in a fireman's carry. His bloody stump pressed down on her face and she tasted his blood and sweat. She couldn't see or hear much for a time as she was carried over mud, dirt, and bodies. The demon's pounding feet matched her racing heart.

I'm going to die, I'm going to die. Oh, crap, what did I do? Her armour chafed badly in her groin and shoulders and it felt like something bit into her right foot, but she couldn't scream.

Something knocked the wind out of her shield-bearer and she was launched forwards onto the ground, narrowly avoiding the pointy end of a broken spear. Her world spun around her while she rolled and tasted dirt. Pain shot up her right leg and she screamed. Her vision blurred and a rough red hand held her down before she could try to get back onto her feet. A red fence erected itself around her before yellow blobs assailed them.

Her fence crumbled quickly and a round shield blocked her view. She could still hear meaty thuds and terrible grunts beyond that shield, but then something heavy battered at the shield. Her last shield-bearer struggled under the pounding and yellow hands reached around to tear the shield away. She searched with a hand and grabbed an axe, preparing to help her last shield bearer.

"We've got you," Peter said into his mic.

Still dazed, she saw Peter at the head of a tightly packed group of red horsemen. Using spears and leather-padded horseflesh, the horsemen crashed into the disorganized yellow formations and sent them flying for metres around her. A second group of horsemen crashed into the yellow forces from the opposite side, trapping them in a pincer movement. Jessica leapt to her feet and hacked at a yellow soldier while it was staring at the horsemen, then embedded her axe in the neck of another before four of her last demons could come to her aid. Several of the Yellows still tried to reach her, but they lacked cohesion and her demons cut a path through to safety.

In the confusion, Jessica was carried far from the battle and a horseman accompanied her, running down any strays that tried to attack her little group. The Yellows eventually gave up trying to chase the main group of horsemen and elected to regroup at the castle. They were harassed all the way back by Peter's expert use of the cavalry, losing dozens of soldiers each time Peter called a charge.

Once they reached the fort, the Yellows found that they could no longer climb the walls. The remaining defenders had won against the few Yellows inside the keep and had regained the walls. The ladders had been destroyed or taken inside. The defenders now took up bows and started firing arrows at the mass of Yellow soldiers below them.

Trapped between the cavalry and the archers on the wall there were still more Yellows than reds, and they were forming a compact shield-wall. Peter called off his cavalry attacks. They were tired, the enemy archers were still quite dangerous, and any charge would likely see the horses crash against the walls or trip over the bodies lumped nearby.

"Peter, send your cavalry back into the fort, tell the archers to hold their arrows." A small grin formed on her mouth as she remembered some of her history lessons.

"YELLOW TEAM CALLS TRUCE," a voice announced before she could send a new order.

"Georgy, what does that mean?"

"Just a moment," Georgy said, his mic clicked off a second later. Jessica raised a tired hand against the nearest star's glare. She found Georgy's observation platform hovering a hundred metres above the fort's walls. He was gesturing into the air, presumably talking to the observation platform's computer. She sat down and examined an arrow sticking out of her right foot while her guards kept a lookout around her.

A moment later she heard a click, "The computer let me talk to Ammon, he said the wasp-men want to end the game. They don't think they can get any further without losing too many points and they're offering a way out for us because they don't think we can gain any more either."

"Nope."

"Jess?"

"My answer is no. Tell them they need to surrender now."

"Are you—"

"Just do it. Peter, get your soldiers to fetch buckets of oil and grab some logs from the keep's fireplace."

"Ah, I see..." Georgy said.

A few minutes later, black smoke and the smell of burning flesh filled the air.

"YELLOW TEAM SURRENDERS."

"Perfect," the Trustee whispered to itself.

CHAPTER 5

"Our allies will not be too pleased at this insult. Beaten and burned by my upstart humans after such limited training. Such a turn of events. If it weren't the wasp-men's troops I'd be proud."

"Shall I punish them?"

"Punish? No-no... this result furthers my plans. Instead, let them know of our ally's displeasure. I will smooth things over with the wasp-men, then I'll come see our commanders myself."

***

Jessica's smile was slowly curving downwards under Ammon's hard frown. "A disaster," he was telling them on their way back to the *Inveigled Ambassador* from the Shellworld. "A humiliation."

"Bull," Peter said. "We won, we *GAH*!" Ammon slapped Peter on the side of his head.

"My translators indicate that 'bull' is an indecent slur. Show respect to your teacher, Peter Dorn, or you may not live to see the next game." Peter rubbed the side of his head and frowned in silence. "You humiliated your superior opponents spectacularly. Yes, this battle was won, but at such cost. Ninety per cent casualties, loss of both the main field *and* the fort's walls. Your game was being watched by millions of observers. Do you understand this term? Millions? I see that you might grasp the figure.

"Jessica, such a stupid gamble to enter the games, humanity's fate could have been sealed had you been killed or captured. There would have been no more wargames for humanity unless the impossible was achieved in the next two rounds. No chances for furtherance on the intergalactic stage."

"Humanity has gotten *this* far without any help," Jessica said.

"Has it? Would humans truly be alive without the efforts of your predecessors in these games?"

"We put people on the moon," Peter said.

Ammon raised an eyebrow, "An interesting development. So, some advancements have been made, *finally*."

The three competitors looked at each other before Georgy said, "Are you inferring that a long time ago, another team of humans somehow... won some prizes and gained some technology?"

"Hmph, I would have thought the answer an obvious one. I confess I do not know how your predecessors applied their winnings once they returned to Earth."

"How long ago was this?" Georgy said.

"Over two thousand, three hundred and forty years ago, by your reckoning. A marvellous team they were, adaptable, philosophical, great learners." Ammon raised his head and closed his eyes as he spoke. He opened his eyes again to give them each a long look. "What you three have done is... terrible. Under normal circumstances, it would be something of a jest, a good laugh at the misfortunes of our enemies. These are not normal times. The wasp-men offered a fair truce after you humiliated them, but you," he pointed at Jessica with a crooked fingernail, "*burned them alive*." He took a deep breath and sighed loudly, "I managed to collect your winnings, you were also awarded a bonus due to a handicap the Shellworld Games Masters have placed on humans as a minnow team. Interest in your unusual victory is quite intense. I was almost crushed by curious citizens while I was trying to collect the points. But there is another issue now."

"The wasp-men are pissed off and want some revenge?" Jessica said.

"They are unhappy, yes, but they are respectful and are playing in an area that was not their expertise; it is a minor loss for their team overall. No, the issue is that our Trustee's opponents, who are leaders of a powerful faction amongst the Shellworld's caretakers, have taken a keen interest in you. They have petitioned the Arbiter's Guild to enter a team against you for the next game."

Jessica looked around at the broad shuttle, taking in the sparse numbers of still-functioning demons arrayed in lines. The demons were facing the front of the shuttle, oblivious to the conversation taking place in front of them. The bodies of the fallen were packed into large blue crates for transport back to the *Inveigled Ambassador* where they would be brought back to life. "So, these opponents are better than the wasp-men?" She imagined the entire shuttle full of blue crates.

"Jessica, they are champions of thousands of games over tens of millennia. If the petition is successful, we must counter-petition for a forfeit or risk total failure. Your winnings are barely enough to give you some paltry gifts. All the winnings will be lost, and our Trustee will find it very difficult to recover."

Georgy looked thoughtful. "Tell me, Ammon, what will the next game consist of?"

Ammon looked at them all, worry creasing his already wrinkled eyes. "A battle that no humans could ever fully prepare for in the time allotted."

***

"Ammon has little grasp of human history in the last few hundred years," Georgy told them while they tried to sleep on white form-fitting mattresses. "This next game sounds much like World War Two. Or the Cold War. We will be given things like diesel-powered tanks, machine guns, jet aircraft, warships. This must be why I was chosen to lead this round."

"You fought in World War Two?" Peter asked with a sneer. "You must be a lot older than I thought."

"No, you idiot. I was a weapons officer aboard a Russian warship. I have had little military experience, but I assure you, I am very capable. We will *not* lose."

"So certain are you," Peter said in an oddly familiar voice. "What about these... what were they called?"

"The Plinth," Jessica informed him.

"Yeah, Plinth. They sound invincible; wouldn't you say?"

"'Smart, eight feet tall, claws like long knives,' I think the description was," Jessica added. "Like big, brown werewolves. They've won aerial battles, underground cave wars, underwater battles, space battles, hunting contests, eating competitions. Yeah, I made that last part up."

"Who are also tens of thousands of years out of their comfort zone. This sort of war I have first-hand experience in, but to them, it's ancient history."

They all looked at a noise in the middle of their sleeping chamber. There was a hissing sound and a hole appeared in the floor. Liquid steps dripped down, and the room's lights increased their intensity from moonlight to midday sun. They shielded their eyes for a moment and heard someone enter the room from the red-rimmed doorway. "Up," Ammon told them. "Your Trustee approaches; get up."

It navigated the white steps up into their sleeping chamber.

It was dressed in familiar red clothes but stood on large legs that reminded Jessica of a frog and smelled like a rotting, moss-covered tree. The thing's top half looked like a snail's head with arms sticking out of the base of its neck. Its four eye-topped stalks twitched and snapped around to look at her. She heard the others gasp.

"Welcome, Team Earth, I trust you are well," the monster spoke to them with a soft, melodious voice, like a mother calming her brood. "Please, don't be shy, take your time to adjust to the light."

"Well, it's about time," Peter said. "Why couldn't you have come to see us earlier?"

Ammon frowned at him.

"Calm," the monster said, holding up its two small arms in a gesture of peace, "I did not mean to upset you." It turned to one of the walls and pointed at it. The entire wall morphed from soft padding into a large flat screen. A picture of the infinitely flat, wide Shellworld quickly formed on the screen. "This plot of land you see before you is Games Central. I've brought you all here for the one hundred thousand, five hundred and forty-second Inter-Galactic Wargames."

"The one hundred thou—" Jessica started to say.

"Yes, yes," the monster told them, "you are aboard my private cruiser, above Games Central. You have had an upsetting few days. For that, I apologise. I must properly introduce you to your involvement here. The, ahem, 'planet,' which we call the Shellworld, is an artificial construct, approximately five million times the size of your sun. Somewhere around one hundred quintillion people live on the surface, many times that live on the inside and there are thirteen million tame stars to light its surface. Built for a great many reasons, for many years it has specifically been used to host the grandest war games in the galaxy!" The monster pointed at the screen again and the Shellworld disappeared, replaced with a wall of text, the top few words were in English, "This is my name, 'Hubunker.'

"Now, introductions for the rest of you are in order. Hmm," Hubunker studied the wall of text for a minute before continuing. "If only they would give us more time... but oh, hey, I have an idea; you could all state your own names and occupations, that would help me greatly."

"Wait, you don't know who we are?" Peter said.

"I have been a little busy of late, seeing off ruffians, keeping our friends happy, and what have you. I have been watching you from afar, though. Well, hmm, it would help me to know who you are, and then to, ah..." it hesitated, "sort you into your roles."

"Haven't we already done that?" Jessica said, getting more and more worried.

"Silence," Ammon said. "Yes, Hubunker, as this child states, their roles were chosen by your probes already."

The four eye-stalks turned to regard Ammon, then to look at each of the humans at the same time. "They were?"

"Apparently." Peter looked side on at Ammon.

"Fascinating." Hubunker sat down next to Ammon. "Earth team, I am your benefactor, your species' Trustee as it were. You do know what this is all about, don't you?" It paused for a moment. "Is that... are you all giving me the blank face？" Hubunker sighed, "As I said, this is the one hundred thousand, five hundred and forty-second games, which are held once every, maybe, seventy Earth years, so by your relatively short lifetimes the games have been going for quite some time."

"Seven million years," Georgy whispered.

Hubunker heard him, "Ah, yes, close enough, I think... Anyway, each team entered into the games acts as the commanders of armies, each of which is given technology equivalent to different eras of development. For example, the first battle you fought was conducted using technology very similar to that of your Medieval ages, while the last battle will take place over great distances in orbit above the Shellworld."

"Look, we know all of that, but what exactly do we need to do to go home?" Jessica asked.

"I wouldn't mind knowing too," Peter said.

"Uh, there is a slight problem with that particular question." Hubunker held his three-fingered hand up to stop more queries. "There's the question of funds required to send you back. It is a considerable sum and your winnings so far are a small fraction of what you will need."

"Could you just take out a loan to send us back?" Peter said.

"I'm afraid that's not possible. No entity would dare loan me the vast amount of funds needed to send you back. I am quite wealthy, as such things go, but it has taken me a hundred of your years to acquire the funds to bring you here. It would cost even more to send you back."

"Why bring us here in the first place?" Peter asked. "How does it benefit you?"

"As your planet's Trustee, I stand to win or lose certain things that I might desire: more friends among the Shellworld factions, satisfaction in guiding a minnow race of bipeds, and currency of course. I could not run things around here without some *points*. You are fortunate I have continued to take an interest in your species. There are much crueller trustees out here who also have a desire to use your race and tamper with your development. Fortunately, I raised enough funds this time before someone else took away my privileges and I was allowed to send a probe to search for viable candidates.

"The candidates, by which I mean you three, had to meet certain criteria as demanded by the Games Masters. The trouble is, the probe had to select candidates at random, and I'm afraid you three were it." Hubunker made a coughing noise, possibly clearing its throat. "I had little involvement in the selection process."

"So, you paid for three random people to be kidnapped?" Jessica asked.

"To represent your people in a game of inter-galactic importance is a grand honour and *not* something I would have considered a kidnapping. Perhaps it's best you understood that for all our sakes. Much of the remaining funds I have I used to purchase your soldiers. I have little currency left and my fortunes rest with your successes or failures. Ammon, did you not inform them of these things?"

Ammon bowed his head. "We had little time, master."

"Stop calling me, master." Hubunker shook its four eye stalks back and forth in what looked like an imitation of a human shaking his head. "Such a dour fellow. Ah, but where are my manners? Please, tell me about yourselves."

***

"Ah, good, good," Hubunker said after hearing their stories. "So the probe has done well, I see." Hubunker cleared his throat and turned towards Jessica. "A martial artist? Hmm, and a historian? Not sure about you but you had a satisfactory command in the first game. I shall have to review the recordings." He turned to Georgy as if brushing her away. "Mr Ivanov, have you played many non-static games? Think-on-your-feet quickness?"

"Depends on what you mean, but ten-second chess can really keep you on your toes."

Hubunker nodded "You may have some potential, especially with the planning stages for the second game."

A little annoyed at being brushed aside, Jessica interrupted. "I majored in ancient battle strategies and tactics, most of which are still in use by the military today."

"Yes, yes, of that I have no doubt." Hubunker said, "Both of you should do well. Burning my friend's soldiers was a tad ill-considered, perhaps, but the wasp-people assure me there are no hard feelings. Now," Hubunker turned its eyes on Peter, "you, sir. Ammon's praise is very high of your quick-mindedness. I saw some of it on my way here; marvellous job. Excellent use of the cavalry, where did you learn such tricks? You are not of Earth's militaries, just a... a what?"

"Theoretical physicist."

"Ah, science type; to study nature instead of being taught it must be wonderful. Much of what you learn is already known among the factions of the Shellworld, but I cannot fathom more than a drop of that ocean. You must have some special mind to work in that stuff; little wonder you have such command of troops on the field."

"I tell the demons to do something and they do it; and forget morale." He looked at Jessica. "These demons just don't care about dying."

"Why do they look like... demons?" Georgy asked, "I can't imagine our predecessors took too well to how they looked."

Ammon smiled while shaking his head.

Hubunker ignored Ammon. "I fashioned them in this way to be similar to your body shape, so you would know their basic capabilities. The red skin is to match your team's colours. Their resemblance to your 'demons' is a coincidence that I was not aware of. This did present... issues for your predecessors, but you don't seem to have the same qualms." The creature clapped its hands, satisfied at its explanation.

"How long do we have until the next game?" Georgy asked.

"Three days."

CHAPTER 6

"I need all the most recent recordings of the Plinths' battles, specifically those battles in the arena we'll be fighting in. I need a psychological profile on each of the enemy commanders. I need a detailed map of the battlefield and its victory conditions." Georgy was sweating, thinking of all the preparations they would need in less than two days.

"Very good," Ammon said, "we will supply you with these resources."

"An interesting character," Hubunker said to Jessica and Peter while they watched Georgy work at a table in the ship's main hall. Ammon stood next to Georgy and holographic images popped into and out of existence all around them. "He reminds me of some previous competitors from Earth, all business-like, very professional unlike you two; you're so... *emotional*."

"He's worried," Peter said while leaning over the observation deck's railing.

"He should be. Since your first game, more eyes will be turned to your team for the second game. The stakes are raised. You fight the Plinth in two days."

"No, I think he's worried about his dogs," Jessica said, "I'm worried about my parents. We've been gone from our homes for a couple of days now."

"Your absence being noticed is unlikely," Hubunker told them. "Don't you remember what you agreed to when my probe negotiated your entry into the games? I could show you the conversation if you like."

"No thanks," Jessica shook her head, feeling her eyes tear up. "I don't remember much at all. I can't imagine what my friends and family are thinking right now."

Hubunker looked Jessica up and down with two of his eye-stalks while still watching Georgy below. "I can see you are rather upset, Jessica Stanner. A curious choice for the probe to have made. I do not believe, as you may think, that you were chosen by the probe to lead the first game. While I would have liked to use Peter as our second in command for the next game, he was already assigned that role by Ammon for the first. Hmm," Hubunker brought a hand to his lips and started pulling at his wide mouth, thinking something over.

"Well, I'm hungry and tired. Mind if we find some food?" Peter asked.

"I do not mind, let us three gain some sustenance and we will talk of Earth. The probe gathered vast amounts of information while it was scouting but I have little time to assimilate it all and I prefer to hear it from the cat's mouth."

"You mean the horse's mouth?"

"Horses can talk?" Hubunker asked before burping.

***

The image of a Plinth filled half his vision as it stalked across an ash-filled battlefield from a recording several centuries ago. It wore some sort of advanced, silvered armour and started firing a gauss rifle at some unseen opponent. Jessica was right; it looked very much like a werewolf, even with the armour covering it from head to toe. In the corner of his eye, Georgy noticed Hubunker and his fellow humans leaving the observation platform. "Tell me, Ammon, what is the significance of fire? Why is it so upsetting?"

"Mr Ivanov, have you been burnt to death before?"

"We're dealing in demons, not real people. Why does it matter?"

Ammon sighed and wiped his face with his hand. "Mostly, it is tradition. Since before Hubunker was granted Trustee status over humanity from my old master, before the great Pyramids were built, it was poor sportsmanship to use too much fire. The first games were once fought between fully sentient combatants who preferred a swift death over the fear of flames. It's also a little harder to repair soldiers if they are burnt."

"We don't lose any points for using fire, though. If it pisses them off, we could use it to our advantage."

"No, you don't lose points..." Ammon raised an eyebrow at Georgy, "but the political consequences could be severe."

"How so?"

Ammon sighed again and looked towards the ceiling, exasperated, "Never have I been asked to give a lesson in Shellworld politics."

"Well, you're telling me politics affects the games. I want to know how."

"Hmm, while Hubunker gathers what you need, we have some time. Come."

"Where are we going?" Georgy asked after Ammon's receding figure. He was headed for the shuttle bays.

"On a tour, to the Shellworld."

***

Jessica felt as though she was in a dream, floating among the stars, watching pretty lights as they flashed before her.

She occupied one of the *Inveigled Ambassador*'s space battle simulators. Peter floated in another simulator, his red clothing replaced by form-fitting black underwear trimmed in blue. Jessica had taken the baggy red clothing off as well, allowing her more freedom of movement within the zero-gravity sphere of lights.

"So, if we're meant to be preparing for the next battle, why are we dressed in this strange gym gear floating in a battle simulator on a spaceship?"

"Because, dear child, Hubunker thinks we could do with a quick course in zero-gravity. Until Georgy can come up with a plan, we'd just get in the way. Also, that gym gear is a pretty advanced form of spacesuit. I think we'll be using them to go swimming, too, if we need to, in the next game. To be honest, I thought you would have lost your breakfast by now."

Jessica tapped several of the holographic circles within her simulator, then grabbed a bar attached to the simulator's edges and spun over to find more holographic circles, smiling as she did so. "I feel fine. In fact, this is the most fun I've had for a long time." Even as she said it, the horrors of the battle against the yellow aliens were fading to the edges of her mind.

"Well, I'm not," Peter said weakly.

"I thought you used to crew on submarines."

"I did," Peter replied before stopping to hold his mouth. "But at least on a submarine there's gravity. I think I need some nausea tablets."

Jessica laughed at him while spinning to find her next holographic targets. She tapped the holographic circles and with the ends of her fingers flicked the lights in a new direction. Red coloured lights started to encircle the blue lights she'd just flicked, quickly engulfing them in until the blue had disappeared. Jessica frowned, realising her simulation wasn't going very well. A moment later she shrugged and spun sideways to get a good look at a screen where she could see Peter in his simulator. He looked as pale as a ghost.

"Looks like I lost. How are you going?"

Peter peaked over at her through his corresponding screen and grimaced with the effort of keeping his stomach's contents intact. "Well enough."

"I've been thinking, who decides the rules in these games?"

Peter grabbed one of his simulator's bars and covered his mouth again while closing his eyes. He opened his now bloodshot eyes after swallowing loudly and looked at her. "Not the Plinth."

"Well, how do you know?" Jessica asked.

"Because I like to read," he replied.

"Smartarse. You remind me of some of my students."

Peter cracked a small smile. "Glad I could be of service. Anyway, as for who controls the Shellworld? Well, it's kind of like on Earth. The difference is that where we have different countries, the Shellworld has a lot of different factions, like groups of species with common goals who control different territories. Some of the factions control the dwarf stars, others control parts of the outer shell or parts of the thousands of shells and hollow bubble worlds on the inside. Other factions might control large data banks of artificial beings enslaved to do their mathematical bidding."

"The Plinth don't control the place?"

Peter shook his head, then appeared to regret the act and remained as still as he could for several heartbeats, again trying to keep his food down. "No. They don't even control a large minority. The computer told me the Plinth form the central contact point for several million allied races. They have a lot of friends but aren't terribly important by themselves. Other species are much more powerful, living near the Shellworld's innermost shells. They're freaky looking, too, like moon-sized octopuses. They're the ones called the Games Masters. I got the feeling they don't much care about the games anymore, but they did put all the rules in place."

"Talk about freaky-looking, so is your hair," Jessica said with a laugh. Her own hair was waving around in the zero gravity of the simulator in graceful waves. Peter's long curly white hair, normally falling flat on the back of his neck and over his ears, looked like a tangled monster, splayed around his head like a large starfish.

"I'm guessing these wargames help the factions gain more friends?" Jessica asked before turning back to restart her battle simulator on an easier setting.

"That's the basics, yeah," Peter replied. "I didn't get much further than that before Hubunker put us in these torture chambers. Oh, apart from one faction that everyone else seems to be scared of, that is. They're called the Arbiter's Guild."

"And what do they do?" Jessica prompted.

"Well, they judge people. Or whole races, or factions if they want to. If you interfere with the games, you may as well start building a coffin for yourself and all your family and friends."

"That bad?"

"Yep. They're like terminators. Don't annoy them."

"Don't break the rules, got it," Jessica said. "Speaking of family, where are yours?"

"Dead."

"Oh. I'm sorry."

"Yep. I quit the military when my wife died, only for both my sons to die in Afghanistan. Bit annoying, really."

Jessica stopped directing holographic sprites in her simulated battle. "A bit annoying? I'd be devastated."

In the corner of her eye, she saw Peter shrug. "They did me proud. What else can a man do, but keep on living?"

"I guess so," Jessica said, surprised at Peter's calm acceptance of the deaths of his wife and children. It must have been his way of coping, treating it all as if it was a non-issue.

"What about you? Where are your family?"

Jessica felt a pang of guilt as she recalled her parents, both alive and well at home. "They live in Sydney. Dad's a solicitor and Mum's an accountant. A match made in hell if my childhood was anything to go by, but they seem to make it work."

"Your childhood? You're still a kid yourself."

"Tell that to my students." The memory of one her larger senior students saying 'Miss Stanner' in a snivelling tone was still fresh in her mind.

"No thanks, you can keep your annoying teens, I'd rather keep learning here."

"Commanders?" Hubunker's odd voice called to them from a connecting corridor.

"Yeah?" Peter asked, his face turning green as he tried to look back at the corridor.

"Please come. I've decided to try to accelerate your training."

"More simulators?" Peter asked, visibly gagging at the thought. They put their red jumpsuits back on while they talked.

"Yes," Hubunker replied. "This will be a... different experience. These simulators will accelerate your minds while you practice in a digital space.

"Oooh, we're going inside a computer? Just like the Matrix," Peter said, his mouth splitting across his face like a smiling clown.

"A what?" Jessica asked.

Peter's grin vanished and he stared at her. "You've never heard of the Matrix?"

Jessica couldn't help herself. She tried to look confused but started laughing. "Just kidding, old man. I've seen Aliens."

"That's not what I'm... Oh, you're a funny one. Almost as funny as myself."

Hubunker coughed, drawing their attention back to him. "Please, time is thin, follow me."

They walked down, around and up long corridors filled with white light. Moments later they arrived at a dark room that stretched into the darkness. Near the room's entrance, two raised beds that glowed red waited for them.

"Lie down, please."

"Don't mind if I do," Peter said, still looking a bit green.

"Okay," Jessica said. She slid onto one of the beds while Peter hopped onto the other. Something shifted in her vision when she put her head down. "I'm seeing stars."

"It is a digital overlay," Hubunker replied. "You are seeing nothing, but the ship is creating images in your mind. Don't be alarmed, Commander Jessica, but you're already inside the simulation."

***

Two fat snakes, larger than a human, slithered past Georgy and Ammon. Their heads were covered in electronic devices that they manipulated with long tongues. The tongues were forked, and where the forked tongues ended, they split into long tendrils.

The two humans, flanked by a dozen demons, walked further along the white street and Georgy gawped at what he saw. Towers, reaching kilometres into the sky, reflected the light of dozens of stars, feeding the light down to the streets below. White, blue and gold colours surrounded them wherever they went. A short bridge connected the city to other sections of the Shellworld.

What Ammon had called a 'short' bridge covered an area that was several kilometres wide and ran into the horizon. Short was certainly a relative term, here, as the horizon extended tens of thousands of kilometres into the distance. The bridge held trains as tall as the largest battleships Georgy had ever been on. The trains were as long as the city itself and floated on superconducting magnetic rails, leaving the city-sized station every five minutes. Megayachts floated on a higher level of the bridge, churning their way through the water on the top of the bridge at a much more leisurely pace than the supersonic trains.

Below the bridge were battlefields of yellow and purple trees and grasses.

Hundreds of battlefields.

Dozens of kilometre-long starships, each representing a different Trustee of the battling creatures below it, hovered above the battlefields. Some of the ships were pointed arrows, others looked like doughnuts and yet others resembled floating cities.

"Those ships are carefully arranged so as to not upset each other," Ammon was telling him. Georgy was distracted by a small group of beetles, half a metre tall, scurrying towards them. The beetles carried multicoloured backpacks and came to a sudden stop in front of the humans. They seemed to stare at the humans for a moment before scurrying away again. Another alien, much like a jellyfish, floated past them on a puff of air.

"Are you listening?" Ammon asked.

"Yes, sorry."

Ammon cleared his throat, annoyed. "As I was saying, the starships you see up there are clustered to be closer to their own factions. There, those three, they are within five kilometres of each other but overseeing different battlefields. They look after the interests of three different species, but all three Trustees belong to the Deconstructors Guild. Those two over there? Those are part of the Million Star League, the Plinth's faction."

"Just how many factions are there?"

"Too many to count. A faction might control two hundred thousand stars and all of their planets and resources, yet they would be considered a small faction. Most factions are much smaller than this and don't have stars of their own. The more powerful factions control large swathes of the Shellworld's stars, its surface and more importantly, its internal systems. You have to remember, Ivanov, most of the Shellworld's citizens live inside it. Hubunker's Advancement Alliance own five hundred thousand stars and a good portion of the surface, but they are yet to penetrate far into the politics of the internal factions. Come in here."

The two walked inside an open, white archway.

"What's this place?" Georgy asked as he looked inside. It resembled some sort of large, dark, night club. It was empty.

"I'm thirsty," Ammon replied. "Beer, two," he snapped at a black, silver-lined wall near the entrance. A hatch opened to reveal two silver bottles for him. "Here," he shoved one of the bottles in Georgy's hand. "It's good, drink it. Relax."

Georgy burped. "Oops, excuse me," he said while covering his mouth. "These beers are wonderful," he grinned madly, enjoying the odd sensation of the alien beer interacting with the pleasure centres in his brain.

"According to the probe's research of Earth's electronic web ways, most Russians prefer vodka."

"Hah, that's a bit of a falsity. Beer suits just *fine*," Georgy said while slurring his words. "I don't mind Tchaikovsky either but I much prefer the Beatles."

"Hmm, I could request the bar play such songs from the ship's archives if you like?"

Georgy's eyes widened, "You can do that?"

"Can't you on Earth?"

"Well, yes, but not so easily. Please play Here Comes the Sun."

"Original language?"

"English, please." The song immediately started playing through hidden speakers throughout the nightclub. Georgy searched for the source of the song, taking notice of the large number of rounded alcoves in the walls and recesses in the floor where lounges of different colours and sizes all lay empty. The two humans sat in a recessed circular space on red lounges. A small, round black table occupied the centre of their recessed area.

"There must have been a thousand creatures on the footpath we passed earlier, why is this place empty? Not even the demons came in."

Ammon held up a finger. "Pieces. Soldiers. Clones. Not demons, they have no mystical powers."

"*Piercers*, then, I mean... Pieces. Why aren't they in here with us?"

"The question isn't why *we* are in here. The question is why we came. This place is for Trustees and their teams only. It is a place to discuss secrets and strategies, a private creative arena."

"Ah, we would call that a briefing room."

Ammon shrugged. "It is why we are here. We are here to discuss politics. I am drinking because I despise politics."

Georgy chuckled and ordered another beer from the black table. "Don't we all?"

"I'm not supposed to hate it. Back on Earth, before I was convinced to join the games, I was in training to become a king. It was not much fun. The games are more to my liking."

"A king, eh?"

"Pharaoh."

Georgy squinted at the bald man. "You, a Pharaoh?"

Ammon shook his head and swirled the beer around in his cup. "Not anymore. Now, to business: I brought you here to give you some appreciation of the power of this world. The city we have visited is small but contains over a billion individuals, most of whom have similar requirements for a particular type of air, temperature and light. A single starship floating above the battlefields out there has ten times the wealth and influence of this whole city."

Georgy spat out some beer. "So Hubunker really is rich?"

"Unimaginably so. Hubunker is also a ruthless politician. He's using us, Ivanov. By bringing the human race into the games, he's showing the more powerful factions he's an underdog. He's playing the victim to garner support for his Advancement Alliance, to make changes to the Shellworld."

"To change... what?"

"To change the rules of the games and, if possible, to remove the games altogether. But to do so means we need more support. These Plinth, are you sure you can defeat them? They are very good at these games."

Georgy nodded. "They'll be arrogant. It should be easy to unnerve them."

"Good. You need to anger them in such a way that their trustee will call its allies to watch your wargame. If you can anger them enough and their allies come to watch the battle, it will attract the attention of more trustees and other citizens. Those city-sized starships out there? You may notice them drifting towards your battle from those that they're meant to be watching, to get a better look at you."

"This helps us... how?"

"It will distract the Plinth. Interest in this battle will already be heightened, but if you can draw more eyes to your wargame, the Plinth commanders will become very self-conscious. They'll second guess themselves, make mistakes."

***

"I think I'm getting the hang of this," Jessica called over the laser-linked communicator on board her star fighter. She rolled her fighter left, then counteracted the spin by applying an equal amount of thrust in the opposite direction. An entire squadron of star fighters flanked her, keeping a distance of at least ten kilometres from each other.

"Stay on target," Peter said.

"What?"

"Stay on target. Damn, always wanted to say that. Seriously though, you're coming up to within range of the enemy capital ships. Remember how to arm your missiles?"

"Uh... yeah," Jessica said. She watched more than felt her digital arms flip a couple of switches to arm the missiles. "Seems so primitive, shouldn't we be able to control these ships with our minds or something?"

"Then what would be the point of playing wargames? Might as well just let the computers do everything."

"Good point." Jessica scrunched up her face and grabbed her star fighter's stick. The enemy capital ship must've been over twenty kilometres long, huge compared to the hundred-metre-long star fighters. She feared for her wingmen as the capital ship started firing at them with missiles and canon shots.

Alarms screeched in Jessica's ears and she pushed hard on her star fighter's control stick, sending its crescent-shaped nose down, arcing out of the path of an enemy missile.

Two of her wingmen got caught in the firestorm and their anti-matter-fuelled engines detonated. They held just a few micrograms of anti-matter, but the resulting explosions might as well have been nuclear bombs going off.

Jessica's star fighter went into a spin. Stars twirled around her view. Explosions scattered debris and the lights of missiles and other star fighters streaked past.

Her star fighter's HUD suddenly went red and for a fraction of a second she felt a thousand nails sticking into her back.

Her vision returned to normal, the HUD reverted to green and the pain disappeared.

"Dead again?"

"Yep," Peter said. "For the fifteenth time."

Jessica thought she heard a hint of annoyance underneath Peter's normal sarcasm and good humour.

"I'm getting there."

"I suppose. I went ahead and finished the battle without you. We won, thanks to my vastly superior usage of our destroyers."

"Well, sorry," Jessica said, getting annoyed with Peter's arrogant tone.

"It's fine. Let's try it again. The idiots we're blowing up don't seem to mind. One of them even tried cracking jokes before I put a laser into his ship's bridge."

"Oh really, what was the joke?" Jessica asked. "My naivety?"

"No..." Peter said, sounding thoughtful.

"Wait, are you saying they really were telling jokes?"

"Yes. They haven't been speaking to you?"

"Only my wingmen when I give them orders. They've been giving me advice as well."

"Yeah, they're helpful, even when they want to die."

"No, you're not really saying they're actual people we're killing in here?"

Silence answered her.

"Oh, come on," she said, thinking Peter must be laughing at her.

"They're real. Real digital beings who used to have real lives. I think they might be trapped in here, on Hubunker's ship."

"You mean they're sort of... prisoners?"

"More like slaves. They seem to be happy to die. Hmm, I have an idea, let's go kill some and get you some more practice."

Jessica shivered. *Slaves, happy to die...*

***

With the humans distracted, Hubunker pleaded his case, and it appeared this time he may have convinced the various representative creatures to join his alliance.

"Wait a moment," one of the two stick-thin aliens interrupted. "You let a probe pick all three of your commanders for you? Hubunker, the selective process takes months, years on occasion, to sift through a species to locate the perfect commanders. Why did you entrust a probe with this task? I note that none of the three are military personnel."

"Are you belittling our artificially intelligent friends, Chort of the Fifty?" Hubunker replied. "Yes, the probe chose my commanders, but only after five hundred years of tweaking the algorithms. They're not currently of humanity's militaries, but I assure you, they are very capable as the recordings have proven."

"You've said this once before," a robotic spider clicked at him. "Our representative observed your 'Jean' lose an un-losable battle, or had you forgotten that, Hubunker?"

"Jean was useful. Is *still* useful," Hubunker declared. Ammon turned his head sharply and gave Hubunker a warning glare.

"*Still* useful?" Chort asked. "Are you implying that your Jean still plays a role in the games? I was of the impression that humans were a short-lived species, or are they all like your pet here?"

Ammon's eyes moved to slits at the insult.

"Ah... no. Jean is not *directly* involved," Hubunker replied. He snapped his fingers. "Just get me those plans. My friends, the waspmen, are heavily indebted to my cause; they have the funds to see that you are paid for your services. But tell me, if my commanders can indeed force a truce, or pull off a miraculous victory against the Plinth, will you join the alliance?"

A creature, much like a giant bat from Earth, screeched at him and flapped its vestigial wings. "You make me laugh, Hubunker. You truly believe your humans have a chance at defeating the Plinth? Nobody has defeated the Plinth in a million years."

"That's an exaggeration," Ammon said quietly. Hubunker wagged a finger at the human, telling him to be silent among the assembled beings.

"Gentlebeings, I assure you it can be done. When was it the last time that the Plinth were tested? This is the very problem with the games. The Plinth pick their battles and humiliate all challengers to retain their power. Just give me this one chance - if my lowly humans can hold the Plinth to a truce, or defeat them, the Plinth will lose much of their alliance. They'll be distracted, weakened, and my agents will strike. What say you?"

"Fine, Hubunker," one of the robotic spiders clicked in response. "Provided your humans can achieve this feat, we will move our vessels in support of your own. Too many times have we seen the Plinth use their influence to become Trustees and abuse their beneficiaries. Too many times have the Plinth ruined our plans for expansion within the fifth shell. We will provide you with the information you seek, but until your humans prove themselves, our presence here was just a dream."

"I understand." Hubunker turned to the rest of the assembled beings, seeking their answers.

"You want a war, Hubunker? We'll join you if the Plinth are beaten," the bat said.

***

With Ivanov safely aboard a shuttle on his way back to the *Inveigled Ambassador*, Ammon decided to pay his old friend a visit.

The elevator, a hundred paces to a side, ascended a shaft on the inside of one of the city's tallest buildings. He wondered what his old friend would say when Ammon saw him. It had, in fact, been several hundred years since they'd had a chance to meet. Hubunker had kept Ammon very busy, laying the foundations for the new alliances.

Ammon ignored the various floors as they flickered past on the other side of the wide elevator's clear doors. Beings of many shapes, sizes and colours on each floor glanced at him, curious at what being would be allowed to use the tower's central elevator. Their business resumed the moment he passed their floors.

Even as he sat at the elevator's centre, approaching his old friend's top floor home, Ammon wondered why he bothered to come. Was he looking for comfort? Or for reason in the approaching madness of his master's designs?

The elevator stopped and the glass doors opened onto wide, windowed walls that overlooked much of the white city. As Ammon approached the windows, he saw airships coming and going throughout the bustling city. The top floor of the tower stood over ten kilometres tall and clouds obscured much of the view of the city but he could still see endless needles poking through the clouds that represented the tops of other skyscrapers.

"Ammon, you came."

Ammon turned and bowed. "Yes, old friend." He sniffed, smelling the sweet scent of berries wafting from his old friend's diminutive body. Ammon kneeled down to meet his friend at a similar height.

"It has been a long time," his friend said.

"Yes, Trustee Lodis, it has. It still would be longer if I had not had this rare chance to meet with you."

Even though Ammon kneeled down, Lodis stood a head shorter than him. The Trustee resembled a large rat standing on its back feet, with a flat, expressive face and stubby, finger-length tail. Lodis wore purple robes, trimmed in golden circuits that flashed with each movement. The golden circuits, Ammon remembered, connected directly into Lodis' nervous system, greatly expanding his mind from that of a simple rodent to one of the smartest trustees Ammon had ever met.

Lodis sighed. "Are you drunk, old friend?"

"No," Ammon said and shook his head, a little too vigorously. He tried not to breathe too much so that Lodis didn't have to smell his breath. "I took some supplements, I am sober. Or will be soon."

"Then you have not come to drink with me and something is troubling you."

"Yes," Ammon replied. He wanted to lie, to say that he'd simply come to greet a friend, but that was pointless. As former champions in the games all trustees had access to the greatest gifts the Shellworld could bestow. In fact, only gifted beings could become Trustees.

Had Ammon lied, Lodis would know it.

"Come and sit," Lodis pointed to the wall next to where the elevator doors were. They could have moved elsewhere to talk, but there was little point, one spot in Lodis' large circular home was as good as any other. Two seats moulded themselves from the white walls, perfectly matching Ammon and Lodis' sizes. The window view of the city shifted and grew downwards to cover the floor so that they appeared to be sitting on the edge of a tall mountain. Ammon winced when he remembered the first time the view had changed like that, thousands of years ago. He'd clung to the walls like a scared child.

He wondered how the current human competitors would act; they seemed used to, or at least understood, some of the Shellworld's technology.

"Lodis, I have to ask, how are your new beneficiaries?"

Lodis glanced sidelong at Ammon before replying. "They progress in the games in leaps and bounds, as do many others. My chosen commanders have won many gifts and their people have grown in stature as a result."

"You treat them well."

"As I treated you."

Ammon nodded and almost lost his composure, saddened by recent events. "I remember well. If only you were still humanity's trustee, I may be home as we speak, ruling my homeworld as benevolently as you guide your beneficiaries."

"You worry, then, about your current trustee?"

Ammon nodded. "Trustee Hubunker is ambitious, as you know. I feel more like a tool than a member of a minor race."

"You disagree with his methods, young Ammon?" Lodis stared at him, trying to read his mind.

Ammon remained silent for a moment, choosing his words carefully. "My people need guidance that I fear Hubunker is not adequately providing."

Lodis stood from his small chair and walked across the windowed floor, as if floating in the cold air beyond. "I cannot provide what you seek, my friend. My duty is to my current beneficiaries, not to the derailment of Hubunker's mischievous plans."

Ammon's mouth opened a little, startled as he was that Lodis knew something of his master's plans.

"Yes, I know Hubunker's mind. I'm small of stature and small of wealth, comparatively, but I am not small of mind or power, in my own way. This... Advancement Alliance he has been gathering... it signals a dangerous shift in the surface factions, one that I wish to have no part in."

"But master—"

"Silence, Ammon," Lodis said while holding up a scrawny, four-fingered hand. Ammon's next words were choked off as if Lodis had reached out and slapped him in the throat. He reached for his mouth to try and pull an invisible hand from it, but the feeling vanished. "Yes, I know Hubunker's roots run deep into the Shellworld. His cause is a worthy one. To think, if he succeeds, the rules could be re-written. We could start exploring the universe as you and I always wished to do. The wonders we could discover... I hear rumours of other shellworlds, other empires bigger than ours at the edge of the universe. Imagine that. Alas, a planet a day arrives through the wormhole gates above us to be torn apart and used for spare parts instead of being explored and admired. Yes, Hubunker might put an end to the stupidity but," Lodis punctuated his speech by poking the air with two clawed fingers. "His enemies have roots further and wider than he could hope to imagine. If tensions continue, expect serious repercussions from my old Plinth masters."

Ammon frowned, irritated by Lodis' obvious fear. "If you will not supplant Hubunker as humanity's trustee, and you will not join the alliance, then you would let the games continue and all developments and science stagnate. You say yourself a planet a day is brought here to be dismantled by the world crushers. You could help us convince the Games Masters to stop this, once and for all..." Ammon hung his head, feeling defeated. "You survived the teachings of the Plinth once before; you can survive again."

Lodis walked back over to Ammon and patted his hands. A small surge of energy seemed to freshen Ammon's arms with each touch of the small creature's claws. "I survived, that is correct. I prospered under the Plinths' brutal teachings. My family? My world? My species? They were not so fortunate. This is why I gave up the trusteeship over humanity - the further you were from the Plinth, the better. I did you a favour, my friend. I fear for this world, Ammon. I fear that the games may end but the war will remain if Hubunker's machinations continue."

"I... I'm sorry."

"Don't be. You pleaded your case. I have now rejected it. Let us be friends once again. Besides, the Games Masters no longer care what we do up here and no amount of convincing will help. They sleep and wither away while we play wargames in their honour. Tell me of your plans again, for when you return to your homeworld. How you're going to conquer your people through love and brilliance. Tell me again of those funny hopping creatures, they remind me of a fellow I met some years back."

"I will. I'll even tell you what became of my family. The people of my world have finally rediscovered them. Just promise me, please."

"Promise what?"

"If Hubunker's plans fail and humanity survives, help my species in the times to come."

Lodis closed his eyes and slowly shook his head, then growled quietly to himself. "I will do what I can. But you owe me in return."

"What is it?"

"There's a rather expensive bottle of my finest beer, seventy-thousand years old, still vacuum fresh after all this time. I'll need some help to drink it."

Ammon's mouth watered at the thought. "Brewed in the seventeen-hundredth shell below this city?"

"Give or take a few shells, I can't remember exactly where I bought it but it's good stuff. The last bottle's in my private study beneath the tower observatory. It's meant to last me several months but with your help I suspect it may just take the afternoon... and part of the night. Please go fetch it."

"With pleasure," Ammon said and almost jumped to his feet, the unpleasant business of a few moments before all but forgotten. He started off towards the giant tower's kilometre-wide observatory to hunt for Lodis' precious beer.

"Don't forget the cups. I can't drink from a bottle twice my height."

Ammon grinned as he walked.

***

She heard voices.

The room was dark when she woke up. Her mouth was dry and tasted foul from the broth she'd eaten while recounting Earth's history to Hubunker. She thought she could smell bile. It was always light when she woke up, but, this time, the only light came from the red-rimmed doorway to the main hall. She looked around the dim room and saw Georgy and Peter asleep on their form-fitting mattresses. Georgy snored quietly, and Peter's white pony-tail rose and fell on his belly.

Where are the voices? she thought. She sat up. *There,* they were coming from the main hall. Quietly, without disturbing the others, she crept out onto the observation deck. The voices got louder, and she could make out different syllables in alien tongues. *Why isn't the ship's translator working?* she thought. When she reached the observation platform, she peered down at a small group of creatures bathed in the red lights of ship's night time. Hubunker and Ammon were addressing six other aliens, one of whom seemed to be of the same species as Hubunker. A wasp-man was among them as well as a couple of metre-high robotic spiders, a giant bat, and two stick-thin humanoid figures twice Jessica's height.

Hubunker burped and barked, the wasp-man rubbed its arms together to whistle and the bat screeched a reply that made her jump. She could hear Ammon's grating tones but could not make out the words, he was speaking his native language in a quiet manner. There seemed to be some tension in the group, it was hard to tell. It was the strangest conversation she had ever witnessed.

After a few minutes, the visitors started filing out of the large hall into one of the side rooms where Jessica knew a shuttle would be. Ammon turned around and saw her watching them. "Come down, Jessica," he said as if to a frightened child. One of Hubunker's eye-stalks looked at Ammon and then at the observation platform.

"Yes, come, Jessica, you no doubt have some questions," Hubunker waved off the last of the visitors with one hand and beckoned to her at the same time with his other. White liquid shot out of the observation platform, cascading down to the floor of the hall, solidifying into the shape of steps.

"Wow," Jessica mouthed while moving down the stairs. To Hubunker, she said, "Who were they, your visitors?"

"An assortment of like-minded individuals, allies you might call them. Backers, investors, creditors. We form something of a web of support."

"So, they're your friends? Just them?"

"Remember some respect, child," Ammon warned her.

"She is only curious, Ammon. Yes, friends of a sort. They, in turn, have many other friends among them, many individuals of great influence who are sympathetic to my cause. Together, as a group, we form the Advancement Alliance. We were once small but we're growing. We now control half a million of the Shellworld's stars, enough to challenge the more powerful factions."

Jessica frowned. "Your cause? What exactly are you trying to achieve?"

"Control of the Shellworld, of course. We want the power to say how the world and its many resources are used. But first, the Plinth need to be put in their place."

"Oh. That sounds ambitious..."

"Come, sit," Hubunker motioned with one hand and a table with three seats formed from the floor. "None of us today, none of our allies or the Plinth or anyone else, have the smallest inkling of why the Shellworld was built, and it is likely that the Shellworld will exist far into the future after we are all gone. There are many theories as to why it was built, one of which states that to survive some future calamity the races of this galaxy and those around us must band together to find the greatest minds. This is done through the games, to sharpen minds, to further creativity and preparedness for potential challenges in the future. Those races that do well are rewarded. Those that are unbeaten? They control how the games are run."

"That seems a little unfair," commented Jessica.

"That's the problem - The system is stagnant, those at the top, such as the Plinth, make the rules. Minnow races, such as humans, are given high barriers to entry so that they cannot compete. There is no creativity anymore. I am trying to break this stagnation and end these games for good, to seek better means of creativity and the strengthening of minds."

"Why not just give other races like humans these 'gifts' yourselves?"

"The reigning factions would not allow it, it would hinder their power here. If that were done, the Plinth would have your race wiped out at the first opportunity and have you branded cheaters. It has been tried before by others. Ha. There is too much potential for this world to be wasted on wargames. There is still so much we could learn of the universe. Ah but these matters should not concern you, your future lies in the games themselves and the glory they hold." Jessica thought she heard a touch of sarcasm.

"So why were your friends here?"

Ammon cleared his throat, "Perhaps we—"

"No, my friend, one more question will not hurt. Mr Ivanov requested some rather sensitive information in the preparation of your next wargame. This information is difficult to come by and while not illegal to obtain, there is a great deal of hoop-jumping to slide through."

"Hoop-jumping?"

"Indeed, the Plinth will be quite upset if they knew we had obtained detailed plans of the next battlefield and psychological profiles of their commanders. I adore Mr Ivanov's thinking. Fire, burning. Haha. He will advance my plans more than I could have imagined…" Hubunker hiccupped and held his stomach; Jessica smelled mouldy cheese on his breath. "If you can win, that is. Perhaps, Jessica, it is time for you to sleep now. There is a lot of material to cover, and Mr Ivanov will require what aid you can give him, once you're well rested. Goodnight."

"Goodni—" she was cut off by a buzzing sound. One of the ship's multi-coloured probes dropped from an opening in the ceiling and sung at her with blue fire. Pleasant perfume filled her nose and her limbs went limp.

CHAPTER 7

"Did you sleep at all in the last couple of days?" Peter asked Georgy as the *Inveigled Ambassador* and its small flotilla of black shuttles descended towards the waiting battlefield, "I swear you were drilling the poor devils non-stop."

Georgy snorted. "How could I have slept with such snoring from yourself? Besides, I'm a sailor, an officer of the Russian Navy; I can do without sleep for quite some time."

"You forget I've crewed submarines, Ivanov. Still, you sure you won't fall asleep while tanks are rolling towards us?" Peter asked with a grin. "Should we have one of the shield-bearers pull a coffee cart around behind you? You're looking a little dark under those eyes."

"Ha, I'm old and fat, Dorn, not tired."

Jessica ignored them and looked over the equipment their team would be bringing to the battle. Most of the soldiers and equipment were in the shuttles, assigned to land in different areas instead of all together as they did in the first battle, but there was still plenty to gawk at in the *Inveigled Ambassador*'s main hall.

They had a sea-going warship. Taking up half the hall's length, the 115-metre vessel was immense inside Hubunker's ship. It had been delivered by the Games Masters' servants mere hours earlier, matching specifications chosen by Georgy a day ago. The warship would be used in the opening stages of the battle. Once the sea battle took place, a land invasion by the victor would follow. The bow of the destroyer-class ship towered above her and she felt claustrophobic underneath the metallic weight.

Jessica was concerned about Georgy's choice of weapons. Arrayed along the walls of the hall were row upon row of incendiary grenades and Molotov cocktails. The warship was mostly loaded with incendiary shells, and she'd seen primitive flame throwers being carried onto the shuttles alongside small tanks and basic rockets. *What is he doing, pissing off the Plinth like this?* she thought to herself. Ammon had not been happy to hear of Georgy's choice of weaponry but had been overruled by Hubunker.

"We are almost there, commanders," Ammon said. "Remember this: the Plinth are ruthless masters of battle. They have won more games than all the wars ever fought on Earth. You defeated the wasp-men, our Trustee's allies, and by defeating you, the Plinth seek to humiliate our allies. Fight well, for even in defeat there is honour and points to be won."

***

The arena was far larger this time.

The opposing forces were fighting for control of two separate islands at each end of the rectangular arena. The arena stretched a hundred kilometres from one end to the other, yet, using binoculars, Jessica could still see the enemy fleet approaching from the other side of the vast area.

The 'ocean' was flat, not curved over the horizon like on Earth, and the water lapped softly against the edges of the ship like a calm spring day. A light mist gathered above while two starships, themselves the size of small cities, floated above the arena, keeping a respectful distance from each other. Hubunker's *Inveigled Ambassador* took a defensive posture over the island the Terran forces were defending, while the Plinth's yellow, crystalline behemoth of a starship loomed above the centre of the arena.

Distant white walls, several kilometres high, marked the arena's rectangular edges, where giant spires reached into the sky. Jessica knew there were millions, maybe hundreds of millions of beings packed into those spires and all along the walls, recording everything that happened and broadcasting it to the billions or hundreds of billions of spectators.

Apparently, this was a momentous event in recent Shellworld history.

Jessica almost laughed. She felt hysterical, scared, amused; she wasn't really sure. She was in the captain's chair of the destroyer, facing down a much larger enemy ship and a small fleet of twelve troop carriers behind it. *"Chase the splashes, Jessica,"* Georgy had instructed. *"Don't worry; they're not used to this sort of warfare."*

Well, neither am I, she thought and clung tightly to her chair while the ship swung in almost forty-five-degree arcs.

Chase the shots... Every time the Plinth battleship fired its much longer-ranged guns at Jessica's destroyer and hit the water, her demons would steer towards the splashes. By the time they reached the splash, the Plinth crews had re-targeted at a shorter range, trying to predict where Jessica's destroyer would be. It seemed to be working so far.

It would be a couple of kilometres before the human destroyer could fire with any sort of accuracy and by the time they could fire, the Plinth would be able to bring their own shorter ranged guns to bear. They'd made it this far though, surviving twenty minutes of gut-wrenching turns to close the distance.

The Plinth were using soldiers identical to their own genetic makeup, saving huge amounts of points.

The Plinth considered themselves the perfect soldiers. Up to a third of the human team's points for the battle were used up in the demons themselves, so they were already at a disadvantage. Georgy had to cut costs somehow, which meant an inferior fleet. He'd clearly expected the destroyer to be defeated and had thoughtfully told Jessica to put a wetsuit and scuba-diving gear on.

The oxygen and nitrogen tanks currently sitting on her back chafed and twisted her back every time the ship violently swung from side to side.

She heard a whistling sound before water splashed half a ship's length in front of them and fresh-water sprayed over the ship, carried over them by a strong breeze. A few drops splashed against the bridge's forward windows and Jessica flinched. "They almost hit us that time."

"Stay calm, Jessica. Are you in range yet?" Georgy asked from back on land, almost twenty kilometres away.

"Damn." She almost hit her head when the demon at the wheel made a random turn. "We there yet?" she yelled. The demon manning the range finder nodded at her. "Yeah, we're in range," she replied to Georgy.

"Okay, they've probably worked out what you're doing. Have your sailors move in the opposite direction to the shots. It won't work for long, but you should be able to get a good salvo off, maybe slow them down."

Another splash sprayed the side of the ship and she almost fell out of the chair from the demon's manoeuvring. "I really wish you had put the torpedoes on the front of the ship."

Jessica could almost hear Georgy shake his head. "No point. Just start firing the incendiaries." She groaned but gave the order to fire their first salvo. When another enemy shell splashed down behind the ship, she ordered the demons to stop dodging and level out the destroyer to give the gunners a steady position to fire from. Demons on the deck then cranked the ship's main turret to a higher elevation and swivelled it towards the distant target.

"Cover your ears," her range finder told her. She did so, just in time. The guns fired. Jessica felt the shock of the shots and saw bright flashes and smoke escape the muzzles of the guns. She coughed when the black smoke wafted over the bridge.

"Why don't our personal shields work for noises and smells?" she asked out of frustration.

"It's a battle simulation," Peter said. "You have to be a part of it *somehow*." Peter's platform had been floating several hundred metres above the ship the whole time and Jessica envied his comfortable position. She gave him the middle finger as if he could see it.

"The enemy vessel is manoeuvring," the bridge's spotter told her.

"Will we hit it?"

"I do not know, it is slow. They are firing again. There, a hit."

"Holy crap, did I hear him say a hit? From the first shots?" Georgy asked them.

"That's what he said. Spotter, any damage?"

"A little, the shell hit the bow, I see some smoke but nothing critical was hit. Maybe some small guns."

"That's some damn good shoo—" Georgy's comment was cut off by a loud bang when something big and fast slammed into the destroyer. Jessica was knocked to the bridge's metal floor and some demons lost their footing. Her ears were ringing when she got back onto her feet. She held onto a nearby railing while the ship took more evasive action. Down on the deck below was a gaping hole on the ship's port side.

"The ship is hit," Peter said for Georgy's benefit, "not bad thou—" Another explosion cut them off, smaller this time but much closer. Jessica peered out of the bridge's port side door at a smouldering machine gun and tasted toxic fumes.

She snarled, "Return fire."

"Keep your cool, Jessica," Georgy said.

"Shut the fuck up."

"The enemy vessel is manoeuvring for a broadside," her spotter said.

At two kilometres apart, the ships passed each other. Shells fell around the ship, some slamming into its side. Hot fragments and demons went flying. The ship listed to starboard as its lower decks took on water from torpedo damage. The starboard side was unrecognisable by the time the ships had passed. Holes littered the deck and demons raced to quell multiple fires throughout the ship and patch man-sized holes with spare scrap metal.

They were fortunate, most of the enemy shells were armour piercing and had gone right through the human ship's thin hull instead of exploding inside it. Jessica could see many small holes in the Plinth's battleship but they were pin-pricks compared to its overall size. Smoke engulfed the enemy ship while chemical fires raged across its superstructure.

The Plinth were ignoring her, leaving her destroyer to die. "Deploy torpedoes," she called out from her ruined bridge. "Fire the whole salvo. Tell the engine room to put out more smoke. Everyone else abandon ship and bring the explosives with you."

With hisses of compressed air, ten torpedoes dropped into the water and streaked away towards the enemy ship's rear. Having dismissed the destroyer and distracted by the fires on their deck, the Plinth noticed the torpedoes when it was too late. Three of the torpedoes hit their target, destroying almost all the battleship's engine turbines.

Jessica swallowed water when her demon bodyguards dragged her into the artificial ocean. With their help, she managed to get the breathing apparatus attached before they pulled her under the water.

"Beautiful work, well done, Jessica," she heard Georgy say in her earpiece. She couldn't reply while she was being dragged by her demons several metres below the water's surface, but she didn't have to.

"Their troop carriers are going ahead without the battleship," Peter said.

"Good. You've pissed them off, Jessica. The arrogant bastards think they can take our beach without naval fire support."

"They still have the numbers."

"Yes, for the moment."

***

"The Plinth Trustee is moving. They've started signalling to their allies." Ammon told Hubunker.

"Good. We have their attention now. Send the word out to all who will listen, have the Advancement Alliance broadcast it; the Plinth are trying to intimidate us and our commanders, yet again."

Ammon hesitated before answering, "The whole Alliance, master?"

"All of them. The Plinth will want revenge for my commanders burning their troops. We need to provoke them further."

Ammon frowned. "Is that wise?"

Hubunker stayed quiet for a moment, watching the wargame unfold below them while paying attention to the yellow bulk of the large Plinth starship bearing down on the *Inveigled Ambassador*. He flicked a single eye-stalk in Ammon's direction, annoyed that he would question humanity's Trustee.

"You are afraid for your students. I understand. I need you to understand this: this is the moment we have been waiting for. This is the moment you need, Ammon of Earth, to achieve your goals. Remember that. This is what we have been building towards for centuries"

"I..." Ammon shook his head. "There will be consequences."

"I know this. As head of the Advancement Alliance, I have always known. Will you comply?"

"It will be done," Ammon turned on his feet and headed for the *Inveigled Ambassador*'s bridge.

"Good."

***

Goosebumps started to form on Jessica's arms and she shivered in her wetsuit while she held onto one of the Plinth ship's wrecked propellers. The ship was dead in the water while Plinth soldiers worked mere metres above to clear the wreckage and try to fix one of the turbines. She pointed up at the enemy soldiers and drew a finger across her neck. Her demons ascended toward the Plinth repair crew who were taken completely by surprise. As the purple blood spilled out around her and her demons, she wondered how many more Plinth were still alive and did a head count of her own troops, coming up with around fifty dark-suited demons still with her.

As quietly as they could, they surfaced and unstrapped their scuba tanks. They let the tanks float away and started to climb the ship's port side near the bridge, hoping the Plinths' attention was focussed on the starboard hull and the few small fires that had managed to spread below decks. The demons dug their claws into the rims of large bolts and climbed to the top. Under the cover of smoke, the lead demons took out pistols from within their wet suits and quickly searched the area before throwing down some ropes and hiding under the bridge's outside stairwell. After ten demons had climbed over the ship's side, they headed for the nearest gun emplacement to plant explosives.

The deck was quiet while Jessica was lifted onto the ship. The wind-blown smoke stung her eyes. She ordered a handful of her troops up the bridge's stairwell and they crept forward with pistols pointed towards the bridge's hatch. More demons reached the deck and headed for hatches leading to the decks below to plant explosives in the ship's armoury.

One of the demons near the guns used hand signals to communicate with those closer to her.

"What is it?" she whispered to her small group after they received the message.

One of her guards nodded towards the demons at the guns, "They spot Plinth troops, perhaps twenty of them, going over the ship's starboard side. Others are coming from below deck. They may have spotted the dead repairmen."

"Go," she hissed, "go-go-go." Her demons charged the rest of the way up the bridge and she heard an ear-splitting screech coming from somewhere above her. The bridge's hatch swung open and her demons opened fire at the Plinth troops coming out.

The battle erupted all over the ship. Her demon's explosives detonated with a boom loud enough to deafen her and the 'pop-pop-pop' of pistols were met by the roar of much larger rifles. Her lead demon reached the bridge's hatch before it could be closed and tackled the nearest Plinth, disappearing inside. More demons piled through the hatch. Jessica reached the bridge and watched as the Plinth and demons shot and tore at each other. The Plinth were half a metre taller than the demons and lashed out with three-inch claws.

It was the first time she'd seen a Plinth so close; she stood in shock at the sheer size and ferocity of the werewolf-like physiques. A demon's face was torn to shreds by a single swipe of a Plinth soldier's claws and another fell from multiple rifle shots but it wasn't long before the demons overwhelmed their larger opponents.

Three demons lay dead among five Plinth who had been unprepared for the attack. "Lock the hatches," Jessica said. "We need to give our troops downstairs more time." Even as she was giving orders, she saw Plinth stalking towards the bridge from outside, firing across the main deck at someone near the closest exhaust stack.

From a ladder leading to the ship's fire control room on the next deck up, she saw a Plinth peer down at her, "Up there," she said while pointing. The nearest demon grabbed a grenade from a dead Plinth and threw it up the ladder.

Jessica covered her ears, but the explosion was far louder than she'd expected. A tremor vibrated the floor of the bridge and a demon ducked for cover. Glass shattered from the explosion and shards licked against her personal shield in yellow and red flashes of energy. This was more than a grenade explosion. Her demons had succeeded in blowing up the ship's armoury.

It took a whole minute before she could hear anything again. She looked around at the bridge and thought she saw pretty red flowers and fireflies, but slowly realised an intense gunfight had erupted around her. "BROWN TEAM SECONDARY HAS ENTERED THE GAME," a loud voice announced over the top of the carnage.

"What's going on?" Georgy said.

"She did it," Peter said. "Their ship is gone for good."

"How? Why? And why did a Plinth enter the game?"

Jessica didn't hear the reply; two Plinth soldiers killed her last demon inside the bridge. The demon managed to cut the jugular of one of them before the Plinth's claws slashed his stomach open and they both fell to the floor. The final Plinth stared at her.

"Did you hear me?" Peter was asking her.

"Oh, damn," she whispered before crawling over broken glass towards a corner, her heart racing. It kept staring, opening and closing its bloody fur-covered hands.

"It happened right after a dozen city-sized space ships blocked my view of the sky," Peter continued talking. "The floating castles up here must be the Plinth's buddies, cheering it on. It's like the thing wants to prove something to them. The rest of the Plinth have been acting oddly, too. It's like they're not sure what to do, or they're showing off."

She looked for some sort of escape. The ship started tilting and she finally saw the damage on its superstructure. The whole first third of the ship had been split open and oily black smoke blanketed everything. She looked back at the Plinth, which was slowly stalking towards her with its large fangs on display. "Breathe," she said to herself. "It can't hurt you."

"What can't, Jessica?" Peter asked.

"The Plinth," she stood up while it towered over her. She wrinkled her nose at its meaty breath.

"Get out of my way," she said and tried to step around it. It stepped in front of her while growling to force her back into the corner. "It's not letting me get out of here. It's blocking me from moving out of a corner on the bridge."

"What colour is its fur?"

"Ah..." she paused while looking at the fur under the thing's grey body armour, "light brown, almost blonde."

"That's him, Jessica," Peter said with a hint of frustration.

"Him who?"

"Didn't you hear the announcement? The enemy Secondary is a light brown colour, not purple; you're looking at him."

"Well, crap," she said while shaking from adrenaline. "Isn't blocking me like this sort of... cheating? The bastard stinks worse than the smoke up here." She heard distant gunfire, and the Plinth commander looked down at the smouldering ruins of its once-mighty battleship. With a suddenness that made her jump, two bird-shaped aircraft roared over the ship, heading towards the human beach. "They have jets."

"Understood," Georgy said.

"How many points is killing an enemy commander worth?" she asked as she fingered the knife at her back

"Oh wow, the silly girl's at it again," Peter said. "How do you propose you do that? The Plinth must be five times stronger than us."

The Plinth commander was watching her closely, taking in every word she was saying and ignoring the gunfire and explosions below them. "I'm going in. Peter, enter me into the game, now before it's too late."

"No, Jessica, they'll kill—"

"RED TEAM SECONDARY—" She didn't hear the rest as she kicked off the wall behind her to dive on top of the Plinth commander. Searing agony embraced her back as claws dug through her wetsuit. She screamed. Giant teeth gnashed at her face, but she held them away with one hand and a knife that she'd plunged into its neck.

Several heartbeats later, it was dead.

She felt hot liquid roll down her back and legs as she unlocked and stumbled out of the bridge's port-side hatch. She tripped over a demon's body on the way out and fell onto the stairs outside. She noticed movement below her and picked up a nearby pistol. She tracked the movement until it was below her and saw the red skin and white crown of a demon's head. She dropped the pistol and let the demon pick her up. Two more demons waited for them at the bottom of the stairs with captured Plinth rifles raised to their eyes.

One of them started firing but she didn't hear it, she couldn't hear anything.

She was starting to lose colour from her vision. Everything was turning to shades of grey and she heard blood rushing around her ears like white noise.

Coldness engulfed her body. She was floating.

Something dark and rubbery covered her face, blowing air into her mouth.

Strong red arms dragged her down into the water's depths.

Darkness.

CHAPTER 8

Jessica came to full consciousness as if someone had flicked a light switch. "Drink," a demon told her, she blinked at the bright light around them. The demon helped her sit up and she found herself on a sandy beach littered with smoking ruins and bodies. Cool water slid down her throat and she coughed up a small glob of red mucous. Multi-coloured orbs floated back and forth around the beach and demons helped load dead troops from both sides onto waiting white sleds.

A shadow briefly covered her and the demon tending to her wounds stepped back to give her a better look at the scenery. Peter's circular observation platform touched down a few paces away, he waved at her. "How's death feel?" he asked her.

She frowned, "I died?"

"Technically yes, but only after the game was finished. We won Jessica, we won by a lot," he seemed anything but cheerful as he walked over and helped her onto her feet. Hubunker's starship hovered several kilometres above them, as did a dozen other starships of various shapes and sizes. She heard Hubunker's distinctive croaks and hoots further up the beach and saw an assortment of creatures gathered together.

"What happened?"

Peter pointed at the wreckage. "They surprised us with their jets, which helped them take the beach, but our land mines and trenches slowed them down. Our artillery and tanks couldn't do much to their better armoured tanks, but they lost half their troops here. Once they got to our town, Georgy trapped them inside the streets and burned them alive. They tried to regroup their soldiers on the eastern side, but Georgy had machine gun crews and rocket launchers waiting for them. We mopped up the remainders and used their landing boats to send some troops and capture the Plinth town."

"Then why so glum?" Jessica ran a hand up her back where it felt numb. She felt torn cloth but smooth skin underneath.

"Georgy's been accused of cheating. Hubunker's arguing against the accusation as we speak." Flanked by several demons in advanced combat gear, they headed off towards the small crowd of beings.

"We have a bodyguard?"

"Tensions seem a little high," Peter motioned above at the red, black and orange orbs zipping past them to encircle the arguing aliens. As Jessica and Peter neared the gathered creatures something embedded in the very fibre or air of the Shellworld started to translate for them.

"It is inconceivable that this primitive being could have so vastly defeated our Plinth colleagues."

"And they burned most of my soldiers, they burned them." The Plinth commander was visible among the crowd, pointing large claws at a kneeling human. Georgy had his knees buried deep in the yellow sand while two purple orbs latched onto his hands with red glowing tendrils. Hubunker raised his hands in a placating gesture.

"I assure you, there has been no—"

"Your commander mocks us," the Plinth commander screamed at Hubunker. Ammon stepped forward in front of Hubunker as if to defend him.

"Soldiers are burnt in war," Georgy said quietly. "Your troops were ill-prepared." He looked up from the sand to stare at the Plinth commander. "*You* were not prepared."

The Plinth roared and several creatures jumped back in fright. "Arbiter, they must be punished. Can you not see it?" The Plinth looked at something that resembled some sort of purple tree trunk with thick green tendrils coming out of the top.

"Your plight seems reasonable." Its tendrils vibrated as it spoke.

"No, please, arbiter, hear my case," Hubunker said and waited for a response. At a signal from the arbiter, Hubunker continued, "Thank you. Humans have no knowledge of these games; he would not have been able to learn about the systems in place in the short time he has been aboard my vessel. Arbiter, you know of me and my kind; subterfuge is not our way."

"Then how in the million-stars did he do it, hmm?" A short blue elephant with two trunks asked. "No one could have defeated our Plinth colleagues so viciously."

"It's called planning," Georgy said while a tear rolled down the left side of his face, "and experience."

"Human," the arbiter addressed Georgy, "what experience do you speak of?"

"War, battles. I've been in real naval engagements. I've studied war for most of my life. I assume that's why I was chosen to lead this game."

"He lies," shouted the Plinth commander.

"No, I speak the truth. Hubunker, can't you show them?" pleaded Georgy.

"He would only fabricate your records," the blue elephant said. "He's guilty."

"Guilty."

"Guilty," several others called out.

"I'm afraid I must be the judge of that," the tree-like arbiter said. "In all the history of the Shellworld, no minor race has ever achieved total victory over a major player. None have ever come close. It would seem as though you have deployed some nefarious device to gain an advantage. Until the game can be reviewed in detail, I am withholding half your team's winnings. Furthermore, as recompense for your deliberate targeting of your opponent's game pieces with combustible weaponry, you will enter your pieces for the next game in the minimum required time," translators interpreted several alien sounds as gasps from the shocked crowd. "Take your commanders and pieces, Hubunker."

"Not enough," the Plinth commander said.

"This one needs punishment," someone else said.

Two stick-thin humanoids crossed their arms. "That's quite enough; you have no proof of any wrongdoing."

"He must be punished. Pieces and points mean nothing next to the price of respect; the human must be responsible for his actions," the blue elephant insisted.

"Respect forms no part of the rules—"

"Execute him," the Plinth roared, cutting off Hubunker's response. Georgy's eyes bulged, and a cacophony of noises erupted from the crowd while creatures jostled and gesticulated at each other. Silence followed several moments later and all eyes turned to the arbiter. It lifted a single tendril towards Georgy.

Hubunker raised his voice, "Stop, arbiter, consider your actions. This game will be analysed to the microns, quadrillions of beings across the Shellworld must be watching this momentous event this very instant. Yes, this 'primitive' chose flame throwers and incendiaries, but all is fair in war; it is written into the rules. You will see; there was no cheating involved." The arbiter seemed to pause as its tendril hung low at its side.

"Demons," Jessica called to the four power-armoured soldiers flanking her and Peter, "could you stop them if they tried to kill Georgy?"

One of them turned towards her and replied, "Momentarily, yes, Commander. We may all be executed thereafter."

"Jessica, no," Peter hissed at her. Ammon looked at them with red-rimmed eyes and shook his head at her.

She looked down at her feet, feeling helpless.

"Do it, arbiter," the Plinth commander said while clenching its high-tech rifle in brown muscle-corded fists.

Georgy looked over at Peter and Jessica, the skin under his eyes sagging. "Look after my huskies for me..." The arbiter's tendril cracked the air like a whip and the red rope attached to the purple orbs pulsed.

For a brief moment, bright white flames replaced what had once been the body of Georgy Ivanov.

CHAPTER 9

"Damn that arbiter, Plinth puppet," Hubunker fumed as he paced back and forth in front of the stunned humans. Jessica was seated in a vast Shellworld elevator, large enough to hold an army, and her heel kept tapping the clean white floor. The ride to the next arena was going to take up most of their remaining time while the elevator shifted from zone to zone within the Shellworld's internal shells. "The games masters will see. The neutrals will all see. The Million Star League and their Plinth overseers will all pay for this outrage." Jessica barely heard him as she tried to concentrate on the technical details on the elevator's wall, showing them battle options, starship configurations, and arena details.

Her eyes blurred, and her mind felt fuzzy. They'd just lost Georgy and were now expected to fight another battle in an arena no human had ever encountered.

"I suppose you could say it's a bit like submarine warfare, just... with air instead of water, and no gravity," Peter was trying to tell her while he slurped red soup from a brown mug. Ammon sat next to them drinking green tea. "My submariner days are long over so I'm a little rusty, but I could try and brush up on some old sonar calculations. I used to be really good at it, I'll just have to adjust for air instead of water. That should be fine..." he said a little sarcastically. "I've got my nausea tablets this time. So, what do we have to do to win?"

"It's a timed deathmatch."

"A... deathmatch, you say?" Peter tilted his head at nearly forty-five degrees and raised his eyebrows at Ammon.

Ammon ignored Peter's mock astonishment and nodded. "We have approximately ninety-seven hours to locate the enemy force and annihilate it. The arena is weightless, filled with air, and without light. Stealth is of the utmost importance; there is little terrain for defence."

They all heard a chime coming from a device on Hubunker's left wrist. He brought the device up closer to his eyestalks and touched it with his right hand, "Ha. We're in luck. The new arena's games master is allowing Ammon to join the wargames as our secondary."

A small smile formed on Ammon's wrinkled face, "Thank you, master Hubunker."

"Don't mess it up this time," Hubunker said as he pointed at Ammon. "Forget—"

"Forget the redoubt manoeuvre; I understand, master."

"You've fought these battles?" Peter asked Ammon.

"Of course he has. A long time ago, perhaps, but he keeps in practice, don't you?" Hubunker said.

"Yes," Ammon replied, nodding.

"He can help you choose a fleet. In fact, I believe he has been working on such a scenario for quite some time."

Ammon nodded, "I have several fleet configurations already prepared for just such an occasion. I can place the order with the games master's entourage and the fleet will be waiting for us when we arrive."

"Glad to have you aboard," Peter said with what may have been mock enthusiasm, his red-rimmed eyes staring at nothing.

"You must have been praying for this moment your whole life," Jessica said. "You must have hoped one of us would die so you could take our place." She fought to keep the stammer from her voice. The flash of white light that had once been Georgy was still fresh in her mind.

"Calm, Miss Stanner; your assertions are not quite correct. This is part of Ammon's function in case something like this happens. He's a sort of... spare, among his many duties. Mr Ivanov's incineration will not be in vain. Ah, but where are my manners? I must now leave you to choose your battle craft. Before I go to collect your winnings from the central exchange, may I suggest the mark twelve power armour this time?"

Ammon put his hands together in a thoughtful gesture. "The mark twelve failed us last time."

"Its capabilities are superior to the thirteen and fourteen."

"It takes more practice, master. For Jessica, I would favour the mark fourteen, it's the most intuitive."

Hubunker growled before snapping a finger at them. "Suit yourself; I don't have time to waste on these frivolities."

"Then go, please," Ammon dismissed their Trustee with a wave of his hand. The alien stomped off to the rear of the gigantic elevator where small transportation orbs waited for him. Out of the thousands of demons packed into the elevator Hubunker took almost a hundred with him as bodyguards. Tensions must have been high at the central exchange.

Jessica had almost no idea what they had been talking about, deep in grief and shock as she was, but a thin smile formed on her lips anyway. "You just told Hubunker to piss off, didn't you?"

Ammon grinned. "And it was glorious. Hubunker deserves respect as our Trustee but he has no place telling us commanders how to prepare for our games. Peter is our game three commander, so the responsibility is his, but, unlike our Trustee, I believe I can make some well-informed suggestions..."

***

"Hubunker, your humans impress us. Our friends have finally seen the truth of the matter, they move to execute our plans," a wasp-man said through Hubunker's wrist communicator.

"Excellent. Is the operative in place?"

"Not yet. While much of the Million Star League is distracted by your humans' next game, your Jean will infiltrate their ships aboard my trade vessels. Are you sure Jean's mind was the right one for copying into your soldiers' bodies?"

"He will succeed, or we fail."

***

A demon, named Jean, crept in the shadows of a Plinth starship. He was naked, apart from a thin black belt that shielded him from the starship's sensors. Thousands of other demons, all with Jean's memories, infiltrated other starships belonging to the Plinth and their allies. Tortured for centuries, enduring his existence within the body of a demon, the army of Jeans relished the thought of death. His torturer, the Trustee known as Hubunker, would not be able to resurrect him this time.

In the darkness of the ship's cargo bay, he moved towards his ultimate destination. The power station beckoned him. He could *almost feel the tiny anti-matter bomb, hidden in the black belt, hum with approval as he approached the target.*

He heard long footsteps behind him; they suddenly stopped. "Who are you?" a Plinth soldier growled at him.

Jean smiled, then ran. He made it a dozen paces before the Plinth soldier shot him in the back of his head. Sensing its host had been killed, the anti-matter bomb detonated.

Moments later, thousands of more bombs exploded aboard their target ships. The conflagration and carnage was the signal for millions of ships within Hubunker's Advancement Alliance to attack. Hubunker's allies opened fire.

The war for the Shellworld had begun.

***

If it weren't for the holographic displays in front of her, Jessica could have sworn she was in an empty abyss. She felt like everywhere she looked darkness peered back. There were no stars in the arena, no lights. All the airships that the humans and their opponents were using were covered in light absorbing paint and were all in stealth mode, not risking the slightest hint of exhaust fumes for their opponents to detect. She had barely seen the ships when they'd slipped into the dark arena, but they looked like streamlined rockets with multiple wings that flapped and waved like silk in the dead air, as silent as ghosts.

The mark fourteen power armour that she wore did its best to make her comfortable, but it was too large to allow her to find a proper perch on the observation platform. She had to stand with straps holding her down due to the arena's weightlessness. It was hard to believe they were somewhere at the centre of the endless Shellworld, where, gravity was non-existent. Peter had worked out they must have been travelling at almost two per cent of the speed of light to get to the centre of the world, yet they hadn't felt any changes in direction on the elevator. She should have been surprised, but after seeing the other wonders of the Shellworld and its inhabitants, she could readily believe in almost anything.

Now it was the human team's turn to use such advanced technology.

The arena itself was a relatively "small" sphere with a radius of almost ten thousand kilometres. She wondered how they were supposed to fight over such distances, let alone find their opponents. Ammon had assured her their enemies would find them fast enough.

Hundreds of blue glowing arrowheads that represented allied ships on the holographic displays crawled forward in small squadrons that had split up into search parties. The formation resembled a patchy hemispherical glob with a larger reserve force at the centre of the glob. Dozens of large capital ships sat at the centre of the glob, surrounded by hundreds of small fighters.

Without wings, the capital ships moved slowly, dragged along by smaller frigates until the moment they would abandon all stealth and bring their engines online. Looking like a giant spear on the holographic displays, Peter's flagship sat at the very centre of the capital ships, large sound scopes deployed, listening for enemy movement.

"Sound sensors report movement at sector eight-five," she heard Ammon say.

"Eight-five... oh you mean top right central. I see it," Peter said. A tiny red dot appeared on Jessica's holographic display in front of the human fleet, showing her where Ammon's scouts had detected movement.

"I shall send seekers; they will create an echo that will bounce off their hulls."

"Echo-location? Yeah, I got it, thanks."

"Keep talk to a minimum, their scanners may see our communication lasers."

Minutes passed. A small group of seeker drones deployed near the red dot. Jessica's eyes were fixed on that one spot and she couldn't tear her attention away.

"Too quiet," she whispered. The first of the drones activated and screamed into the abyss, searching for an echo.

Nothing.

The second drone went ten kilometres further before activating.

Nothing.

Three more went further and spread out.

Red dots filled that entire section of the holographic displays. "Hold fleet," Peter called from the command ship. "Fifty-seven contacts."

The probes were quickly destroyed by enemy railguns.

"They're spread pretty widely," Jessica said.

"Correct, I suggest sending more probes into all sectors."

"You think it's a trap?" Peter asked.

"They must have seen our communications and deduced our formation."

"How?" Jessica asked.

"They've played many games before," Ammon said quickly. Probes entered the darkness in a large spherical pattern. While she waited she ordered the observation platform to move closer to the rear of their fleet, thinking she could get a closer look at the enemy ships with her suit's sensors rather than relying on the interpreted holographic images the platform chose to show her.

The probes reached their destinations and simultaneously screamed into the darkness. "Not good," Peter said. The enemy fleet looked like a giant octopus with its arms slowly closing in on the human fleet. The octopus' head was directly behind them. "They're behind us."

"Repeat my commands to the fleet," Ammon said without pause, "all ships forward at full speed, repulsors to the rear, deploy smoke screens, maser and x-ray laser craft target enemy craft in front of the fleet, deploy tactical probes and scatter one wave of mines." Peter relayed the orders as quickly as he could and Jessica watched as the firefight started. Smoke and tactical probes filled most of her view, punctuated by bright flashes when the probes fired off different types of countermeasures or were destroyed. The enemy 'octopus' fired hundreds of small missiles that looked like red teeth to her eyes. The missiles streaked towards the smoke and spiralled through as they searched for their prey. Some exploded less than a hundred metres from her and deadly shrapnel sparked off the observation platform's shielding. Jessica flinched from the sounds and noises, helpless against the sudden onslaught.

"Danger," she heard while a shrieking alarm pierced her eardrums. She tried to cover her ears with her suited hands in a vain attempt to shut out the noise and looked up just in time to see a missile streak towards the platform. The platform wrenched hard to turn her away from the incoming missile and deployed a yellow umbrella of defensive energy.

"Urk—" she uttered, winded by the platform's manoeuvre. The missile slammed into the umbrella and she was thrown into the darkness, ejected by the platform. She bit her tongue and tasted blood before losing consciousness.

***

Elsewhere inside the Shellworld, far from any wargames, Plinth pilot Clawpit stepped into his starfighter and awaited the command to launch. It came seconds later. Ascending from the darkness within a secluded area of the five hundredth shell, thousands of kilometres below the surface shell, Clawpit and several hundred thousand starfighters made haste.

"The Warmonger's Alliance has struck. Defend our stars, wipe out the aggressors. Die with pride."

"Die with pride," thousands of Plinth pilots replied all at once.

A relatively small hatch, over a hundred kilometres wide, opened in the five-hundredth shell's ceiling to allow the starfighters to rise. More hatches began opening. The hatches appeared to move at a snail's pace, but were widening at several hundred metres per second. More and more starfighters joined Clawpit's armada. Bigger ships followed.

Shellworld citizens scrambled for cover as the Plinth ships roared skyward. Over and over again, if neutral ships were caught in the Plinth armada's path, they were shredded by the uncaring guns of the armada. Shell after shell whipped past the Plinth vessels as they rose upwards and Clawpit snarled his approval.

"Out of the way," Clawpit yelled at a large taxi train unlucky enough to be hovering over an open hatch. Clawpit fired his starfighter's missiles, as did a hundred others, and the taxi train felt the Plinth armada's wrath. Debris and bodies glanced against the superheated plasma shields of Clawpit's starfighter. "Too slow."

Capital ships waited for the armada in the Plinth section of the top few shells.

"Arise, Million Star League, defeat the Warmonger and his Alliance," the Plinths' Trustee called to them from its city-sized ship above the Shellworld.

Millions of starfighters and capital ships breached the surface of the Shellworld's top shell and were immediately engulfed in a storm of enemy fire.

***

"Battle is joined, my allies," Chort of the Fifty's image said, relayed to several hundred thousand vessels located around hundreds of different stars. "Hubunker's Alliance needs our help. Charge your weapons, steel your minds. Head to the battlefield. The games are over."

Chort of Fifty's fleet launched from planets and moons surrounding its territory's stars. Hubunker's main fleet were engaged with Plinth reinforcements from the Shellworld.

A flanking force of motley ships, representing the Plinths' unprepared allies, headed to cut off Hubunker's fleet from above, trying to surround them.

"Intercept those," Chort of Fifty said on the holographic displays of thousands of different ships.

***

Planetary guns and other large guns hidden in asteroids scattered around the Shellworld opened fire, attacking ships and each other. Within moments, whole planets were engulfed in flames.

"Hubunker," the planetary governor of Ash-Two, a small world overlooking a distant part of the Shellworld, demanded the trustee's attention.

"Yes, governor?" Hubunker asked, slurring his words a little.

The governor of Ash-Two shivered its leafy tendrils, surprised that Hubunker himself had answered the call.

"The Plinth were well prepared. They have guns like us. My world crumbles."

"I see. Keep fighting."

"My world burns."

"Fascinating. I must go now." Hubunker's image disappeared.

"Hubunker?" the governor asked weakly. Quakes rocked the governor's palace as anti-matter powered missiles rained down.

***

For millions of kilometres across and above the surface of the Shellworld, lightning flickered at an ever-growing rate. Each flash of light heralded the destruction of another capital vessel, coming at over a hundred flashes every second. Those observing from the Shellworld's surface had to cover their eyes for fear of going blind.

A wormhole, located some two hundred thousand kilometres from the shellworld's surface, disgorged a ship in the form of a green lattice basket. The lattice slid out of the mirrored surface of the wormhole and its black urchin-like occupants paused what they were doing.

"Big wargame?" a subordinate asked its superior.

"Scan for communications." The superior activated the ship's tactical overlays and a holographic image appeared in the ship's observation bubble. The ship's computer started tagging battling ships with different colours and smells, sorting them into opposing battle groups. Yellow Plinth, blue Arbiter's Guild, red Advancement Alliance, brown Fifth-Shell Oppressed League, and hundreds of other factions seemed to have joined the battle.

"Report?" the superior demanded from its subordinate.

"Our Plinth allies call for help."

"I smell you are right. The Hubunker Warmonger has struck, just as the Plinth said he would." The superior extended its black spikes, sniffing out different control panels located within the green-lattice ship's observation bubble.

"Your orders?"

"Send for reinforcements."

"That will take quite some time. We have no military."

"I smell this battle will *take* quite some time, my inferior. Perhaps hundreds of years. We will have time to build more ships. Do it, send the probe and ask for reinforcements."

Moments after the probe was sent back through the wormhole to the black urchins' home galaxy to seek reinforcements, a rogue missile slammed into the green lattice. The superior and inferior, along with several hundred artificial intelligences and cloned slaves died in the fiery wreckage.

***

Hubunker sipped on a blue drink his species considered alcoholic, but would taste like salt to a human. The *Inveigled Ambassador*, safely tucked away inside a shell much closer to the human's current wargame, relayed messages back and forth, updating him on the battle's progress.

"Master, the game has taken a devious turn. The Tentacle-Twelve have attacked but we are regrouping," Ammon said.

"Fine, fine," Hubunker muttered.

"Are you paying attention, master?" Ammon asked.

"Yes, of course, friend Ammon."

"It's the battle, isn't it?"

"I... what? Yes. The battle above us. You are right," Hubunker said as he took another sip and tapped the control band on his wrist to bring up a better view of part of the battle. "The battle is also taking some loopy turns. We're winning the opening moves, I think. There are many variables."

Ammon sighed, loud enough for Hubunker to hear the human's annoyance. "Speak up, Ammon."

"I worry, master. You promised me power. What good is power if humans are punished for this war you have instigated? Will I be the ruler of a dead species, like so many others?"

Hubunker spared two of its eyes for Ammon, keeping the other two fixed to watching the holographic battle above the Shellworld. "No, no. You fret when you should be worrying about your wargame. No harm will come to your species."

"I disagree. The Plinth know I am complicit in your plans, despite my protests. They'll ensure the Arbiter's Guild puts my species on trial, there's too much evidence for them not to."

"Nonsense, my friend. I have covered all bases."

"And if not, I'll be an immortal champion ruling over dust."

Hubunker rocked back on its form-fitting chair and gulped down the blue liquid. It rolled its eyes around the dark room of the *Inveigled Ambassador*'s simulator room, thinking of all the time it had put into these plans of action. All the worrying, the fretting, the deals it had made and the secrecy required for thousands of years. Hubunker started getting angry with its human slave. Ammon's indignancy had always been a thorn in the legs, but now, at the very moment it needed Ammon's full support and trust, Ammon continued to question, to probe and attack Hubunker's plans.

"Then, my poor human, you better hope this battle is won, if not for my sake, then for yours. Begone now." Hubunker ended the conversation and Ammon's annoying face disappeared. "Ship, open a communications channel to Trustee Nine-Fifth of Dark City twenty-three hundred, Shell Five."

Moments later the holographic image of an ape with a shark's mouth appeared in front of Hubunker.

"Ah, Trustee Nine-Fifth, there you are."

The ape opened its mouth to reveal row upon row of sharp teeth. Clearly, Nine-Fifth was annoyed. "Trustee Hubunker, what have you started?"

"A battle, a true battle," Hubunker said while waving its hands in the air in triumph.

"So, you really are a warmonger. I suppose you want assistance of some kind?"

"How did you come to that conclusion, Nine-Fifth?"

"Because it has been five hundred years since we last spoke, and war is all you would speak about. Just because the Plinth occupy a territory next to my city, does not mean I dislike the Plinth enough to fight with them."

Hubunker affected a grotesque, wide-mouthed smile, much as the humans would do. "You forget, Nine-Fifth, you owe me."

"I owe you a city, not a war."

"And cities have soldiers, millions of them."

The ape wagged its large, teeth-filled mouth in front of Hubunker. "They are for games and protection, not war."

Hubunker wagged a finger at the hologram. "My allies are winning, Nine-Fifth. I demand you throw open the Plinth barriers and attack their fleet's hub. Otherwise, if my allies win, you'll be next."

The ape clicked its fingers in frustration and snapped its jaws. It growled at Hubunker. "You play a dangerous game."

"The games will soon be over, my friend. Will you comply with my wishes?"

"Damn you, Hubunker. We will gather our armies and attack the Plinth fleet bays, as you request. Don't expect my city to be intact in a year from now."

"Fine, fine," Hubunker replied before cutting the communications link and reaching for another cup of blue liquid. "This is *fun*," it said to itself. It opened another channel, this time to another powerful trustee in the sixth shell. There would be several hundred more trustees and territorial officials to contact.

The war would continue. Hubunker had plenty of time.

***

It couldn't have been long before she regained her senses; her tongue and mouth were numb and her right leg felt funny. She looked down in a sudden panic but couldn't see what was wrong in the blackness. She tried to ask her suit what the problem was but it felt like her mouth was glued shut.

"You seem to be in some distress," a calm male voice said. "With your permission, I shall scan your neural impulses and we will communicate non-verbally. You can move your head, if you agree to the scan, please nod your head."

She nodded. "Good, to aid with communication follow these instructions: form a thought in your mind as if it were are text across your eyes, then nod to send the text to me. I will attempt to decipher the thoughts."

Who are you? You sound like a human. She thought the words as if they were bright white lights across her vision.

"Please repeat," the voice said. She repeated her question. "I am your mark fourteen safety vessel. My mind template was taken and modified from a former human commander. You are currently under my protection."

Oh, thanks. What happened to me? Why can't I talk?

"The observation platform ejected us to save us from a missile strike. Your ankle is broken and you bit off the tip of your tongue. Do not despair, your injuries are minor and will be repaired at the conclusion of this game. I have administered numbing and stabilising agents to the affected areas, so they cannot be moved."

Well, that explains that. How far is our fleet? Could we signal them?

"Signalling is not recommended."

Why?

"We are being hunted."

Jessica's eyes widened. *But we haven't entered the game.*

"Irrelevant. We were illegally targeted and will be again. You must be brought to mental parity before we can continue. Please describe how you feel."

How do I feel? How do you think I feel? Why can't we hear Peter or Ammon's orders to the fleet? Are you blocking the signals?

"I cannot speculate on your feelings, I do not know your particular chemical or electrical structures within your neural network. As for the fleet, I am not blocking the signals, as it appears there are no signals for me to block."

Jessica twisted and sent her body into a slow pirouette while she searched the spherical black arena for any signs of light. "Your heart rate has increased."

I'm scared.

"Understandable. You are isolated within a wargame where the threat of death is quite possible. What are your other thoughts?"

Are you some sort of shrink suit? she asked sarcastically. *I'm lonely and afraid that I'm going to get a railgun slug to the face from an alien warship. I'm tired, I haven't had any sleep, I want to go home, and...* she paused.

"You were going to add something before you paused. What was that thought?"

Her eyes started to sting as she fought back tears, *I... I miss my parents. They must think I'm dead now.*

The suit held a short silence before replying, probably coming up with the most appropriate thing to say to calm her down. "That must make you a little... angry, perhaps?"

What the hell do you think?

"I think you are angry at those who have hurt you. I believe you are angry with the bastard who brought you here." Jessica blinked, confused. "You're pissed off with Hubunker. You're pissed off with the Plinth."

Uh, yeah, I suppose so. You're not sounding much like a robot anymore.

"There's no 'supposing' about this Jessica. I'd be pissed off too, especially since these morons cheated and shot at us. In fact, I *am* pissed off." The suit's calm voice was steadily getting faster and louder with an angry growl crawling into its synthesised voice. "They shot us against the rules. They want to kill us. They're going to stop you from going home. Home, Jessica. These bastards are stopping you from seeing your parents."

Jessica's eyes narrowed. *So, what do we do about it?*

"Good, determination is good. I am administering a concoction directly into your spine and the base of your skull. This will increase your senses and allow for deeper integration into this mark fourteen safety vessel. It will also remove much of the neurological damage caused by stress and lack of sleep."

Sounds good; then what?

"We track them down—"

And kill them.

"Precisely."

CHAPTER 10

How did the enemy surround the fleet so easily?

The arena, Jessica found, was not an empty black space. With soft flaps of the mark fourteen suit's ghostly wings, she floated through a squall of near-black objects that the suit's sensors detected. They were rocks of various shapes and sizes. Asteroids. She did her best not to conjure up an image of one of those old Star Wars movies while she slipped between the rocky objects. The suit gave her a visual representation of the field using infrared. It all looked like grey shadows to her. Shadows upon shadows. One of the shadows appeared to be a small planetoid, hundreds of kilometres across.

"Roughly translated from the Shellworld's deep archives, your enemies are the 'Tentacle-twelve,' or the twelfth race of intelligent tentacled beings that were ever encountered by denizens of the Shellworld's libraries. At least in surviving records." An image popped up on Jessica's face-plate with the label 'Tentacle-twelve.' It looked a lot like a spherical jelly-fish; a blue translucent ball with numerous dark blue tentacles equally spread across its body.

Looks like a primitive octopus.

"Primitive but old. They have survived where the species that discovered them, and many others, died off hundreds of millions of years ago. Few races can claim such age or power. This arena is like their natural environment."

So, if they're so old, they've had a lot of practice in here.

"Correct. It is likely they helped formulate the very rules that govern this arena and know its loop-holes. I believe this is why they were able to attack the observation platform." They were nearing the edge of the squall and Jessica thought she glimpsed a shadow against one of the larger asteroids on the suit's infrared sensors.

Was that...?

"Yes, it's possible you saw a hunter-killer craft. It has been tracking us since we reached the rock-field. It may be looking for an excuse to fire upon us and it has been moving with such intent that it may, in fact, be the enemy commander or its second in command, I believe now is the time to give it a reason to attack."

You're going to enter us into the game?

"Yes. It is unlikely we can defeat such an adversary, but we shall deny it from attaining one of the game's minor objectives, namely, possession of this rock-field. A secondary outcome is both positive and negative."

Jessica, breathing rapidly, waited for a few heartbeats for the suit to continue its explanation *...and what is that secondary outcome?*

"Sorry my dear, but my mind was elsewhere. We're going to draw the attention of the fleets."

Oh... she thought for a second, *you're bringing the battle here on purpose? How is that a good thing?*

"You were able to spot the enemy amongst the rocks. Your fellow commanders and playing pieces will also be aided by such an advantage; the Tentacle-twelve will gain nothing. We shall even the playing field a little. Are you ready?"

The voice in her head was starting to sound almost... familiar. *Wait... who are you? Besides being a 'safety suit.'*

"You mean my human consciousness? As I mentioned I was a former competitor from Earth. Who I was is irrelevant; the real me died centuries ago and much of my personality was stripped and enhanced when scanned and stored for use in the games."

Well, before we both potentially die, I'd still like to know.

The suit sighed, a sound so human it gave her goosebumps. "I was a member of parliament in sixteenth-century Paris."

A member of parliament?

"As well as philosopher and professor of the law. An interesting choice for the games, wouldn't you say? My brothers, the demons, are me as well. They have my mind at least, just altered. I possess the memories of Jean Bodin, as do all of the demons. This, the manipulation of my mind as use for the games, I suspect, is punishment for my disastrous role in the wargame I was involved in."

Jessica shrugged. *I bet you did better than I did in my commander's role.*

"Your knowledge of ancient warfare aided in your choice for the games, but it was not the main reason. You earned your place here due to the correct balance in your reflexes, athleticism and... emotional state."

She frowned. *But I'm not an athlete.*

"Nor was I, yet here we are. I shall now enter us into the game. As a condition of entry, you will have complete control of this mark-fourteen safety vessel and all its faculties. Your neural pathways are now fully integrated, and you should discover more senses and options becoming available to you.

"Merely wish for a movement or a function to happen and it will, as much as I can achieve at least. You have micro-mines, magnetically-propelled grenades and slugs in plentiful supply as well as chemical propulsion that should increase our speed up to twenty times the force of our home world."

You mean twenty G's?

"Yes, 'gravities' or G's. Ready?"

Do it.

"RED TEAM OBSERVER HAS ENTERED THE GAME."

***

"Jessica, what are you doing?" Peter's voice was faint in her ears while she hugged desperately to the side of a car-sized asteroid. She used the suit's tiny suction cups to crawl towards the asteroid's edge and peer into the black field beyond. Her scanners searched for signs of abnormal movement. She instinctively leapt away before the scanners had registered the sound of a gauss-rifle swivelling towards her. The car-sized asteroid gained a large hole where she'd been hiding and the super-sonic crack of the passing projectile hurt her ears before the suit dampened the sound. Two more projectiles broke the sound barrier in rapid succession, each shot coming closer than the last.

The suit added graphics on her helmet display, showing her where it thought the enemy was firing from. She raised her arm and a small barrel automatically raised itself from the suit's forearm. It fired a five-second burst of tiny pellets at the larger hunter-killer. She was rewarded with the sound of several pings. "Tracer rounds are embedded, target locked," her suit told her. "Kill the bastard."

She almost asked the suit how she would go about killing something that must have been a hundred times the mass of her suit, but the thought seemed to come to her of its own accord. "This mark fourteen suit is the most expensive power-armoured suit in the fleet, it is well prepared for just such an occasion." She raised her left arm and a larger barrel assembled itself. The suit painted several red targets across her vision, she aimed at them without hesitation. Thump-thump-thump, small grenades left her arm-barrel at high velocity.

"Watch out," her suit said. She kicked her legs out wildly and rockets attached to her legs came to life. Her wings guided the sudden momentum in a tight arc, one of them snapped off when she hit an asteroid.

A missile streak past her, she spun out of control and hit another rock. The impact wasn't hard. She leapt off again, firing her gun in earnest at the red dots while the dots moved across her vision. "Calculating trajectory," the suit told her. The red spots grew dotted lines. "Splitting vision now," it told her. Her vision blurred for a second before her left eye could see the red projections and her right saw the infrared shadows of the asteroids in her path. "Continue firing, Jessica."

She fired more grenades, at least she thought it was her firing them. A lot of her concentration was on the asteroid field that she was hurtling into. It felt as if she'd been split into two people but was conscious of both halves. She punched a smaller football-sized rock with her right hand and activated the rockets on her feet to send her in a new direction to avoid a larger rock.

"RED PLAYER SECONDARY HAS ENTERED THE GAME."

"We are coming," she heard Ammon say.

An asteroid exploded somewhere above and rained debris on her head. She kicked off in a new direction and fired more grenades at moving dots. As an afterthought, she discarded a small explosive mine from her back.

Come and get me, she thought at the hunter-killer.

"Come and get me, you coward," her suit screamed into the darkness on her behalf. Projectiles cracked past her in response. More and more projectiles filled her aural senses until she could no longer hear.

"I have blocked all sound, many more enemy units have arrived," the suit said.

Okay, she thought before raising both arms at the projected red displays. Mines discharged from her back and pellets and grenades ruptured the enemy hunter-killer's hull.

"Enemy craft disabled." She kicked off towards the hunter-killer, intending to kill its occupant but felt a sudden sting in her left leg. "We are under fire."

Something hit her. She somehow knew the exact amount of blood she was losing with every heartbeat.

She knew the suit was working to supply her with more oxygen and to block the blood-loss.

She knew she should have tried to dodge in another direction.

Somehow, she just didn't care.

Grenades, mines and pellets filled the void between herself and the projected red dots of her new assailants while she travelled towards the disabled hunter-killer. When she crashed into the enemy vessel it *hurt*. She must have been travelling nearly a hundred kilometres an hour. The suit softened the blow.

Winded, she clung onto the black surface of the enemy ship like a Koala that had found its favourite tree. Almost unconsciously, she ejected the last of her mines and flares and a thousand tiny needles of light sprang from her lower back.

"Target acknowledged," she heard a demon say. Moments later the space around her lit up in cascades of fire and hails of deadly rain.

Arrow-headed ships suddenly darted in and out of the asteroid field while the more rounded vessels of the Tentacle-twelve smashed the rocks to pieces. Jessica held on tightly to the alien ship and sweat stung her eyes.

"Hang on, Jess; I'm coming for you," Peter said over the radio. Moments later, a fifty-metre-long vessel smashed through a large asteroid and impaled itself against the hunter-killer Jessica was clinging to.

"Correct your targeting sensors for sector fifty-two," the mark fourteen safety suit broadcast over the general channel.

"Oh, fu—"

"Acknowledged, firing," Ammon cut Peter off before explosions erupted in Jessica's right view-point. Jessica fired a few pellets in the same direction and swore she saw one of her mines cripple an enemy probe. "I have successfully flanked our enemy," Ammon said.

Jessica heard a clatter of movement to her right. "BLUE COMMANDER HAS ENTERED THE GAME." She instructed the suction cups on her arms to let go of the hunter-killer before a metallic whip sliced the air where her arms had been. The 'whip' tore small chunks from the craft and almost ricocheted into her helmet.

"Now you're mine," she said using the suit's synthesised voice. The voice projected throughout the asteroid field where it filtered up to the opposing fleets around them. Purple and orange fire flickered across the heavens in response.

"Challenge accepted and exceeded," the Tentacle-twelve commander said to her. It was a chilling, freezing sound.

"Move, Jessica. Attack," the suit said, she leapt at the enemy commander. Her legs twisted around and her rockets fired on impulse, sending her straight at the enemy commander.

She crashed into the enemy commander and caught it in her armoured hands. Armoured tentacles wrapped around her arms and legs, but no matter how hard they strained, she would not let go of the near-perfect spherical shell. She strained as hard as she could, using the suction cups to try and pull apart the enemy commander's shell. The motors driving her suit's mechanical muscles whined in her ears.

A crack appeared in the tentacle-twelve's shell and something inside it shrieked in alarm. She ignored the alien shriek and plunged a fist into the dark sphere before it could close again. It wasn't long before the gelatinous monster inside the shell stopped writhing and the pressure on her arms and legs finally abated.

"BLUE COMMANDER IS DECEASED."

"F squadron come about to sector seven, B squadron hold where you are. Ammon, cut their tail off," Peter yelled. He started talking to himself, manually calculating trajectories and distances. Peter did not trust the sensors on his ship, the Tentacle-twelve were using too many light-emitting decoys, so he was manually guiding the fleet, using nothing but sound. His calculations were far more accurate than their enemies expected; one after another, Tentacle-twelve warcraft were being shot to pieces.

Jessica heard the battle chatter but couldn't respond. The enemy commander had severed her spinal cord. She could still move if she wanted to but the suit had administered so many pain-numbing drugs the explosions from the battle were starting to look like pretty butterflies. The Tentacle-twelve responded to the onslaught with fresh reserves that slashed through the asteroid field.

Rail guns sent slugs pounding the rock-filled battlefield and were answered by human missiles and gauss-rifle fire. Mines detonated and sonic charges shattered swathes of the local arena, scattering hundreds of tonnes of rock in all directions.

"Drink deep, Jess-ic-ha," a demon said.

The voice was much like her suit's. Her faceplate opened wide. She inhaled stale, smoky air that tasted like sulphur. A flask of vile liquid invaded her lips.

Clarity returned quickly. It seemed a sort of bodyguard of similarly suited demons had managed to surround her.

Ships pummelled each other at point-blank range. Blue and red dots emerged on her heads-up display. Both the enemy second in command and observer elected to enter the game to more directly command their forces.

Peter did his best to keep the enemy contained within the asteroid field where sensors could better detect the orb-ships of the Tentacle-twelve. Ammon and his small squad of fighter craft duelled with the opposing second in command and its bodyguard to keep them distracted from the main battle.

Let's go, she suggested to her bodyguard. *We need to rally with the reserves and re-enter the battle.*

They left. Away from the battle, until the battlefield looked like fireworks instead of a local firestorm. The demons dragged her towards the waiting reserves. There were almost twenty of them; small capital ships over a hundred metres long, ready to deploy fusion drives and enter the fray, rail guns blazing.

They were so far from the battle now that the conflagration receded into a pinpoint of destruction

Take me to that one, she told her bodyguard while pointing at the nearest fighter-carrier.

"You wish to pilot?" one of the demons asked.

I need to get back to the fight.

"Jessica, no, you're in no condition to help us," Peter said quickly between canon shots aboard the flagship. "The Tentacle-twelve are too fast for you and you're injured."

I'm fine, the blue gel is like magic, I'll be back to normal in minutes. We trained for this in the battle simulators, Jessica replied while a demon crewmember pulled her inside the carrier's heavy top hatch. *We must have been in there for months.*

"It was a few hours."

But our minds were sped up. I can do this. I'll lead our reserve wing of fighters and pick off the Tentacle-twelve's bombers.

"That was a space battle simulator. Jess, don't be stupid, this isn't space."

Stupid? Her eyes became slits and her mouth clamped shut. *We logged at least two hundred hours of atmospheric flight. I can do this.*

"You're an idiot."

Peter?

"What?"

Shut up. She heard Ammon laughing quietly over the communications channel.

Demon hands tore broken pieces of armour off her back and others produced new pieces. The light in the carrier's hangar, while a dull red, seemed bright to her eyes. She couldn't help but squint as the demons pushed her through the air and guided her into a sleek, fusion-powered fighter. Peter continued plotting firing solutions, guiding guns and missiles at large, unseen targets lurking among the asteroids.

"You will be spotted the moment you launch your fighter," Ammon informed her. "The reserve fighters are not stealth craft. They are a final solution, a brittle hammer. You will need to keep your distance and strike only when the opportunity presents. Do you understand?"

Jessica nodded. Her suit interpreted for her.

"Enemy capital ships have been spotted moving towards the battle zone. Are you ready?"

Point me at them.

"Alright Jessica. Fine. R squadron is yours to command. Make it count," Peter said.

Demon pilots floated over to other sleek fighters and sealed the cockpits around them. Jessica tapped on her fighter's control stick and squeals of compressed air alerted her to the presence of the fighter's micro-fusion drive forcibly exhaling out of multiple thrusters. The fighter swerved and pitched under her deft movements.

She could feel the raw power of the fusion drive as it powered up, mere metres behind her. Excitement enriched her tired mind.

Hey Peter, you know those silly old movies you keep quoting?

"What about them?" Peter asked distractedly.

Since we're the red team, I want to be Red Five.

"Ha, funny. You ready or not? The enemy capital ships are looking scary right now."

The carrier's hangar bay doors slammed open, revealing pure darkness on the other side.

R squadron, launch.

"R squadron launching," her demonic co-pilots replied.

The fusion drive's exhaust roared in her ears and the acceleration slammed into the back of her head, neck, spine and legs.

As Jessica's small squadron of eight fusion-powered fighters screamed into the darkness, the allied capital ships started turning to head into the battle. Engines as big as entire fighters ignited. Twenty-metre-long guns swivelled towards the battle and loaded flak and armour piercing rounds. Another squadron of eight fighters deployed behind Jessica and swept downwards, their exhausts marking them like bright, moving stars as they sped away.

The human fleet must have looked like a supernova.

"Jessica, get away from the capital ships as fast as you can."

Why?

As if replying to her, flashes of light heralded the unwelcome sign of canon-fire from the enemy capital ships lighting up the darkness from the opposite side of the arena. Plasma shields on the allied capital ships activated and decoys deployed. Seconds later, the enemy shells slammed home.

The surviving ships, their armour plating burning and shattered, returned fire. The demons in control of the main ship guns set them loose. Sensing their freedom to fire, the guns shouted their rage at the distant Tentacle-twelve vessels, scoring hit after hit.

The Tentacle-twelve capital ships, much quieter but weaker than their human counterparts, quickly scattered into the darkness. Jessica's squadron locked onto a wounded vessel and tracked its smoky entrails.

Arm missiles.

"Missiles armed."

Fire.

Sixteen missiles lit up the noses of eight fighters. Seconds later they slammed into the enemy capital ship's bulbous exterior. Chunks of advanced materials and red-hot dust scattered into the air. Secondary explosions ripped open the Tentacle-twelve ships' midsection, setting loose orange, red and white fire.

One hundred points to us, Jessica thought, trying to keep a mental tally of her personal kills.

***

Trustee Nine-Fifth of Dark City twenty-three hundred, Shell Five, impatiently waited for the Plinth gate to open. Located several hours from Nine-Fifth's city, he had nevertheless managed to transport an army several hundred thousand strong to the gate.

Reaching fifty kilometres from the fifth shell's surface to the ceiling, the gate stood tall, denying the shark-mouthed ape soldiers entrance to the Plinth hangar beyond.

Spiked, purple plants as tall as oak trees waved slowly in the slight breeze. The only sounds were of officers communicating orders and of Nine-Fifth's own observation platform as it hovered over the heads of his army. Hundreds of transport ships, aerial combat fighters and multi-coloured orbs stayed fixed to their positions in the sky.

It was night in this section of the fifth shell and simulated stars replaced the glow of the ceiling lights. Infrared and aural sensors supplemented the basic glow of thousands of lamps attached to soldiers in the packed formations.

"What's taking them so long?" Nine-Fifth asked one of the officers riding in the observation platform with him.

"Perhaps if we give the mercenaries more power from the city grid?"

"They have too much already," Nine-Fifth replied. "Damn digital dimwits..." he cursed the mercenaries. He'd paid an army's worth of points for the digital beings to hack into the Plinth gate. Even as he tapped an armoured foot on the observation platform's deck, the mercenaries, hailing from a shell many thousands of levels deep, waged a silent war in the digital spaces surrounding the true-lifers. Crystalline computer systems embedded within every nook and cranny of the fifth shell was a potential battleground for billions of mercenaries fighting against the Plinth firewalls.

The digital army should have been enough to overwhelm the gate, yet it stood shut against them.

Nine-Fifth briefly considered giving up, packing up his army and returning home. Perhaps he could sue for peace before the fighting started? But then he remembered how the Plinth had treated him and his beneficiaries in the wargames.

The Plinth won every game they fought and every time they defeated Nine-Fifth's chosen commanders, they had gloated. Their arrogance knew no bounds... until this day, when Hubunker's humble humans had finally managed to humiliate them.

It seemed the Plinth and their Million Star League could be beaten.

Nine-Fifth drew a deep breath. The Plinth would be defeated, one day, but he doubted he'd still be around to see it.

He thought he heard a soft hiss coming from the gate. He listened harder and opened his eyes to the darkness, searching for a sign that the gate had been breached. Then, when he thought he must have imagined the sound, he heard a mountain splitting in half.

"The gate is opening," he exclaimed for the benefit of his officers.

"Yes, sir."

A vertical sliver of light appeared in the gate's mid-section, reaching kilometres into the sky.

"Get ready," he told the officers. They continued watching while the sliver of light widened.

Then, with the suddenness of a lightning strike, the gate slammed open. For twenty kilometres to each side, the gate had practically vanished into the walls, moving almost too fast to see. The white light of the Plinth hangars washed over Nine Fifth's army. Many soldiers had to cover their eyes, despite the eye-protection their suits of armour provided.

"Forwards, soldiers of Dark City twenty-three hundred, move into the enemy's hangars. Kill the hated Plinth. Kill them with missiles. Kill them with your guns. Stab and bludgeon, smash and destroy them. When all is done, burn the survivors!"

One of the officers looked at him with her jaw shut, staring a little longer than was truly necessary. She shrugged and touched a control on her armband. "Okay, Trustee Nine-Fifth. That's what we're here for."

He looked back into the Plinth hangar beyond the gate, seeing the rounded white shaft that serviced the Plinth armada emptied of most of its fighters and shuttles. The individual landing pads, leaf-shaped around the cylindrical hangar, numbered in the thousands, just like tree leaves on a very large, inside-out tree.

"Tell the soldiers to get in there and blow up the refuelling stations and control mechanisms for those landing pads, now—"

A powerful gust of wind blew the nearest officer from the observation platform's deck and slammed Nine-Fifth to the control panels where he clutched at glass screens. One of the other officers had also disappeared over the observation platform's walls.

The platform was so far from the front that it had taken almost thirty seconds for the change in air pressure to affect it. Without realising it, when the Plinth gate had slammed open the army below them was sucked forwards several metres by the vacuum created by the decompression between different sections of the shell. The higher pressure of Nine Fifth's territory rushed into the lower pressure of the Plinth hangar.

It was as if a black hole had appeared, drawing the entire army towards the waiting jaws of the Plinth warriors on the other side.

Shark-mouthed apes closest to the gate were pulled right through it. Once they'd skidded to a halt they struggled to their feet and realised, too late, that they were surrounded by Plinth soldiers. Personal shields immediately started glowing red from rifle rounds hitting them.

Designed specifically to penetrate a personal shield, the Plinth rifle rounds laid waste to the Dark City's soldiers.

Plinth warriors armoured in green and silver powered suits charged forward, carrying staff-rifles that featured molecular-bladed cutting edges.

The bladed staff-rifles cut through shields and tore off hairy brown limbs. Nine Fifth's soldiers started fighting back.

Smaller but far more numerous, Nine-Fifth's soldiers surged forwards, trying to break through the trap that the Plinth had laid for them.

Mortars and canons rained down miniature explosives at a tremendous rate of fire, decimating rank upon rank of apes caught out in the open. Plinth aircraft leapt out of the vertical shaft of the hangar and started duelling opposing craft from the Dark City.

Nine-Fifth's multi-coloured orbs crackled with energy as they approached the Plinth hangars, but before they could assist their ape-like allies, bigger, red, powerful orbs descended from within the hangar, wrapping tendrils as long as skyscrapers around the multi-coloured orbs.

"Fight them," Nine Fifth screamed when he regained control of his observation platform. "Kill them!"

Up and down the vertical shaft of the Plinth hangar the same scene played itself out. Hubunker's allies outnumbered the Plinth at least fifty to one, but for every Plinth killed, twenty allied soldiers fell.

"Move it, Red Five, they're closing in," Peter said.

Where are they? My HUD's messed up, she replied. Flickering ghosts of ships moved across her HUD. Her fighter's sensors informed her the enemy were fifteen kilometres away as well as forty-five or more.

Peter muttered something under his breath, doing some calculations. "The nearer signatures to you are the decoys. Target the further ones. Hurry, those are the bombers."

Still trapped inside the asteroid field, Peter's flagship had taken a beating. With so many out of control fires on board his ship and damage to its hull, it was easy to spot and vulnerable for any enemy ships or fighters eager for a few points.

Jessica could see Peter's ship with her own eyes. Even at seventy kilometres away it was large and rimmed in red fire. Flashes of light winked in the darkness each time it fired flak rounds at unseen targets.

One of her wingmen disappeared from her HUD.

Coming, she told Peter, ignoring her lost wingman.

Squadron, target bomber signatures at forty-five clicks. Fire missiles at will.

"Firing missiles," her wingmen replied. Guided almost entirely by sonar, the missiles locked onto the distant targets and rushed away.

Her aural sensors dampened the sound for a moment before turning the volume back up. She wished the sensors hadn't turned up again, the pounding and screeching of alien shells hitting allied capital ships alerted her to the destruction of another vessel.

Moments later her squadron's missiles hit the bombers.

Ten points.

"Jessica, my strike force and I are engaged in a hunting mission against enemy stealth fighters. Peter is vulnerable, you must ensure no others get near him."

Understood, Ammon.

"Uh, you might be too late."

"What do you mean?" Ammon asked Peter.

"Bombers."

Jessica was so close to the asteroid field now that she could see individual asteroids glowing from reflected firelight.

Switching to guns. Squadron, follow me. Jessica banked hard, turning from her patrol route to head directly into the asteroid field. The fusion engine screamed louder as she dialled up the power.

"Not good," Peter said, sounding strained. Jessica heard alarms on Peter's flagship. "Enemy missiles incoming." The flagship's guns started firing again. Smoke lit by orange and red fire blanketed the ship while Jessica and her squadron flew past.

"Whoa," she said, forgetting her ruined tongue.

Missiles streaked through the clouds and hit the flagship, detonating on impact. Reacting on instinct she fired her fighter's guns through the smoke.

As her squadron flew past the burning flagship, orange tracers from her fighter's guns lit up the area. The fighters flew through the smoke and flashed past three bulbous-looking alien bombers on the other side.

Split up and pursue, she ordered her fighters.

The bombers attempted to flee among the asteroids. One of Jessica's fighters, confused by the light and smoke, smashed into a small asteroid.

"Get out of there," Peter yelled at her.

Jessica ignored him, dodging in and out of asteroids on the hunt for her prey.

Two of the bombers were caught by her wingmen and smeared across the asteroids. "Jessica, disengage, your fighter is not designed for close action," Ammon told her. "The flagship's defences are down. Three enemy marines were seen heading for the flagship; they are very dangerous and will overwhelm Peter's crew. I will engage them and stop them from capturing Peter while you hunt outside of the rock field—"

Something pinged against one of her fighter's six ailerons and jolted her fighter enough to send her spinning.

She lost her grip on the fighter's control stick and her face jammed up against the inside of her suit's face plate.

Jessica breathed like a hummingbird and fought for control of the fighter. Alarms protested and sweat flew like rain inside her suit's helmet.

Asteroids large and small flew past the spinning fighter, fast enough that it looked like dark grey hail stones, each one promising her death if she hit them.

With one final effort she lashed out with one hand and grabbed the stick. Her suit guided her actions, helping her bring the fighter under control.

The fighter's engine cut out and she started drifting. She slowly brought her breathing under control and tilted the fighter back towards the flagship.

I'm better equipped to deal with the marines, she told Ammon.

"Ridiculous, you almost got yourself killed. Those marines are wearing very strong armour."

My safety suit is worth as much as a capital ship. Cover me old man, I'm going in.

Moments later she spotted them, three silver-armoured Tentacle-twelve, swimming through the burning air towards the immense flagship. She slowed her approach to a crawl and fired her fighter's machine guns at the aliens, dislodging one of them from the flagship's hull and taking a limb or two off another. Both the survivors slipped into a crack in the flagship's armour, close to its bridge.

"Peter?" her suit asked on her behalf.

"I'm... here," he said, sounding weak. He coughed and sounded like he was breathing hard.

"Get to an escape pod."

"Can't... get out."

Jessica frowned, then, and slammed a fist against her cockpit's armrest. *Open up.* She ordered her fighter. Her suit relayed the command and the fighter's cockpit opened for her. Her straps automatically fell off and she jumped out of the fighter and into the darkness.

R Squadron, continue your patrols and assist Commander Ammon, I'm going to get Commander Peter.

"Acknowledged."

Jessica's suit deployed its ghostly wings and guns. Rockets attached to her legs fired and she flew towards the breach in the flagship where she'd seen the enemy aliens go in.

CHAPTER 11

The corridors of the flagship were hot and twisted from the heat of the explosions outside and fires inside. The infrared visuals were useless, so the suit switched almost exclusively to sonar. Bodies of unprotected demons lay strewn around the corridors in unnatural poses. One or two had died recently, torn to pieces by the enemy marines.

The passive sonar of her suit appeared to show the images in black and white, fading in and out of clarity with every new sound that echoed throughout the corridors. The sounds of distant gun fire and robotic marine suits lit up her sensors, guiding her towards the fighting.

She flinched when a broken pipe hissed at her, brightening the HUD for a moment as she floated past.

"Jess-ic-ha," a demon addressed her from a half-closed hatch that she had already passed. The demon shone a light that was attached to a black rifle into the corridor. The demon's red uniform was torn and blood slowly seeped out of a bandaged wound, but the demon itself seemed alert.

Are there more survivors? Jessica asked.

"Not in this section, commander."

We have to stop them from reaching Peter.

"I am yours to command."

They heard gunfire, not far away, quickly followed by screeching and tearing sounds.

Peter?

"They're here," he replied.

Jessica fired the rockets on her legs, pushing her towards the end of the long corridor where the bridge was located in the centre of the ship. Just as she was about to reach the open hatch to the bridge an amoured tentacle shot out across her path. She hit the tentacle with her right shoulder and hit the walls of the corridor with her head and chest, followed by the rest of her. The enemy marine came crashing after her, torn from its perch on the wall when it had hit Jessica with its armoured limb.

The safety suit briefly took control and clung to a metal panel that had been torn from the walls. The enemy marine floated past and spread its remaining tentacles across the corridor, slowing its momentum. Jessica stared at it in the red light from the bridge, taking in the damage the alien's suit had already sustained. Half the Tentacle Twelve's limbs were missing.

"Orient yourself, Jessica. Kill it before it kills you," her suit told her.

Okay. She took back control of the suit and pointed the guns attached to her arms at the marine.

Before she could fire, the marine flicked a long arm at her and hit her in the stomach. The blow was absorbed by her suit but sent her backwards through the air of the long corridor. She fired anyway, tearing shreds from the walls and splitting the marine's armour.

The marine leapt after her, grabbing her flailing arms before she could bring them back to fire at it. A third tentacle coiled up, ready to strike. Jessica brought her feet down to point at the marine's spherical body and fire the rockets.

Let go, she told the marine.

"Objective acquired," the marine replied. Its tentacle grabbed her torso and started squeezing.

Her rockets burned the marine's armour, warping it and turning it different colours as the material started to melt. The armoured tentacle tightened and she felt the air leave her lungs.

The demon that Jessica had left near the hatch she'd found it appeared by her side. It looked at her, trying to make out what was happening in the darkness. A second later it took aim with the rifle and fired on the enemy marine.

The bullets were tiny but packed full of explosive rounds. The rounds shattered the marine's armour where Jessica had heated it and the explosive rounds turned the marine inside the armour into formless jelly. The tentacle around her chest slackened and she drew in a deep breath.

"Are you functional, commander?" the demon asked while helping her unwrap the armoured tentacle.

I'll live, she replied, still gasping for breath. *Peter?* she called on the communicator using her suit's synthesised voice. There was no response. *We have to find him,* she told the demon.

Something tore open near the ship's engines. The loud boom of the torn object reverberated throughout the ship, brightening her suit's aural sensors for a moment. She thought she saw spidery tentacles moving within the spherical bridge and mentally shuddered.

"Yes, Jess-ic-ha. I can scout the bridge while you recover."

She nodded and held her chest and stomach. She felt the suit apply numbing agents to remove the aches and pains but it left her feeling hollow. *Stop*, she told the suit. *I need to be able to feel to fight.*

"You have three broken ribs, Jessica. The enemy marine hunting for Peter is fully functional, I suggest we retreat."

And let it kill or capture Peter?

"To stop it killing or capturing *you*. Peter is smart, probably the smartest competitor to have ever come from Earth, he should have found safety by now. " She saw the ghostly shadow of the demon slip quietly into the bridge's open hatch, hugging the walls as it did so.

Peter's not wearing a safety suit, he needs all the help he can get. I'm going in.

"Very well."

Jessica floated into the bridge, passive sonar online, listening for the smallest of sounds. Jessica searched with lidless, white eyes and held her breath to keep from making any sounds that the enemy marine might hear.

It probably already knew she was there. She imagined it slithering around the darkened ceiling, slowly reaching out with its long tentacles to wrap around her chest and finish the job its comrade started, removing the life from her. She twitched, scared of her own heartbeats.

Her suit brought the infrared sensors online, helping her see the various smashed screens and cooling bodies of demons as they floated around the bridge. She couldn't see the demon, which must be hiding behind the various alcoves or ruined seats.

Jessica extended her suit's black wings a little and beat the air once, slowly, moving her at an angle away from the bridge's centre. She held her arms at different angles, the attached guns fully deployed, trying to cover every possible route of attack. She beat the air again, avoiding a dead body that blocked her path.

There it was. A tentacle. She couldn't see it directly as it blended into the room's temperature perfectly and made no sound, but there it was. The tentacle lay like a shadow across a formerly active display screen that was still cooling down. She brought an arm up to fire at it but stopped herself. She had no idea where Peter was.

Peter?

No answer, but neither did her suit's sensors pick up any sound from Peter's communicator. If he was in the bridge, either the communicator was dead or it was turned off. Most likely he wasn't in the bridge at all.

The tentacle had not moved and she doubted what she saw. Maybe it was a pipe, a girder or a dead demon's arm.

If she was wrong and the alien marine was somewhere else, she would lose the element of surprise.

You're hesitating, she told herself. *Just do it.*

She pointed her arms at either end of the tentacle, hoping to hit the marine's body, then fired.

Noise and light exploded to life within the bridge, allowing her to see the carnage the marine had wrought. Anywhere up to twenty messy bodies littered the air, along with bits and pieces of electronics and crystalline data displays.

Jessica's rounds hit the armoured tentacle at both ends, shearing it off on one side and denting the armour on the other. She barely noticed. The enemy marine's spherical body was so close to her head she could have leaned forward and kissed it.

A split second after she fired, the marine's tentacles started closing around her, caging her in like a fly caught in the spider's embrace.

Jessica panicked and kept firing while igniting her rockets to try and get out of the trap. The explosive rounds chipped the marine's armoured body. It recoiled from the onslaught. Debris from the blast embedded itself into Jessica's right arm and the gun on that arm stopped firing.

She slipped through the marine's cage and flew directly into the path of bodies and smashed electronics, then hit the spherical ceiling. She quickly turned and pointed her still functioning gun where the marine should have been.

It wasn't.

Tentacles reached for her.

Explosions erupted from the far side of the marine's body. It was the demon, firing its rifle at the marine while it was distracted.

Caught between the demon's rifle and Jessica's powerful arm gun, the marine reversed course and reached for the demon. The demon broke cover from behind a dilapidated console and kicked off the bridge wall, sending it flying to the ceiling faster than the marine could catch it.

Jessica fired again, breaking a tentacled claw from its armoured limb.

The marine ignored her and took off after the demon. The demon kicked off the ceiling, trying to put as much distance between itself and the marine as possible.

"Go, commander. Peter is safe now, you are not."

Good idea.

She turned and rocketed towards the bridge's entrance hatch, grabbing its open lip with her damaged arm and swinging out into the corridor beyond.

She felt something snag her good foot and looked down to see a claw attached to her ankle.

It was dragging her back into the bridge. More tentacles moved towards her.

No-no-no, she thought and fired her rockets at full strength. She started moving out of the bridge but the marine held tight. She brought her functioning gun down and fired at where she thought the marine's body was.

It screamed. Frustrated or in pain she couldn't be sure, but it let go and she rocketed away, hitting one of the corridor's walls and sliding along it.

She hit the open edge of a side room's hatch and stopped there, feeling light headed. *Where's my foot?* she thought when she realised why the marine had let go. It hadn't. She didn't have time to ponder the problem.

The marine followed.

She fired, again and again, blowing limbs, claws and sections of corridor panelling to pieces. The marine slammed into her.

It had three semi-functional tentacles left by the time it got to her, with what seemed to be half a body. Still, it managed to wrap her up with one of the tentacles.

The marine turned and Jessica saw, behind the marine, the demon's white teeth glinting in the reflected light of the burning corridor.

Jessica strained against the tentacle's grip but felt too numb to move. The marine threw pieces of debris at the demon but missed. The demon bounded from wall to wall, avoiding the thrown objects until it was within the marine's lashing tentacles.

A tentacle embedded itself within the corridor's ceiling, right where the demon had been. The demon kicked off the ceiling, flipped mid-air and hit the corridor's floor before jumping again to avoid the last tentacle.

The demon slapped the tentacle with one of its hands. Jessica thought she heard bones snapping in the demon's hand. Blood splattered from the demon's fingers and coated the walls dark red.

The demon grunted from pain and kicked off the ceiling again to dive into an open hatch, pointing the rifle at the marine's ruined body. The demon fired, hitting the marine's tentacle that was still embedded in the ceiling, shattering it. The marine unwrapped its tentacle from Jessica to try and defend itself.

Free from the tentacle's crushing grip, Jessica did the only thing she could think of and grabbed at the marine's ruined armour with her left hand, then spun the alien body and punched it with her right hand.

It was the distraction the demon needed. Realising its mistake, the marine re-wrapped its tentacle around her, then turned its attention back to the demon.

The demon was already on top of it. It shoved the rifle into one of the many cracks in the marine's armoured body and fired.

The tentacle around Jessica immediately slackened. The fight was over. Jessica chucked the tentacled being's ruined body away from her.

Thank you, she thought at her demonic saviour.

The demon acknowledged her thanks with a nod.

What happened to Peter?

"Another piece escorted him to the hangar while we distracted the marines. We must leave this vessel. More marines may be coming for you."

My foot, she almost screamed when she remembered her severed foot.

"It will be replaced. Our forces need to regroup. Both the Terran fleet and Tentacle-twelve have been decimated."

Okay, I understand. But... even if we regroup. is there much left to fight with?

"Some few ships and transports remain in both fleets."

She heard a loud ding in her communicator. She frowned, waiting for the inevitable announcement.

"BLUE TEAM REQUESTS TRUCE."

Wait, what? Jessica asked, surprised that the Tentacle-twelve would want to stop fighting.

"The enemy have failed to capture you or Commander Dorn," the demon explained for her. "Their objectives are now harder to obtain; this may seem like a logical conclusion to the game to our opponents."

She heard Ammon over the communicator. "I suggest we acc—"

"Truce accepted," Peter said, sounding tired.

"TRUCE ACHIEVED IN ARENA FIFTEEN-A."

CHAPTER 12

They'd lost the game. The Tentacle-twelve had beaten them by a small margin. It was still a surprise; Peter's manually calculated firing solutions had almost turned the tide. Her demon saviour, the same one that had fought two enemy marines by her side, was applying blue-goo to her stump of an ankle. Blue goo covered its severed fingers on its right hand.

The demon's voice, though twisted and grating, still sounded much like her suit.

"You're Jean Bodin, aren't you? Or were?" she asked the demon. He seemed to ignore her question, but, as he checked on her repaired tongue, he looked directly into her eyes.

"I am not at liberty to discuss." He winked at her. Ammon looked over at them from his cross-legged position while demons attended to his wounds. He stared at Jessica's demon as it stalked off towards Hubunker, who was waiting for them near the arena's cavernous medical bay.

"Interesting fellow, isn't he?" she said.

"All pieces are tuned to their role in the games," Ammon answered while he continued to watch the demon, one hairless eyebrow raised. He looked back at her and smiled with a crooked set of teeth, "Rejoice, child. We have lost the greatest battle in known Shellworld history. The Tentacle-twelve are noble adversaries, so your homecoming is assured under their protection. The Plinth cannot touch us here."

"Ho! Friend, Ammon, I must stop you there," Hubunker called out to them, he crossed the hall of broken red demons and black aircraft in hops and steps while more demons doled out blue liquid and multi-coloured orbs to the wounded around him. "The Tentacled-twits will attempt to protect us within the confines of the halls of the exchange, but outside of the halls, maybe even within them, I'm afraid things have... changed."

***

The Hall of the Exchange of Points was an endless cylindrical shaft. Kilometres-wide white spindles formed the skybridges that connected the rest of the Shellworld to the Exchange offices at the centre of the shaft. Each spindle was semi-translucent, with the white floors eventually disappearing as the sides curved up to form a clear ceiling. Ten separate spindles extended from the outside walls of the cylindrical hall towards the central white hub. They stood at the entrance to one of these spindles, one that was suited to oxygen-nitrogen breathers. Jessica peered upwards and suffered a sudden onset of vertigo.

The Hall of Exchange of Points had hundreds of layers of spindles, going up into an endless vertical hole. "Don't look down," Peter said next to her. He was staring down through the floor, wide-eyed. She saw why - more spindles, as many as there were above them. Beings from a thousand different worlds packed the oxygen-nitrogen spindle ahead of them, peering at the human team with many types of different eyes and other senses.

Most were there to see Team Earth.

Just as many aliens must have been trying to get a look at them from each of the other spindles, where the air was different. "Wow."

"We appear to have a crowd," Ammon said, deadpan.

"Hmm, yes. I hope our security measures will be enough," Hubunker said from in front of them. He looked regal in his red gown, flanked by demon bodyguards in red energy-suits that made them look like they were encased in red fluid. The three humans, now fully healed, walked slowly behind him in their formal red tracksuits. More demons in red fluid suits surrounded them while more of them wore mirror-like armour, hefting weapons of many different types. Dozens of Hubunker's multi-coloured orbs floated around the edges of the group and the surprise addition of several Tentacle-twelves started pushing through the crowds in front. The Tentacle-twelves were using armoured suits much like the one Jessica had fought in the last arena.

Jessica felt like the bulls-eye on a target board. She could smell the foul odours coming off the crowd around their group, like rotten eggs mixed with methane, wet-dog, decaying flowers, and mouldy cheese. She started gagging and the sounds and colours of the crowds whirled past while they pushed through. "I've got you," Peter had to shout for her to hear, he held her arm and gave her a quick smile. She smiled back to let him know she was okay. Halfway across the spindle, the commander of the Tentacle-twelve raised three of its armoured limbs.

"We are being asked to stop, something is blocking us," Hubunker interpreted for them. Fluidic demons closed around the humans and their Trustee. Jessica looked through the masses of armoured aliens to where the Tentacle-twelve had raised itself up on multiple limbs. Several of its arms rapidly formed different shapes in the air, and Jessica thought she heard something growl back at it. "The Plinth are here in some numbers," Hubunker said.

With the suddenness of a leaping snake, the Tentacle's armour changed from silver to black and cracked two of its limbs over the crowds. The crowd recoiled from the menacing gesture and slipped away to the sides. Jessica could just make out what was blocking their path. It was the Plinth, thousands of them standing rank upon rank across the width of the spindle. They were not armed or armoured but it was clear they were trying to stop the humans from reaching the central hub, locking their arms together. "Disperse or the Games Masters shall be informed," Hubunker shouted at them.

"We invoke the right of protest," said the Plinth leader. Ammon translated the Plinth's response. "You bring excessive force into this peaceful Exchange; we protest your actions." The Tentacle cracked its whip-like limbs again and more of the crowd moved away. The Plinth did not flinch.

"We respond to multiple threats and past actions; we believe our actions are lawful. Disperse!" Hubunker shouted again.

"Reduce your forces and we shall open our ranks."

"The Games Ma—"

"You know as well as we the Games Masters and their appointed arbiters are engaged in conflict, a conflict you designed, Hubunker Warmonger."

"Warmonger? Nonsense. I am a single being. How could I have started such a conflict?"

"You have done your damage Hubunker, over many years. Your human pawns we will not damage, they may pass. No one else is getting closer to the central hub. We'll have you banned from the

Exchange for your crimes, and your new friends, the Tentacle-twelve, had best leave before the same happens to them."

A buzzing sound filled Jessica's ears and multicoloured orbs faded to reds and oranges. More Tentacle-twelves headed for the Plinth blockade, changing to black as they stepped over other beings in their way.

"We must leave our allies if we are to go through," Ammon said to the other two.

"Won't they hurt us?" Jessica asked.

"No. They have given their word that we will not be harmed if we leave our protectors behind. They have much to lose if they do not keep that word. Despite their prior treatment of us, they are law-abiding members of the Shellworld. Their quarrel is not with us."

"This dour fellow is quite correct, as are the Plinth," Hubunker said, "though they do not know to what extent they are correct... Hmm, I fear this is where we part ways. I do not know what will happen to me once you have gone, but it is, perhaps, prudent that I do not tarry too long. A conflict has already started on the outer reaches of many of the Shellworld's star nets." Hubunker sounded very happy with the announcement. "In fact, it started after Mr Ivanov was executed. His death, regrettably, became the trigger for my friends and their allies to begin their campaign. Jean has finally proven his worth; with the bodies I have given him, he has wiped out the Plinth's grand capital fleet and their Trustee is in full retreat. The conflict may even reach this very Exchange, but not for a few hundred years, I imagine."

Hubunker looked thoughtful for a moment, ignoring the posturing Tentacle-twelve, the belligerent Plinth, and the protective orbs above. "When you do enter the Exchange and choose your final prizes, I advise you to choose things for the betterment of your species." Ammon nodded impatiently. "Do not focus too much on yourselves. Now that the residents of the Shellworld know of your potential, it is likely that some of them may try to... *manipulate* you and the rest of humanity with no small amount of force. I do hope that there will be no need for such worries. The conflict may distract them for quite some time. Oh, but I do waffle on, don't I? Go, my beneficiaries; enjoy your prizes. Ammon, get lost."

Ammon smiled and bowed, "I intend to, master."

"Oh, shut up and go, you idiot."

They made their way towards the long lines of Plinth soldiers until they stood at its edge. "Let us through," Ammon said. One of the Plinth looked at each of them and snapped its large jaws. It unlinked its arms and moved to the side. The next soldier behind him did the same, as did more and more until a path appeared.

"Go," the Plinth leader growled at them in English. They stepped through the tight corridor and did their best to ignore the hot breaths at their necks. When they made it through to the other side Jessica started shaking. The whole way to the hub was now clear, not a single being stood between them and their destination.

"The Plinth cleared the way for us," Ammon said.

"To create a killing zone?" asked Jessica.

"As a sign of respect. Georgy humiliated them. They know he didn't cheat and they learned some valuable lessons these past few days. Do not dawdle lest we lose the respect they are showing us."

Jessica found she didn't need any encouragement to go faster. If it had been up to her, they would have run the rest of the way. She still might have if she could trust her new, artificial foot and her legs didn't feel so wobbly. She kept looking over her shoulders, expecting a Plinth to be right behind her.

They couldn't have reached the Hub quickly enough. Lots of doors waited for them with blinking lights in different patterns above each of them.

"This one." Ammon nodded at a door that was starting to open into the top of its ornately patterned architrave.

Inside was a well-lit room no bigger than Jessica's living room. She felt warmth caress her face and sweet perfumes calm her nerves. Blue walls complemented wooden furniture and grassy green plants. A large alien sat at a desk two sizes too small for its stick-thin figure. It had three eyes hidden in a single long groove across its forehead and a large mouth that almost extended from one side of its head to the other. "Please sit," it said. Jessica expected to hear the slightly delayed automatic translation that would let her know what the creature had said but she realised after a moment she already understood.

"You speak English?"

"Please sit," it repeated for her with a slight purr in its high-pitched voice. It gestured to three wooden chairs. Cushions with floral patterns were tied to the chairs by red ribbons. "We have much to discuss; you have been allotted a great deal of points and it is unlikely a species such as yours has had much experience with so much currency. I will attempt to aid you in your decisions."

"Just get on with it," Ammon snapped. "I've been waiting thousands of years for this moment, Earth will embrace me once more."

Jessica and Peter looked quizzically at their former teacher and shrugged at each other, *strange remark...*

Ammon noticed their shrugs and said, "I was meant to be a Pharaoh, a god amongst men. I will be again."

"Very well," the alien said. "We'll start with your primary desires, then work on miscellaneous options based on those desires, plus a few you may not have thought of for yourselves. I will now dive into your neural pathways, hold for one moment..."

***

Jessica felt like she was lying naked on a bed of grass. *Where are my clothes?* She looked up at a clear blue sky. She eased herself up and looked around to find she was in her backyard. The wooden palings of her old fence were as worn as ever, but the clothesline was missing. She stood up and felt dizzy, newly-gained knowledge weighing her mind down.

She took one wobbly step towards the house and noticed discarded police-tape in the green bin down the side of the house. With a frown she stepped into the house's unlocked back door, walking into the too-neat laundry and continued to the kitchen. She tested her new infrared vision and saw heat radiating from her chrome-coloured kettle. A spoon clattered to the kitchen floor and she turned sharply to see what had moved it. She crouched into a defensive posture and felt the ends of her fingertips crackle with energy.

"Jessica?" her mother said, her voice quivering. Her mother held tightly to the doorframe between the kitchen and dining room.

Behind her mother, her father was sitting at the dining table, nursing a warm cup of tea. His face started to turn white.

He leapt up from the table to race past her mother and grab a towel from the laundry. Jessica abandoned her defensive posture and covered herself with her hands. She leaned heavily against one wall and shook with relief.

"Here," her father wrapped her in a brown towel. "Jessica, where have you been?" Tears started falling from his cheeks. Her mother, still holding the doorframe, stood in shock, eyes wide and mouth hanging.

"Mum, Dad, I... I think I need to talk to NASA."

***

Ammon awoke to find he was lying atop some dusty tiles underneath an overhanging shelter of some sort. He turned on his side and looked across a black river of melted rocks. A wheeled metal vehicle roared at him as it rolled past on the black rocks.

"A road, a truck" he said to himself. He felt the knowledge come as consciousness returned. "A shop. Restaurants. Morning sunrise. Pyramids.... Pyramids?"

He stood up quickly when he realised what he was staring at. The ancient memories did not gel well with this modern reality. The pyramids should have been smooth, glittering monuments to his father's greatness. These miniature mountains were crumbling and dull. The smells of the vendors were all strange to him and even the dust tasted different to how he remembered.

Yet, this was Earth. He was home.

He smiled.

"'Ezzāy hàdretàk?" a man asked. He wore glasses and had a concerned look on his face.

"How am I?" Ammon replied, instantly recognising one of Earth's modern languages. He imagined himself through the middle-aged man's eyes. Ammon must have looked like a frail, bald, naked man, sleeping on the sidewalk of a street in the middle of Cairo. The man was trying to be helpful, he surmised.

"How am I?" he said, this time in the man's native tongue. Ammon stretched out his hands and watched them glow. Small, purple sparks arced between his fingertips. "I feel great."

The man's mouth gaped open. He dropped the odd-smelling food he had been holding.

"Your hands..." the stunned man said, mesmerised.

"And my eyes," Ammon said. His eyes started glowing purple.

The man's eyes widened. He turned and started running.

Ammon laughed.

"Must be serious, now," he told himself. The war for the Shellworld would grow, in time. Not only that, but before he'd been whisked away from the Shellworld a case had been brought against humankind in the Arbiter's Hall. The Plinth were trying to install a new Trustee. This, Ammon could not allow.

He would have to work quickly. First, he would have to take over the various governments of Earth using his newly acquired gifts. Next, he would enforce a new law, one that would allow him to quickly distribute new, very advanced technology to the world.

Things might get messy for a while but it would be necessary if Earth's inhabitants were going to survive. The Shellworld's war might not affect the Earth for ten years, a hundred, maybe a thousand. But there was one thing that was certain, the war would reach it.

There were just a couple things standing in his way.

The girl was young, prone to anger, and naive. She would be useful, but she'd made the mistake of choosing other, deadlier gifts over the more expensive gift of immortality. Very likely Jessica would die before she would be of use in defending humanity in the coming war. He should be able to capture her easily enough; he would just have to do it before she realised her full potential.

The man was another matter. Brilliant and quick, it would not take Peter long to acclimate to his new gifts. He was arrogant and obsessive; perhaps Ammon could use that against him...

***

"Alina, Illia, don't stray too far," Peter shouted after the two huskies. The dogs bounded happily in the snow surrounding

Inverness Castle. Peter never thought he would be walking around the Scottish highlands with two Russian huskies in the middle of winter, but here he was. It was a far cry from the heat of his mother city of New Delhi.

Despite the freezing temperatures, the cold of Scotland just didn't bother him anymore.

He found he could do a great many things he'd never been able to do before. Yet, as amazing as doing things like being able to breathe underwater seemed, he was dissatisfied.

There was so much more he could learn.

He looked to the cloudy, grey sky and pierced it with his enhanced vision, staring at the stars beyond, trying to search for that strange world that had given him these gifts.

"Peter."

Peter frowned when he heard the gravelly voice by his side.

"Ammon, I wondered how long it would be before you came to see me. It's only been two days since Jessica disappeared from that military installation in Australia. You move quickly." Peter turned towards the ancient man. Ammon had dressed in a black business suit, complete with a white button-up shirt and black tie.

He wore sunglasses. There was no mistaking him, though.

"So, have you come to kill me?"

"Kill you?" Ammon looked genuinely shocked.

"Isn't that what happened to Jessica?"

"Jessica is safe," Ammon replied. "I'm quite fond of her, but her gifts are needed in the future, beyond the limit of her natural life. No, I dare not harm her. I have come to give you a deal."

"A deal?" Peter asked, not trusting him. Subconsciously he raised his defences. His personal defences were gifts from the wargames, added to his genetic makeup.

"You want to go back there, don't you?"

Peter looked back to the skies. "To the Shellworld." He nodded and said, "How do I get there?"

"I'll show you."

EPILOGUE

"Hubunker Warmonger," the arbiter at the centre of the Arbiter's Hall addressed him. The Arbiter's Hall was beige in colour, a hundred kilometres in diameter, with billions of observers taking their seats and other comfortable positions on the spherical wall. They needed monitors or telescopes and other scanners to be able to observe the trial. Hubunker noted a hundred-metre wide hole, tiny at this distance, where some of his allies had tried to smash through the hall and rescue him several years earlier.

Since then, the battle above the Shellworld had escalated in size and the security systems around the Arbiter's Hall strengthened. The hole was slowly being repaired, millimetre by millimetre, back to its original strength by microscopic machines.

"I am no warmonger," he finally replied.

"Hubunker Warmonger," the head of the Arbiter's Guild repeated. Being tree-like in nature, the head of the Arbiter's Guild had grown to immense proportions, allowing itself to grow to almost a thousand paces wide. The arbiter's speech was not audible to the average citizen's ear, it's voice was so low in pitch it had become sub-sonic to most beings. Hubunker, nevertheless, felt the giant creature's voice reverberate through his body. "Judgement has been made," said the electronic translators embedded in the walls around him.

Hubunker sighed. "And what is my fate?"

"Execution, of course. There is more, though, that has been covered in a separate trial parallel to your own. You claim to have used and abused your human beneficiaries to start this war as if they were not complicit. This, we have determined, is a lie. The humans known as Ammon and Georgy Ivanov were recorded in a bar, planning to help overthrow the established order and sow chaos."

Hubunker's eyestalks contracted, surprised at the revelation. "The Trustee Bars are sacred ground; you have broken your own laws to take those recordings."

"So, you admit it then?"

Hubunker covered his mouth. "Shit," he whispered.

"Noted. This is the sentence we hand to the humans: Your beneficiaries are found to be guilty of collusion in your plans. An arbiter will be dispatched to judge the race of humans whereupon a new trustee will be appointed. As you know, Hubunker Warmonger, the rules have changed. The human race is to be held hostage on the surface shell until they prove themselves worthy in the next wargames. The rest of the human race is to be expunged from their normal place of residence."

"You can't," he said, defeated and saddened by the thought of his human pets being slaughtered and the survivors being forced to migrate to the Shellworld. "The actions of two beings should not impact on their entire race."

"If the rules were changed, as you have wished, that may be the case, but they have not.

"The humans are primitive, arbiter, they're not aware of the rules."

"Hmm, that may be so. Yet, as trustee of that race, you should have informed them. Their punishment is your fault, Hubunker Warmonger."

The fight left his eyestalks. "I'm sorry," he said, as if those two words would absolve him of humanity's doom.

"Execute," the ponderous voice echoed through his body. In a flash of brilliant white light, Hubunker was no more.

***

Jessica dreamed a hundred thousand nightmares. She couldn't breathe, couldn't escape. The dreams kept coming, over and over. She felt as if she was constantly fighting waves in the ocean. She could see the surface, but every time she breached it into wakefulness, a new wave of nightmares came crashing down.

Restless sleep assaulted her for what seemed like a hundred years.

Her parents turned to dust. The doctors that had whisked her away, vanished. Aliens invaded her mind, torturing her, burning her as an act of revenge. Her skin melted, her eyes burst from the heat and she upchucked bile.

Tears flowed like a river.

The Earth turned ever faster until she thought she watched a perpetual twilight, where night blended into day.

The hand of her teacher broke the surface.

"Jessica," a voice croaked from beyond the nightmarish veil.

"Ammon?" she whispered. Her eyes opened. She awoke on the floor inside a small, white room with no windows or furniture. "Where am I?"

"Jessica, you're alive," Ammon's voice continued. "You're aboard an arbiter's starship, in orbit around Earth."

"In orbit?" Jessica frowned and looked into Ammon's eyes. The small man was resplendent in white, silken gowns. Trimmed in gold, the gowns concealed all but his bald head.

His purple eyes struck at her heart as if she were looking at a monster. Then she remembered.

"You."

"Yes. I trapped you in a cocoon. For a hundred and thirty years you have slept, Jessica. For that, I am deeply sorry. It was a grave error on my part."

"What...what has happened? A hundred and thirty years?" Shock and fear took hold of her senses.

Ammon looked sad, his eyes drooping where they had once been hard as diamonds. "The war for the Shellworld drags on. Hubunker was captured in one of many battles and put on trial. Obviously, they found him guilty. Unfortunately, this means a new trustee has been appointed."

"Tell me, Ammon, what have you done to Earth?"

"What have I done?" Ammon's mouth juddered, almost smiling. "What *haven't* I done? I have done a lot, child. The Earth is united under my rule. Humanity has advanced tremendously under my guidance, but..." he looked to the side. "All the sacrifices I have made, the lives sacrificed to progress... it has all been for nothing."

Jessica raised her arms, noticing yellow mucous covering her skin. It was then, her head shivering, that she noticed the colour of her hair as it fell across her face. Normally brown hair fell like a red curtain across her eyes.

Her arms glowed a soft green. The more she woke up, the brighter her arms glowed. "What. Have. You. Done?" Green fire started flickering from her fingers and her eyes felt as if they burned.

"The Games Masters themselves have decided our fate. The Plinth were denied the Trusteeship but the Arbiter's Guild were ordered to appoint a new Trustee for us. They found one."

"Me? Is that why I'm being taken?"

"No," Ammon reached for her flickering hands and grasped them, instantly calming her with his touch. "I exiled Peter from Earth, sent him towards a star gate that should have taken him a thousand years to reach. This is my folly; Peter... he betrayed us, as I betrayed him. He has taken it upon himself to become the new trustee. Jessica, I'm afraid he has agreed to the Plinth's terms. As a condition of Peter becoming trustee, Peter asked for two commanders. I offered Aislyn Reigns as one of them... that's *you*. You're now a young woman named Aislyn Reigns. I could do nothing to stop it. My only hope is that the arbiter does not recognise you." Ammon turned away and wiped his eyes. "To keep you alive I have altered your appearance and your genetic makeup. You are our only hope, Jessica. You need to challenge him, stop Peter before he ruins everything my master built. You can't allow the Plinth to rule over us with Peter as their puppet. You need to become the trustee and reverse the Plinth's terms."

Jessica's mouth suddenly felt dry. "What terms?"

"The Earth and all of humanity are to be reduced to a small sample and kept on the Shellworld until the new games are over. Yes, Jessica, you're right to be horrified. Earth is to be annihilated."

"The Earth... what?"

"The rules have changed, Jessica. Since humanity has broken the rules, or so the arbiter decreed, our species cannot remain as an independent enclave from the Shellworld. The arbiter will scour the Earth of life, nothing will stop that now. You can save our species though. Become our trustee and throw off the Plinth's influence."

"H-how can I challenge him? Peter's had a hundred years head start," her head spun at the thought even as she said it. While she slept for a hundred and thirty years, Peter had learned, day by day, how to use his new gifts.

Ammon gently pushed her head down into the yellow goo she had been lying in for the past century, forcing her underneath it.

She spluttered as she choked on the mucous substance. "You will have to try. You chose the deadlier gifts while Peter chose immortality. Your name, from now on, is Aislyn Reigns. Remember that and they will not suspect who you really are. I'm going to embed Aislyn's memories into your mind so that you remember who you have become. At the first chance you get, request assistance from the Reigns Syndicate, they will try to help you."

"Who the hell are the Reigns Syndicate?" she asked.

"Your new family." Ammon's hands engulfed her red-haired head with purple fire.

Jessica screamed as the nightmares closed in. A new childhood, that of a young, dead woman's who had lived over a hundred years into Jessica's future, started unravelling in her mind.

Ammon's lips drooped low. "Good luck."

END OF THE LINE

Madame Elaine Amplebottom was a wiry old lady, yet, as her servant had discovered, her claw-like hands did not lack for strength. As old as she was, Elaine had gathered quite a lot of wealth over the past three hundred years. She had spent almost all of the money on her new starship: a two-hundred-kilometre-long vessel she liked to call a 'Light Chaser.'

Davious Goodspeed, despite being hired as a nurse, may as well have been her slave. She'd hired him to look after her bodily needs, while the two of them made the greatest journey ever made by mankind. The problem was that Davious had been assured it would only be a couple of months. It was not.

The starship, registered under the name *Pretty Pebble*, quickly accelerated. Davious felt a continuous nudge from the acceleration; it was enough to keep his feet on the floor. Faster and faster, Mr Goodspeed's beloved Earth fell behind them, until it was nothing but a small blue spot of light. A day later the Solar System had receded to the size of a thumbnail.

"Davey, come here you lazy man-thing," Madame Elaine told him ever-so-sickeningly-sweetly "Give me a backrub."

Davious shuddered. He had entered his own private hell as soon as he'd stepped on board the *Pretty Pebble*. *See the sights*, the advertisement had said. *Live forever*. What the advertisement failed to mention, was that he would often be waist-deep in a large bath, filled with questionable brown liquids. In the bath, he was made to massage Elaine Amplebottom's wrinkly old body. She loved her backrubs.

This happened, daily, all the way to the edge of the universe.

He could think of better things to do with his time. If he'd done some research on who Elaine Amplebottom was, and what her goals were, maybe he wouldn't have been suckered into this mess.

"Coming," he said, trying to mimic her sweet tones. He hated every syllable he spoke. It was going to be a *long* trip.

The days and months, spent accelerating away from Earth, crushed his soul. Outside of the ship physics worked its magic, and they seemed to travel past the stars much faster than they really were. As they came closer to the speed of light, time came to a screeching halt for its passengers. In the few months they had spent travelling across the universe, entire empires had flourished and dwindled. Stars were birthed in the dark void, bursting like sparklers across the viewscreens. The sparkling stars ignited the emptiness of deep space. Some stars inflated as they died, or slowly dimmed.

Davious was despondent when he realised they must have skipped millions of years. *My dogs*, he thought, *my birds.* He hoped they'd lived a good life.

He doubted he would live past the next two years due to his heart condition. The *Precious Pebble* had little in the way of medical equipment; Elaine had explained that she simply didn't need it, and hadn't bothered to acquire any for her employee/slave.

To distract him from his misery - an impossible task while they were in the bath, I assure you - Madame Elaine Amplebottom tried to teach him Einsteinian Physics. It was a losing battle. He could grasp the basics but gave up on the math.

"Wait a minute," he interrupted her on one occasion. The ship's speakers played some sort of obnoxious music that hurt his ears, while he rubbed water-wrinkled fingers against Elaine's hard, flaky skin. "You're saying nothing can go faster than light. But if we're travelling at the speed of light in one direction, and someone else is travelling in the other direction at the speed of light, then wouldn't we be travelling at twice the speed of light?"

He found out just how quick she was when she turned around and slapped him with her claws, leaving red welts across his face. "You're not thinking of the perspective of the passengers. My good idiot, remember the perspective. Bah. Maybe tomorrow."

He persisted, "And if we're travelling towards a planet, isn't it travelling towards us at the speed of light too? Wouldn't time be slow on the planet as well?"

"Perspective," she yelled at him.

He held up his hands and tripped backwards over the bath's lip, hitting his head against gold-trimmed black tiles before choking on some brown liquid that splashed into his mouth.

He almost vomited inside his mouth when the putrid stuff lodged at the back of his throat. After a couple of minutes, he stood back up and stepped into the bath.

"But perspective is what I'm talking about, isn't it?" he asked, raising one arm to stop her striking him.

"You're not the sharpest tool in the shed, are you?" she said.

He grinned behind her back. "Probably not, I do make for a bloody good hammer though," he replied. Elaine glared at him.

He laughed as he ran away from her steely claws.

Ten years of shipboard time, and billions of Earth years later, he was in such a state of depression that all he could do was stare at the stars and galaxies. They seemed to whiz past, like car lights on a busy highway; blue as they approached, red as they receded.

While in one of these depressive moods he spotted *it*. The End. Or at least, he hoped it was. "Look," he shouted to Madame Elaine. "There's something funny over there."

"My word..." Elaine's speech faltered. "What is that?"

The stars ahead of them disappeared. What looked like the brightest object in the universe, a large ring of blue light, shone on the *Precious Pebble*'s gem-encrusted surface.

The ship's communicators were flooded with messages of hope, fun and excitement, for eternity. Elaine and Davious were drawn towards the bright ring like flies to some rather seductive manure.

"Hello," a strange voice said from behind the two passengers. Davious Goodspeed jumped with fright, and Elaine Amplebottom stiffened like a statue. A strange creature the size of an elephant, but with the body of a praying mantis, appeared aboard the *Pretty Pebble*'s bridge. "My name is Tanis Rock," the black-suited praying mantis told them. "You appear to be approaching the blue circle. I assume you would like to enter?"

"Who are you, and how did you get aboard my ship?" Elaine asked, her voice failing.

"Please answer my question, do you wish to enter?"

"I..." Elaine faltered again. "Of... of course I do." The thought of eternal youth licked at her mind.

"I see," Tanis said and turned slowly to Davious. "And you?"

Davious thought back on the long journey he'd been forced to take, and of everything he missed back on Earth. "I just want this trip to end."

Tanis regarded Davious slowly, and then looked at the distant halo through the viewscreens. "I am afraid I cannot allow either of you to enter. You see, you're not on the list." Tanis held out a large golden scroll so that they could see its considerable size. "You must leave."

"What?" Elaine was stunned to silence.

Davious clutched his chest. Heartbroken, he fell to the floor. He felt like he was having a heart attack.

"Oh, Mr Goodspeed, is it?" Tanis asked him after a minute of silence.

"Yes sir, that's my name," he said, through a wall of tears. The pain in his chest disappeared.

"I just found you on the list. Here, hold my arm and I'll take you there." Davious leapt with joy and touched the strange creature's arm. A brilliant white light, matching the blue halo's intensity appeared, and he was gone.

Wide-eyed, staring at where her man servant's body had been, Elaine couldn't believe an idiot like Goodspeed could enter the halo. What had he done to earn eternal youth? "Check that list again," she demanded.

"I'm afraid you still aren't on the list," Tanis told her.

No amount of pleading would elicit a different response from the strangely-perfumed monster.

"But, where should I go now? This is the end, isn't it?"

"Turn back," Tanis said warmly. "Keep going until you get back to Earth. By the time you return to the blue halo, a spot may have opened up for you."

"Hah." She stuck up her nose. "What a rude suggestion."

"Well then, if you continue to the other side of the universe, there is a place much like the blue circle where they may be happy to admit you."

"Perhaps I was a little cruel," Tanis Rock said to Davious. "That is a long way to go."

Davious shrugged, he was distracted. They were in a large alien park, with food and friendly people aplenty. Not one of them was like Elaine, and this made him happy.

"I'm sorry, what were you saying?" he asked Tanis as he picked a cherry from the garden. "Why is it cruel?" The cherry smelt sweet.

"I neglected to tell her where she was going."

"Where's that?"

"Ah, it doesn't matter. I'm sure she'll find what she needs."

It took twenty more years for Madame Elaine Amplebottom to reach the other side of the universe. Billions of years passed on the outside of the *Pretty Pebble*. The stars were getting older and there were fewer of them.

The universe had become a dark place by the time she reached a red halo at the other end if the universe. Without her comforting idiot, that 'Goodspeed,' the trip had been oh-so-hard. It had been especially hard without her backrubs.

"Welcome, Madame Amplebottom." A small beetle-like creature, wearing a dark green cape, appeared on the ship's bridge. She would have stepped on it but was taken aback by its deep, rumbling voice. "You're a little early," the beetle told her.

"I'm early for what? How do you know my name?" Elaine asked.

"You're early for the eternal party. Hmm, I'm in a good mood today. I could let you enter before the festivities begin. Here, touch my antennae."

Hope flared brightly within Elaine's beating chest. "Does that mean I will live forever?"

"Uh." The beetle hesitated before saying, "I suppose you could call it living."

"Oh, thank you, thank you."

"For what?" the bug said, genuinely surprised.

Madame Elaine Amplebottom disappeared in a flash of red light and entered the world beyond the red halo.

"Oh dear," she said as she saw where she had been transported. The largest, ugliest creature she had ever seen, sat in a bathtub as large as an Olympic swimming pool. The creature was as large as a blue whale. But where a whale had smooth skin, the pink beast before her had fat rolls up and down its entire length. The fat rolls were only broken by craterous pimples.

The red tub was lit from no light-source she could see. All the walls were pure darkness and the floor, as far as her failing eyes could see, was blood-red.

"Where is this?" Her claw-like fingers quivered with disgust. The bath stunk of pus and rotten eggs. She could hardly breathe. "Is this the end?"

"SHUT UP," roared the pink monster. She cowered and looked for somewhere to run. "GIVE ME A BACKRUB, NOW."

THE REAPER'S CRUISE
CHAPTER 1

"We lost contact with another paradise today," the apparition to Elias's left said while he lay on the sun-soaked beach. Waves of dark blue water dumped people into the soft sand with what must have been a bone-breaking force. Elias smiled at the cheers and laughter that filtered up to the beach from the swimmers. "Are you listening to me? This is serious, El."

"I heard you," Elias said. He waved limply at the green apparition and raised another glass of mind-altering liquids to his lips.

"You understand what this means don't you? Three paradises lost, gone. Millions of souls."

"I'm sure they're out there somewhere." Elias raised his sunglasses to get a better look at the glowing apparition, 'What are you so worried about Fenik? It wasn't a human paradise. Go pester the captain about, and get a new body while you're at it. That green glow doesn't suit you.

Fenik changed to a deep red, showing its annoyance, "Put that glass down and think for a minute. It's only been a month since the first paradise portal disappeared. People are starting to panic."

"There are hundreds of other portals." Elias frowned; the beach was forgotten while Fenik stoked his annoyance, "At least a hundred paradises, dozens of university portals, hundreds of game portals and carnal domes. If something did happen, the souls would have been downloaded into the ship's core and the captain will oversee repairs."

"Repairs? How can the captain repair that much real estate if the ship keeps losing more data stores at this rate?"

"Fenik, go home. Relax, then write up some more bad music, stick to what you're good at. I have a tournament to go to."

"Bah." Fenik turned yellow in disgust and scattered on the winds. "Go lose your silly games, El."

Elias shook his head and downed the last of his tasteless drink. He swung his legs over the side of the reclined wooden chair and planted his feet in the sand.

The game wasn't due to start for another hour but Fenik had ruined his mood. He stomped across the beach's soft red sand towards the distant rainforest and ignored the sparse crowds of beach-goers stretched out along the endless coast.

As he looked off into the distance at the people, pets and apparitions, he couldn't imagine the captain would let three entire paradise portals drop from the mainframe. He'd seen the news as soon as it had happened but it seemed like some sort of trick.

It was nothing he had to worry about in any case.

Well then, he might as well log out of the portals and reset, maybe even do some clothes shopping and order a feast.

He logged off and the red sands disappeared, replaced by the relatively Spartan confines of his personal white palace.

The feast, which was full of every kind of delicacy he had ever enjoyed back on Earth, was already laid out on his favourite long table. Candles on a beautifully decorated chandelier hung in the air without any visible cables.

He dialled time up by a thousand inside the palace. Now he would have all the time he needed while time slowed to a crawl outside of the palace.

To his dismay, he found the feast as tasteless as the drink on the beach. He could smell the lovely flavours and feel the textures, so it wasn't too bad. It did start to worry him though.

Damn Fenik, distracting me even from my meals.

Fenik the fool worried too much and sucked the joy out of everything by trying to make everyone else worry. Fenik had been Elias's guide when he first came to the ship's data cores, but that didn't mean they had to be friends. He'd had to tolerate that thing's presence for what must have been centuries now.

A ringing bell caught his attention and he looked for the nearest palace communicator. Information overlaid itself across his vision when he looked directly at the communicator. It chimed again, then again. The chiming almost became a constant ringing and text streamed across his vision at unreadable speeds.

"What are you doing now Fenik?" Elias said aloud. Then he swore; time inside the palace had been dialled down by one thousand, not sped up as he had requested.

"Normal time," he called out. The messages speeding across his vision halted. He'd missed his game, plus half a dozen other social engagements.

"Five minutes at one-thousandth time..."

He did a quick calculation in his mind, "Three and a half days?"

He jumped up from his long table and accidentally knocked several plates onto the floor, scattering lobster and grilled steaks under his feet. "What the hell, Fenik?"

He brought up the ship's main newsfeeds and the most popular story was of the number of portals lost over the past week as well as small ship-wide degradations. One such degradation was the loss of taste for most inhabitants.

Fenik arrived in a puff of grey smoke, stinging Elias' eyes with what smelt like charcoal.

"Three and a half days?" Elias shouted at Fenik. "What the hell for?"

Fenik changed to a smoky dark red, annoyed, "That was not me El. You know I have no control over your personal spaces. The ship is in trouble."

"The ship... impossible. Nothing can touch us."

"Incorrect, you ape brained moron. The inhabitants of the cruise ship's destination planet have become somewhat hostile. The captain is calling for the aid of the ship's best game players to stop these horrendous attacks. You have been summoned, against my wishes. Apparently, a dim-wit who does almost nothing but play games for a few centuries is of greater assistance than Fenik."

"Uh... the captain itself has summoned me?"

Fenik turned a shade of grey so dark it may as well have been black, "As I said. Things are not good."

They met at the highest tower of Elias' great white palace. It wasn't the captain. At least, it wasn't the Captain's living, breathing mind-self. It may as well have been the captain though – everything in this meeting, in this white room, would be recorded and fed directly into the Captain's mind for storage and judgement.

Elias was sure he should have been shivering with nerves. Decades had passed since any humans had interacted with the captain.

The all-seeing, infinitely benevolent tree-monster may as well have been the ship's god. Without the captain, nothing worked. Hundreds of billions of souls depended on its guidance and millions of the true-living depended on it to keep them alive through the decade long voyages between stars.

"You are among a few I have chosen," the captain told him.

It wasn't using speech. Elias received the captain's words as text planted directly into his mind, words that were automatically translated from subtle movements from many of the captain's branching limbs.

The captain's brown trunk was twice the size of a normal human, held aloft by dozens of thick, flexible branches. It wasn't a tree, of course, but many inhabitants believed it was descended from a carnivorous plant species or some sort of crab. Elias decided it had to be something completely different but more importantly, why should he care where the captain came from?

"Ah, yes sir, Fenik mentioned that. I was chosen because of my involvement in the games."

"Yes," The word came almost half a minute later. "You are aware the ship is under attack?"

"I am, yes but—"

"Good. You have demonstrated great flexibility in the games. Do you remember your homeworld, Elias?" The words were gentle, putting Elias at ease.

"Earth?" Elias said. "Yes, I remember Earth, bits and pieces. Nice place, but you rescued us before the attack."

"Have you enjoyed your time here?"

"Yes sir, immensely. I'd never leave if I had the chance."

"Interesting..." Somehow Elias got the sensation of sadness when the captain continued. "Then it may upset you to know that this task will require you to leave the ship for some time."

"Oh I know, sir. I guessed from the loss of the portals and the situation in the true-life areas that you might need some of us virtuals out there."

"Yes. We have lost more than just the portals. Entire sections of the ship were damaged. Billions of souls have been lost and many more may follow. Are you ready to replicate some of your more aggressive games within true-life?"

"When do I start?" Elias said without hesitation. "Will I get a new body?"

"A device will be provided for your locomotion. More will be revealed once you are underway. For now, though, I must suspend your thought patterns, you will awaken once your task commences."

CHAPTER 2

Space. Heat. Ground.

Hundreds of tons of dirt and rock reached for the sky after Elias' entry pod slammed into the planet's surface. Metres of ablative material from the entry pod's shell were vaporized and the cushioning interior shifted violently as it sunk ever deeper into the ground.

The explosion was engineered to hit a small tectonic plate in such a way as to cause large earthquakes across the land.

Dozens of his friends slammed into the tectonic plate every few hundred metres, throwing up a large wall of dirt and sand for several kilometres.

As Elias emerged from his cracked descent pod he immediately identified the enemy installation he'd been tasked with attacking. Enemy anti-aircraft weapons spewed hot lead into the alien sky as more of his friends poured down like red rain. Some of them blossomed into red flowers when they were hit.

Elias extended one fifty-metre long arm, then another and another, until all sixteen spidery legs had found the alien ground. The legs levered his three-metre body off the ground.

One of his legs lost a large chunk out of it when an enemy gun started shooting at him. *Time to move*, he thought, and in a blur of motion, he skittered across the barren, sand covered landscape.

It was night-time and the muzzle flashes of the enemy guns were clearly visible to his spherical-body's enhanced sensors. He dodged left-right-left until he was less than a hundred metres from his target and leapt forward. He crashed into the gun and its alien operators with such force that they died on impact.

"Elias, watch your legs." One of his friends called to him. One of the aliens emerged from the gun's wreckage with a small rifle and started shooting at his main body. The shots plinked off his body without any effect.

"Haha, not a problem Shima," he called back.

The alien that was shooting at him was a furry brown in appearance, standing on two legs, about two metres tall. It hooted loudly at him from a small trunk where a nose should be. He brought down one of his giant arms to swipe the critter from its perch.

"Ouch," he said involuntarily as his arm was lopped off. Stunned by the loss of the arm, he jerked back and swatted at the creature as if it were an aggressive hornet on his face. The creature ended up in several pieces.

"It's the rifles; they have molecular cutting blades along their sides. Read your briefing notes," Shima told him.

"Yeah, thanks," Elias inspected the rifle and the damage it had done to his legs. He looked towards the enemy installation and saw at least a hundred enemy soldiers spreading out before them. "I have an idea."

"Oh no, not the rocks," Shima said. She was within arms-reach behind him, watching as he picked up handfuls of small rocks with his three-clawed feet. "We can't risk damage to the installation."

"Watch me." Through a hail of alien bullets, Elias skittered the short distance and sliced his way across the alien lines until he was at the bottom end, parallel to the building the aliens were protecting. The nearest enemy creatures raised their rifles as if they were ancient battle axes. Elias smiled in his mind, took aim, and pelted his rocks at them.

"Haha I see," Shima said before replicating his maneuver at the opposite end of the alien formation. "Why didn't the captain just give us guns?"

"'Too impersonal,' I think was the answer in our briefing notes," Elias said.

Shima snorted. Together they picked apart the alien defenders until the aliens in the middle broke cover and ran for their lives. "I'll round them up, boss. You take the installation," Shima said.

"See you soon."

Shima went to chase the scattering aliens with her rocky arsenal.

Elias considered the building they'd been fighting over. It was large, round and sand-coloured. It blended in with the surrounding environment.

There were seven or so similar buildings, all several stories high. He quickly made his way to a central building, bowling over several enemy combatants on his way. *This must be it*, he thought. The enemy command centre.

There was a large circular door a few degrees around the building where he saw what must have been some support personnel fleeing towards. The door clanged shut and he extended his legs to start walking, taking a measured approach in case it was a trap.

He reached the doors without incident.

The doors were thick and as big as a small house, but there were cracks where he could jam his claws into.

Elias anchored himself to the ground and stabbed at the cracks with most of his clawed legs. The claws slipped a hand-length into the cracks and with all of his engineered might, he started to pull the doors open.

He shook with the effort, but with every second another few centimetres appeared until, with a sudden surge, the doors sprung open like a trap.

Despite having sixteen legs, he lost his balance and momentarily fell to the ground. He quickly got back to his feet and shifted his attention to a large hole, the size of a human skull, pointed directly at his body.

Oh, he thought before jumping to one side.

Too late.

A metal slug as long as a human arm delivered a blow that tore a hole clean through one-fifth of his body and spun him to the ground. Several spidery limbs forcibly detached from his body and armour and internal circuitry scattered over the ground.

A lone alien soldier approached from the inside of the compound, its bladed rifle raised high.

Still in shock from the gunshot, Elias flopped around like a fish out of water, trying to get away. The alien hacked one of his claws off and he recoiled.

"Help." he screamed over the communications channel to his friends nearby. "Help," he repeated as he tried to roll backwards. Nobody answered and the alien soldier continued advancing on him.

He activated his external speakers, "Stop," he yelled at the alien. It stopped.

It shook its head, "You know our language?"

"Please just stop."

"Die, monster."

Elias screamed as another leg was hacked off.

"No." He lashed out with one of his damaged limbs and smacked the soldier in the back. The soldier was knocked to the ground and Elias slapped it again.

The soldier stopped moving.

"Close the doors. Fire, Fire." Someone from inside the building yelled.

Having regained some control, Elias charged forwards at the enemy gun. Two soldiers were operating it.

A large metallic slug cracked the air where he had been. He picked up the alien soldiers and threw them against the far wall of the cavernous building. They came to a screaming halt against delicate-looking equipment.

Surprised at the openness of the building, he nevertheless made quick work of a handful of other aliens before pinning the last one to the floor of the well-lit room.

Most of the aliens wore desert browns and yellows, but not this one. The last alien was dressed in a light green cloak and looked smaller than the soldiers.

Before he could deliver the killing blow, he caught a flicker of light coming from some of the surviving equipment at the far side of the building. He focused his optical sensors on the flickering light and zoomed in until he could make out shapes and colours on some sort of primitive television.

"What's that?" he asked his helpless prey.

Frozen in fear, the green-suited alien couldn't reply. Elias, dealing with damaged, spasming tentacles, pushed himself closer to the screen while holding the alien in his claws, careful not to accidentally kill it.

Elias was fascinated by what he saw. On the screen, in a dark uniform, was a human speaking into some sort of camera. The human appeared to be a middle-aged man, floating as if he were in a spaceship.

"It's speaking English," Elias said, "but I can't understand the words. I know English, why can't I understand him?"

His prisoner looked at his spherical body, more curious than frightened, "You know this language? You have invaded its worlds?"

"Invaded... what are you talking about?"

"That is what it is saying, that your ship attacked its homeworld."

Confused, Elias continued watching. After a few moments, he grew frustrated at his inability to understand the language he had grown up with. "Translate for me."

"I... cannot. I can turn on some text if you would let me go."

Elias stared at the creature in his claws and weighed up the risks of letting it go. "What is your name?"

"Call me Green."

"Green, you understand that if you call for help or delete those recordings, you will die a rather painful death?"

"Yes, I would expect so," Green said while looking at the dismembered body parts of the soldiers scattered over other pieces of equipment.

"Hmm," Elias took a moment longer before slowly releasing his grip.

He didn't think Green could cause any trouble, but even if it could, Elias was curious.

Green moved on shaky legs towards the screen and started manipulating some dials and conical buttons. Alien text appeared on the screen, text which he found he understood with perfect clarity even though he'd never seen the language before.

"—and this is footage of my homeworld during the initial attack," the uniformed man was saying.

The picture on the television changed to that of a devastated city. Smoke filled the sky, blanketing giant white skyscrapers in black soot. Hundreds of people in strange clothing ran in a panic in all directions, screaming as they did so. A lone soldier encased in power armour waved for people to get out of the way before pointing a long cylindrical stick - some sort of silver rifle - at something in the distance.

Elias froze with shock as he realised what the soldier was firing at. It was *him,* or something much like the mechanical body he currently inhabited. The spherical alien monster dwarfed the humans and the lone soldier.

With the swipe of a single one of its sixteen long tentacles, half of the humans were knocked off their feet and the soldier disappeared in the mess of bodies.

There were other scenes of carnage that floated across the screen, but Elias was too shocked to pay much attention.

"The enemy vessel looks like this," the human continued.

"Oh..." Elias felt like his heart had been ripped out of his old body. The image was a grainy one. It was as if it had been recorded from a great distance against the blackness of space. A long, dark shaft formed the ship's backbone. Dozens of egg-shaped environment pods hung off the central shaft from thick arms. The arms independently rotated around the central shaft, providing gravity for the beings that lived within them.

It was the captain's ship.

CHAPTER 3

"Why aren't you replying over the communicator?" Shima said with her external speakers. "What are you looking at?"

Feeling lost at the implications of the recordings, Elias barely registered Shima's presence until she grabbed a couple of his damaged arms and forcefully moved him aside.

"It looks like an ancient television, wh-whoa. You ok?" Shima finally noticed the large hole in Elias's shell."

"He's the enemy."

"What? Elias, what are you talking about?"

"The captain. He is the Reaper of Earth."

"You're hurt, Elias." Shima held him fast and started doing a deep scan of his body's circuitry. "You're not making sense."

"They're not our enemy, Shima."

"You mean this critter?" One of Shima's arms snapped out like a whip and grabbed the alien in its claw. "They *are* our enemy, El. they murdered millions of beings in the ship's core codes, they killed thousands of true-lifers when they hit one of the habitation pods. Those were real people, El, peaceful people. Murdered."

"We were defending ourselves," Green hooted at them.

"Liar," Shima yelled at it.

"Watch the recordings, Shima, it's true. The captain destroyed Earth. It destroyed our Empire and took us as slaves." Elias shifted under Shima's weight to free a couple of his limbs.

Shima felt him tense up. "Now I know you're cracked. It's propaganda, El, nothing more." As if she were casually shrugging, Shima snipped the alien in half. "There, problem solved—"

Elias exploded into a writhing froth of metallic motion.

"What are you doing, El?" Shima screamed at him. He ignored her while he tore chunks from her armoured shell and lopped off limbs. "No El, Noo."

He hammered at her shell over and over again until one of his claws slipped into a crack and tore apart vital internal machinery. Shima's thrashing limbs went limp.

He'd done it; he'd killed his friend for the sake of an alien.

It didn't take long for the rest of the captain's forces to wipe out all of the anti-starship weaponry.

Elias made his way to the extraction point, avoiding both the locals and other spidery droids. He was the first to the extraction point and that suited him very well. He powered down and sat in silence, watching the stars rotate slowly above while he contemplated his revenge.

How? How did the captain convince everyone that it was their saviour? Elias couldn't recall the details of what had happened to Earth, he'd never felt the need to remember it, but now it seemed like the most important issue of his entire existence. Had he ever actually lived on Earth? Or was he just a computer program conjured into existence?

How old was he, truly? Had he really lived inside the captain's ship for centuries, or was he only a few hours old with memories implanted?

No, he must have lived all that time. The captain wouldn't bother implanting all of these useless memories if all it needed was a mindless killing machine.

"Your creativity is your friend," Fenik had once told him. *"Harness it, practice new techniques. Paint a canvass. Learn to juggle. Who knows, you might even teach the captain a trick or two..."*

The Captain's learning from us.

Using us.

Damn, Elias thought.

I wonder if he's learnt mutiny yet...

Spidery soldiers started arriving at the extraction point, excitedly blaring congratulatory remarks at him and at each other. He ignored them, showed them the damage to his spherical shell and pretended not to hear.

An extraction shuttle arrived shortly after, firing missiles and coil guns at distant targets. Plumes of sand whirled away from the star-shaped shuttle's exhaust fumes and wafted over the waiting troops. The shuttle's doors opened and dozens of spidery soldiers raced up the ramps. Elias, as one of the most damaged soldiers, took his time and arrived last. The others had retracted their clawed limbs and sat in spherical cradles that held them down.

Curiously, the shuttle was deathly quiet. Where moments earlier there had been a cacophony of excited chatter, not a single spherical soldier remained active.

He reached out and tapped the nearest spidery sphere, trying to provoke a response.

Nothing.

"Shuttle," he called, "are these people asleep?"

"Negative. These units have been wiped upon recovery."

"Explain, what do you mean by wiped?"

"Memories deleted. You must return to your assigned cradle for debriefing and deletion."

Elias mentally shivered, "I... I've been damaged. I won't fit in the cradle."

"Unacceptable. Applying override measures," the shuttle's intelligence said. He heard a sharp click and waited for the shuttle's computer to take over his body. It didn't happen.

"As I said, I'm damaged. Please, just let me stay like this for now. I'd like to watch as we head back to the ship."

Silence followed.

The shuttle's ramps quickly folded up into the shuttle and he held on to the walls. A rumble reverberated around the clinically sterile ship and gravity increased dramatically.

Elias moved towards the shuttle's command centre. It was sealed shut by a large airlock but the designers had thoughtfully added a display screen and controls to use them. He tapped at the controls, recognizing the schematics from one of his many simulated adventures. It was an easy thing to find an internal view of the shuttle's command centre. He saw alien beetles, each a metre long, overseeing the shuttle's progress.

True-Lifers, not machines like himself.

Good.

Elias started cutting into the large airlock.

Having commandeered a powerful set of electronic binoculars, Shima shook from the damage she'd sustained while she watched the shuttles return to the captain's starship, their home.

"Why, Elias?" she said weakly. At over a million kilometres away, even with the powerful binoculars, the ship was little more than a dark pin against the vast starlit background.

When it happened, though, the flash of light that had been Elias' shuttle was clearly visible, perhaps even to the naked eye. Large pieces of the captain's ship slowly started coming apart.

Shima refocused the binoculars after the blast. She saw that several of the ship's mountain-sized engines had been smashed by Elias' suicidal ramming.

The looped recording of the human admiral could be heard over the approaching alien artillery and running troops.

With sudden clarity she could understand the admiral's words, "...it calls itself an arbiter from a place named the *Shellworld*. Do not trust it; do not let it near your planet. It will take your people and copy your minds. It will destroy your world..."

Afterword

Thank you for reading Starships and Apocalypse Volume One. If you enjoyed it, why not leave a review? As an independent author reviews are gold and even a short review, just a few words, can make a huge difference.

Made in the USA
Monee, IL
19 June 2021

71776019R00177